C000098542

Hacienda Moon

KaSonndra Leigh

Published by TriGate Realm Press, 2023.

This is a work of fiction. Similarities to real people, places, or events are entirely coincidental.

HACIENDA MOON

First edition. February 19, 2023.

Copyright © 2023 KaSonndra Leigh.

ISBN: 978-0615668239

Written by KaSonndra Leigh.

Hacienda Moon
Expanded Edition
A Gothic Paranormal Romance
© 2012, 2013, 2017, 2023 by KaSonndra Leigh
Published by TriGate Realm Press

Fourth Edition License Notes

This ebook is licensed for your personal enjoyment only. This ebook may not be re-sold, copied, or given away to other people. If you would like to share this book with another person, please purchase an additional copy for each reader. If you're reading this book and did not purchase it, or it was not purchased for your use only, then please return to Amazon.com and purchase your own copy. Thank you for respecting the hard work of this author. This is a work of fiction. All characters, organizations, and events are products of the author's imagination. Any similarity to real persons, living or dead is coincidental and not intended by the author.

www.kasonndraleigh.com[1]

Cover Art © 2023 by Asterielly Designs
ASIN: B008QAY0BQ

PREFACE

I'm excited to bring you this new expanded edition of Hacienda Moon, one of my top selling novels of all time and the story I love most out of all my literary babies. I truly appreciate your patience while my team and I worked to revamp this story. This latest version contains more gothic suspense, intrigue, and of course romance.

The Gothic Romance novel is special in that the storyline not only features a love affair between two people, but it also takes you on a walk back in time and showcases a connection between the main character and a historical house. The plot is part mystery with a paranormal element and an epic romance that crosses through time. This is why it's so important to introduce both the love interest and the house in such a way to help the reader transport themselves into the story as well.

Having said that, my editor and I decided to release this edition in the way that it was meant to be experienced. I've included the original opening chapter that had previously been deleted due to its sensitive nature. However, I felt that its inclusion was necessary in order to help the reader experience and understand Tandie's losses before her investigative journey begins. Due to the complicated and oftentimes graphic nature of this story, I'd suggest you review the content warnings in the following section before moving ahead with your journey.

I hope you enjoy this expanded edition of Hacienda Moon.

Sometimes the Darkest Soul Can Have the Brightest Heart of All...

Love, obsession, and betrayal, the most powerful human emotions are spun together in this gothic novel. Hacienda Moon is a seductive tale of one woman's journey to confront the demons of her past and find the courage to face her future. It is a mesmerizing novel that explores the deepest depths of human nature. This novel is loosely based on the true story of a warship called the Fortuna that attacked the region now known as Brunswick County, North Carolina, on September 4, 1748.

Content Warnings: blood & gore, death among people of all ages, graphic violence, kidnapping, derogatory terms, weapons, murder, discrimination, intense sexual situations.

For Mom and Grandma...as always.
We love and miss you.

Part I

When deep down in the core of your being, you believe that your soul mate exists, there is no limit to the way he or she can enter your life...

...Arielle Ford

Dear Diary,

I dream of a man, someone who lived a long time ago. He has eyes filled with warmth, dark jewels that penetrate my soul each time I glance into them. As I drift along this cycle of pain, this fight that I call life, I think of him, my mysterious lover. And when I close my eyes each night, I imagine his face just before I fall asleep. He touches me, holds me, and loves everything about me. I understand this is only my imagination, but it's something I believe has crossed the boundaries of another era to reach me.

Inside ~~this memory~~ this dream, we sometimes lay together on a mattress inside a small cabin, a tiny but cozy place with only one room and a bed made of hay. I realize these are stolen slices of time, yet it doesn't matter. His love fills me with desire, makes me feel invincible, turns me into the conqueror I've always wanted to be but was too afraid to become. At dawn, I sneak away and leave him sleeping soundly. However, doing so causes me pain. And then, the dream ends.

Why do I yearn for him?

How can I obsess over a stranger?

My phantom lover is only an image inside a dream, but his touch seems so real that I wake up and feel lost after I realize he's gone, leaving me to face life without her, my soulmate, my little girl I lost so many years ago.

Sighing deeply, I lift my body up, get dressed and head out to work. Life's cumbersome trials have become difficult to face every day. I have lost the two greatest parts of my heart, and the will to live sometimes escapes me. But no matter how much I hurt, I find courage when I think of his face, and in my darkest hour, I discover the will to carry on. Just because life has tossed me onto the wheel of chaos and has taken everything I ever held close to my heart, doesn't mean I will allow the agony to consume all of me.

Grief, loss, and pain, I have this to say to all three of you: "I'm taking back the key I gave to you—the one you used to lock my heart inside your dark chamber."

My life still belongs to me. I understand what you don't want me to see. You don't want me to believe or hope... or live. However, I'm going to do my best.

I must try.

Somehow I will survive. ~~For him~~

For now, I wait.

Chapter 1

T *roy, New York State*
    July, 2010
    Tandie

"I DON'T KNOW, TANDIE. It's like you're two different people these days," my husband's voice said through the car's speaker.

I scoffed and focused on the road ahead. Curvy, dark, slippery roads, typical upstate New York travel challenges, met my gaze. We'd headed out early that evening to avoid the pending thunderstorm. However, the rain came fast and hard. The trip to our family cabin was supposed to bring us closer. Everything was going wrong, including the weather.

"Only you would say that right now. Blame it all on me. Great."

"I didn't mean for it to happen."

Famous last words. How many times had the women in the office told me about their husband's infidelities? And how many of those stories began with the phrase: "I didn't mean for it to happen"? If they paid me each time, I'd be a rich woman by now. That was for sure.

I refused to cry. Instead, I focused on the road ahead. The rain had eased up a bit so now a dewy veil obscured my view. From in the backseat, my five-year-old daughter, Breena, hummed her favorite tune, a song from a popular kid show.

"Gotta go. I'll call you back once I reach the cabin."

"Tan... wait. I might be late getting there."

I scoffed. "Don't bother. I'm hanging up now, Jack." My lips trembled.

Inhaling deeply, I turned my attention back to the road, ignoring the rocks perched in my chest. Sure, my work as a police psychic kept me out in the field often. Sometimes the cases consumed me. It took a lot to pull psychic visions from within someone's belongings, and when I did, I gave up a piece of myself. Yes, I spent a lot of time working on my crime memoir. Becoming a New York Times bestselling author required sacrifices.

Still, none of that was an excuse for Jack's behavior. I found out about the affair through a mutual friend. Sure, I could view other people's mishaps and memories. However, my psychic ability didn't work on people close to me. If it did, the result couldn't be trusted.

You don't deserve to be happy.

Everyone suffers around you.

Tell my story, or I'll punish you.

The whispers echoed through the car as though I had a passenger speaking to me. However, there was only me and my daughter in the backseat. The cabin dropped to a deep chill and my breath materialized before me.

"What the hell?" I checked the car's thermostat and frowned. Not even upstate New York was this chilly on a summer night.

Goosebumps prickled my arms. I stole a quick glance behind me. Breena studied her tablet and hummed along with the song. Her pink topaz ring sparkled when touched by beams from the streetlights. She looked up and flashed me a toothy grin, warming my heart. I turned around and gripped the steering wheel.

"We're going to be just fine, Baby B," I said, ignoring the increased chill. I'd given Jack Harrison eight years of my life. How could he throw it all away so easily?

The white flash came from nowhere, searing my eyes and cloaking my vision, the aftereffect blinding me. A brief image of a young girl's face flickered inside the light and vanished. It felt like someone turned up the sunlight for a few seconds and then turned off daylight afterwards, taking my eyesight with it.

"Oh God!" I hissed, "I can't see!" I forced my eyes open wider, willing them to adjust to the situation. Grasping the steering wheel, I blinked and tried to see through the dense blackness that had cloaked me in shadows.

"Mommy, are you okay?" My daughter's voice floated through the air like a beacon of hope in an otherwise dark and desolate world.

I pressed down on the brakes, a mistake on these icy roads. Immediately the car started to spin, and I felt my stomach drop as the tires lifted off the ground. We completed several rotations before landing with a thud and an ear-splitting screech of metal against metal.

"Mommy!" Breena cried out from the backseat. "I'm scared."

"Stay calm, sweetheart," I said, although my own heart was pounding in my chest. As the darkness cloaking my eyes faded, I could see where we were—suspended over the Hudson River! I had somehow managed to lodge the car between the guardrail and the mountainside—a death trap if I ever saw one.

"How the holy hell?" I muttered, my mind struggling to comprehend how we got here. All I could focus on was getting out safely.

The car dipped again and I struggled to unlock my seatbelt with no luck. "Hold on, baby! Don't panic"

Breena screamed and the car plunged further, but all I could do was brace for impact as everything went dark and silent.

21 MONTHS LATER...

"I didn't want you to hear this secondhand, Tandie," the NYPD forensics department manager, George Gomez, said, "so I stopped by myself."

The big man walked into my new apartment and sat down on the accent chair opposite mine. He hunched over, his enormous frame making my chair seem small. Releasing a long sigh, he said, "There's no easy way to say this. We've replaced your position. Found a new psychic. Now, this wasn't my idea. I want you to know. I- I'm... Sorry, Tan. If you need anything..."

I waved off the rest of his sentence. Had expected this conversation. I spent the last 21 months trying to understand what happened the night I lost my daughter. What was the white light that blinded me and the girl's face that appeared inside it? The timing of its appearance didn't seem natural. Perhaps the rain played tricks on me. No, I was certain there had been something supernatural involved. The doctors blamed my injuries and loss of psychic abilities on head trauma. My psychiatrist insisted I was two steps away from the psych ward. I lost my daughter in that accident. So what the hell did they expect?

The inability to use my visions crippled me and rendered me useless to the NYPD. My career as a psychic medium was over, and all I received was a small alimony check from my ex-husband. Thank goodness for the royalties I'd received for my bestselling non-fiction book, *Psychic Minds Demystified*.

"Are you all right, Tandie?" George asked, bringing me back to the present situation.

I scoffed a laugh. The most underrated question ever. "Honestly, I expected this conversation sooner. I know it comes from someone above you."

"I wish there was some other way," George said. I knew he meant well. George had been my champion since the day I took on the job of psychic medium four years ago.

"It's all good. I have new plans for my life."

George's face lit up. "Really? Wanna tell an old man about them?"

I hesitated before answering. "I'm going home. Back to North Carolina. My best friend helped me find a new place. I'll be renting while I save up enough to buy the house. So that's scary."

"I'd no idea you were moving. Makes me happy to hear this news though. And sad."

He wasn't the only excited person. Frieda almost jumped through the receiver when I told her I'd made the rental agreement with the owner via phone. I no longer possessed the ability to see past events, or to touch someone's belongings and see their story. However, I knew something about the house she'd chosen called out to me.

Which was exactly what I needed, as I'd find out soon enough.

Chapter 2

Bolivia, North Carolina, July, 2012
    Tandie

Six years had passed since I last traveled through my home state of North Carolina. Many things in my life had changed, but everything in this place seemed to have stayed the same. Over the past two years, I'd lost my psychic visions and job with the NYPD, my husband and my beautiful daughter.

I turned up the car's radio. Opera music blared through the speakers, calming the voices inside my head, the ones that kept telling me I made a mistake by leaving behind my job as a psychic medium and successful author in New York and moving back to the south, an adventure I chose in order to grieve while writing the next great American Gothic Romance novel.

Yeah, sure. I knew the change from a New York Times bestselling non-fiction writer to novelist would be tricky. However, my soul needed this change. Craved this new venture in life for healing. I'd lost my little girl and my husband within a two-year timeframe. The time for a fresh start had arrived.

I even allowed my best friend, Frieda, to talk me into buying a 300-year-old house, a plantation filled with history and energy, the perfect remedy. Moving back to Bolivia also meant I'd be closer to Frieda again. I looked forward to catching up with my friend. We had lost so many years together, and I wanted to make up for moving away and leaving my female soul mate for a man who turned out to be unworthy of the sacrifice. Being close to someone was just the thing I needed to mend the hole left in my heart. Victory over my ex-husband's attempt to ruin my life was something I could feel, a hint of many good things to come. That was until my Camaro rolled to a stop in front of the large three-story plantation house.

"Talk about needing a little TLC," I said, rolling my window down and staring at the hulk of a structure that stared back at me with its weathered windows for eyes.

With the two top levels surrounded by a wraparound balcony, the 260-year-old Chelby Rose was the queen of haunted houses, the perfect fit for a writer of the supernatural and odd. The chipped wooden siding was a faded pink, and moss and dirt covered most sideboards. The black shutters surrounding the top and bottom windows appeared to be in decent condition, but patches of rust scattered across the metal roof. Overgrown trees hung over the top as if reaching down to protect the house with their mangled branches. The place needed work—lots of it. I imagined the inside posed as much of a challenge as the outside, and I didn't even want to think about the family cemetery I heard about, the one hidden somewhere in the woods behind the house.

Strangely, I felt a stirring in my chest, a pull as if the house were calling to me, beckoning me to come inside. I was torn. My mind wavered somewhere between happiness and freaking out. The day Frieda Sampson's picture of Chelby Rose hit my inbox, I felt an instant connection to the place.

It was still early evening, but the moon had already risen over an opening in the trees, the soft touch of its light cradling the left side of the roof. Moonlight lighting up my new home was an intriguing scene, one that filled me with a peaceful sensation.

Inhaling deeply and holding the breath, I got out of the car, removed my three suitcases from the backseat, walked up the steps, and approached the lock box. The owner, Mr. Chelby, had emailed instructions for retrieving the master key a few days ago. He'd given me permission to go inside while I waited for his arrival, a gesture I truly appreciated. Good old southern trust and manners, a leap away from what I was accustomed to while living in New York.

I punched in the numbers, removed the key, unlocked the door and stepped into the musty hallway, trying not to get freaked out by the creaking door as the hinges groaned a loud welcome for the home's soon-to-be-new owner.

"This is fascinating." My voice echoed through the area. The hallway's dusty pink walls were covered with portraits of women dressed in colonial style dresses and wide-brimmed hats decorated with white flowers. To the immediate left, a door with a missing top hinge waited to be opened and the room behind it explored. A large dining room was situated just off the right side of the entrance door. Taking my time, I explored the rest of the first level and made my way up to the master bedroom. A king-size, four-poster bed with matching end tables took up most of the room.

I set my shoulder bag down on the wood floor, ran my hand along the bed's curvy footboard and closed my eyes, surrendering to vibrations in the house. A powerful gust of energy shoved through my body, winding me. This was the first echo of a vision I'd experienced in two years. Yet nothing else happened. Bummer.

Psychics all around the world called this feeling the heartbeat of the house, the leftover details of a time long gone. Anyone could sense such a thing if they really wanted to do so. Psychic vision wasn't necessary to experience the inexplicable sensation of a house choosing to open up for prospective owners.

There was no mistaking that Chelby Rose held a glorious history. Parties, birthdays, ceremonies, and heartache: all the vibrations filled the air, bringing the energy to sizzling life. If anything could restore the abilities I lost shortly after the accident, then Chelby Rose was most definitely the thing to do so.

A burst of cool air rushed through the room along with a medley of whispers, and the sound of a moan could've just been my imagination. However, the noise sounded an awful lot like a human voice. "Okay. What the hell was that?" I crossed my arms and shivered.

Something tapped on the window beside the bed, scaring the good sense out of me. I turned toward the noise, cradled my chest, walked toward the window and soon discovered the source of my distress. A tree limb was blowing against the pane. "Well, that'll be the first thing to get done. We won't get any sleep with skinny-tree limbs tapping away like that."

"I said the same thing almost a hundred times," a male's deep voice said from behind me.

Inhaling a sharp breath, I spun around. A man, either in his late twenties or early thirties, stood there and studied me with an amused look in his bright blue eyes. He strolled towards me as though he were a king greeting a lowly subject standing inside his palace and towered over my head. Standing well over six-feet tall, he was evenly proportioned... aka built. Striking waves of dark blonde hair were combed away from his face. The tailored dark-gray suit he wore showed he'd just come from a party of some type, or maybe he dressed that way every day. There was only one man he could be—Saul Chelby, the oil tycoon who owned the house I'd be renting to buy.

"Mr. Chelby?" My face flushed for the second time in one day.

"At the lady's service." He walked over to me and held out a hand. "You must be the lovely Mrs. Harrison." My face heated even more. This was the first man who'd complimented me since I left my ex-husband, Jack. I didn't know how to react and felt super awkward.

"Yes. I am her. I mean, I'm Mrs. Harri—I'm Tandie Harrison." I sighed. *What a bumbling idiot. Get it together, woman.*

"Saul Chelby. Your benefactor extraordinaire, Tandie Harrison. Also known as the landlord guy." He gave me a fetching smile, one that lit up the darkening room.

Turning away from me, he walked over to the old night table beside the bed, removed a folded paper, smoothed the document out, his long fingers sliding gracefully across the surface and returned to where I stood. Taking the document, my fingers brushed across Saul Chelby's hand as I did so. A small zap of electricity vibrated off his skin and into mine. Clearing his throat, he said, "Your contract. Look over it in your spare time. The agreement states that after twelve weeks of renting, we'll assess the situation and discuss purchasing. I'm responsible for repairs and such until you purchase the house. I have a contractor in mind. No need to stress over that detail. And don't worry, Tandie. If you ever need extra time to pay—"

"I can handle my bills, Mr. Chelby." Pause. "I know what you're thinking. Struggling writer, divorced, an all-around risky tenant, right? I can handle my finances. Are we clear?" *Note to self: wait until after you buy the house before you tick off the owner.* "I'm sorry. I don't mean to be snappy. It has been a long day. I'm normally not so...."

An amused expression crossed his face, those perfectly shaped lips and cheekbones of a nobleman. He out shined a movie star. "Actually, I had pegged none of those things on you. However, I most definitely believe we're very clear now."

Sighing, he stepped closer to me and stared deep into my eyes, a faraway look in his sad gaze. Why didn't he send an assistant out to handle something like this? "Please understand, Mrs. Harrison, selling this place is like giving up a part of me. To trust someone with something like that is difficult. I'm having trouble finding the right words. Work with me, if you don't mind." Blushing, he stuffed his hands into his pockets, a humble gesture for someone known as an oil tycoon. I wanted to know the story about this handsome stranger. That was until I remembered what he just said: I'm the landlord guy.

"I know all about finding the right words, Mr. Chelby. And I understand what you're trying to say. There's no need to worry. I'll take good care of your family's home." I didn't need to tune into him psychically to understand what he thought. Chelby Rose was a fine house, and I looked forward to spending some time alone with the place.

"You'll do just fine. The house likes you. Also, I've hired a contractor. He should start in a few days," he said, giving me a sad smile.

"Sounds good. But what do you mean when you say the house likes me?"

The faraway look faded, and he blinked several times, meeting my gaze with a business-like face. "You must think I'm the strangest landlord. Either that, or a psychopath." He made a light laugh.

"Are you kidding me? I'm a psychic, Mr. Chelby," I offered a smile. I wanted him to loosen up. The man appeared as though he might jump through the roof at any moment. "I purposely made the odd regular parts of my life." We both shared a nervous laugh.

"Please call me Saul. Mr. Chelby was my father and grandfathers before him." An awkward moment of silence passed as we stared at each other. "Do you need help with anything? Your bags, maybe?"

"No, I'm good."

"All right. Enjoy your new home, as I'm most certain she will enjoy you." Reaching out, he took my right hand in between his firm grasp and slipped a set of keys into my palm, holding my gaze the entire time.

"Thank you," I croaked out. He hesitated as if he wanted to say more just before he released my hand, stuffed his back into his pockets, turned around and walked out the door, disappearing around the corner and walking away without even making a sound. The man reminded me of a phantom. My daughter, Breena, used to be the only other person who could sneak up on me that way.

Eager to discover what treasures waited on the third level, I walked along the hallway until I came to a fifth entry at the end. The door was on the wall between the last two of the four doors leading into the respective bedrooms, so I assumed it led up to the third level of the house. Placing my hand on the knob, I almost let go once the chill of the metal came into contact with my skin. "It's so cold." The old knob didn't turn or even budge an inch. It was locked and didn't respond to any of the keys Saul gave me. "Okay then, Mr. Chelby. We'll have your contractor deal with this first, I think."

AFTER RETURNING TO the first level, I headed outside, wishing I would've taken Saul's offer to assist me, and stopped walking at once. There were no suitcases sitting beside the Camaro. I walked around the car, circling it a few times, my mind racing. I exhaled and tossed my arms up in the air.

"What the hell?" I turned back towards the house and froze. My eyes widened as I struggled to focus on the sight before me. At the front door, the suitcases sat arranged by size from largest to smallest. I scoffed a sigh.

"I can already see we're going to get along well, Chelby Rose."

I headed up the steps and grabbed the largest suitcase. Did I pack the kitchen sink in here? Nope. I smuggled my typewriter into it though. The beautiful thing about a fresh start was leaving behind the possessions you no longer needed.

Heading into the living area, I set the largest suitcase down beside the antique coffee table sitting in the middle of the room, unzipped it and removed my Smith Corona typewriter nicknamed Lilibel. Saul had made it clear he didn't want to sell his old home to just any stranger, although I wasn't sure why I qualified for the role.

My Grandma Zee taught me to never question a gift, as long as the giver didn't provide an adequate reason for you to do so. Chelby Rose had been the answer to my cry for freedom, the first step toward letting go of the pain of the last two years, and discovering the way to regain that vital part of me I'd lost... my psychic visions. Then I'd be able to understand the phenomena that took place the night I lost my daughter.

My agent expected me to send the first draft of my novel in a few days. No pressure. I wanted people to know that just because I wrote nonfiction, didn't mean I couldn't sell fiction. My two books, *Pathways to the Afterlife* and *Psychic Minds Demystified,* had become instant bestsellers. However, that was because I had researched and wrote about the things my grandmother told me. She said my paternal ancestors were a group of shaman women who used personal belongings to see events from and sometimes travel to the owner's past and future. I'd renewed my interest in my ancestral elements since the mysterious white light incident, the one that occurred the night my daughter was taken from me.

Grandma Zee told me the family belonged to a line of powerful Owanechee medicine women. The ability to communicate with spirits walking along certain planes of existence was a gift passed down to at least one female in each generation. Sometimes these women, known as pathseekers, held such a powerful aura that spirits would come to them. That wasn't always a good thing. Sometimes the spirits would get jealous of the pathseeker and her unique power. However, abusing the ability came with consequences. Often, I wondered if I'd overstepped a boundary and angered some mysterious god or goddess who then took my psychic ability.

My father disappeared when I was six and my mother passed away before she had the chance to teach me anything substantial about our lineage and the way my gifts worked. She also didn't want me dabbling in that part of my heritage, and Grandma Zee upheld her wishes. So I winged it.

Tell my story.

Or I'll punish you.

The words that jump-started this journey echoed through the room as they'd done inside my head everyday over the past two years. I grasped the sides of my head and waited for the preceding headache to pass. Whatever thing that haunted me back in New York had followed me here. The thought should've frightened me. Yet it didn't.

"I'll tell your damn story." And then I'll make you pay for what you did.

Chapter 3

T *andie*

THE NEXT DAY, I SAT at my desk and studied the image of Breena holding a large beach ball above her head, taking in every detail of my daughter's little body, my chest constricting and eyes filling with tears. Outside, the Bolivian wind howled through the house. Funny how the sound mimicked the heart of my soul these days.

Sitting inside the silence of Chelby Rose's living room, I closed my eyes and released the hold on my imagination. My head filled with memories. It was like I still felt the sun beaming down on my shoulders as my daughter and I enjoyed our stolen time that day. Back when life was simple, even though the end had already taken roots without me knowing it.

Sighing, I opened my eyes and stared at Breena's photo. "You're still not going to talk to me, huh?" Silence.

The pill bottle by the window beckoned me for the first time in weeks. It was the strangest thing, because I didn't remember putting it there. "We can do this. You're better than that bottle." I repeated the words several times just before a calmness washed over me.

I fidgeted with Breena's pink topaz ring, my good luck charm. I had worn it around my neck every single day. The jewel once belonged to a powerful Owanechee medicine woman on Grandma Zee's side, an heirloom passed down through generations of my father's ancestors. Breena used to say that the rose-colored stone was her magic rock, a way of talking to the fairy people. Now her mysterious token served as a salve for me.

I turned my gaze back to the picture and focused on her smile. "Don't stay mad at me too long, Baby B. Okay?"

After pecking out a mind numbing total of one hundred words, I spent most of the next hour trying a host of other solutions that the big orange do-it-yourself repair book proposed for leaky faucets. Saul still hadn't returned either of the two messages I'd left for him about the issue. Maybe if I called and told him the house was floating away, then he'd move faster.

"All right. The fix-it book says I need some Stop Leak. So guess what you leaky little thing? It's time for me to head into town," I said, feeling odd for scolding a faucet.

Trudging through the hallway, I grabbed my handbag off the desk sitting beside the entrance to the living room and headed toward the front door. I yanked it open and screamed. The woman I almost collided with released an ear-splitting yell too—my best friend, Frieda Tyson.

"Girl, you scared the crap out of me. I thought you were a ghost or some crazy ass thing like that." Frieda pulled me into a tight embrace, winding me. This was the first time we'd stolen some time together since the funeral two years ago.

At 5'9" tall, she was a healthy woman with an equally powerful embrace. She and I were opposites in both style and appearance. Frieda, with her exotic dark skin, made you think of the Nubian goddess statues found in the Harlem museums, and she towered over my pudgy 5'6" frame. Frieda was elected to the homecoming court twice, and the guys flocked to her like bees. While I played the part of the bookworm, the girl who preferred the quiet calm of the library, the nerd in our group. Add to that oddness a pair of bi-colored eyes (one light brown and one green pupil).

"Just look at you! Gorgeous as usual. I hate you so much right now," Frieda mocked and burst out in laughter. The perfume she was wearing reminded me of a flower garden just the way her exotic scents always did.

Frieda, a sex therapist, was a hippy woman. She reminded me of that supermodel, Naomi Campbell, but with more meat on her bones. Still without kids, she and her tax attorney husband, Dom, traveled all over the world on their days off. Frieda always made sure she sent plenty of pictures back to me, making me yearn for a touch of the exciting lifestyle my friend had found.

Being in Frieda's presence ignited the ache in my chest, the longing to have someone listen and understand how I felt inside. To understand the drive to figure out what happened to my daughter, a tragic loss of which I knew wasn't an accident. Shortly after Breena's funeral, Frieda returned to work, and I had mentally prepared for what I knew was going to be the next chapter of my life. If there was one person I could be myself with, then she was the one.

"How much do you weigh now? 100lbs.? 110? No matter, you look fantastic." Frieda spun me around, examining my body and pinching the skin around my waistline.

I clicked my tongue. "I am not that skinny. Geez, Frieda, you have me practically anorexic at 100lbs. And what about you with your designer duds? Look at those fingers. They're filled with rings. I think that hater feeling is mutual."

"Let me get real, girlfriend. How are you, baby? Are you feeling all right?" She placed an arm across my shoulders, staring deep into my eyes as I led her into the house.

Walking into my living room-study, I eased out from under her embrace and contemplated the best way to answer Frieda's question. "Let's see. Other than trying to accept my new status as a plumber, I'm dealing with things." I passed a quick glance to the picture of Breena sitting on my writing desk and fought back the stab of grief that weakened me each time I thought of her.

"This house is ancient. What did you expect? I'm so mad you haven't called me until now. Don't you know how much I love you?" Frieda asked. Before I could answer, she continued talking at a breakneck pace, sitting down and filling me in on the reason she and Dom have a temporary hotel room in Wilmington, a city about twenty minutes away from Bolivia. "This little water-hole town is so strange. You can't be quiet around here. I won't have a clue whether you're truly gone."

"I can't even get a word in edge-wise," I finally said as Frieda paused and took a breath.

My friend placed two fingers on her lips, a way of silencing herself. Didn't last long, though. "Sorry, baby. I worry about you out here all by yourself. I don't understand why you just didn't move back to Castle Hayne. Your grandmother's house is still there."

Thinking about my grandmother's old house gave me goosebumps. Memories of the thing in the woods behind that house haunted my thoughts. I'd never forget the day I got lost in the swampy woods or the terrible events that followed. To forget about that tragic time, the day my babysitter and one of her friends disappeared, was one of the main reasons I moved to New York with Jack.

"200 people live in this town. What could happen?" I asked.

"Bolivia's ghosts. That's what. I almost didn't come here tonight. I love you, Tandie, you know that. But I don't fancy driving around this place. In fact, some of my colleagues take an extra twenty minutes just to drive around Bolivia. Gas companies must love us, right?"

I nodded absently. "It's not that bad." I thought of Saul and had to admit I found it odd that even Chelby Rose's former owner didn't want to live in his family's old home.

"What's it like living in an old plantation house? Aren't you scared the ghosts of Old Jacob Atwater and the other slaves might come back to get you?" Frieda asked.

I smirked. "Frieda, you're so dramatic. There are no slave quarters on the premises. If there were, then they're all gone now. These old houses are rare. Owning one is a privilege. Something to be admired, I would think."

Frieda gave me a wry look. "All right. You might have a point, I guess. The place still gives me the creeps."

"I can't believe you're saying that. This was your idea," I reminded.

"Hey, I didn't think you'd take me seriously. Besides, I sent you hundreds of photos of nicer houses. And what does my little Wednesday Addams friend do? Chooses the creepiest one, of course. I don't know why I expected you to do anything else," she said, tossing her arms up in the air and shrugging.

"This was the best choice for me," I explained, thinking of the way Chelby Rose greeted me with an embrace of energy the first day I arrived. The house and I understood each other. Truth be told, I hoped that some spectral entity existed in this house. What other way would there be for me to understand the light that blinded me and the voices I heard the night Baby B died? I kept silent. Didn't want to scare Frieda, since something already spooked her.

"Yeah, but everybody knows the old Chelby house is haunted. That's why I came to get you out of here."

I frowned. "I just moved in, and I kind of like it here."

"Not like that. We need a girl's night away from this ghost house. Away from the New York Times bestseller you're working on." Frieda stood and pulled out her keys. "There's this cute little bar over in Castle Hayne. It's owned by some friends of mine. We can go there."

"But I really need some Stop Leak."

Frieda gave me an incredulous look. "Tandie, stop making excuses for why you can't have fun anymore. Girl, we're only twenty-seven-years-old and you're about ready to grab the crochet needle and a couple of cats, I think. I know losing your baby hurts. I miscarried four years ago. Hell, I still get all teary-eyed when I think about it. But, baby, let life go on. You can't play victim to the past forever."

Tears lined Frieda's eyes, and right away, I realized how selfish I'd been. My best friend had suffered through one of the worst times of her life back then, and I wasn't able to be there for her the way I'd wanted to be. And although Frieda played down her heartache, being the independent woman I knew her always to be, I still felt guilty and seriously needed to make things right with her.

I hugged her again, doing what I should've done all those years ago. There was nothing that compared to the heartache of losing a child. Nothing. We embraced a long moment, the Tick-Tock of the grandfather clock sitting out in the hallway our only solace. Pulling back, I reached up and wiped away her tears. "I'm so sorry. I wasn't there for you."

"Don't even start getting all mushy on me," she said in a tear-strained voice. "Time to have a little fun."

"Okay. Let me grab my bag," I said, wiping away my tears with my fingers, yet feeling somewhat eager to go out and be around other people. The writing life was a lonely one and Frieda's visit provided a chance to get out and be around the living, a vital part of the creative process.

"Uh, you need to change. There is no way I'll let you wear your grandma's gear to a club," Frieda said, eyeing my long, baggy black dress. "Grab some jeans, a sexy shirt, a smile, and some courage. No questions. Now, get to it."

"Yes, Mama Frieda." I said and headed up the stairs to change as a cool breeze swept across the left side of my body.

Chapter 4

E*ric*
Eric stepped out of his Jeep and inhaled deeply, his nostrils assaulted by the salty aroma coming off the ocean. The smell was less dank than the air around the swamplands back in New Orleans, but still held its own little kick. His heart sped up a bit. He never realized how much leaving his hometown of Castle Hayne had affected him until now. He also felt a bit underdressed in his ripped jeans and short-sleeved flannel shirt. There was a slight chill in the air, indicative of summer nights on the North Carolina coastline. His thick, dark hair blew into his face, obscuring the view of his friend's bar and tickling his forehead. *Definitely time for a haircut.* Nevertheless, he was eager to head into the Aeneid and catch up on current events with his friends.

What had happened in his old town since he last visited?

Was there truth to his mother's claim that the upcoming Dark Souls Day was the Ignitor for his family's misfortunes?

Eric stood on the curb and studied the building, a sturdy, two-level structure decked out in a red, green and white color scheme. Eric thought of the Cheers bar when he saw the exterior. The old bar owned by his best friend, Virgil McKinnon, sat at the end of a street and was close to the coastline. The building's exterior faced the shores leading to the ocean.

He walked into the Aeneid and took in his surroundings. On Thursday night, the place seemed a bit deserted. Several booths along the walls remained open and tables set up along the middle aisle were empty. Three waitresses too many waited on the few patrons already seated. The small stage set up diagonally across the room from the entrance was occupied by a woman reading poetry while a male pianist played a soft tune. Leave it to his best friend to know how to run a club that set just the right mood. The tourists ate this little spot up on weekends, no doubt. The boy he used to play lacrosse with as a kid had done well for himself. Eric chose the next-to-last booth on the right side of the bar, all the way in back and closest to the doorway, a dimly lit area with no overhead lights. This way, he'd be able to surprise his friend.

"Eric Super Cute Cheeks," a woman's voice said from across the room. So much for stealth tactics. Before he could turn his head and identify his admirer, a squeak shrilled into his right ear. A set of long arms surrounded him and the scent of strong perfume drifted into his nostrils. There was only one woman it could be—Abby Poole, Virgil's little sister and active member of the *Mystical Aura of the Red Aegean Sea*, or the MARAS, a group of Castle Hayne women dedicated to the preservation of the town's supernatural history. The women also held New Age ceremonies to purge evil spirits from what Eric had heard. "It really is you. Oh, my God! Nobody told me you were back here in these parts."

"I've been lying low. You know how it is around here when I come to town. I always find out I slept with about ten of your friends before I leave."

"Do you think you can hide those sweet cheeks?" She pushed him up against the wall, reached down, and pinched his ass. Glancing around at the Aeneid's three patrons, Eric's face heated. After all these years, Abby could still make him blush.

"Behave. If you can." Eric's face flushed.

"Why should I want to behave with you back here in this town? Should have told me you were coming back. This is exciting news." She scooted her body closer to Eric's as though she were trying to work her way up on to his lap. The scent of cigarette smoke drifted into his nostrils. She was still a heavy user and still wore the same trademark outfit: a tight red skirt, a black v-neck tee shirt, and a scarf covered in a pattern that reminded him of a checkerboard. Abby always had a thing for putting those two colors together. She'd told him after the first time they made out in high school that red and black were her spiritual colors, and when she wore them, no one could make her feel like she wasn't worth anything.

"Tell old Abby how's my favorite pupil doing?" She beamed a smile, the sparkle of a gold front tooth flickering in the low light.

His face flushed. "I'm glad to be back. I love what Virgil has done to the place." He was eager to turn the subject away from talking about their history together. Virgil was preoccupied with tending the bar. He'd wiped the same glass at least fifty times, his eyes glued to the woman reading the poetry. As though he heard the silent pleas in Eric's head, his friend scanned the area until his gaze rested on Abby sitting beside him.

"Don't look now, but more attention is headed your way, Sweet Cheeks. My brother with the chubby belly and that I'm-a-man-on-lockdown grin just spotted you." A wide smile spread across Virgil's face. Virgil set down the glass he'd been polishing, walked around the counter and headed towards Eric and Abby's table.

"What am I paying ya for, gal? My customers need drinks, hospitality. Hell, they might even need food. What they don't need is dick waxings," he said. "Now get outta my way so I can greet my friend."

Abby rolled her eyes upward and slid away from Eric, but not before she ran her hand over his crotch, lingering over it for a moment. And then, she gave Eric the smile that won him over back in his youthful days, a sexy grin highlighted by her deep red locks and green eyes. "Wild Turkey. Your favorite, right?" Abby asked, ignoring her brother's smirk. Eric nodded. "I'll fix you up a couple and have Ginny bring 'em over to you."

Virgil shook his head, rolled his eyes a bit. "Get outta here."

Turning to her brother, Abby narrowed her eyes. "You're just mad because you got the old hag for a wife." She turned back to Eric. "So glad you're back. You know where to find me, Sweet Cheeks." She winked and shuffled off to the bar. Her next victim, a man who appeared to be about six years younger than Eric's twenty-eight years of age, sat on one stool lined up along the counter. Judging from his dreamy expression, he'd fallen right under Abby's spell as she prepared Eric's Wild Turkey.

"That damn gal, I'm telling ya. She hasn't been right since you two had a go at it all those years ago. That Italian feller she was married to didn't stand a chance. You know why? Because he wasn't Mr. Eric Big Time." Virgil pulled Eric up into a bear embrace and then plopped his husky body down in the seat across from him.

Back in the day, the two of them lived in the principal's office. Their friends had even nicknamed them the Chaos Masters. Trouble for one meant extra stress for the parents of both boys. Tests, cars, sports, girls, sex... sisters—scratch that last one—the two boys had shared everything. The move to New Orleans had weakened that bond; but Eric was still happy for his friend.

He signaled to another waitress, a blonde. She'd just picked up the drink tray that Abby had already finished loading and headed their way. Dressed in a white tee shirt and red shorts, she appeared sweet and innocent next to Abby's fiery personality.

Setting the tray down on the table, the waitress placed two glasses of strong-scented drinks in front of Eric and one beside Virgil's hand. She gave Eric a shy smile. "Wow, she wasn't lying."

"Excuse me?" Eric asked.

"Nothin'. Just makin' an observation." She shrugged and averted her eyes.

"Jesus, Ginny. Could you and my sister plot on ways to molest my friend later? Like after we finish our drinks, for example." The waitress passed one last quick smile at Eric and scurried away. On the way to the bar, Ginny passed by two waitresses.

"I remember him. He's the one the police let get away," the black waitress said to the brunette one.

"Takes some nice sized balls to come back after all that," the brunette waitress said. She half-whispered in Ginny's ear, but that didn't matter. Eric's hearing was his best asset. His family teased him about it all the time. The ability earned him the title of the family's most valuable warlock.

"Hush up." Ginny waved them off. "He might hear you."

"Tsk. Doesn't look like a supernatural to me," the brunette said. "But I'd be willing to find out." She winked at Eric, turned on her heels, and sashayed towards the kitchen.

Eric craved a diversion, a conversation with his old friend that would move him in another direction. He had no interest in talking about any of his old flames or the prospect of new ones, either. "What's this talk about a wife? You didn't email or anything. Did you go soft on me?" A slight ache hit his chest. He hated feeling left out of the events in his friends' lives.

Virgil stole a quick glance at the woman reading poetry to a somewhat bigger crowd now. At least four or five more people had drifted into the bar. Eric recognized the way his friend's face lit up. At one time, he had admired his own fiancée in that same way.

"That's my Shania. And that handsome fella at the piano, the one wearing the Harry Potter glasses, that's our friend, Gus, aka the bartender. As for your soft statement, I'll just tell ya right now. She sets me up with something soft every single night, and it rocks, my man." They both shared a good, hearty laugh and the sensation felt good. No one in his family back home found humor in much anymore. With his older brother, Javier, being recently diagnosed with cancer at age 40, Eric didn't expect the situation to improve much.

"Her nickname's Shay. That's short for Shania. I think she spells it the wrong way. I pick on her all the time, and she gets so mad at me. Make-up sex takes care of these little troubles, though. For a guy that spent most of his life doing everything wrong, I think I finally got something right. She makes me feel that way, you know." Virgil turned towards his wife, a calm look on his face.

He'd put on more weight since Eric last saw him. Back in school, people used to say he and his best friend could pass as twins. Now Virgil looked more like Eric's older brother. The bright Hawaiian design on his shirt added to the aura of this new carefree spirited Virgil. Strangely, Eric was envious.

"You can meet her after she's done with her set. She loves me. So, I know she'll like you. The same, you and I are." Virgil winked and grinned.

"This place is hooked, Virgil. You're still surviving after a decade, and expanding, I see."

"Yeah. Yeah. Dark Souls Day brings the money to keep things looking this way. Tonight, there aren't many tourists, though. I don't have a fancy contractor business like you. Just look at you: your fancy watch, your expensive ride." He cocked his head to the side, looked past my head and motioned toward the custom-made Jeep parked just outside the door. "Man. You left here and worked yourself over." He made a small laugh, shaking his head as though he were in deep thought.

"It's not all like that. Not really. The company still has a way to go before I get big-time sponsors." Eric was eager to steer the conversation to the old Chelby plantation and its new owner. Accepting the assignment from Saul Chelby took some guts. He hadn't yet told his family about the new gig. The rivalry between the Chelbys and Eric's ancestors goes back hundreds of years. Still, Eric needed the money and Chelby wanted an accomplished contractor, or so he said.

There was this omen his mother claimed some old witch had cast on his family hundreds of years ago—one that started in the calm little town of Bolivia. She said the spell was the reason his oldest brother, Javier, was diagnosed with prostate cancer eight months ago.

"Go ahead. Act humble. But we've all heard about Eric Big Time and his big renovation company." Virgil gave him a smug but proud grin.

"You give me too much credit." Eric took a sip of his drink. The rum in his Wild Turkey burned going down his throat, and he winced a little.

"Look at you. Can't even hold your spirits like you used to." Virgil made a wheezy laugh and slapped his knees.

"Speaking of spirits, I see someone bought the old Chelby mansion." Eric set his loaded drink down and raised an eyebrow at Abby. Over by the bar, she was scratching her left thigh as she wiped the counters, sticking her butt out each time she bent over, so Eric had a clear view of her assets.

"Oh yeah, you're talking about that weird chic. She used to be a police medium somewhere up north. They say she had a big-time husband. Son of a bitch gave her a hard time after their kid got killed. Almost made the gal lose her job, and everything—a real high-class ass. Don't you go getting all big in the britches like that, you hear me? Hey, that rhymes: high class and ass."

"Yeah, and don't let me catch you up there onstage reading poetry," Eric said.

"You might catch me doing a lot of things on that stage, but reading poetry ain't one of them," Virgil said, still making the wheezy laugh.

"Saul Chelby sent me a work request. It seems I'll be renovating the place from top to bottom." Eric wanted to steer the conversation toward the old plantation.

Virgil studied him for a moment, his smile fading. "You're gonna take it? I mean, those Chelbys are part of what spooked your old man out, right?"

Eric took a sip of his drink. "Look at the situation this way. It's a chance for me to expand into the local market the same way you've done with this place. Maybe Saul's tenant will decide to sell the place to me so I can flip it. That old house would make a damn good bed-and-breakfast." Deep inside, Eric hoped that selling the house and ridding the old plantation home of the Chelby name might help cleanse the omens attached to the place.

"Well, I think her husband should've made her leave," Abby's voice said from beside Eric's seat. He didn't even see her leave the bar. She held the largest beer mug he'd ever seen. "She's probably a witch. That's why she moved back down here. Everybody in that old hick little Bolivia is a witch or a ghost. Virgil, you know it's true. Don't be looking at me like I'm talking out of my ass or something."

"Abby, you act like Bolivia is a thousand miles away. It's not even thirty minutes down the road." Virgil crossed his arms.

"What are you talking about, Abby?" Eric asked. The town's folklore intrigued him. The more things changed, the more they turned into different versions of the same.

"I'm talking about the witches and ghosts haunting that little old town. I can't believe Saul Chelby is even considering giving up his family's place. That house has been on the market like forever. The little psychic guru chick must really be something," Abby said, studying Eric as if she already knew how much he'd thought about meeting the woman. Her jealousy had been one of the main reasons they didn't stay a couple back in school.

Abby's insecurity was a problem then, and he could tell things would be the same way now.

However, he had to stay focused on his goal... renovating Chelby Rose. He'd give anything to help his mother find her spirit again and do the things she loved. Thing like the pies his mother used to enjoy baking every Sunday. That was until his father died. And then she just kind of drifted away into a world of sculpture making and watching old Lucille Ball reruns, forgetting that the rest of her family even existed.

"Thought you should know, Javier's sick," Eric said to Virgil after Abby walked off.

"Man, your family has bad luck with health issues when you turn forty. What are you, cursed?" Virgil scoffed a light laugh. However, his expression turned serious. "I'm kidding. You know that, right?"

"Depends on who you ask around here," Eric said, thinking of the blame thrown his way when his father died. The townsfolk had always riddled castle Hayne with tales of witches and warlocks. The feud between Eric's ancestors and the Chelby families had passed down throughout the generations. Many believed the men in his family to be warlocks who cast spells on helpless damsels, making the women fall helplessly in love. Eric didn't buy the warlock idea. Yet, he fully believed in a supernatural occurrence that affected his family around Dark Souls Day. And September 28th was only two months away.

The piano music stopped and Virgil lifted his heavy frame up, a smug grin riding his face as he stared at his wife. Turning back to Eric, he said: "The missus calls. Stick around so you two can meet."

"You got it," Eric said, amazed by the way marriage had changed his friend.

Watching Virgil slow dance with his wife filled him with joy; but hearing Abby's words about the witches and ghosts of Bolivia had also jerked him back to a reality he wasn't ready to face.

Chapter 5

andie

T "How many months has it been since you last had sex?" Frieda asked while taking a sip of her limoncello. I nearly spit out my Bahama Mama as I glanced around the Aeneid. The club was halfway full, and I was thankful Frieda and I sat close enough to the stage where an accappella duo played, but far enough away so we could still talk without shouting. Thankfully, no one heard her question.

No one will ever want you. Danger... Danger... Danger!

Oh God. Not here. Not now. That voice. The same one that had plagued my thoughts since the accident sprung to life. I squirmed in my seat, bit my bottom lip, and glanced around, looking for the source.

My hesitation to answer Frieda's question earned me the raised right eyebrow, a look I imagine her patients got when they held back answers during a session. "It's okay to say: 'Frieda, I haven't had sex in ages. My ex-husband was a royal bastard who made me feel like the ice queen. So, I didn't want any.'"

Frieda took another swallow of her drink. Correction. She gulped her cocktail. I refocused on my friend as the voice faded and was glad to own the role of designated driver. "Must we talk about something like that in a club?"

"Like that? Do you mean to say sex? Let me hear you speak the word," Frieda teased.

I rolled my eyes upward and crossed my arms. "You know what I meant."

"If we weren't in a club, you would still clam up. Mental note to me: Must take my bestie out more often before she forgets how to have any kind of fun at all. Deal?"

"All right, deal. Anything to keep you quiet." I studied our surroundings, taking in the club scene and thinking of how I had been nowhere near a dance floor like this one in almost six years. Getting involved with someone hadn't even crossed my mind, especially while I still grieved for Breena. In the presence of a cute guy, I either stuttered or dropped my tampons at his feet. But my best friend had a point. Maybe someday I'd listen to the little voice that wanted me to believe I deserved to be happy again.

"Frieda Tyson. You made it," a dark-haired woman with a braid sweeping her waistline announced. She was wearing a black form-fitting dress and had skin almost as pale as milk, reminding me of a Gothic princess, but with an air of humility about her, a subtle gesture in the way she held her hands clasped together in front of her. A gangly man stood behind her, scoffing. Dressed in a white tee, black pants and an apron, he was the thinnest male I'd ever seen. Spiky brown hair gave him a rock star look and the thick-rimmed glasses he wore reminded me of a character in a movie I couldn't quite finger.

Frieda stood, embraced the woman, and stepped back to admire the enormous diamond on her left hand. "Whoa! You must've really whipped up on him, Shania."

"It was those tips and pointers you gave me. Now, I know why you're such a good therapist." The two women exchanged laughs, while the gangly man standing behind them shook his head and sighed.

"Excuse me. Need to butt in here," he said to Frieda. "Shania, where do you want this box of glasses? Feels like I'm holding an elephant."

"Gus, my fearless multi-tasker. Meet my therapist, Frieda, and her sidekick I haven't met," Shania said. Her voice was light, and her carefree attitude made me want to know more about her. Frieda turned to me. "This is my good girlfriend, Tandie Harrison. She recently moved to Bolivia. Monitor this chick, Shania. She intends to be a bestselling novelist."

"Ah yes. I've read one of your non-fiction pieces. I especially enjoyed the one where you explain how you channel psychic energy from a person's belongings. Excellent piece of literature," Shania said and turned to Gus. "Put those over behind the wet bar. Those are for the upcoming Dark Souls celebration."

"It's about time," he muttered and turned to Frieda and me. "Nice meeting you, ladies. Try not to be strangers." His eyes locked on mine and lingered too long for an introductory gaze, making me feel uneasy. Maybe he'd overheard Frieda's sex therapist question. I could only imagine the conversations busboys heard regularly. Embarrassment raged through me, heating my face.

"Thanks," I said. Gus nodded and moved on toward the bar.

"Don't tell me we still celebrate Dark Souls day," I said to Shania. The celebration, a town tradition, involved a purge of evil spirits from Bolivia and its neighbor Castle Hayne. In the past, I avoided the festival. Didn't need to attract any more spirits than the ones I'd already called to me in the past. However, this year, the prospect intrigued me.

She raised her eyebrows. "I can't believe you asked that question. Course we do. Brings in tons of patrons. Both Dark Souls Day and the Macon House Charity event do. Having said that... Frieda, I'm hoping you'll still be available to help?"

"That's right," Frieda chimed in, taking a sip of her drink after doing so. "We'll need to discuss the Macon House guest list, Shay."

"You got it," Shania said and winked at me. "Come along as well, Tandie. We could use a best-selling author's touch on the program wording."

The invitation blindsided me a bit. I wasn't sure if attending events excited me as much as they did in the past. However, I needed to get my name out there. To put myself in the heart of Bolivia's paranormal society. My agent would agree. "Sure. Why not?"

"Fantastic. I'll be in touch as the event date draws nearer," Shania said.

While listening to Frieda and her friend gab about sex in marriage, I let my gaze drift off to the right side of Shania and toward the bar at the front of the Aeneid. At once, my heart leapt into my mouth, and I questioned the accuracy of my eyes. A dark-haired man sitting at the bar had his gaze locked on me. I looked away, pretending not to notice him. *Chickenshit.* However, each time I turned back in his direction, he was still watching. My breath hitched, my pulse increased, and the next time our gazes met, neither of us looked away.

He was tall and broad-shouldered. Even through the plaid shirt, his muscles rippled and moved as he did. Beneath his worn jeans, he wore work boots that echoed against the floor as he stood and nodded to the bartender. Could the words that had assaulted me as soon as I stepped through the door have something to do with this man? Damn my visions for going silent and teasing me with little slices of light.

The man stood, raked his free hand through his luscious dark hair, and slapped the man standing beside him on the back. And then he turned towards me. Our eyes locked, and the music slowed down, as did everything else around us. My stomach flipped. He was achingly handsome, and I found myself caught in the rapture of something hard to describe. He gave me a half smile and a slight nod. My eyes widened as he turned away. I fidgeted with the straps to my thin, black cami tank and shifted in my chair.

There was a strong sense of familiarity surrounding our eye lock moment.

With my arms crossed tightly enough to cut off the circulation, I fought a sudden urge to leave the table. Frieda and Shania were preoccupied with their own conversation, so I had no problem easing out of the booth and slipping away.

I had wanted to investigate the rooftop dining area ever since we arrived, so I strolled through the aisles of patrons eating and conversing and headed up the steps leading to the balcony, inhaling a tiny breath when the cool nighttime wind bit into the top Frieda made me wear. A July night at the beach sometimes packed the same ice-cold punch as a September one. Yet strangely, I felt warm enough to repel the slap of the chill in the air.

Yeah, you know why that's happening. Could your newfound bodily heat have something to do with Mr. Mysterious sitting at the bar?

Silencing the mischievous voice in my head, I headed toward the rails running along the back of the balcony, the part closest to the ocean, and took in my surroundings. Fewer people sat at the tables outside than the ones on the inside.

I leaned against the rail, feeling the cold metal against my fingertips. In front of me lay an abyss of darkness, with only the sound of the waves crashing against an invisible shore as company. I tried to focus on the peaceful sound and take comfort in it, but something out there in the waters was stirring, and I couldn't shake my sense of unease. In the distance, a set of lights flickered.

At first glance, the lights resembled a cruise ship sailing along fully lit. I moved over to the telescope attached to the rail and studied the vessel. Inside the lens, the form changed. The odd shape was more like a blurry silhouette of a battleship, an ancient one. Straining to focus on the outline, I stretched my eyes until they felt dry.

And then, like magic, the strange vessel disappeared completely from view. No lights. No blurry outlines, nothing. "Whoa. Too much Bahama Mama tonight, I think."

"Nope. It's not your drink. Not that you'd be the type to get drunk," a female's deeply accented voice said from behind me. The woman dressed in a red skirt and a black top was pretty in an old-time movie star kind of way. Her dark red lips blended in with her deep auburn tresses; but her eyes lined with a thick ring of black makeup reminded me of a burglar. "There's really a ship out there, but only certain ones of us can see it. Creepy, right?"

The woman studied the ocean, lost in her thoughts. I always attracted strangers who would suddenly start spilling all their secrets. This ability to hypnotize people into revealing their innermost secrets had been that way for me ever since I was a little girl. But this woman's strange words, along with the disappearing ship I just saw, made me jittery. The chill in the air increased and the thin tank top I wore tonight did a lousy job of blocking any wind.

"Wow. It's freezing up here. I'm heading back inside."

"Don't you wanna know why you can see that ship?" the woman asked.

An invisible force stopped me in my tracks. There was no way she referred to the ship I just saw. "Not really, I'm good," I answered truthfully, turning to face the woman.

"I can see that ship because I'm touched by death. And you..." she eased toward me and narrowed her eyes. "You got the witch's mark. I can smell dark magic on somebody all the way from my house."

Feeling anxious, I turned to go back inside the club. The woman moved in my path, her movement slick and fast like a cat, and leaned closer to my face. "You stay away from what's mine, witch. Do you hear me?"

"I don't even know you. It would be hard to take something from a person I don't even know," I said, inching back toward the telescope. I really wished my psychic intuition still worked.

"Hmph. Figures you wouldn't remember me. Well, I know all about you," she said, narrowing her eyes.

"Abby! What's going on?" a male's deep voice said from behind the woman. She flashed a bright smile just before she turned around and said, "Not a thing. We girls were just having a little chat."

The voice belonged to him, the man from the bar. He strolled toward us, his dark plaid shirt and blue jeans giving him a strikingly mysterious appearance under the balcony's lights. With his gaze locked on my face, I suddenly understood the woman's warning. Sure, he was drop-dead sexy; but his looks were more like the turn-me-into-a-vampire-you-sexy-beast kind of death. That way I can come back and kidnap you when I'm ready.

"I'm sorry, ma'am. Abby doesn't mean to be this way. We still have to keep child locks on the cupboards because of her."

Abby clucked her tongue and crossed her arms. "Don't you dare talk down to me, Eric."

Eric... his name is Eric. Why does that name ring familiar to me?

He wasn't paying attention to Abby's scold, though. His gorgeously mysterious eyes locked on my face and my heart fluttered. "*Eres la chica mas Bonita de aqui.*" His beautifully accented words floored me, and he beamed a smile that knocked me senseless. My mouth opened and closed a few times and the wind cut through my shirt like an ice pick. Yet nothing cut through the spell Eric held over me.

"Beautiful," I said before I thought about it. "What did you say?"

His smile deepened, which highlighted one dimple on his right cheek. The wind whipped through his dark hair, lending him an intriguing, yet comforting air of mystery. He shoved a hand in his pocket and said: "You're the prettiest girl here. Top of the line pickup. I know."

"I wasn't thinking that at all," I whispered, holding our gaze.

He took a step towards me, and then the night wrapped us in its embrace. "I'm Eric. And you are?"

"Well, let me just tell you somethin.'" Abby stepped between us, breaking the hold Mr. Mysterious held over me. She turned to Eric, blocking his view of me. "Witches use spells to control people, so they don't believe in nothin.'"

I scoffed and stepped around her. "Look, people. I don't have a clue about who you two are, but you really need to work out your problems. I'm heading back inside to get my friend. Try to have a good night." I headed back into the club before Eric could say anything else, and before that Abby woman accused me of being a witch again.

Chapter 6

*T*andie

The next morning, I pecked out a significant chunk of my manuscript. The caffeine from my cinnamon flavored coffee kicked in and pushed my muse out of the bed. Satisfied with the progress I'd made, I sat back and flipped through the pages, my mind drifting back to thoughts of my encounter with the mysterious Eric from the Aeneid. What was his story? Especially his accent. He was the type who haunted the dreams of many females, I'm sure.

I couldn't afford to get distracted. Regaining my visions and understanding of what happened the night of my accident held priority over everything else. How else would I determine the reason behind the apparition who caused my accident? This novel was the key. The one with the love interest named Eric.

I stopped flipping sheets and focused on the words. The connection that escaped me on the previous evening hit me like a lightning bolt. I flipped back a few pages and re-read my hero's name... Eric Fontaine. No fucking way. I started writing this story shortly after the accident. How could my protagonist's guy have the same name as someone I just met? Yeah, sure, Eric was a pretty common name. However, given the circumstances of the reason I started writing this novel, I knew this couldn't be a coincidence. No visions needed to understand that one.

"Too bad I'll never see him again." The thought dampened my spirit a bit. While mindlessly flipping through the next pages, I noticed something about the manuscript.

"Wait. What?" I was tired. That would explain the reason I read page 20 and then page 41. I flipped through the manuscript again. Same deal. Twenty pages of my manuscript were missing... 3 days before my agent's submission deadline. I closed my eyes and inhaled deeply. "There must be a logical explanation."

I tossed the papers on the desk and shuffled through the pages. My breathing increased as I fought back a panic attack. No pages 21-40. "Okay, Tandie. Time for a break. Then come back and try again." I stood and walked out of the study.

Passing the window beside the entry door, I caught a movement out the side of my eye. A young blonde girl around seventeen years of age was shuffling around Chelby Rose's neglected rose beds, the ones that lined the property's borders. No one but Saul and Frieda had stopped by since I arrived a few days ago. Even though I knew Bolivia's population was small, I'd believed I was the only resident at this end of town.

I opened the door, stepped outside and walked towards the girl. She was wearing a strange costume, a brown prairie-style dress complete with a shift that lifted fabric up at her waistline the way women wore their clothing back in the 18th century. The dress had an apron on the front and a collar made of lace. The design looked as though she ripped it straight out of the colonial period. I stopped just before I approached her.

The ground beneath my feet seemed to sway, making me lose my balance. My lungs felt constricted, like I was being choked, and the numbing sensation in my toes and fingertips made me feel like I was walking through quicksand with no way out. A wave of dread crashed over me, so powerful that I lost control and could not comprehend or fight it. Then, like a flip of a switch, the sensations abruptly faded away. A boost of wind passed by me, setting the girl's strange clothing into motion.

The girl spun around and caught me off guard, her eyes wide with surprise.

"May I ask who you are and what you're doing on my property? I asked sharply.

"By all means, I do apologize. I'm Ella, the neighborhood gardener." She spoke with a deep southern accent and made a small curtsy, her curly blonde ringlets pinned up in a loose chignon. I repressed an insane urge to laugh and held out my right hand. The girl stared at my outstretched palm and frowned. Slowly, she reached out and placed her slender fingers in mine.

"And you are?" Ella asked. I couldn't see anything about this girl. Skin to skin contact was the best way to connect with my third eye. Nothing. Not one vibration or image.

"I'm Tandie Harrison. This is my place now. Or it will be soon enough." I pulled my hand away and clenched my fist.

"Tandie? Hmm. Why, that sounds just like—candy." High-pitched giggles spilled out of Ella. She covered her mouth and lowered her head as though she'd shamed herself by laughing.

What an odd little pill this one is.

"Yes, I believe it does," I said. Another series of high-pitched giggles erupted from Ella.

"Okay then, Ella, the gardener. Why are we poking around my flower beds?"

"You're gonna need to be thinking about my services real soon. Just look at all these poor wretched souls. You need to hire me right this instant." Ella turned and caressed two dried roses, touching each one as if she were a parent tending a sick child. There was something about her that made me uneasy.

"Tell you what. Since we've just met, and I don't really have any pictures of your work—"

"This is what I do. I did all of this right here by myself. My mother helped me a few times, at first. I got it correct the next time, though." Ella's voice raised a notch.

"I understand, Ella. I'll get back to you when it's closer to blooming season."

A disturbingly wide smile appeared across her face after she narrowed her eyes. "Well, don't wait too long, unless you want them to freeze up and turn black."

"I'll make a note of it."

Ella bowed again and turned around without saying goodbye. I watched the girl bounce away, skipping down the driveway until she turned and disappeared behind the trees.

"Do people around here not believe in cars?" I wondered aloud. I looked back one last time at the place where Ella disappeared. "What a strange girl."

SAUL'S CONTRACTOR SHOWED up on Chelby Rose's doorstep the following Monday. I opened the door and my mouth fell open. My contractor, a wonderfully handsome if not somewhat stoic lover of Latin phrases, stood outside my doorway. It was the guy from the Aeneid. The one named Eric. We held shocked gazes for a long beat before he spoke first.

"Es la chica mas bonita," Eric said in that swoony accent, a smile spreading across his perfect lips. "This is quite the surprise."

Dumbfounded, I opened and closed my mouth a few times before I finally said: "You're the contractor Saul hired?"

His face drooped a bit. "The one and only. Unless, of course, you object."

"You don't look a contractor." What a rude thing to say to someone. It was my default mechanism when I felt vulnerable or shocked in a way that rendered me senseless. Just as Eric's presence did when I opened Chelby Rose's door.

"Should I call Mr. Chelby? Tell him you want another guy instead?" He raised his left eyebrow and smirked a bit. I had half a mind to say yes and call his cocky bluff.

Instead, I crossed my arms and lifted my chin. "That won't be necessary. Provided the one he hired knows his shit."

"Oh, I think he can handle your expectations." His eyes smiled while my cheeks flushed with enough heat to singe the rosebushes. Time for a comeback.

"Also, if he doesn't mind a bit of guidance along the way." Right back at you, Mr. Contractor. Two can play the bluff and blush game. He furrowed his eyebrows. "This is going to be my home. I'll be assisting you."

He cleared his throat and shuffled on his feet. "I don't think so. This man works alone."

"Not on this house, he doesn't." I said, lifting my chin higher and holding back a smile. Mission accomplished. "Do we have an understanding?"

"We do indeed." He held my gaze a moment and turned towards the front yard. "I'm going to inspect the outside. You're welcome to come along... boss."

Giddiness erupted in my stomach and I found myself assaulted by something hard to explain. I didn't dare admit my blossoming curiosity.

"I'll go change. Then meet you back out here."

Eric nodded a few times, lifted his lips in a slight smile, and gave me a two-finger salute just before he walked off the porch.

I got ready in no time. Dressed in ripped jeans shorts, an old black tee-shirt, and a gray bandana that held my hair back, I walked outside and scanned the front yard until my gaze landed on the contractor. Eric set down his armory of tools, waved at me, and got right to work. Curiosity was killing me. Paying attention to his advice and recommendations was going to be difficult.

Eric Fontalvo was calm and ruggedly handsome, but he also had an underwear model's appeal: high cheekbones, a gym-ripped physique, and a body decked out in jeans and a blue plaid shirt. After looking over the exterior, he came inside. He examined the faucets, adjusted a few washers, and stopped the leaks. I watched him while he worked on each area, a quiet intensity surrounding him.

"You have a lot of structural damage. Some pipes look ancient. Maybe around ten decades in age." He rattled two rusted pipes underneath the kitchen sink.

"That's almost a hundred years," I muttered, feeling stupid for repeating the obvious.

"Exactly. I'd recommend replacing them, along with that old disaster-in-waiting awning on the front porch. It looks good enough from a distance; but the fascia boards supporting the frame are rotten." He flipped bangs out of his face and gave me a small crooked smile. His hazel-brown eyes lit up with warmth. "No offense to you, ma'am."

"Not a bit taken," I said and went back to chewing the inside of my lip. If he was trying for a ticket to get a remodel job out of me, then his one-sided smile was well on the way to winning the spot.

"The exterior needs a new paint job, too. And the roof issue." He stood and pointed up to the brown stains splattered across the kitchen ceiling. Heat spread over my cheeks and I could tell the blush showed from the way he smiled and looked away. He shuffled on his feet twice and ran a hand through his hair. Why was he so nervous? Surely a man like that had women falling all over him. "I've already made a few minor repairs. Tomorrow I can start prepping the exterior for paint."

"Sounds like a good plan," I said.

I wanted to know more about this handsome stranger. One thing Frieda was right about: there wasn't a shortage of eye candy in my life at the moment.

The next day, Mr. Intense Contractor came prepared with all his renovation gear. I met him outside the front door. He bent down and pulled a loose board out of the deck, his muscles rippling underneath the fabric of his shirt.

On the first day I arrived at Chelby Rose, I'd promised myself that I would put my personal touches on any renovations, and I intended to hold steady to my word. Armed with a set of recently purchased paint brushes, I strolled past Eric and headed down the front steps.

"Um, Ms. Harrison, what are you doing?" Eric stopped pulling boards and turned towards me. His face bore an amused smirk underneath his smile. At first, the undertones in his voice came across as southern. But after listening to him longer, I thought the syllables hinted at more of a Puerto Rican or South Columbian accent.

"Isn't that obvious? I'm going to paint," I answered, waving my pack of paint brushes. "Do you have issues with that?" I asked, slightly annoyed by his smirk.

"Course not. It's your place. I just thought you'd—want to review the issues and head inside. I'm sure you'd rather be writing." He flipped a strand of hair away from his face and stood. I wondered if he was going to move the loose lock beside it, too.

"That's exactly why I need to be out here. I need inspiration." I pranced over to the four five-gallon paint buckets Eric had lined up along the front porch, pulled out my paintbrushes, and counted them. One of the six brushes was gone. "Crap. One is missing."

He cleared his throat before speaking. "Far be it from me to keep a lady from her mission, Ms. Harrison. But you're going to paint with those?"

"What's wrong with my paintbrushes?" I asked, looking down at the pack in my hands. I took my time picking these out at the hardware store.

"Not a thing if you're doing a paint-by-number job, that is." A grin spread across his lips. "Those are touch-up paint brushes. As in, you paint little tiny sections with them. Not the best thing for covering 200-square-feet of siding or even a porch."

I frowned and studied my brushes. They were super small compared to the ones he had laid out on the ground. We shared an amused look as Eric burst out laughing first.

"Well, thanks for pointing out the fact that I'm a total amateur," I said, grinning widely.

"Sorry, Ms. Harrison," he said and tried to straighten out his face.

"And please, lay off all the Ms. Harrisons. I mean, that sounds so grandmotherly," I said. He gave me a tight smile and nodded, the amusement of my dilemma still clear on his face. Embarrassed beyond words, I bent down and lifted one bucket, my muscles straining against the weight.

"All right, Tandie it is. At least let me help you with that." He walked down the steps and grabbed the pail, much to my relief, and set the container down on the porch. "Painting can be trickier than it looks. The porch has to be sanded first."

"I appreciate your offer, but I suspect painting doesn't come anywhere close to writer's block." I didn't want to let him see me squirm in this moment of renovation stupidity. Translation: I completely depended on the contractor. Plus, there was something about this guy that comforted me and made me believe I could lower my infamous emotional guard.

He moved the rest of the heavy buckets out of the sun and on to the porch, wiped his face with the back of his hand and turned an intense chameleon-eyed gaze on me as he strolled my way. Yeah, sure, people admired my strange two-toned eyes all the time, but the windows to Eric's soul did amazing things. The pupils changed colors depending on the way and the type of light that hit his face.

"Somehow, I believe you can handle some pretty fierce writing issues." His voice came out low and raspy and the dark tee shirt he wore today stuck to his abs, all six glorious packs of them. Perfect wasn't a word that came anywhere close to describing Eric.

"Thank you for that vote of confidence, Mr. Contractor."

"Ooh, I get it. You can use old-fashioned greetings on me, but not the other way around," he said with a smile spreading across his heart-shaped mouth.

I shrugged. "It doesn't count for work titles, only when you use someone's last name."

Eric smirked and made a small laugh. "How convenient." Releasing me from the intensity of our stare down, he moved his gaze to his waist, adjusted the tool belt on it, turned his attention back to me and stepped closer, leaving a small amount of space between our faces. He was ruggedly handsome, minus the cockiness that made Saul Chelby so intriguing. But even without Saul's confidence and rich boy looks, this guy held his ground with ease.

"What's so convenient?" I asked.

"That I'm stuck with an assistant who makes words and rules up for a living." Moving around me, he said, "I'm heading inside to take another look at those pipes. I'm sorry you got all dressed up in those shorts for no reason." He turned and strolled toward the house, leaving me standing there with a handful of useless paintbrushes.

"Okay. Maybe I gave you too much praise, a little too soon," I whispered and headed toward the house.

Chapter 7

E*ric*
    Eric grinned as he walked back to his Jeep, his mind awhirl with the thoughts of Tandie's smile. His head spun with a desperate intoxication, something he hadn't felt in years; not since that one fateful night when he'd been so blind to the truth of what lay before him. His heart raced, sending waves of heat through his body; all for a woman he'd just met. He could still feel her gaze on him, her bi-colored eyes burning into his soul and her gentle smile despite all of the pain that weighed on her shoulders. What secret did she hide? Was this just a distraction, or something more? He had to find out.

And then the growl slipped through the evening like a chainsaw, hacking its way through a beautiful wooden structure. He stopped a few feet away from his Jeep and studied the woods surrounding Chelby Rose. The trees shuffled in a strong Bolivian breeze and teased him with silence. Every cell in his body went on alert, and he found himself unable to move. Cold chills swept across his backside, even though sweat beads erupted across his forehead.

"No fucking way." The growl rattled his nerves. Because Eric knew what the noise meant. Even though his family had moved far away from the small town of Bolivia, his father still heard the growls just before he died of a heart attack. However, his father survived almost a complete decade after passing thirty-six years, the age when men in Eric's family expired. Javier's fortieth birthday happened in a few months, so he was going to do the same.

Would Eric be immune? Or did this growl mean that his brother's time had lessened?

Could he learn enough from the elusive residents in this town fast enough to save Javier?

Eric was jittery, anxiously waiting for the growl to draw nearer. The deafening silence was what he heard. He stood still, listening intently for any sound of life. It killed him to leave the defenseless woman alone in the house that his family's misfortune began, a worry that intensified with each step. But he had learned his lesson the hard way in the past, being branded an outcast in Bolivia as a result of his last doomed relationship. Could he dare to put his faith in someone new again?

His brother, Javier, warned him about coming back. Along with coincidences, Eric was never one to heed warnings and unsolicited advice. He'd never have helped turn the family business around if he gave in to those two weaknesses.

A buzz vibrated at his hip. He pulled out his cell phone and studied the screen. There were a few text messages from Abby.

Eric! Where r u? I'm at the Aeneid.
Come fast. It's Virgil. Something bad happened.
Oh God, no.

***

ERIC PARKED HIS JEEP just outside the Aeneid and jumped out. Eyes glued to the scene ahead, he fought back the terror clouding his mind. "It's Virgil. Something bad happened," Abby's text had read. No fucking way! He refused to believe the negative thoughts racing through his head and figured he'd find his friend waiting to explain how he had busted up his leg or something. The yellow police tape strewn around the outside of the club told the silent tale he didn't want to hear.

"Where's Virgil?" he shouted at Detective Leroy Newman as he approached his old classmate.

"You can't see the body. I'm sorry, Eric," Leroy said in a monotone voice, his accent bland.

"The body?" Eric croaked, his fists clenched.

"Virgil's dead. Appears to be a robbery. I'm sorry, Eric," Leroy confirmed. They had never been friends. Leroy lost two girlfriends to Virgil back when they attended high school. Tonight Leroy seemed almost happy to deliver the verdict that someone attacked and killed Eric's friend.

Shoving past Leroy, Eric stalked toward the ambulance parked across the street. The paramedics struggled to load the stretcher, a black body bag strapped on top. Just one look was all Eric needed. Closure never came for him until he saw the person in a lifeless state, a self-serving confirmation, he guessed. The same way he had gazed at his father lying in the coffin during his wake.

"Hold on! Wait!" he demanded, startling the man lifting the gurney. Eric unzipped the bag and gagged at the sight before him. Doing so exposed layers of blazing red flesh on his friend's throat, as if someone or something peeled them back in pieces. Virgil's mouth gaped open, his face frozen in an eternal ode to the pain he must have suffered. Memories of the way his mother screamed the night his father died surged inside his mind, and he felt like doing the same thing.

"Could you move back, sir?" the youngest paramedic said to Eric and nodded to his partner. Eric took a step back, allowing the men to lift his friend's body into the ambulance, and struggled to comprehend the events taking place around him.

"This happened because that witch moved back down here." Abby's voice said from beside him. She stumbled over to Eric and collapsed in his arms. "She's the reason something stirred all those old Bolivian spirits up."

"Abby, what the hell? You shouldn't still be here," Eric snapped, moving her away from the ambulance and back across the street. "Your brother is dead, and the only thing you can think about is an old wives' tale?"

"Don't you be chastising me about what's real and trying to make me think I'm crazy. I saw her. She stood on the rooftop, watching for that boat again."

"You're delirious. What are you saying?" Eric demanded. Yet, deep down, the smallest ember of doubt stirred awake.

Abby started pounding on his chest. "Don't you do that to me, Eric Fontalvo. You and your cursed family should have just stayed away."

"Calm down, Abby," he said, restraining her arms. "Stop acting like this and get your head together."

At once she collapsed in his arms, her body pressing into his, sobs jerking through her thin frame. Leroy walked up to them and motioned toward one paramedic, the same guy who had just finished loading his friend's body into the ambulance. The paramedic nodded toward his partner and made his way over to where Eric and Abby stood.

"Come with me, ma'am. Let's get you something to help you feel better." Somehow, he coaxed Abby away from Eric. Medicine might soothe her nerves for a while, but nothing like that would work for him.

"The psychic will need to stay in town," Leroy said to Eric. Just what had Abby told him about Ms. Harrison?

"What? Come on, Leroy. Don't tell me you bought tickets for the witchcraft train too." Eric tried to laugh.

"No, I'm saying strange things have happened since she moved into that house a few days ago. But in this case, a witness placed her at the scene of your friend's death."

Eric's blood pressure shot up. "That's a fucking lie! What witness? I just left her house."

"This was earlier in the evening when Abby spotted her." The detective glanced at Virgil's sister.

Eric scoffed, but he had to consider Leroy's words. He had arrived at Ms. Harrison's house later in the day. However, she couldn't have done something like this. Sure, she was a fit woman. Only a man comparable to the Terminator would've been able to lift his friend's body and break bones. There was a logical explanation. He now understood the meaning behind that damn growl.

"She wasn't the only one who saw the woman. Virgil's old lady, Shania, also said she saw our fortune teller walking along the beach."

Abby was jealous, her motives transparent; but Shania's observation threw him. "I'm sorry, Eric. I've always respected you and your family. Hell, our mothers crocheted together before your father moved you all away. I'm just stating the facts. People are uneasy. This time of year always brings out the freaks. But some of those fears are valid."

"Right, but Ms. Harrison isn't a freak. She's a grieving mother. Somebody who's trying to put her life back together. I can understand that. You want to pick on her for being human or because she's different?" Eric demanded, his body trembling and nausea inching up his throat. A siren blared through the air. The ambulance pulled off, taking Virgil's body away to be deposited in a cold, dark morgue.

"Chill, Eric." Leroy moved closer to him. He always stayed remarkably controlled. Eric had never been that way. He supposed if he would've been, then maybe he'd still be engaged.

"Didn't you see your friend's body? Something ripped his throat out. It's not like anything I've ever seen before." Leroy paused, his expression softening but still serious. "I can bet your pretty waitress's ass over there the coroner will come back and say there's not an animal around here that makes blunt cuts like the ones on your friend's neck."

Eric's heart sped up. "What are you saying?"

"A large fork or..." Leroy sighed and massaged his neck. "Human teeth made those marks."

"You're trying to tell me we've got a man running around who thinks he's an animal?" Eric asked.

"Could also be a woman," Leroy said, his gaze locked on Eric's face.

Eric threw his hands up. "I know what to do. Even better, I'll help you figure out your next move. Find the son of a bitch who killed my best friend and leave Ms. Harrison alone."

Leroy's dark eyes lit up. "Go tell that to your buddy's sister. You two are close. Explain to her how you want me to axe suspects just because you're sweet on one of them."

Eric glanced back at Abby sitting on the edge of the sidewalk, her legs pulled up to her chest as she rocked back and forth. She looked so fragile and innocent, reminding him of the way she was during their high school years. It was a time when he and Virgil got together after studying to discuss lacrosse, volleyball, and, of course, the school's hottest girls. If it weren't for Virgil, then he'd probably be flipping burgers instead of running his own business.

But then, his father moved the family away, his solution to running from that damn heartache that haunted their family. "You will not win," he said under his breath.

"What's that?" Leroy asked.

"Nothing," Eric muttered and headed over to check on Abby.

THE DAY OF THE FUNERAL brought more drizzle. Eric's mother always said that rain at a funeral was a good thing. Tears from the sky meant that the soul being laid to rest had floated away to Heaven. The attendees at Virgil's funeral stood under umbrellas as the grave keepers lowered his friend's casket into the earth.

Shania leaned on Gus the entire time, her right arm shaking so badly that Eric almost walked over to steady her himself.

Eric's family pastor, Frederick Jeffries, gave a fine eulogy the way he always did for all people in the coastal cities. The musical undertones in his voice and the raw passion in the way he delivered Virgil's final portrayal brought tears to Eric's eyes.

Abby stood beside Eric the entire time, her face frozen in an empty stare. Their mother, Mrs. McKinnon, shouted at the grave keepers, a scene to break even the hardest man as they lowered her son's body into the ground. Several agonizing wails later, she collapsed into her husband's arms. Several family members rushed over to lift the grief-stricken woman and carefully ushered her back to the limousine waiting at the head of the line. She was like a mother to Eric too, and each wail pushed harder against his chest as if his limbs would explode from the heaviness he carried.

Pain always eased in to his life at some point. Heartache made him commitment-phobic and ruined his engagement. It also took his father and made his mother go insane. Now the crafty agent of death had taken his best friend. He stared at the grave keepers tossing dirt on top of the coffin, wanting the pain to end, vowing to drink enough Wild Turkey to make him sleep until the next year.

"Staring at the coffin won't bring him back," Abby said in a flat voice. She remained remarkably calm throughout the ceremony. There wasn't a tear anywhere on her face. How much did he truly know about the woman standing beside him?

"What do you suggest I do, Abby? Stand there like you and pretend nothing's happening?"

She smiled, but her shoulders trembled. "My dear, sweet little Eric. You've always been so hateful to me. I can see that now. My friends, the MARAS, will take care of everything. Just you wait and see."

"Do I even want to know what you mean by that?" Eric asked, feeling odd standing so close to the woman he once thought was a sex goddess. Something about her had changed. Even the tone in her voice and the way she carefully pronounced each syllable. Sure, they all grieved for Virgil, but Abby's eyes held something that reminded him of a wild animal.

"You don't wanna know what I'm thinking. You can't handle it. Besides, I hear you'll be working with the witch, fixing her house up and all that." She sounded more like herself, but the crazy look was still in her eyes. Moving closer to Eric, she ran her hands over his arms, massaging them.

"That's right. I should tell you, though. I'm not sure who you and Shania saw on the beach that night. Tandie was at home," Eric said.

"Tandie? She's a first-name bitch for you now, huh?" She snorted and moved her hands away from him. "Well, she's evil. This is all her doing. It's always her fault." She lowered her eyes as if she wanted to keep herself from saying more.

"Why do you act this way? All petty and hard when you know you're upset," Eric said, annoyed with Abby and disgusted with the small part in him that wanted to hear why she considered Tandie a witch.

"Tell me. Why do you always go after the wrong woman? First the tragic model girlfriend and now the witch. I hear you got tough competition, though. Kinky Saul Chelby's hot on her trail. That's the problem with men. You think with your dicks and not your chipmunk-sized brains." Her voice faltered for the first time since they arrived at the funeral. She stumbled a bit and her lip trembled.

"You're just like my brother. No wonder the two of you got along so good. Go on and run away to your little witch living in her ghost house. All of y'all deserve each other." She turned and headed toward the cars parked along the side of the road, not even bothering to lift her umbrella.

Upsetting Virgil's sister during a time like this wouldn't have made his best friend happy. He owed it to Virgil to remain civil with Abby, even if she was losing her mind. He knew little about the MARAS. However, if they planned to take advantage of her, then he intended to stop them.

"Abby. Wait!" Eric ran toward the family car and touched her arm. She turned to face him, the stony look back on her face. "I don't want to fight. We need each other now. I'm upset too. I just don't understand how you can act this way, so calm about everything."

"It's easy enough," she said, shrugging.

"I'm asking as a friend, but have you gone mad?" Eric asked in a gentle voice. He didn't want to further upset Abby. If anyone understood the pain this experience had delivered her, then he did. How many times has he experienced the death of his loved ones in the last decade? Too many to count. Each time, the experience numbed him, yet triggered the fight inside his soul at the same time. He wanted Abby to understand she could do the same thing.

"No. I'm not crazy. When I think about it, I'm actually kind of... glad. Like I said, the MARAS will handle things from here. No worries." That being said, she smiled, walked toward a separate car from the rest of her family, got in and drove off.

Eric watched the black sedan's taillights disappear over the hill, wondering which night he fell asleep and wound up drifting through a nightmare.

Chapter 8

T*andie*

    A more subdued Eric returned five days later and got right to work, concentrating on everything I noted. He installed the deadbolt I'd requested and stepped back to admire his creation a few times. He was intense and didn't half step on any request, no matter how small.

"Thanks for getting this done so quickly. After living in New York, I feel safer this way," I said.

"Not a big deal. It's best to be cautious. Especially right now in case you haven't heard about the murder." He studied me with an intense gaze. Fine stubble outlined his mouth and his warm eyes turned sad as he looked away. I wanted to know why, but didn't dare ask.

"Very true. I heard about that poor man at the Aeneid."

"His name was Virgil. Someone murdered him." He said the name with such passion in his voice that I winced a bit. His look softened as we stared at each other. "Have you been back to the Aeneid recently?" Was that a slight accusatory tone in his voice?

"Nope. I don't care to be around crazy people who think I'm a demon," I stated.

"Then you haven't been there since the night we unofficially met," he said more to himself than as a question for me.

"Should I be asking you why I feel like I'm on trial?"

Sighing, he ran a hand through his thick wavy hair again. I imagined what it would feel like to mimic the gesture. Black sheep reputation aside, I found myself intrigued by the man standing before me now. He was cloaked in mystery. Yet, I stilled my fluttering heart and concentrated on the issue at hand.

"I didn't want to say anything. Don't get upset, all right?" he said.

"Continue, please," I said.

"A couple of people claim they saw you walking outside the Aeneid right before Virgil disappeared."

My heart flipped. I wasn't ready to be the town's gossip board again. "What? You're joking, I hope. Wait a minute. I can only guess that one of those people might be—your waitress friend, Abby."

"Virgil's wife claims she saw you too."

I held his gaze, controlling the heat rising in my chest. His eyes demanded both the best of and worst parts of a person's soul as though stripping you bare with one somewhat menacing look. "Then maybe they need glasses because I was here at this house fighting stupid plumbing issues and trying not to drown while waiting for you to arrive. Now, if we're done with my interrogation, I believe you were hired to do a job."

"I didn't mean to make you feel uncomfortable. I'm pretty sure they made a mistake in who they think they saw. But it's not every day that my best friend gets killed. Forgive me, ma'am," Eric said in a factual tone and turned back to his work.

Feeling like an ass, I craved a way to ease the tension. I understood the pain of losing someone close to you and the agony of enduring life thereafter. "Well, now that those tidbits have been covered, it's like this. I keep finding loads of issues.

Are you in the market for a full renovation?" I shrugged, my painful shyness raging. I couldn't ever recall feeling so insecure about talking to someone. All those years spent with Jack had dampened my personality more than I realized.

"I accepted Saul Chelby's offer as his contractor, not as his renovator," Eric said, the offensive look on his face softening into curiosity.

"But his soon-to-be new owner needs a complete makeover on her house. There are more issues than I can count on three hands. Surely, Saul would understand that."

"He might think I'm a moonlighter and fire me if I poach on his territory," Eric said, moving just a bit closer, his handsome features still guarded, but more relaxed. "I know I would feel that way."

"You don't seem like a man who gets intimidated easily," I said, crossing my arms. His presence although uninvited comforted me. I'd felt this way when we first started working on the house. However, we now shared this kindred bond, the undeniable link that came with the arrival of soul crushing loss on one's doorstep.

Now you're flirting with the repair guy.

Just what will you do if he returns the gesture?

"Good observation. You've got yourself a deal," Eric said, holding my gaze a long moment before backing away. I held back the urge to follow him.

"It's okay to wait another week or so. In case you need more time."

He gave me a slight smile that didn't reach his eyes. Shaking his head a bit, he said: "I'm right where I need to be."

Experiencing fluttery sensations about another man besides my ex for the first time in almost a decade made me feel different, but strangely alive too. It was as if I stood outside myself and was watching my body move along in life.

Eric passed a card to me, brushing his hand across mine, allowing his calloused fingers to linger a moment. "Um, in case those issues pop up again sometime soon. Those might be somewhat expensive to repair if left unchecked too long."

"Is there anything I can look forward to in this makeover?" I asked.

"The plumbing issues should only take another week or so to finish. The structural elements will take time. I'll be back the day after tomorrow," he said.

"Great. Chelby Rose is eternally grateful, Mr. Contractor." I reached out my hand. He took it in a firm handshake. His palm wasn't as rough as I had imagined it would be, but his grip was strong, a good sign. Or so I thought...

Later that evening, a car pulled into the driveway, the bright lights blinding me. The man who got out of the driver's seat was average height, medium build, and he wore a trench coat over gray slacks. He reminded me of Inspector Gadget for some odd reason. Considering the unnerving conversation I'd just experienced with Eric, I struggled to control my anxiety.

"Good evening, Mrs. Harrison," the man said, approaching me. Right away, I figured he must be the detective Eric had told me about, the one who investigated his friend's death. He held out his hand and said: "Detective Leroy Newman."

I ignored his offer to handshake. "It's Ms. Harrison, Detective Newman, and soon to be Ms. Jacobson, thanks for making a note of that."

"Quite the lady, you are. Those folks up north taught you how to kill every bit of southern charm you had left in you, I see," he said behind the large mustache on his face.

"Am I under arrest, Detective? I don't recall seeing a subpoena or any type of formal document."

"I have a few questions for you, if you have the time. You lost your daughter a couple years ago, right?" he asked, ignoring my question. I was dirty, annoyed, and still shaken up by Eric's news about people seeing me at the Aeneid.

"Everyone knows my situation. Your point?"

"Breena was her name, right?" He held my gaze, but I stayed silent. I had spent enough time around his type to understand that he'd already made a conclusion about something. "She had a nickname. What was it, if I may ask?"

"That's none of your business," I heaved.

He moved closer to me so only a foot of space separated us. "Don't make this any tougher on yourself. I already have two witnesses placing you at the scene where Mr. McKinnon died. We have no leads. The higher ups are coming down on my ass. I'm feeling just a tad desperate, Ms. Harrison." He paused and inhaled a shaking, angry breath before he continued.

"As a former police medium, I'm sure you understand how things deteriorate for suspects when that happens. The only reason I didn't have you brought in for questioning was because of Shania McKinnon. Poor woman. She literally lost everything in one night. Still, she tells me not to harass the local celebrity—something about her tourists associating the Aeneid with negative publicity. Yet, I'm willing to bet my entire monthly wages that you know something."

I frowned and crossed my arms. Not only was the detective hyped up about this case, but he was also right. I'm fairly certain that Shania's desire to protect my identity was mainly because of Frieda.

Shaking his head and grinning, he stepped back. "Was your daughter's nickname, Baby B?" My heart made a small leap. "The old nose never steers me wrong when it comes to my leads, Ms. Harrison. For some reason, the word Baby B was written in blood near the body. A little tidbit we kept out of the papers. You know how that works, don't you? Given your history with the NYPD."

"I need to call my lawyer," I whispered, shaken by this new information.

"No. First, you'll answer my questions. Second, you call your attorney," the detective snapped and closed the distance between us.

From beside us, a male's familiar confident voice broke through the tension. "Detective, you shouldn't be rude. You'll either allow Ms. Harrison that one opportunity for council or provide a warrant saying she's to be arrested. Or, you can feel free to choose a third option," Saul stated, coming to stand tall beside Detective Newman. Dressed in a white knit shirt that was opened at the collar and beige khakis that almost matched his messy sun-kissed hair, he sent my mind a whirling.

"Saul Chelby. Where's your car? Last I checked your company squandered enough money out of its clients to buy an island. Seems kind of strange to see you walking around out here without wheels," the detective said, fidgeting more than he did before Saul appeared. "And just who the hell are you to be giving me orders?"

Detective Newman was right about the missing car issue, but I was relieved to see Saul. If anybody could handle domineering and rude then that would be Mr. Alpha-Male Chelby.

"This is still my house, and I don't really like it when misguided detectives come around harassing my tenants without due cause," Saul said.

Detective Newman stepped toward him. Saul didn't flinch or appear the slightest bit intimidated. Instead, he stood there, glaring at the detective with an expression somewhere between savage and school-boy mischievous.

"Who the fuck do you think you are, Saul Chelby?" the detective spat at him.

"Watch the language, Detective. We're in a lady's presence." A boyish smile spread across Saul's face. The wickedness in that small gesture and the insanity behind those eyes made me want to step back and toward him all at the same time.

The detective kept going. "You and your family left enough scandals behind to see us all through the next hundred generations. And you have the nerve to step up on my beat like some kind of king and start bossing me around? What is she? One of your bondage girls?"

Saul threw his head back and laughed as if he and the detective had shared an inside joke between friends. "I'm sure you'd love to know." And then Saul spoke in a low, but firm voice. "Unless you want to deal with my attorney, which judging by the ragged way your department operates, you obviously couldn't afford to do. Then, you'll need to remove yourself from my property, Detective Newman."

The detective's brown skin turned several shades of crimson. Working his jaw muscles, he took a step back and turned toward me. "Don't leave town, Ms. Harrison. Or I'll have you arrested. Good night." He turned without looking at Saul, got into his sedan and kicked up gravel as he pulled out of the driveway.

Now. Time to deal with Mr. Take-a-Walk-in-the-Woods standing here beside me. Turning to Saul, I said: "Did I miss a payment? That why you're here?" I smoothed out my black dress and did my best to hide my rattled nerves.

Saul stuffed his hands in his pockets, tilted his head to the side, and gave me a boyish grin. "Can't a landlord check on his tenant without suspicion?"

"Perhaps. Better watch yourself, though. Apparently I'm some menace at large wannabe." I turned and headed towards the doorway. The people of Bolivia suspected me of foul play. What I wouldn't give to experience even a slight tingle of a vision.

"I doubt that. Seriously, you're fine? Some psychopath is on the loose. I wanted to check... to see if you need anything."

He shuffled his feet, stuffed his hands into his pocket, and hesitated before speaking. "I wanted to warn you. Someone was killed. Virgil was an idiot at times, but it's messed up how he died." Saul shook his head and continued. "The Aeneid's regulars are all shook up about this one."

He moved his handsome, but boyish gaze over my slip dress. Frieda told me he was a player hidden behind southern charm, a man known to be a swinger in kinky sex circles. I found it hard to believe the humble person standing before me could be anything other than a businessman who worked too much, a powerful man targeted by the local gossip mill because of his last name. That was until he glanced at me as if I were a new dessert on a forbidden menu.

As though he heard my thoughts, he slowly lowered his eyes.

"You want to know what's odd about all this? I dreamed that I was standing outside the Aeneid a few nights ago." I recalled the details that were as clear as if I had experienced the events in person.

Saul moved closer to me, leaned in and said, "With all due respect, Ms. Harrison, I don't think I'd make an awful lot of fuss about having a dream like that. Our friendly neighborhood detective might get the wrong idea."

And he was right. According to Eric, I already had people accusing me of being a witch, even going so far as to confront me without saying a word in introduction. Just as Detective Newman had done. Even New Yorkers weren't that bold.

"I'm shaken, of course. But I'd nothing to do with that man's murder."

"No worries. I've got your back," Saul said and held my gaze.

Breaking our staredown, I craved some alone time. Didn't want the landlord to consider me a witch or a loon as well. "I'm fine. If you don't mind it's been a long day."

"Of course. Talk to you soon." Saul nodded in true southern gentleman style, turned and walked back to his car parked just outside Chelby Rose's front gate. I hadn't noticed it sitting out there before.

Shivering as a breeze touched my shoulders, I turned, headed back inside, and did my best to ignore the howl slicing through the night behind me.

Chapter 9

*T*andie

Over the next few weeks, Eric threw himself into his work and tackled Chelby Rose's renovations one painstaking project at a time like a true professional. And I did my best to handle the accusations being thrown my way by Detective Newman.

Eric handled the mid-August heat with ease, unlike me who'd gotten spoiled by New York's cooler temperatures. However, there was a diminished presence hanging over him. It was as though someone had turned a light off and left a hull of the man who I'd first met. He barely said a word to me before hopping into his routine, and I found myself missing the intriguing man I'd first met.

The mysterious leaky plumbing wasn't the works of a ghost in the house. Instead, loose washers on the main line leading from the ancient well, something I thought was a hunk of mangled stone sitting in the backyard, had caused the chaos. And the leaking roof in the kitchen was fully restored. I had to use a chunk of my book advance to help with the materials, but the end result was beautiful. The beauty of the home began to shine through the rotten wood and chipped paint I first saw the day I arrived at Chelby Rose.

The results of Eric's handyman skills were beautiful. The final perk was the light rose-colored exterior paint, a shade considered original to the house. Eric didn't say a word about my upgraded paintbrushes. He was too busy making sure I didn't catch him watching me as I bent over to paint the lowest boards on the house. However, I turned around at the perfect moment on paint day and caught him staring. His face flushed so badly, I couldn't resist doing something to celebrate my small victory.

"Wow, it's so hot out here today." I stretched my arms, lifting my tee-shirt up until my belly button was exposed, basking in the warmth of the late summer sun. Eric's mouth fell open. Success! That move totally stole Mr. Intense's attention. Tucking my lips, I made a move toward an even more creative tease, bending over to pick up one of the three paint brushes I'd dropped.

"What are you doing?" he asked.

"What does it look like? I dropped my paintbrush." I shrugged and waved the brush between us. "Did I not use the proper technique for bending over and picking it up?"

He gave me a dimpled grin and moved closer to where I stood beside the house. Glancing down at the brushes beside my feet, he said, "They do look somewhat dirty. You sure you can handle that task? You strike me as somewhat of a nice girl. With that much paint and dirt all in the heads, you have to get a little rough with cleaning them." His gaze bore into mine, smoldering me under a hazel brown sugary-colored look this time.

I held his gaze. "Oh, believe me. I have plenty of ways to clean dirty things."

There was about a foot of space between us now. "Is that right?"

"Oh yeah," I answered, hoping that the pulse line on my neck didn't show the way my heart thumped inside my chest.

His gaze drifted from my eyes down to my lips and finally ended at my left shoulder. "Then why don't you start by cleaning that big red spider off your shoulder?" An amused smile spread across his lips, but a scream shrilled out of mine.

Eric slammed his hands over his ears. "Damn it, Tandie."

Adrenaline spiked through me. He might as well have said my breasts were hanging out. He would've gotten less of a response than he did with the spider statement. "Get it off me! Do you see it? Is it still there? Get it!" I shrieked, jumping around and spinning in half circles.

"I won't help you until you stop trying to burst my eardrums," he said, still half-way smiling. He came over and put his arms around me, pulling me into his embrace. "Calm down, Tandie. It's gone, all right?"

Vowing to never tease Eric ever again, I waited for my breathing to normalize and for my trembling limbs to steady as I was pressed against Eric's chest.

"Wow, you're arachnophobic," he said after a long, but charged moment.

"You think?" I said, still too embarrassed to look up at him. His thumb circled around the small of my back, and that tiny gesture alone ignited several neglected parts of my body.

"I'm sorry. I did not know that would happen," he muttered in my hair.

This time I did look up at him. "What do you mean, Mr. Contractor?" I said in measured words, anger quickly replacing my nervous fear. His silence said it all. I pushed back from his shoulders and glared at him. "You sneaky mean person. You tricked me."

"I'm sorry. I know. It was a terrible thing for me to do. Do you forgive me?" He made begging hands and put as much sadness into that gorgeous face as he could muster.

Are you insane? Of course I forgive you. "Nope. I'm afraid it's not quite that easy, Mr. Contractor." I crossed my arms, turned my head and tapped my right foot, refusing to look at him.

He took a step closer, closing the distance between us again. "What if I make you a forgive-me-offer you can't refuse?"

"Nope. Not even then."

"You don't even know what it is," he said.

"I don't care." *Are you insane, woman. Stop telling this Spanish Adonis that you don't care.*

"I can cook for you. One of my favorite Cajun dishes," he teased.

"I'm listening," I said, twisting my lips in an effort to hold back a smile.

"Seriously, let me do this for you. I won't tell you what it is unless you agree to it."

"Okay, fine." I turned and stalked off toward the house before I lost all control of the power he seemed to have over me.

THE INFATUATION WITH my novel's main character in the flesh blossomed to dizzying heights. It had been a long time since I'd enjoyed any genuine male company, and I savored the moments I spent painting with and then watching Eric from my writing room's window.

During that time, I discovered he cooked fabulous meals. His forgive-me dish was blackened crawfish, served with cornbread and French cut green beans on the side, a dinner his family often made in New Orleans, he said.

The contractor was also quite the comedian at times. So there was plenty of joking at my expense. He made fun of my paint clothes. Annoying. The way I attempted to put my own spin on the crawfish dish didn't turn out well. Rude. The fish was burned beyond the ability to eat it. Eric laughed until he cried. Annoying again. But even I had to admit the crispy thing sitting in the pile of Stove Top stuffing looked pretty ridiculous.

In the end, I didn't stay mad and laughed almost as hard as Eric. It was almost easy to forget we had both recently experienced such bad misfortunes. Yet, it felt good to get a break from grinding out the great supernatural novel for a bit. I was fairly certain Eric appreciated the diversion from his woes as well. He'd lost his best friend. I couldn't even imagine what asylum would be able to hold me if I were to lose Freida after Baby B.

"Okay. I don't get out much," I admitted.

"Tandie, I don't think you've ever gotten out. Forget about adding the much to it," he said and grinned.

Even though he was somewhat aggravating, I couldn't deny how much I enjoyed his company. The bulk of August went by so fast that I didn't even stop to consider I hadn't heard from Saul the entire time.

After about another week, Chelby Rose's final repair consisted of restoring the exposed areas on the roof. The adventure with Eric was almost over. My heart ached at the thought of spending agonizing stretches of time sitting alone at my writing desk and reading myself to sleep while listening to crickets and frogs... and ghostly voices warning me of impending danger.

On the evening before the roof repairs were scheduled to be completed, I realized something: I was truly, deeply, but not quite madly intrigued by the workaholic man known as Eric. A small part of me was still upset about the spider joke. However, he sometimes put sixty-hour weeks into the restoration project. I had to know more about what made him tick. For all the talent he'd been given, Eric held a secret. I could tell. It was in the way his eyes sometimes glazed over and he stared in space at times caught up in some thought only he understood.

One evening he came inside for a drink and we situated ourselves in the study.

"I'm really happy with the results. You're amazing. I mean—your work is amazing. Almost as good as that blackened crawfish you introduced me to." I broke the ice since I could see he wasn't about to do so. A nervous energy surrounded Eric today and he kept shuffling his feet for some reason.

Eric took a look around the study, a curious expression on his face. He shifted in his seat and set his glass of Duplin on the table. "My client's happiness is the goal. I do what I have to do to make sure it happens."

"Why do you always look around that way? You do so every time you come in," I said.

"It's a fascinating house," he said, focusing his gaze back on me. Bolivia's howling wind whipped across the rooftops, putting Eric's handiwork to the test. Eric jerked his head toward the clock chiming on the seventh hour. He was nervous and jumpy this evening, completely different from the way he'd been acting.

"I promise I won't let the boogey men under the stairs get you," I said.

"That's very comforting to know," he said in that smooth but sarcastic way that only Eric could pull off without making you feel like an idiot.

I wasn't going to let him get away with being elusive this time. "You have a beautiful slight accent. It sounds, um, different."

"Okay, thanks, I think." An awkward moment of silence passed. Eric clasped his hands together and then moved his fingers apart.

"Say something in Spanish," I said.

"What? Why?"

"I love the language. It's gorgeous." I shrugged and held his gaze.

"Want to hear something funny?" he asked suddenly, still not breaking our gaze.

"As long as it's not at my expense again," I answered.

"Maybe it will be next time," he said with a smug grin. I reached over and shoved his shoulder a bit. It was kind of like pushing against a wall. "Seriously though, I don't speak fluent Spanish. Only a few phrases here and there. My father was born and raised in America. And my mother's family moved here when she was four."

"How does someone with such super sexy pickup lines not know how to fluently speak one of the main languages of love?" I covered my mouth and muttered, "Oh, God, I can't believe I just said that."

He shrugged, but his eyes lit up. "I guess it's kind of similar to a psychic who has to ask a lot of questions," he said, working to hold back a smile. "Aren't you supposed to have all the answers?"

"Ha ha. I'm working on that, thank you very much," I said, feeling a bit frustrated because I could never outwit him. "Well then, do you want to tell me how your family ended up in Bolivia, North Carolina?"

He sipped from his glass and looked around before he said, "Not really. But I will if you threaten me with that paintbrush."

So annoying. "Funny. Keep it up and I might just do that."

"My ancestors arrived here in the mid-eighteenth century. Satisfied?"

"Wait. So you can trace your history all the way back to your very first relative?" I asked.

"Is that so strange?"

"Your family must've paid a fortune to have that done," I said.

"My family takes our ancestry seriously," he said, his smile fading.

"I don't want to sound like I'm criticizing, but, yeah that's different."

"My family has a unique history," he said and held my gaze. Something was at war behind those eyes: sadness, loss, pain, and some other thing I couldn't identify. "Would you like to hear the rest?" I almost didn't hear his question because I was caught up in reading his eyes.

"Sure, I would," I said, forcing my mind back to our conversation.

"Our first ancestors opened a turpentine business and started a large family."

"Did they know much about the Chelby's? That would've been around the time the plantation was built."

He shrugged. "You worked for a large police department. You're the expert of finding information on people. Shouldn't you know all of this?" he asked. I couldn't tell whether his wry grin was a scoff or a smirk.

I inhaled deeply before speaking. "I'm not such a guru these days. I was fired because I lost my visions."

"That seriously sucks. I'm sorry." He held my gaze this time without looking away. Tears welled in my eyes, stinging my nose. I blinked them away. This wasn't the right time for those little demons of sadness to start nagging at me, not here in front of Eric.

"Don't apologize. You're not the one who fired me." I used sarcasm, hoping the ploy would hide my true emotions. The trick didn't work.

He scooted closer to my side of the sofa and cupped my hands in between his large ones.

"Let people care for you if they want to. That won't hurt anything," he said in a seductively low voice. Sitting there caught up in the rapture of Eric the contractor, I lost myself. His eyes were dark pools filled with a mysterious past, and my ability to read them faltered, the same way I'd failed during the last few months of my NYPD stint. The same way I fell short of helping my childhood friend, Chelsea, and Baby B. However, I enjoyed experiencing this softer side of Eric, a welcome distraction for us both. I had begun to think the man was all muscle, sarcasm, and nothing else. More ticks from the grandfather clock sitting in the hallway clicked through the silence, a reminder that time moved on even though sitting here with Eric made me forget such a thing existed. He released my hands and stood. I did the same.

"Tomorrow, we finish the roof," he said. I was happy to hear he'd taken to my assistance in such a positive way.

"I can hardly wait," I said, following him into the hallway by the entrance. *Oh, and by the way would you like to go out with me sometime? I'm extremely sex-deprived. Can you help me out?*

He stopped just before he walked out the front door and turned to me, narrowing his eyes. No way. He didn't hear what I just said. The gift didn't work that way. "Listen, if you ever need anything—um, any help even after we're done with the renovation then don't hesitate to call. I'm not too far from here." His gaze bore into my eyes and a wildfire of thoughts spread through my mind.

"I'll remember that," I said my face heated with blush. Eric nodded, walked out the door, got in his jeep and drove away into the dim evening.

I returned to my writing. However, I was distracted by the wind. A scratching noise trickled across the roof, stealing my attention yet again. I made a mental note to speak with Eric about fixing whatever was loose up there during our renovation adventure tomorrow.

Turning back to the manuscript, I focused on editing. I edited my story around the missing parts because I couldn't remember what the pages contained.

I read the next passage and typed: 'Darkness in human form remains an enigma unseen by any woman struck by cupid's mischievous arrow. As Eric held Maud close, she felt his heartbeat, thudding in sync with her own. What does this mean?

Handing one's heart to a beautiful stranger, when deep down inside regret tears at your soul?'

THE NEXT MORNING, FOG clouded my mind and brought along a familiar sensation I'd waited a long time to experience again. Only something was different this time. Embracing the newfound sensation with eagerness, I gave in fully as the after effects of the initial shock slivered through my body.

I trudged up Chelby Rose's dark wooden staircase, one bare footstep at a time, my world consumed by a trance. Right away, my subconscious mind knew what had happened. I was walking inside a vision or maybe a dream, and the reverie took place right inside Chelby Rose. I didn't know how or when it had happened. However, the important thing was that it did.

The foggy trance led me upstairs. Music. No wait. A woman humming a tune drifted into my ears as I trudged up the stairs one careful step at a time. The upstairs hallway seemed familiar in all aspects except one: the four bedrooms were now spread apart, separated by no less than ten extra yards of wall spaced in between the old wooden doors.

I glided past the first door on the left, my bedroom and let the invisible hand of the dream as Grandma Zee called this method of movement, pull me along the hallway. As I moved toward the door next to it, a sharp sensation of dread washed over my body. The thought of entering the room behind this door showered me with coldness, the same feeling I first experienced when I entered this part of the house a month ago.

Tonight the first tease of a vision I'd had in years led me back to this room again. I willed my feet to turn around. A slither of light glowed underneath the one inch gap at the bottom of the door. The lady continued to hum even though I had stopped just outside the room. Chest heaving, I stood with my nose so close to the door I almost felt as if I were part of the wood. With hesitation, I put my hand up and pushed against the rough surface.

At once, daylight surrounded me, stinging my sensitive eyes. I flinched, held a hand up and parted my lids just enough to focus on the room's new look. The dust-covered hardwood floors in my version of Chelby Rose now shone brilliant and shiny. A small bed was pushed up against the left wall. The covers were decorated with purple and pink flowers, trinkets of a little girl's room.

Sitting in the window facing Chelby Rose's neglected gardens was an old woman in a white rocking chair. She stopped humming for a moment when I entered the room. Tension filled the next few moments and I didn't dare move a muscle. The woman resumed humming in a raspy voice as she sat staring outside, her gaze fixated on something in the garden.

"Who are you?" My voice echoed. More humming.

I crept closer to where she sat and reached out to touch the old woman's shoulders. Her long silvery gray braid started to flap as if a gust of wind passed through the house. No way. She lifted one wrinkled, blotchy hand, pointed toward the window and said: "Your baby needs you. Her spirit cannot rest." And then she continued humming. I stole one quick look at her face moments before the woman disappeared.

The fog surrounding my vision faded, revealing a sunny day. The vision or whatever craziness I just experienced had ended. I snapped out of the trance as if a switch turned reality back on inside my head. I stood in the same locked room, but it was empty now. The walls were covered with dust and dirt. It was as if the old woman was never there.

A chop chop chop sound came from outside. I walked over to the window overlooking the garden. Ella. She stood beside the largest rose bush and was cutting dead branches off by the dozen.

I had never experienced a walking vision before where I interacted with a spirit in a dream. The thought held me mesmerized for a moment. I found myself caught up between wondering where Ella had been hiding over the past month and trying to figure out what the old woman wanted me to know about my eager gardening girl.

I walked down the stairs, out the front door and approached Ella. The girl offered me a glowing smile.

"G'Day, Ms. Harrison—I mean, Tandie."

"Hello, Ella. I thought we agreed you'd call before coming over."

"Well yeah, but my garden needs me today."

"You mean, my garden?" I corrected.

"But of course that's what I meant." She turned on the innocent-girl smile.

"If you're going to work for me, you'll have to respect my schedule," I said.

Ella stared hard at me for a long moment. Her smile faded and her vivid blue eyes turned icy. She dropped the sheers and started trembling.

"I've always been responsible for these roses. Now you're telling me I can't work with them?" Her southern accent deepened. The girl transformed into Ms. Hyde within a few seconds.

"That's not what I'm saying at all," I said, feeling a touch edgy.

She moved closer to me. "They think I don't know. You think I don't know."

I considered her words before speaking. "Ella, you're done for the day." I used the stern voice I had perfected from my time with the NYPD.

Ella glanced up at the window where I had just left the old woman's spirit. A wicked smile spread across her heart-shaped lips, sending chills through to my core.

"No, miss missy! You're the one who's about to be done." Ella spat on the ground by my feet.

"What's that supposed to mean?" I demanded, thinking I was going to have to call the authorities if Ella kept up with this behavior. How long would it take them to get to the house? Since arriving in Bolivia I hadn't seen a single police station or even a sheriff.

Ella turned around without answering my question. Instead, she slammed her hands up on her cheeks, making a whack that startled me. With flared nostrils and a pinched face, the girl turned and ran screeching like a wounded animal down the driveway and through Chelby Rose's gates.

"It's not fair! Not fair!" Ella screamed over and over again as she ran down the road, out of sight and into the forest.

Part 2

Virtue and taste are nearly the same, for virtue is little more than active taste, and the most delicate affections of each combine in real love...

~Ann Radcliffe, The Mysteries of Udolpho, 1764

Chapter 10

E*ric*
    Eric took the long way to Leroy Newman's office. He wanted to clear his head so he could think over the last four weeks he'd spent with Tandie. No. He wanted to beat the crap out of himself for not having the nerve to ask her out. But first business. This trip to see Leroy was a necessary item on that agenda.

He already learned several things: she wasn't psychotic, crazy, or vicious enough to murder someone in cold blood. Hell, she was almost ready to call the police on Eric when she saw the live crawfish he bought for cooking.

Whoever it was Abby and Shania saw on the beach outside the Aeneid sure as hell wasn't Tandie. However, if she were somehow involved then he'd most certainly find out.

Eric belonged to a family where the eldest males didn't live past the age of forty. Word around town was that a spell caused all this misfortune. His father cheated the curse by an additional eight years. Did his family moving to New Orleans slow the process? Or did they piss off whatever put the curse on the family and now it was waiting patiently for a shot at revenge?

Eric's family lineage was strange. Their history even came with its own mythology. One of his ancestors named Enrique had sailed to the island on a Spanish warship that attacked

Brunswick Town back in September of 1748. It was called the Fortuna. Soon, his ancestor set up a shop and met the wealthy Chelby family who quickly became his best clients. Later on, Enrique had told his customers that an evil spirit brought him across time, and that his name in the previous life was Tobiah, proving his sanity was questionable to say the least.

Eric had pushed thoughts of his time traveling relative to the back of his mind, and resolved to focus on Saul Chelby's decision to sell the old mansion, even though he was renting it at the moment.

Tandie Harrison was the key to finding his answers. Eric felt the truth in that statement even though he didn't understand why. Maybe her psychic abilities would be of some assistance. Either way, she was connected to his family's dilemma in some way. Why else would she have chosen Chelby Rose?

Which made Eric believe Saul also had a role in this game of bastardly deeds. It wasn't like the man lived in the house or even in Bolivia. He hardly ever came to town anymore. Everybody knew that. Why out of the blue did he decide she needed Eric's assistance?

Coincidence?—one of the two things Eric lost faith in ages ago. However, he did believe in its more reliable sister called synchronicity—the thing that was happening with Tandie Harrison.

He walked into the building that housed Detective Leroy Newman's office, making his way past the police officers' stares, and headed down the hallway to the last door situated at the end.

"Eric, my man. Thanks for coming out to meet me." Leroy settled down in the chair behind his desk, giving off a sigh as he did so. Eric settled in one of the guest chairs. "How goes the Chelby house project?"

"Small talk about a reno? Really, Leroy? The project's going is all I'll say." Eric wanted to get down to business. "Any suspects in my friend's murder case?"

"You know I can't go into details."

"Then why drag my ass down here."

"I have to cross and dot all the letters," Leroy said, his gaze focused on Eric's face.

Eric scoffed a laugh. "You mean, I'm a suspect? Me? The best friend, might I remind."

"Your reputation precedes you, Eric."

"Son of a bitch, does it ever end?" The past was reaching out to claim Eric's inner peace yet again. Didn't he already have enough going on? He couldn't shake the rumors about the ghost of his ex-girlfriend, Jenna, and the events that surrounded her death. Or that his father had went out searching for Eric the day he died. In a town that savored the ghostly and dark, those two events trailed Eric like a cheetah stalking its prey. Would he ever be able to claim his true identity? Or shake the supernatural stigma that his ancestors were warlocks? If that were true then Eric would've conjured up an identity spell by now. The fact remained, his brother needed him to stay focused. Self pity wasn't an option.

"Now that you've hit a wall, do you have leads? Genuine leads?"

Depends on who you ask," Leroy sat back, opened his drawer, and pulled out a blow pop. He removed the wrapping in one skilled swipe. "Best shits ever. Beats the hell outta cigarettes anyday. Want one?"

"I'll pass. Enlighten me on the suspects?"

Leroy smirked and gave me an incredulous look. "So no candy then. Got it. More for me."

"Come on, Leroy. You grew up with Virgil, too. Give me something." Eric hoped their childhood connection would be enough to get some sort of update. He didn't want to jeopardize Leroy's job. Yet, he needed to understand who targeted his friend and why.

"What did you mean by that last statement?" Eric asked.

Leroy took one last swipe of his lollipop and set it down. "It's like this. The leads are well... something you'd expect to get coming from Bolivia."

Eric pressed on. "That would mean what exactly?"

Leroy sighed, leaned forward, and propped his elbows on his desk. "According to one lead it was a wild animal. Another claims a serial killer from New Orleans made his way to Castle Hayne. Of course, the MARAS have their own theory."

"Let me guess. Our local neighborhood writer is a witch. Oh, and she magically lifted a man three times her weight. That's how she did it, right?"

"In a nutshell, yes," Leroy answered. Eric laughed. What else could he do?

"Which of these leads will you pursue?" Eric asked.

He knew Leroy couldn't give him any details. Instead, the detective said: "Tell you what. I'll get in touch once we have something concrete."

ERIC WALKED INTO A different version of the Aeneid and regretted the decision at once. The walls were covered in black silk drapery, highlighting the black and gray checkered flooring. Blood red tablecloths donned the tables in the middle of the club. Dark Souls Festival was almost a month away. Yet, Abby had already lent her signature style to the decoration.

More patrons filled the club tonight than when he first arrived. That night he first met Tandie. She reminded him of a delicate doll the way she stood on the rooftop and hugged herself.

Eric headed towards his favorite booth on the far right side of the club. Unfortunately doing so gave him firsthand chance to hear the things people were saying about him once again.

"That's him. He's the man she died for," one patron whispered.

"I say he's involved in this one too," another customer said.

"Didn't his father die trying to save him?" the waitress named Ginny asked her colleague.

The stares. The whispers. It was as though his hearing improved to a deafening level. Something snapped inside Eric. How many times would these rumors follow him? It didn't matter that he'd been away for almost a decade. Didn't anybody care about his friend's fate?

"Fuck this shit," Eric said and turned towards the exit.

"Eric! Wait up!" Abby's voice called from behind him. He turned and faced her. "Where ya going? You can't leave already."

He sighed and fought back the annoyance assaulting him. "Coming here was a mistake."

"No, Eric please don't leave," Abby said, grabbing his forearm. She wore all black and her red hair was pulled back in a tight ponytail. Black circles surrounded her eyes and she wore minimal makeup.

"I should've called before now. Sorry."

"No worries. I've something to show you. Follow me." She led Eric through the club and to a room located behind the kitchen. Inside the room, Eric felt as though he'd stepped into a shrine dedicated to Dark Souls Day. Photos of war ships from the 1800's decorated the walls. A large framed black and white photo of the Macon House plantation sat in the middle of the wall opposite the doorway. The owners stood just outside the doorway, posing in typical late 1800s style with the parents behind the children. The faces had blurred a bit even though Virgil chose a quality frame. The ode didn't stop with the decoration. A large mahogany desk sat in the middle of the room, taking up most of the space. Papers and photos were strewn across the surface along with a scarab amulet that caught Eric's attention.

"Dios Mio," Eric said. "What is this room?"

"What's it look like? It's Shania's ode to Bolivia and Castle Hayne's history."

Abby's black and white tuxedo cat hopped off the file cabinet and pranced towards Eric.

"Nettles likes you," Abby beamed. "Can't say I'm surprised."

Eric shook his head and scoffed a bit. His friend truly loved his wife. Enough to have created an office ripped from the past. Outside the room, music from the Aeneid's jukebox drifted into the space, creating the perfect mood for a club owner.

"I'm short on time," Eric said, anxious to discover the reason behind Abby's invite.

"This here scarab comes from an old school group called the Enochians." She held the scarab up to the light. Beady eyes met Eric's and damn if it didn't feel as if he were under observation.

A chill settled over him. "It can sense all kinds of bad things. The MARAS use it all the time."

"Explain," Eric said.

"The Enochians used scarabs to assist with seances. Like the Egyptians they believed these little beetle babies held powerful magic. See there. It has wings and eyes made of ruby. But the legs and body is obsidian. How cool is that?"

Eric sighed and crossed his arms. His patience wilted. "You brought me here to look at ruby bug?"

Abby twisted her lips and tilted her head. "No. I wanted to show you our demon detector." She picked up the scarab and held it in front of Eric.

"Demon tool." Eric scoffed a laugh and shook his head.

"That's right. You can place the scarab somewhere near Chelby Rose's front door. It'll scare off the evil spirits and attract the good ones. That witch inside—"

"You're kidding, right? Seriously Abby. This is low. Even for you."

"Why? Tandie Harrison is a witch. Everybody knows it. I'm giving you a chance to prove she's a good one. That's all. What's wrong with that?"

"I've lots to do. So if you'll excuse me." Eric turned and stepped over Nettles who'd settled on the floor behind his feet.

"She's gone and put a spell on you too. I can see it all over you." Abby crossed her arms and glared at him as if he were the one doing something wrong.

Something inside him snapped. He squeezed his eyes shut a moment and fought back the heat surging through his body. Blood rushed to his head and the room closed in on him.

Spinning around, he said: "Damn it, Abby!" Eric's fist slammed down on the desk, shaking the antique on its wobbly legs. He had done enough trying to make people believe him, seeking out answers to questions no one wanted to answer. He felt like he was alone in this fight, and he wasn't sure if he could take it anymore.

At once, the room seemed to stop; the lights flickered and the jukebox outside of Abby's office stuttered over one phrase of a Leonard Cohen song until someone silenced it. Eric felt electricity spark through his veins as Abby stepped back away from him, her face twisted with shock and disbelief.

"What was that?" She whispered.

Eric shook his head, feeling more lost than ever. "I-I don't know. All I know is that you need to trust me–I know what I'm doing."

Chapter 11

T*andie*

The next evening, I drove to Brunswick Town, Bolivia's historic county seat, my mind still shaken by the previous night's events. Experiencing a sleep walking moment was the breakthrough I craved.

The setting sun created shadows that stretched across the road like creatures from a horror movie, proof that I was probably losing my mind faster than I already believed I would do. The mission was to find a can of Stop Leak, the perfect remedy for temporarily fixing any lingering plumbing issues.

The Abby woman's accusations cut me to the core and I had no idea of what Detective Newman was playing at. People around Bolivia embraced the strange and odd. That much hadn't changed throughout the years. However, Abby had indirectly accused me of being a witch the night we first met. What could it mean that both of us saw the ship in the water? Even more strange, how did Abby even know I'd seen it? The woman obviously had issues. However, if I had a boyfriend that looked like Eric, then I'd probably act psycho about him too.

Images of his smile flashed through my head and comforted me. A tinge of hope pinged my chest. I wanted to see him again. There was no denying it. For now, I needed to stay focused. Breena's spirit wasn't at rest and neither was mine.

I focused my attention back on the road ahead. The darkening streets started to look the same as I drove along the deserted country back road and the lack of streetlights didn't help the situation. "It's definitely going to take some time to get used to navigating in the black dark of night."

I turned onto Brunswick Town's Danford Road and passed several deserted stores. After driving a few more miles, I began to suffer from the weariness associated with being in a strange town. I'd driven out too far, and my cell phone's signal faded by the second. The lakes became larger and the scenery merged together as I drove around the small town in what felt like a complete circle. After passing the sign reading Boiling Springs Lake for a third time, I concluded that I'd gotten totally turned around.

"Okay, city girl. Just how do you get lost in the trees when you're used to skyscrapers?" I eased my metallic blue Camaro to a stop at the beginning of the fourth lap around Danford Road. "Okay, you got this. Keep going. Look for something different next go-round." I pressed the gas pedal and trudged forward.

This time an old store came into view, and two of the windows situated on the lower front side glowed with soft yellow light. Success! I eased the car to a stop and parked across the street from the weathered building. The beaten up sign on top of the store had the name Catsburg painted across the front. The structure was two stories high and chipped reddish-brown paint covered the outside. The streetlights highlighted a faded Coca Cola mural beside the entrance. The windows on the second level were completely dark, giving me a strong sense of someone watching me.

I inhaled, held my breath a moment and stayed in my car. The store appeared old like it was built about the same time as

Chelby Rose. The brown wood siding and tattered metal roof along with the gaping front door secured only by an insect type screen sent shivers up and down my spine. The entire storefront reminded me of a jack o lantern's face with four old windows as eyes and a raggedy door instead of a mouth.

In the distance, howls pierced the air. Goose bumps rose on my arms and eventually trickled over my body. I swallowed, studied the deserted street, and once again found myself wishing my sighted abilities would spring back to life.

I checked my watch. 8:25 p.m. on Saturday evening. There should've been at least one or two people strolling out and about.

Whack! Whack! I jerked my head back toward the driver side window, my heart skipping a few beats. A little boy with a pale face and dark circles around his eyes stood with his head pressed against the window. I reared back with a gasp, inhaling sharply.

The boy smiled, his wide grin showing two missing top teeth. I rolled the window down a quarter of the way. Goosebumps crept all along my neck, Grandma Zee's creepy chills. She always said they were the first sign of developing the sight. Maybe my psychic visions were starting to come back. Perhaps this ghost boy jumped out of my head. I made a light laugh, celebrating a short moment and turned back to the current situation.

'What's wrong with you? It's just a little boy.'

"Are you looking for your parents?" I asked.

The boy's eyes were hidden by the moonlight. He kept silent and stood still as if a zombie had presented himself before me, this boy with eyes hidden in shadows. He shook his head in a slow motion without saying a word. More howls rode across the wind. They'd gotten more frequent and louder since I eased to a stop and my young friend arrived.

'Damn you, Tandie Harrison, for being overambitious and trying to buy a house in need of serious repairs. Oh, and you can add driving along the back roads of a small town where any homicidal maniac could be on the loose to that list too.'

"You'd better get home. It's not safe to be out here all by yourself." The boy stood there and stared. "Do you need to call your parents?" He shook his head again as the wind whipped glossy black hair around his face.

"I have to open the door. I need to get some Stop Leak out of that store; or something close to it, anyway. They might have a phone that you could use. Mine doesn't have a signal." The boy tilted his head to the side before he took two slow steps backward, allowing me just enough room to open my car door without hitting him. I didn't want to leave him in the street all by himself; but I couldn't get him to say anything. Maybe the people inside the store knew who he was.

I stepped out of the car, the wind whipping my shoulder length hair around my head, blocking part of my view. I had forgotten how far the coastal gusts reached inland. Sweeping hair away from my eyes, I locked my door and studied the boy's clothing for the first time. He wore a long-sleeved plaid shirt paired with brown coveralls that rode his ankles. He lifted his arm in slow motion and pointed a pale finger at something further down the deserted street. I peered in the direction he indicated. A dark, empty street with no cars or people or any living creature met my gaze. Instead, a fog swirled in the darkness, moving toward me as if it were alive, sending a shiver through my body.

The boy lowered his hand as I inched toward the store. "I'd love to stay and chat, but I've got to head inside and get back," I said and gave him a nervous smile. He tilted his head to the side, his gaze locked on me as I headed toward the entrance. I turned and prepared to climb the steps leading up to the doorway.

At once two tiny hands as cold as ice grabbed my left hand. The boy tried to pull me away from the store. I peered down into his shadowed eyes, my mouth drying out, and my skin growing cold against his touch.

"Stop that! Let go of me." I pulled my hand free as I caught a glimpse of the boy's eyes under the splash of moonlight that hit them. Silver specks flashed inside the pupils. I didn't need any psychic intuition to know that he wasn't a normal boy. Gasping, I turned around and scurried toward the entrance.

I stumbled up two broken concrete steps by the front door, straightened up, and then turned around just before going inside. The boy vanished as if he'd been a ghost drifting in the night. "You are seriously going to be okay." I swallowed and headed through the door, a tinkle of chimes echoing through the silence of the night.

The smell of a musty façade and mildewed wood enhanced by a baseboard heater's metallic odor surrounded me. The store had an old-fashioned design complete with wooden shelves lining the walls. The few items scattered across the slabs of wood were covered in dust. The only modern thing about the whole setup was the country song drifting through the speakers.

"You must be our new psychic celebrity?" A tall woman with dark blonde hair and large gray eyes said in greeting. She spoke in a hard southern drawl and wore a flannel shirt over a long pleated dress. Like everyone else I'd met so far, her outfit screamed outdated.

"Not quite a celebrity," I said, anxious to get back on the road before it got too late. Still feeling jittery, I returned my focus to the task at hand. "I need a can of Stop Leak."

At once, a loud thunderclap rumbled through the sky, shaking the store. Soon rain pattered loudly across the rooftop. I peeked out the door's window and swore under my breath.

"You might wanna wait this one out, sugar. These country roads ain't no place for pretty city girls like yourself to be getting lost on." The woman walked past a mini Coke fridge on her way to a shelf behind the checkout counter. She removed a dusty can of Stop Leak and turned around. I was surprised the store had water bottles let alone Stop Leak.

Mental note: drive all the way into town next time and stop taking the paranoid recluse person's type of short cut. I checked my watch and peeked out the door at the rain. I thought about the phantom boy and wondered if he made his way inside before the storm started. "Looks like it's just a shower. I'm sure this won't last long."

"Don't count on it," the woman stated. "Name's Minerva."

"Minerva? Okay. I'm Tandie Harrison." I couldn't bring myself to say the "nice to meet you" part. The store smelled dank, and the creepy chills had ignited my claustrophobia.

"Minerva's a kick-ass name, right? So I hear you're the newest Chelby Rose experiment." Minerva studied my face with an intense gaze.

"That's right. I'm the newest tenant." I handed her the money for the Stop Leak.

"The place is kind of run down over the years since old Pontus Tomlinson died. Been a long time since that old house had some TLC. Kind of funny when you think about it, cause I remember Pontus had problems with the plumbing just like you."

"Really?" I asked, wondering how she knew about the faucets.

"Yep. Old hooter was convinced the Chelby kids were running around there at night." Minerva dipped my cash into her pocket and started wiping the countertop around the ancient cash register. I couldn't believe such a thing still existed.

"Are you telling me that my house is haunted?"

"Well, I should be asking you that." The woman's cat colored eyes seemed to stare right through me.

"Why would you be asking me?" I asked, feeling anxious to leave.

"Fancy pants psychic, books published on that and all. You should of connected with whatever scared old Pontus to death by now. You look shocked. Guess Saul Chelby didn't tell you about all that when he showed you the place."

"No. He didn't tell me someone died in the house," I said.

"All of that stuff is probably second nature to you, though. Big police psychic and everything," Minerva said, easing around the counter and moving closer to where I stood. "Your poltergeist relief." She held out a bag for me, her gaze locked on mine.

"Right. I think I can weather that storm now. Thanks for the history lesson." I folded the brown paper bag with the Stop Leak inside and turned to leave.

Another thunderclap rumbled the store, startling me. I peeked through the small window of the dirty wooden door and checked the rain's intensity. A figure stood beside the driver side door to my car. Lightning flashed and bathed the street in light, making it easy to see the shadowed figure belonged to a man. And then the street darkened, covering his shadow. A few seconds later, lightning flashed again, showing how empty the street was now.

"Mighty brave thing you doing, sugar. Spending time all by your lonesome in Chelby Rose," Minerva's husky voice said.

I already felt anxious about trying to find my way out of the endless circle of back roads; and the woman's hard stare made me uneasy. "Something wrong?"

"There was a—I saw a man standing near my car," I said, eyes wide so I didn't miss a thing and sweat beads prickling my underarms. "He was standing there beside the driver's door."

Minerva's voice fell silent, and I no longer felt her cat-like gaze boring holes through the back of my head. I turned around and found an empty area behind the cash register. A new country song blared through the speakers of a radio, the tune crackling under the influence of a bad reception. However, I was able to hear a few of the words to Garth Brooks' song When the Thunder Rolls.

I tapped my keypad, unlocked my car doors, trotted to the car in the rain, and kept watching for the shadow people.

FLUMP! FLUMP! FLUMP!

The Camaro's tires chugged along the lane.

I pulled over to the side of the road and eased the car to a stop. "Oh shit, you've got to be kidding me," I said aloud, glancing back at where I had just left the store. There were no streetlights and my phone's signal bar was empty again.

Opening my door, I stepped out and examined the car. Both the front and back tire on the driver's side were flat. I would either have to risk driving on them and experiencing a blowout or stay put in the car until morning; and unfortunately, I had one can of Fix a Flat and absolutely no knowledge of how to change a tire.

Taking a good look at the forest surrounding the area, I patted my chest, a quick way to calm my racing heart, My thoughts returned to the image of the man from the store, the one who was standing beside my car. The woods around me chimed songs of frogs and crickets, and certain dark areas in the trees appeared to be moving.

"Okay. Now your eyes are playing tricks on you, woman," I said, my voice carrying over the forest's nature songs.

Danger! Danger!

I told you not to come back.

You didn't listen. You never do.

I slammed my hands over my ears and waited for the voices to stop. After several rounds of repeating the same words, the whispers cutoff as though someone suddenly pushed a button.

At once, a light lit up the trees growing along the sides of the road ahead of me. Either a large truck or a vehicle with a diesel engine was headed my way. "Oh shit." I scurried towards my door, shuffled back into the car, hit the lock button and tried to calm my racing heart by telling myself everything would be fine.

Coming closer now, the truck's lights blinded me. I held an arm over my eyes, blocking the glare. A pickup truck, a large one with protruding tires that looked too big for the body loomed into view on the opposite side of the road, and slowed down to a stop. My heart thudded, making me feel as if my mouth were filled with the missing beats.

"You all right there?" a man's voice called out, a familiar one. Oh no.

For the second time in one night, I rolled my window down just a notch and said, "I think so. I'm waiting for someone to come pick me up." Yeah sure, I lied; but I had to tell the person something. My tall-tale didn't work. The guy opened the door to his truck, hopped out and started toward my car. Heartbeat thrashed in my ears, a thundering drumbeat of distress. All of the night's excitement was beginning to wear me down.

"Oh God. Please don't hurt me," I whispered furiously.

The guy had almost made his way over to the car. An image of me cranking up, speeding away, and taking my chances on the two flat tires came to mind when a light flickered into my face.

"Miss Harrison? Is that you? It's me, Gus, from the Aeneid." He turned the light on his face so I could see his geeky, but handsome face. The light reflected off his big glasses in a different way than the shadows did for the little boy back at the Catsburg Store.

"Gus. Of course it's you." I made a nervous laugh and released my death grip on the steering wheel. My hands felt so clammy that I didn't even want to shake his hand.

"Got a problem or two, don't ya?" He looked at my wheels and stepped back, giving me room to open my door.

"Oh yeah. I got double trouble. Or maybe triple trouble depending on how you choose to see it," I joked while stepping out of the car.

"I guess you don't have two spares, huh?" he asked.

Standing beside Gus, I found out he wasn't as tall as I originally thought. "Miss Harrison, are you quite sure you're all right?"

"Huh? Oh yeah, I'm fine now. Thanks, Gus. I have a can of Fix a Flat and a spare tire in the trunk," I answered.

"Well if you can fetch the can and open the trunk, I can knock those puppies out for you," Gus said.

"Sounds like a plan." I walked over and opened the trunk for him. Handing me his flashlight, he lifted my spare tire and car jack out of the trunk and set to work right away. He was so polite, humming a familiar tune while he worked. There was no talk of my so-called celebrity status, or the witch's mark that some other people in Castle Hayne seemed to think I had.

Shining the light on his hands, I noticed welts running along the length of both his arms. Although the marks had long since healed, the deep gashes still looked very painful. "I think that about takes care of the last tire. You might wanna—" His gaze landed on me studying his arms, and he stopped talking at once.

"What happened?" I asked.

His demeanor changed, and his bright face turned in on itself. "Life happened, Miss Harrison."

All types of images came to mind. "Life?"

"Yeah, that's right. It's tough being a mechanic's son. No time to primp ourselves like the college boys do." He returned the car jack to its slot in the trunk and rolled my old tire over to where I stood. The prospect of knowing the story behind the gashes on his arm intrigued me. "I can get rid of this old tire if you want me to."

"That would be great," I said.

Gus started toward his truck and stopped, turning to halfway face me. "Mighty kind of you to ask about me like that. Nobody else ever did."

"I'm the one who needs to be thanking you, I do believe," I said.

"You know life is kind of like a flat tire. It gets you excited, takes you to all these fancy places, and then leaves you stranded someplace down the road," he said.

"I guess life does do that, doesn't it?" I said, thinking of the way my world without Breena had changed over the past two years. I felt exactly the way Gus described.

"Better make sure you buy a new tire soon, Miss Harrison, "because life is out there waiting to see if you forget."

"I'll remember that. Thanks again, Gus," I said and hopped back into the Camaro. While driving away, I turned on the radio. The country song playing on the station made me remember the tune Gus was humming. It was the Thunder Rolls, the same song that was playing on the radio at the Catsburg store when I left.

Chapter 12

T*andie*

Vigorous taps drummed against my head. That was how the sound of someone knocking at my door made me feel anyway. I'd hardly had any sleep last night and now some idiot was out there, disturbing the rest of my morning. I opened my eyes and regretted the sudden movement. The day after the storm brought a sun bright enough to light the entire house.

Sitting up and slipping into a soft pair of bedroom shoes, I grabbed my robe off the chair beside my bed, stood and headed toward the hallway. Head pounding, I trudged downstairs to the front door and ripped it open.

"Didn't I tell you I don't need any damn services!" I snapped, regretting my words right away.

Saul Chelby stood outside the front door, his gold hair gleaming in the morning sun. I thought he was another vacuum cleaner salesman. He raked an amused set of eyes over my bed clothes and averted his gaze.

At once, I stepped behind the door, hiding my body. Hmph. True gentlemen really do exist in this day and age. I'd almost given up hope.

"Mr. Chelby. I mean, Saul. I'm sorry. I thought you were someone else."

"I only stopped by for a moment," Saul said, his gaze slowly rising away from the porch, a boyish smile spreading over his full lips.

"Oh?"

"I wanted to make sure you were all right. That was quite a storm we had last night."

"Yes. I—I'm fine, thanks."

"I do appreciate you taking the time to stop by... again, Mr. Che—Saul."

He beamed a grin that lit up his face and his entire aura seemed to radiate sunshine. With his thin top lip, pouty bottom one, and a smile that swam in his bright blue eyes, it wasn't hard for me to see exactly what Freida meant. A person like Saul probably won business deals and the hearts that gave in to his conquests on a regular basis.

"Where are my manners?" I should invite you in. I mean, this is still your house," I said, feeling exposed under his iron-tight gaze.

"Actually, I wanted to ask how things were going for you two," Saul said. I made a light laugh.

"What is it? What's funny?" he asked.

"Nothing. It's just the way you talk about the house. I feel like I should be telling you about a new relationship rather than talking about repair issues," I said. "I guess you could say it's coming along, but very wet in the process."

"I see. Getting a little wet every now and then can be interesting, with all due respect, Ms. Harrison." The most devilish-sexy grin I'd ever seen played across his lips. A blush crept across my brown face. This time, I lowered my eyes. "I do apologize for embarrassing you."

Is there no shame in this man's game? "I'm not embarrassed," I lied, working hard to refocus my thoughts.

"My apologies for taking so long to check up on you."

"You apologize a lot."

"That's because I'm a southern gentlemen. My kind is rare." He bowed his head a bit.

"Okay. Feel free to be even more humble if you like," I said. "Besides, my grandmother always told me that actions speak louder than words."

"Why, Ms. Harrison—"

"Call me Tandie. Ms. Harrison was an old woman somewhere who wasn't even related to me by blood." We both shared a laugh at my reference to the joke he made the day we first met.

"All right, Tandie. Allow me to demonstrate your philosophy. I'd be honored if you'd accompany me to the Governor's Dinner this Saturday."

My smile faded, a surge of dread rushing through me. "I'm not sure—I don't know about a date. Going out with the rent man is like bagging the boss. Is it not?"

Holding back a smile, Saul took one step closer. "Then don't consider it a date. Call this a pre-requisite for a landlord who wants to make sure his best girl is in the right hands." He glanced around at the house before moving his amused gaze back to my face. "You can't hide behind her walls forever."

"I'm not hiding," I scoffed.

"Then I'll pick you up at 6pm. Oh, and wear something that's royal blue," he said, turned around, and headed toward his car before I was able to turn him down.

"Did I pass Saul Chelby's car?" Eric asked as he walked towards me. He set his tools down, the metal items clanging against each other as he did so. The question annoyed me.

"How about 'Good morning, Ms. Harrison. How goes it for you today?' And then we launch into the interrogation." The statement was crass and I didn't mean for it to come out that way. However, I'd tossed and turned most of the night while visions of toothless boys chasing me down a deserted road peppered my dreams. I'd gotten nowhere with the ventures into my supernatural investigation and the lack of progress annoyed me. It was a bit hard to concentrate on writing a ghost's story when people around Bolivia accused me of witchcraft and murder.

Eric held up his hands. "Dios mio, estas en un mal humor hoy."

I pointed a finger at him. "Don't hide behind the Spanish. I've no idea of what you said. You know that."

"I'd wave a white flag but I left those at home today," he said, lowering his hands.

"Yes, for the record. Saul just left. Anymore questions, detective?" I crossed my arms and squinted. The morning sun's rays slanted and hit my eyes. Great. Just what I needed right now... blindness on top of writer's block.

He smirked a bit and blinked a few times. "Did he say what he wanted?"

I gave him an incredulous look. "He's your boss. Didn't he call and show you any love today?"

Eric held up his hands as though he'd surrendered. "I think I'll just go ahead and get started." He bent down, picked up his tools and started walking away.

"I'm sorry, Eric. It's been a long week."

He stopped walking and turned around. "A set of hammer and nails awaits your frustration when you're ready." On that note, he turned and walked towards the side of the house.

"I'll go change so we can get started."

"Right. I'll meet you at the gate," he said without turning around.

I walked back inside the house, got dressed in my infamous contractor's suit—jean shorts, a black tee, and a bandanna—and headed back outside. The agenda included swapping boards on the wooden fence flanking either side of the house. We got to work right away even though unspoken words lingered in the air. After about an hour of working in silence and listening to Eric's Spanish curse words, I gave in.

I removed my bandana and waved it in the air, swatting a few pesky flies along with the gesture. "Time out here. Not sure what's going on but I'd appreciate some type of evidence of life in my contractor."

Eric set down the board he'd just positioned and turned towards me. "Do tell what you're going on about."

Without coming right out and making the wrong statement, I said: "Saul asked me out on Saturday. Some kind of ball." I wasn't sure why I felt the need to explain myself.

"Sounds like fun. Kidding in case you didn't catch on." He turned back to the fence and scanned the boards beside the empty slot. A diversion. I could tell.

"What's the deal with you? Saul's your boss." I was getting dare I say the words? Jealous vibes.

Eric ignored me and continued measuring his boards. "I can feel you staring," he said without looking at me. I crossed my arms and debated my next words.

"That's because I want answers. You're not giving them to me. Is this broodiness about your friend?"

The board Eric had been working on slipped and flipped up from the bottom, striking his chin after doing so. "Fuck me!" he yelled, massaging his chin. I moved over to him and used my dry bandana as a solve against the blow.

"Gods. This will bruise, I'm sure." I held the bandana up with one hand and cradled his neck with the other, a gesture that always calmed Breena's nerves when she had an accident. At once, I thought about what I'd done and snatched my hand away. Our gazes met and held a long beat.

"Don't worry, Ms. Harrison. I don't bite," Eric murmured.

"Neither does Saul." And just like that the cupids stopped singing as crows squawked and killed the mood. Eric braced my bandana and turned away. "I don't get it. If you feel so—so whatever way about Saul then why take this assignment?" He blinked twice and squinted, a sign that I'd hit a nerve.

Turning to me, Eric said: "There's a history. Not a good one. Satisfied?"

"Not quite. More info please."

Eric sighed deeply. "There was a rivalry. It happened a long time ago. Like hundreds of years."

"A rivalry from hundreds of years ago? What kind?"

"A man and a woman fell in love. Townspeople didn't like it. The Chelbys broke them up over something. And the rest is history. Can we get back to work now?"

Absolutely not. This news piqued my curiosity more than ever. I wanted to know more. "So one of your relatives fell in love with a Chelby woman. Found out she was pregnant out of wedlock and spurned both families. All this happened hundreds of years ago, and people are still sour?"

Eric stopped massaging his chin and stared at me. Slowly, he furrowed his eyebrows. "I never said it was a Chelby woman or anything about a baby. How did you know? Been reading up on me?"

His revelation startled me a moment. Had I channeled the information from Eric? Were my visions breaking through the haze? As much as I wanted to believe that were true, I knew it wasn't. Somehow, I just knew the missing links of the story without envisioning anything. "I'm not sure."

"I think we've done enough for the day." Eric turned and started gathering his tools. I wasn't ready to let him off the hook. He'd left out a chunk of that story and I wanted to know why.

"Why did you really take this job? There's something in this house, isn't there?" I asked. No response. "Talk to me, Eric."

He spun around. "Look, Tandie. My time's short."

"Your time for what?" I asked, eager to hear more. Eric was hiding something. Not telling me the entire story behind his words.

"I've already said too much. The less you know the better. Trust me."

I scoffed. "You're making that a little hard to do."

"Forgive me, madam homeowner. I'll make it a bit easier." He reached into his shirt pocket and pulled out a black business card. "My phone number's on here. If you need me, you know what to do."

I snatched the card out of his hand without looking at it. "Nice. But Saul has me covered, I believe."

"Dios ayudame," he whispered and clenched his jaw. God help me. I didn't need a translator for that one.

Chapter 13

T *andie*
      The deserted coastline stretched along the ocean, the water a shadow in the grip of nighttime. I floated in a dream on the beach I'd dreamt of many times since I arrived at Chelby Rose. Running along the illuminated white shores, I fought the panic rising inside my chest. "Breena! Where are you, Baby B?"

The wind whipped dark hair across my eyes, and a long white dress flowed around my ankles. The scent of the ocean stung my nose with its ancient saltwater smell. A bed of lavender colored roses covered the beach. As I walked further along the shoreline, the roses dissolved and dark sand formed.

In the distance, a ship fired a canon. Right away, my feet sunk into the sand, unable to move as if they were glued to the spot. I swiveled the top half of my body towards the sea where the canon had blared. A chill rode across the air, biting at my bare arms with its frigid embrace, and the hazy veil of thick fog clouded my view.

From inside the murky scenery, an old-fashioned ship loomed into view. The vessel was the kind that had the sails stacked on top of each other as if it were taken from a pirate movie. The ship sailed toward the shores, moving quickly, and a strange horn blared through the air, ripping into my eardrums. I slammed my hands over my ears.

Another canon shot blasted through the night, sending waves of fear through my body. I now stood in the midst of a battle between the mystery ship and another vessel approaching from the left side of the harbor. The area sprung to fiery life under the cannons as the ships opened fire on one another.

I grabbed my leg and tugged at my stubborn feet but they refused to budge from the sands. Tears streamed down my cheeks, clouding my view, and I feared for my life as I stood in the midst of a war, terrified that Breena was lost among this madness.

I focused on the ship to my right, the one closest to where I stood. The men standing on the decks were dressed in red uniforms and shouted in phrases that warbled together like a song playing in slow motion. The general standing on the deck shouted orders at his men. However, I couldn't make out the words, but I knew the instructions had something to do with the rival ship.

That was when the general turned his gaze on me, his expression turning sour. Frowning, he directed his men to move towards me. Panic seized my chest as I struggled to get free of the sand, and I yanked at my legs so hard that I lost my balance and fell backward, tiny grains blowing into my eyes and scratching them.

I screamed. A silent wail. I had no voice. More sand blew around me and formed a funnel, suffocating me until I fell into darkness.

Bolting upright, I focused on catching my breath. While not as predictable and readable as before, this new type of vision both intrigued and worried me. The sight was no longer predictable. Where before I had to touch something owned by the subject, I no longer experienced that obstacle. However, the snippets felt more like dreams instead of psychic vibrations. I closed my eyes and focused on the darkness. "Come back to me. Please. I need to understand." I couldn't let Baby B down. Silence... and then...A screech echoed through the room, piercing my eardrums. I slammed my hands over my ears and studied my surroundings.

I woke with a pinching ache in my neck where I had fallen asleep on the sofa. I placed Breena's photo back on the side table, glide walked out of the living room, and headed upstairs as if I walked in a fog.

I had only spent a few nights in the master bedroom. The darkness along with the tree limbs tapping against the window at night freaked me out. Yet, I once considered myself the queen of creepy sensations.

Caught up in a daze, I reached out to turn the ancient brass knob and found that I didn't close the door all the way. With hesitation, I pushed the creaking door open, flipped on the light, and gasped. Thirteen notebook-sized pages lay side by side across the bed.

"What the hell are you trying to tell me?" I whispered and analyzed the rest of the room, half expecting to see a shadow demon hovering in the corner. Was I doomed to suffer the same fate as my father, a man who went insane after my mother was killed? I inched towards the bed, picked up one of the middle pages, and skimmed the words.

"This can't be." I turned the paper over and confirmed my suspicions. Trying to calm my thudding heart, I peeked at each of the other pages.

"Thirteen of my missing twenty pages. This is all a bit much."

I looked around the room, walked to the windows, set the page down on the dresser and pushed upward on the top wooden panes, making sure it was locked. No movement.

"What are you trying to tell me, Chelby Rose? I'm listening. So hop to it. I need to know." I turned my gaze back to the lone page, the one I'd just placed on the dresser. My gaze landed on Eric's card lying next to my manuscript page. I picked it up and read the handwritten name on back. Eric Fontalvo. Why did his last name seem so familiar? That question nagged at me. Grabbing hold of the middle page, I returned to the bed, sat down, and read it aloud.

Darkness in human form remains an oddity unseen by any woman who gets hit by cupid's blinding arrow. I knew from the moment I met him, we'd be locked together within his blackest secret. I love you, Eric Fontaine.'

The paper fell from my hands, and I swallowed hard. "Eric Fontalvo...Eric Fontaine. They're almost identical." And so was the physical description of my male villain, the serial killer in disguise...a man I'd dreamed about off and on since I was a teenager.

Chapter 14

T*andie*

    The next morning, I studied my manuscript, flipping past the newly returned missing pages for the hundredth time. Thirteen pages had been returned and seven were still missing. Many thoughts cluttered my mind. A good old round of research was long overdue. However, I learned a valuable lesson from my last experience with driving around Brunswick Town at night and chose to travel during the day instead. By the time evening arrived, I will have completed my research on Chelby Rose's history and be settled in for the night. A trip to the library was long overdue.

Eric Fontalvo, Saul's sudden infatuation with me, Chelby Rose, and its ghostly inhabitants were all somehow connected. They had to be. Although hating to admit it, I also tied my dreams of Breena in with that lot along with Virgil's death.

Two people had placed me or someone who resembled me at the crime scene the night Virgil McKinnon was killed. I couldn't help but think that my sudden intimacy with Eric came from his desire to figure out what happened to his friend. He had called this morning and told me he had a family emergency and would need to be away for a few days, assuring me this new trip had nothing to do with what we discussed. I wanted to believe him and intended to stand by my resolve to help him. Solving mysteries was what I'd spent the last seven years of my life doing. The time had come to put that expertise back to work.

Something terrible happened in his house, and even though Saul never admitted to his knowledge of the subject, I was pretty sure he wanted me to do a bit of research for him too. Even though Saul's bold invitation and outfit request bothered me, I still found myself mentally scanning my wardrobe. The last time I wore anything remotely close to sexy was at the Aeneid the other night. A part of me felt guilty about accepting Saul's offer; but then, I snapped back to reality. I was a single woman now. Get over the past already.

I stretched, stood up and headed outside, my stiff bones desperately craving a break. Opening the front door and stepping out on the porch, I eyeballed the yard and sighed. Trigs and leaves lay scattered across the front lawn, the victims of Bolivia's latest storm. Walking back inside, I eased the door shut and strolled over to my desk guarded by Breena's picture sitting on top and eyeballed the card sitting beside her photo. Time to get to work. Clicking the red record button on my tape recorder, I sat down and began reading my manuscript.

Eric Fontaine's muscular frame towered over Maud's petite one by almost a foot. His brooding, exotic demeanor intrigued her, even though her instinct and common sense clashed in a battle, a war to determine his true intentions.

I peeked at Eric Fontalvo's card sitting beside the picture of Breena's smiling face. I attempted to pick it up; but a snip snap noise outside the window caught my attention.

Taking a look outside, I quickly found the source. Ella. The girl held a large pair of shears that were almost the same size as her petite frame. She chopped at the rose bushes with a manic fervor. I got exhausted just by watching the girl work as if she were on a deadline.

"All right, little girl. That's enough." I headed toward the front door, stepped outside, and trudged out to where my uninvited gardener worked at pruning the branches, unaware of my presence.

"Hello, Ella. What are we up to today?"

Ella swiveled toward me, her striking blue eyes hard, her hands and arms bloody from cuts. She wore the same type of long brown colonial-style dress covered by a lace apron as she did the first time I saw her. Today the fabric hung close to her hips and she wasn't wearing a shift underneath the skirt, the piece that hiked the waistline up the way women did in the old days. Then as if she'd recognized a long lost relative, she beamed the sunny smile I recalled from the first day we met.

"See what that storm did? That mean old howling wind ripped off all the new buds. It's not a good thing at all, Ms. Harrison," she said in an emotional voice.

"Ella, I thought we agreed we'd wait until—"

"But you can't just leave them out here." Ella's eyes widened. She dropped the shears and wrung her hands.

"I don't need a gardener right now. We talked about this," I said sharply.

"But it's my job to make sure Chelby's roses are taken care of. Do let me stay. My mother will be so mad if I can't do my job. Please." She clasped her hands together as though she were begging and tilted her head to the side. Getting reacquainted with the closeness of southern life was going to take some time.

I studied her face a moment longer and said, "Okay, but on a trial basis, and only twice a week to start."

Ella shrieked a blood-curdling squeal and jumped up and down. "You mean it's official? I get my old job back?"

"Yes, Ella, it's official." I still didn't understand why the girl thought she was getting her old job back. Maybe Saul had used her before, but he never mentioned it.

"I promise I'll be the best gardener. You've just made this the greatest day of my life in over two hund—well, since a very long time."

"Good. I'll be writing for the next few hours. So please keep the fuss down." I turned and walked back toward the house. At the front porch, I turned and took a quick peek at the girl. She was pulling weeds with the energy of a mad artist.

THE LELAND LIBRARY was part sunny yellow ranch house and part brick building, a strange mixture that gave the exterior a unique type of charm. I eased my Camaro into a parking spot and walked inside. Today, my research involved far more invigorating subjects and the change of scenery became a welcome distraction for the writer's block.

I delved into the microfiche files of the Castle Hayne Gazette, searching for articles on Chelby Rose Plantation's original owners, Rose and Thomas Chelby. Images of archived articles that had been transcribed into modern English and entered into the system flickered across the screen—page after page of historical tidbits. One particular item caught my eye. I pressed the silver pause button and read the story.

Castle Hayne Gazette, May 5, 1771

FOR SALE, OR TO BE LEASED for a term of years, the plantation, Chelby Rose on Lockwood's Folly. The house contains five bedrooms and one dining room above; a hall and parlor, below with two fire-places, stables and every other necessary out building. The garden and orchard are capacious and contain a variety of native and imported roses and fruit trees. The plantation contains 900 acres; 400 are under fence; 80 acres are tide swamp, and a part in order for planting. Apply on premises to Thomas Chelby.

"Well the swamp explains the mosquitoes," I said aloud. However, I didn't recall seeing five bedrooms. The house I rented only had four. Could they be talking about the attic? I chose another article that was written before the house went up for sale.

Castle Hayne Gazette, June 1, 1746.

The gardens of Chelby Rose are to be displayed. The fine and elegant gardener, ROSE CHELBY, will open her stylistic creations to the public on Tuesday. Rose will be accompanied by her husband, Thomas Chelby, and their 4 children, Samuel, Joseph, Eliza, and Alice.

I hit the black zoom button, increasing the size of the children's names. Closing my eyes, an image surged through my mind. There was a woman with striking red hair standing in a garden filled with roses. She cut flowers and hummed a familiar tune. Up ahead, three children ran through a meadow filled with flowers. I focused on them. Just a touch closer and I would be able to see their faces. The girl in the group stopped suddenly and turned around. I was just about to get a glimpse of her face when a woman's voice startled me back to the present time and the entire scene faded away.

"I said there's a history behind that there garden," the woman repeated.

I swerved around and faced the middle-aged librarian who'd been eyeing me the entire time. Although I'd gotten used to the stares while I shopped for groceries and handled other daily activities, I still sometimes cringed under the attention. Today, the librarian's curiosity was a welcome asset.

"Really? Where would I find more information on this family?" I asked.

"You're looking at her. Norma Atwater, the unofficial Brunswick Town historian and chairwoman of the MARAS." She held out her hand and gave me a firm handshake. She was a tall black woman with caramel-colored skin, high cheekbones, and a spunky short haircut. She wore an earth-toned poncho covered in a zigzag pattern, a combination that resembled a cross between southwestern and Native American designs. A dark stone the size of a baby's outstretched hand hung on a long chain around her neck.

Her friendly, but strong presence reminded me of Frieda. However, the way she smiled and the nobility in her features made me think of Grandma Zee.

"I'm Tandie Harrison."

"Ah yes, the celebrity buying the Chelby plantation."

"I don't consider myself a famous person," I said.

"Well, Tandie who's not a celebrity, what questions can this old woman answer for you?" Norma asked.

I decided to go straight for what bothered me the most. "What do you know about the history of the Chelbys and Fontalvo families?"

The woman's smile faded and the left side of her face ticked. Swallowing hard, she pulled up a chair beside me. "Forgive me, child. Your question caught me off guard. That's hard to do." A pause. "May I ask what's driving this inquiry? I mean, it's not every day someone walks in and asks me about a two hundred and sixty year old story."

"I, um, well there's this book I'm writing. I need some help with that," I said. The woman stared at me for so long that I thought she was about to tell me to get lost.

"Far be it from me to hinder any type of literary endeavor. I suppose I better start talking then." She sighed and paused.

"That history started as so many others do. With a love affair. The story of Alice Chelby and Enrique Fontalvo is kind of like a retelling of Romeo and Juliet, but southern style. You see, Rose Chelby had a maid named Mary Jean. And the maid's daughter also had her eye on Enrique. Rumors claimed Mary Jean knew the ways of voodoo. But she wasn't a priestess, though. She was something worse." She hesitated and looked around before leaning in closer to me.

"She was a dark witch. When Enrique jilted Mary Jean's daughter, she murdered Alice Chelby. Buried her someplace where no one knows. Most folks think she hid the body somewhere in Chelby Rose's gardens. Then she placed a curse on both the Fontalvos and the Chelbys. But the effects of that curse spread around to some other Bolivian citizens. Old Thomas Chelby blamed his daughter's death on Enrique. He was so angry. Even had the poor boy hunted down and thrown in jail where he stayed until he got sick and died."

"What kind of curse was it?" I whispered, captivated by the woman's hypnotic information.

"I wish I knew. I do know some of Bolivia's dead townsfolk don't realize they were supposed to move on to the other side two hundred years ago. That's why the MARAS was formed. To make sure they crossover. Don't need vengeful spirits roamin' around the place. The good ones are welcome to stay, though. Some Bolivians even found a way to coexist with their spiritual tenants." The woman looked around again as if the empty carrels might be listening to our conversation. The evening hour had arrived faster than I thought it would.

"You're saying the spirits are still around because they're under this curse and can't leave?" I asked, a million thoughts racing through my mind.

"Those poor lost souls are waiting for the one who can set them free. You see, people trusted the Cropseys. And the women took that innocent faith, twisted it and made sacrifices out of those poor people. The souls are too angry to rest. And a betrayed heart can be a dark and powerful thing."

A knot formed in my throat. Parts of the story still didn't link up. Eric's family still existed, which meant Enrique and Alice had a baby together before she was killed. "If Mary Jean and her daughter murdered Alice, then there must have been a baby to carry on the line."

Norma's eyes softened and her expression turned in on itself. "There was a baby. A kind family adopted the sweet little thang—the Atwaters." She stopped and waited for my reaction. "Yes, dear. One of my ancestors took the baby. No one wanted anything to do with the illegitimate son of a fugitive." A shutter flapped in the wind, slamming against the library's exterior window. The librarian jumped and so did I. Something in Norma's story about Mary Jean and her daughter sent chills racing up and down my spine.

"The memories of Mary Jean Cropsey and her daughter's evil deeds are still terrorizing that little town even today," Norma said, shaking her head. "Ella Maud was her name."

Breathtaking dread hit my chest. I opened and closed my mouth several times before I could get the words out. No fucking way. "Ella Maud Cropsey?" I asked, emphasizing each name. The hairs raised on my arm as yet another connection linked my novel to a past event. "That's her daughter's name?"

"That's right," Norma said, eyeing me carefully.

"Can't be. That's yet another person with the same name as the characters in my book," I whispered aloud, my thoughts racing. "It's all connected But how?"

"You say something, honey?" Norma stared at me.

"I was just thinking aloud," I said.

The librarian's gaze traveled from my face to my necklace and back. "There's a powerful soul protecting you, Ms. Harrison," Norma said, giving me a sideways look. "I suspect this entity is attracted to your ability to channel spirits and cross time."

The bold statement both startled and intrigued me. "How do you know I can do that?" I hadn't officially determined I could do those things yet. I hung on her next words.

"My mother had the pathseeker's eye. I can tell when someone is using the gift. Kind of like you were doing when I spoke to you earlier. Don't fight that power, Tandie. Accept it."

"She did?" This made the first time I'd spoken to anyone outside my family about my abilities. I wanted to know more. To understand how to use this blossoming gift to find the cause of Breena's death. I could even help Eric solve his friend's murder. "Why is it called the pathseeker's eye?"

Norma sighed and took a seat beside me. "You don't know how it works? No one ever helped you understand?" I shook my head.

"There wasn't anyone to help me understand. They're all gone."

"Milo take the wheel. Pathseeker power originated from a powerful native american shaman who lived thousands of years ago— Right here in the colonial Carolina times before such a label existed. A woman cursed by a witch. That's why Bolivians call these particular shamans time traveling witches. It's a gift and some would say a curse. Either way, it gives you the ability to travel along time's veil."

"How is such a thing possible?" I whispered, holding my breath as I waited for her answer, afraid to blink for thinking I'd miss something important.

"The pathseeker channels her past lives. In doing so, she can go back in time by latching on to that specific pathway. It takes great skill and a conduit. Not to be taken lightly. Traveling time's veil is dangerous."

I thought about Abby's accusations and felt nausea rising in my throat. Could it be that I'd played a part in Virgil's death and didn't recall doing so? Maybe I'd stumbled onto a pathway and had forgotten. The thought rattled my nerves. "So I am a witch."

"In a nutshell... But mama preferred the term time traveling shamans."

The conversation with Norma left me with more questions than answers. I couldn't make sense of anything she told me. My mother had been dead for over two decades, so how could she have a pathseeker's eye?

Norma must have sensed the confusion on my face because she smiled softly and said, "It's okay, Tandie. Take your time absorbing all this. You haven't had anyone to help you understand these things before now."

I felt like a child as I slowly began to comprehend what Norma told me. My mom's Egyptian ancestors were related to a figure from Biblical times, a woman called Sarah. Mom didn't have the pathseeker's eye. That gift came from my father's side. Instead, Mom had something else— the ability that allows its user to gain access to hidden paths inside the spiritual planes, pulling restless spirits into her embrace while doing so.

But this ancient lineage had also led to tragedy for my family, since somehow Mom lost control of her powers and her car careened off a cliff in the Blue Ridge Mountains. I remembered how Dad seemed determined to prove Mom wasn't gone forever, believing she was stuck somewhere in time within the veil, unable to break free and return home. After a year of obsessively chasing various leads, he wandered off one day never to be seen again. His car was found abandoned in the Blue Ridge Mountains, the place where Mom died.

As I reflected on my family history, I felt an invisible force tugging at me from somewhere deep within myself – a reminder that I too possessed this power my mother had before me. It seemed impossible, but something inside me knew it was true: I was gifted with powerful abilities not many people are blessed with – and it was up to me if I used them for good or evil.

Thanks for the insight." I gathered my things.

"My card if you ever need to talk." Norma stood and slipped a business card in the side pocket on my purse.

I nodded, walked out of the library and scurried to my car. Nightfall would soon fall like a black mist on the small town, and I wanted to be home when that happened on this night more than any other. Now that I understood what Norma meant about accepting this power for what it was, there were other pressing matters that needed attending – such as seeking justice for Breena's murder so that my baby's spirit could rest and helping Eric find his friend's killer by using my newfound ability of pathseeking. I just hoped that when tapping into these forces within I wouldn't awaken a more powerful sleeping beast.

Chapter 15

T*andie*

A subdued version of my contractor returned to Chelby Rose a few days later. From inside the house, I watched him work on the front gate. The iron bars gave him a hard time. The latch he secured didn't hold the gate. Therefore, the left side kept falling off the hinge. It was a two person job, and I didn't need contractual experience to understand the root cause.

I could only imagine what he felt after losing his friend, and then having the murder go unsolved. I was in the same boat. Desperately searching for an answer to an occurrence that haunted both my waking and nocturnal thoughts, and I wanted him to know he wasn't alone. Suffering in silence after experiencing death's hold was one of the loneliest ways to handle grief.

Frieda had filled me in on a few more details. Told me about the connection between my contractor and the man who'd been murdered... Virgil Thompson. Since Shania was also her client, I only received a brief overview. Yet, that was enough. I hadn't expected Eric's hasty return to work. An immense sensation of protectiveness flooded me as I watched him curse in Spanish a few times before shaking his head and turning towards his Jeep.

Inhaling deeply, I left the window and walked out the front door, approaching with caution. The tension radiating from his broad shoulders could smother an elephant.

He shoved his toolbox inside the Jeep, slammed the car door shut and released an agitated sigh. Lowering his head, his muscles tensed and I could almost see the frustration radiating from his body in waves. I wanted to touch him. To help him in that way I've helped so many others who'd lost someone this way. Yet, my damn visions hadn't fully returned. Only odd dreams and other unreliable snippets. I attributed the prolonged loss to my negligence to stay on schedule with telling Maud's story. "Tell my story. Or I'll punish you," the ghostly voice had said. Yeah, I'd done a lousy job so far.

"Ok. Time for a break," I said, my eyes locked on Eric's back.

"I need to keep working." He turned towards me and placed his hands on his hips. "I'm sorry, I lost it that way."

"Work can wait, Mr. Contractor," I said, standing in front of him. "I am the boss, after all. I think my guy needs a break."

He clenched and unclenched his jaw muscles a couple of times, briefly closed his stunning eyes, and reopened them. Pain shimmered in their depths as he voiced his agreement: "You're right."

I had the perfect place in mind for our escape. I'd found it while walking along the pathway leading through the 25 plus acres of forest surrounding Chelby Rose. "I've something to show you. Follow me."

Eric studied me a moment and turned back to the gate. I could almost sense the silent conversation raging through his head.

"All right then... boss. Where are we going?" He turned towards me and crossed his arms, giving me the raised right eyebrow.

"Thought you'd never ask. Follow me." I turned and headed towards the pathway off to the right side of Chelby Rose.

The walkway led to a pond near the swamp I'd read about at the Leland Library. The forest was a mixture of damp earth and wild flowers. There was a slight breeze in the air, the delicate fragrance of lilacs and a hint of pine. The rush of water tumbled over rocks, creating a symphony of splashes and clacks. The walkway was quiet but for the occasional bird or insect. The breeze rustled the leaves in the tops of the trees.

"What made you choose this house?" he asked as we settled into an open area across from the pond I'd nicknamed Breena's Grove. "Chelby Rose has a colorful history, as I'm sure you know."

No way in Hades' haven was I going to tell him that a ghost ordered me to come here and write her story. I shrugged and gave him a diluted answer. "Haunted houses have unique souls. This one hasn't let me down so far. It's perfect for writing a haunted Gothic Romance."

"Could ask you the same thing, you know. Why'd you choose to work on a place with such a colorful history?"

My answer came as a one-dimpled smile. "I have my reasons."

"No fair. You get a full answer from me. Yet, you hide your true intentions." He fiddled with the grass surrounding us just before he met my gaze.

"I'm not hiding anything of interest. Rest assured."

I begged to differ. In fact, Eric Fontalvo was a walking curiosity magnet. "Let me be the judge."

He sighed deeply and squinted. "How about we talk about something much more interesting. Like that psychic pathway book you wrote." I was both flattered and horrified that he knew about my work. "Psychic phenomena expert. That's pretty bad ass. What's your story?"

"It's a combination of things really. My mother told my grandmother some things before she died. She said oddities on the maternal side started with a woman named Sarah and her husband Tobiah. She was a medium of sorts. My father—also deceased—handed down my psychic abilities."

"I'm sorry, Tandie. I'd no idea." He touched my shoulder, his thumb briefly caressing the fabric, allowing the gesture to linger a moment. A small spark ignited inside the touch. Eric moved his hand away. Was that a blush I caught, Mr. Fontalvo?

"It's all good," I said. There was no way I'd go into details about time travel with Eric. Or explain how I believed some mischievous spirit had caused my car accident.

Eric frowned. "Sarah and Tobiah. Aren't those like biblical names?"

"Good guess, Mr. Contractor."

He leaned towards me, his sad eyes suddenly alight with curiosity. "Interesting. Tell me more."

I scoffed a laugh. What would Eric think of me when I told him the gritty details of my ancestral lineages? Oh sure. My paternal side was plagued by Owanechee shamans called pathseekers whose visions eventually drove them insane. While my maternal side descended from a woman who lived during the Biblical times. Yet, somehow I felt that Mr. Fontalvo held his own one-two punch of a secret, one he'd yet to disclose. Something that would make my revelations pale in comparison.

"We came here to relax. Not to be weirded out."

"Well at least you're not related to a blood warlock," Eric said.

I turned to him and frowned. "What? Seriously, you're not telling me..."

"Oh, it's serious enough." He looked away, the Bolivian wind tossed strands of thick, dark hair over his eyes, giving him a mysterious allure. "I'm kind of the black sheep in this family. Things tend to um... happen to the people around me."

"Things? Like what?" I leaned towards him.

He sighed deeply and turned away, the wind blowing his hair around his face as though it were a cloak, hiding the secrets surrounding its mysterious owner.

After a long moment, he turned to me and said: "Bolivia's swamps amaze me. They hold secrets from times long gone." So we were going with an evasive maneuver. Ok. Got it, Mr. Contractor.

"They do indeed. Once upon a time, I could understand their words." The statement escaped my lips before I had a chance to stop it. I found Eric easy to talk to and didn't understand why.

"What are they saying right now?" he asked. Our gazes met.

"I don't know," I whispered, my chest tightening. The inability to sense anything outside my dreams crippled me. "I can no longer envision spiritual occurrences. Not since the accident anyway. That's why I came here. To start over. I um..." I lowered my gaze. Eric placed two fingers under my chin, lifting it so I stared in his face. His rough skin tickled.

"Looks like we have more in common than I realized, mujer bonita." The Bolivian wind kicked up a notch, rustling my long black dress. Eric stared at my lips, his gaze penetrating my soul, telling me everything would be fine yet triggering a reflex that held me back. He had secrets. Something crippling his inner peace the same as it did mine. What was it? I wanted to know. Vowed to find out.

"We should get back. I've held you up long enough," I said, moving just out of his reach.

LATER THAT NIGHT, I opened my eyes and found myself surrounded by a circular wall of dirt, towering about ten feet above my head. I had fallen into some kind of deep hole. "Help me! Please! I'm down here. Oh God, help me!" Sobs wracked my parched throat, while my fingers ached from trying to claw a way out of the hole. However, serenity found a way through the madness in the form of a voice that hummed a lullaby of some type, tiny vocals singing on perfect pitch. I focused my gaze on the opening to my dirt prison. A child's smiling face peered down in the hole.

"Wake up, Mommy. Be strong for us," Breena said, her spirit beginning to fade almost as soon as her apparition had appeared.

"I can't be strong without you, Baby B. Don't go," I croaked through sobs.

The child drifted down into the hole, her white light filling the dirt prison with a soft glow, and touched the pink topaz ring hanging around my neck.

"I'm giving it back, Mommy."

"What are you doing, Baby B?" My heart raced and was breaking.

"Your tattle-tale stories. The ones that—" Breena's spirit began to fade again. "—help you see what happened a long time ago."

"No! Don't go, Baby B!" My voice echoed throughout the chasm just before dirt started falling on my head.

"They're burying me alive. My God! They're burying me alive!"

I bolted upright in the bed and almost dropped the photograph of Breena, a memento I held as I fell asleep every night. Clasping my forehead, I fought mind-numbing anxiety and cursed the headache from hell. "Thank you for saving Mommy again," I said to Breena's picture.

A few more sobs heaved through my chest. The nightmare felt so real, and this time I was being buried alive. These latest dreams, visions, or whatever they were made the thirty second glimpses from before feel like a game. How much longer would it take for me to go completely mad?

Jumbled thoughts rushed through my head: Saul Chelby's golden hair, Eric's friend, the one named Virgil, my missing manuscript pages, the dreams of Breena, Abby's accusations, Eric, the man with the same name as my novel's love interest...and Saul. They all tied together in some way. Well, maybe not Saul's hair, but everything else pointed to Chelby Rose. There was a common element to all those things. My daughter's spirit returning in a dream was the most shocking aspect of them all.

"The trinity of love can stop the witches." Grandma Zee's voice echoed through the room as if she sat next to me.

My heart raced as I heard Grandma Zee's words echoing in my mind. I was filled with renewed energy at being able to connect with her again after the accident had changed my life.

I searched the room, almost expecting her to appear, but realizing that she was gone. My psychic abilities had been severed, but the detective in me was reignited and I had been given a crucial clue. Even if I wasn't sure how to interpret it, this was my chance to make a change.

Chapter 16

E*ric* "Don't look at me that way, Eric. I'm not crazy. I saw her standing on the beach. She kept staring across the ocean," Shania said, her face swollen, her soulful eyes filled with tears. "I thought something was wrong. So I told Virgil to go check on her. About fifteen minutes later, he sent me a text message saying he was headed to the store. I told him to be careful because a storm was headed our way."

"If she was turned toward the beach, then how did you see her face?" Eric asked softly. He didn't want to further upset the woman, but he craved an explanation for what Virgil's wife and Abby said they saw.

"She turned to me and smiled. I looked right at her face, Eric. That long white dress she was wearing made her look a little paler than what I remember; but it was her. She has one of those kinds of faces you don't forget." Shania stared at the shaking glass in her hand. A strong scent of alcohol drifted into Eric's nostrils. Inside the madness of this day, the Aeneid's early morning patrons filed through the doors. "I'm not crazy, but I might be after all this." Shania made a weak laugh.

"You're working too hard, Shania. Virgil would roll over if he knew you were pushing yourself this way. And before his funeral at that," Eric said covering her hands with his.

"I've gotta do something. If I just sit there in that house by myself, then..." She stopped and sighed. "You might find me washed up on a shore somewhere. My father was a working man. He put food on the table for us until he died. My mother called him an old fool. She said he worked himself to death. She's probably right. Like father, like daughter."

"I understand how that works, better than most, I think," Eric said, thinking about how his father sacrificed time away from his family in order to keep the renovation contracts rolling in and the business running profitably.

Deep down Eric didn't feel that the person Shania and Abby said they saw was Tandie Harrison. A lot of things just didn't make sense. Why would Virgil send a text saying he was on the way to the store and then turn up dead on the beach across from his bar over two hours later? If he didn't know better, it might seem as if one of them were setting Tandie up. But the woman spotted on the beach couldn't be ruled out. It was always possible the person the two women identified could be Tandie.

His mother's words about the restless souls wandering the Bolivian streets came to mind. Could it be possible one of them drifted through Castle Hayne? He shook the thought off and made a mental note to buy a gallon of whatever Shania was drinking before he left the club.

"Virgil made me promise that if anything ever happened to him, then I would look after you." Shania reached out and moved hair away from his forehead. The gesture surprised him. "He kept my family from starving, that man did. Taking care of his friend is the least I can do to repay him."

"Don't worry about me. Just look after yourself and Abby," Eric said.

She made a face and scoffed. "That girl is more than capable of looking out for herself." Talking about Abby changed Shania's entire demeanor, making her act more guarded and colder than before. "Can you believe she has already told me I have no right to Virgil's part of the club? I care about this place because he did. Not because his sister is making claims shortly after laying her brother to rest. I don't trust her, Eric. She has been meeting with the MARAS almost every night. She says they're going to help her find Virgil's killer."

"Dios mio. Who do they think they are? Descendants of Nancy Drew? Nobody knows who killed Virgil," Eric said, his brow furrowed. He wasn't surprised to hear Shania's news. "Tell me more about these meetings."

Shania shrugged. "She claims they hold midnight séances at the beach. Virgil knew about it. He didn't tell you?"

"No. He never mentioned it," Eric said, feeling a slight twinge of jealousy because his friend hadn't shared yet another secret.

"Well, see, there's a family there that used to babysit the two of them. But then something happened. Something awful. It's the one thing I could never get him to open up about. And now...Guess I won't ever find out, will I?" She gave him a shaky smile.

"Go home, Shania. You don't need to be here," Eric pleaded.

"Virgil wouldn't want me to let his life's work go down the drain. He'd tell me to stay right here, making sure those girls and Gus don't go hanging out in the back, drinking up his beer." They shared a shaky laugh.

Eric leaned forward. "He'd also want me to tell you that the Aeneid will be waiting for you tomorrow."

Shania blinked away a few more tears, and Eric fought hard to keep a strong face for her. His own emotional chaos swirled like razors in his gut. "You know, I can see why you didn't stay with Abby. You two are like oil and water."

"I don't stay with anyone," he said. It was easy to open up to Shania. There were no pretenses or insecurities to deal with in her the way he had to put up with in his ex-fiancée. He could see why Virgil married the woman.

Taking his hands in hers, she leaned in close and said, "There's a wonderful woman waiting out there for you. No friend of Virgil's could ever be someone who's destined to be alone forever. I'm sorry. The poet in me is acting up again." She leaned back and swallowed her drink in one gulp.

"It's all right. That was a poem I needed to hear," Eric said and made a note to ask Abby about her mysterious trips to the beach.

With Dark Souls Day quickly approaching, Eric's worry over Javier's declining health grew along with it. He made a point to take time for seeing his family's old Pastor, a man by the name of Frederick Jeffries. The nighttime sky over the 300-year-old church looked angry with a cluster of light gray clouds gliding low against a dark sky. The smell of rain lingered in the air and reminded him of Lake Pontchartrain back in New Orleans.

Earlier in the day, he'd spoken with his younger brother, Juno, who'd chided him about being back in Bolivia, terrifying his mother by returning right before Dark Souls Day, the timeframe when most of his people passed away. Fear of the curse frightened his parents to the point where his father had decided to uproot his family and leave.

Eric's family was the last generation of Fontalvos to abandon the confines of Brunswick Town. The move meant that his father had to close the turpentine portion of the business that had been in the family for decades. The decision broke his father down, even though the relocation made his mother happy. Soon after they settled in New Orleans, the wine bottle became his father's best friend and his worst enemy. But hard work made the man, shaping him and securing his place in society. That was his father's motto and now the same way of thinking belonged to him too.

"Eric, my boy. It's such a delight to see you again." Pastor Jeffries embraced him as soon as he stepped through the doorway. He was a tall black man with a plump frame and a calm round face. "Don't tell me. You've come to ask me to marry you and that cute little gal you brought by here last time?" The pastor hadn't changed. He still wanted Eric to have a family of his own. Obviously, he had no idea that he and Lisa had split up.

"No. There won't be any holy unions anytime soon for me." Eric walked over to sit on the first bench facing the pew. "Lisa and I split up a year or so ago."

Pastor Jeffries sat down beside him, a sad look etched on his jolly face. "What happened, son?"

"Life happened. My work and a few other things." Eric hesitated. In reality, Eric wanted to prevent a repeat of his first serious girlfriend's fate.

"What brings you back?"

Eric considered his answer and phrased it carefully. "I'm working for Saul Chelby. Well, technically it's his tenant. She's buying the place after her rental agreement's up."

"Hmm interesting. It's funny how Chelby decided to sell the place, so suddenly. But I'm not surprised that the person he chose happens to be a psychic."

"Why's that?" Eric asked, feeling the same way but wanting to hear what the pastor would say. His parents trusted this man with all their secrets and heartaches and Eric valued his opinion too. "Don't tell me you bought into all that witch talk?"

"No, not witches. But there's something in that house. It brings out the worst in people. Even Saul Chelby doesn't want to live there."

"He hired me to do the contractual work," Eric said. "I got the request from Saul a few weeks before I came here."

A worried look crossed the pastor's face. He studied his plump hands before speaking. "What made you take the assignment? I'd have thought you would've turned it down."

"What? Why? Pastor with all due respect, my company needs the money." And Eric needed to get closer to Tandie Harrison, he wanted to add. It fascinated him that she happened to be a psychic, a gorgeous one too with pain riddled eyes that haunted him.

Coincidence, he didn't believe in. But fate...that was a different story. If Tandie was a means to ending his family's tortures and pains then Eric resolved to find the way. He promised his mother that he wouldn't return without some kind of answer on how to save Javier from the Fontalvo curse.

"I already have to deal with a grieving Shania McKinnon, may the Lord bless Virgil's soul. He seemed lost sometimes, but he was a good man to his wife. I would hate to add your name to that list."

"What happens if I leave? You're the spirit guru. There's no guarantee that the Broken Heart Curse will magically disappear," Eric said, feeling frustrated. "I guess I should just let my family and friends all croak one by one. Real smooth suggestion for a man of God. I'm sorry, Pastor."

During the past ten years, Eric had run. He ran from the nightmares he had of his father's death. He ran from the bullies who pushed him around because he was so frail in build; and he ran from his fiancée, leaving her with memories of the affairs with other women, a flaw he blamed on his own insecurities. Maybe his infidelity wasn't a lack of confidence. Deep down, Eric always knew his family curse would eventually affect any woman he loved. Just as it did his first serious girlfriend. The Broken Heart Curse existed and he intended to end it. He had no choice.

"You're right. I am the expert. My faith gives me the armor I need to conquer anything. But when I visit the sick people who live in Bolivia, there's something that walks behind me. Something that wants to hurt me and force me to stay with the others. I can sense both the good and not-so-good spirits, but I can't see them. I'd help if I could."

"Pastor, every single Fontalvo male except for my father died by the time they reached age forty-two: natural causes, freak accidents, you name it. I don't believe in coincidence. Our ancestors told a story about a man who claimed a witch brought him here. Now either he was crazy, or he knew exactly what he was talking about. A couple of people say they saw Ms. Harrison talking to Virgil just before he was...killed. I don't believe she's a witch, but I can't ignore the police report. I have to know. This contracting job is the way. It's not only about my family anymore.

My good friend is dead. My brother's time is short." Emotion winded him and choked his voice.

Getting closer to the mystery woman had turned into a mini-obsession for Eric. He felt drawn to her, connected to her in some way and he didn't know why. It wasn't only about her striking beauty, the lady with a smile that lit up a room, or her intriguing bi-colored eyes, the ones that hooked him the moment he glanced into those intriguing jewels the first time they met. The oddity of the situation surrounding them made approaching her that much more difficult for him.

"No more running, Pastor. This time, I walk straight into the minefield."

Pastor Jeffries studied him with a sad face. "All right, son. But if you must meet the devil on his playing ground, then you'll need to have your own set of armor ready. "Hold tight."

Pastor Jeffries stood and walked into his office. He returned with a black box covered in velvet. He let out a sigh as he plopped down beside Eric. "These old tired bones." He gave the box to Eric. "It's not rigged. Open it."

"What's in it?" Eric opened the box. A golden shamrock about the size of a 2x2 sticky note lay inside the velvet lining.

"That's your armor, son. Some sort of family heirloom," he said. Eric made a light laugh and frowned. "I promised your father that I'd make sure you get it if anything ever happened to him. He told me you would know what to do when the time came."

"I have no idea what to do, Pastor," Eric said, examining the intricately carved details on the shamrock's leaves. The outline of a lion-serpent's head was etched in the middle; the Fontalvo family crest's symbol. Eric narrowed his eyes, hoping to feel something. Anything. No thunderstorms or magical waves or anything otherworldly crashed into the room.

"Look at me, son. Stand for something. Or you'll fall for anything," Pastor Jeffries said, his eyes filled with fear and worry. "I'm not a superstitious man. I believe the Lord Jesus has all in control. Evil don't stand no chance against a good heart. But I'm also a prudent man. Throughout the years, every single Fontalvo male has died much too soon. Your father was the exception. Now, I don't put a lot of stock into witches and things, son, but I believe your father endured because he left this place. Do the same thing, Eric. Leave. And don't ever look back."

Eric swallowed hard. He didn't want to lie. "I'll consider it, Pastor."

Chapter 17

TANDIE

Saul arrived at 6 p.m. sharp on Saturday evening, and I wasn't the least bit surprised to find him waiting outside my door at the exact time he gave.

I'd spent most of the week chewing the inside of my mouth and fighting an urge to take a pill to calm my nerves. I kept telling myself that just one tablet was all I needed to take the edge off. What would that hurt? Trying to ignore the nervous tension, I placed the bottle back inside the medicine cabinet, the first victory of the night. However, the second one, getting through my first date in almost eight years, was going to be the toughie.

The royal blue dress I wore trailed behind me a bit as I walked to the door. Frieda and I had spent the last two days scouring Independence Mall, looking for the right blue outfit. She also made it a point to tease me about having Jungle Fever.

"Seriously, who uses that term these days?" I had teased back.

"Sex therapists. If we tease our clients about old cheesy terms like that then it works better than a charm, girlfriend. We need some way to make patients loosen up," Frieda said and shrugged.

"Whatever you say." Getting out of the house felt good; but heading out to a place filled with people who called me a witch set the anxiety wheel into motion.

When the tires of Saul's Mercedes SUV had crunched across the gravel driveway, I almost hyperventilated. Taking a peek at Breena's photograph, I inhaled deeply, adjusted my curls Frieda pinned up in a loose chignon and opened the door. Saul stood outside, waiting with a boutonniere in his hand. He wore a dark gray tuxedo with tails trailing behind him. The shirt underneath the jacket was black. The dark clothing paired together with his light hair made a striking combination. A bright smile lit up his entire face as he raked eager eyes over my gown. "You are stunning beyond words."

You can do this. He's human, not a monster.
That means he won't bite or mutilate you.
So calm down.

Saul removed the flower from inside the box and placed the rose in my hands. The color was more of a bluish-lavender. "I've never seen a flower like this before," I gushed.

However, that was a half truth. I'd seen this flower in the dream vision I experienced a few nights ago. Hundreds of blue curiosas surrounded me before the scene turned into a nightmare. What made Saul choose this flower from my dream? Once again, something supernatural had sent me a message. I was meant to be with Saul tonight. There was no doubt about that fact. The question remained though...what awaits me at the end of this venture?

"A blue curiosa. Very hard to find, and very rare like your eyes: one brown, one green. Truly unique," he said, silencing me with his intense gaze.

"I'll be wearing an awful lot of blue tonight," I said, trying to smile through my flushed face.

Laughing softly, Saul said, "It's not for your dress, Tandie. This little beauty is for my suit. That way the other men will know who you belong to. Help me pin it on."

"Of course, I knew that," I joked.

Concentrating on keeping the pointed end away from his well-toned chest, I set to work attaching the flower to the left lapel of his dinner jacket. "There. All done," I said without looking at him. I felt him staring at me. An awkward moment passed, and then Saul lifted my chin up so his deep blue gaze bore into my bi-colored eyes. "It's perfectly all right to live a little. Just a taste of life is all you need. Things will start to get better. I promise." His smile made me want to believe him, but the ache in my chest wanted to keep me a prisoner to the grief.

"I'll consider your suggestion," I answered, holding his gaze.

"Fair enough." Saul smiled, took a step back and opened the front door. "Ready?"

I nodded and stepped outside, inhaling deeply as a cool breeze caressed my face. Saul eased his fingers around my arm and led me toward his sleek gray Mercedes. Opening the car door, he turned and faced me. "I will make every single male envious tonight, and perhaps a few females too."

Face flushing, I smirked and said, "I believe this is the part where I pick on you about how you probably use that line on all your girlfriends."

"Girlfriends? You flatter me with your assumptions," he said, smiling, and opened my door wider.

THE GOVERNOR'S BALL took place in the Thalian Hall, another marvelous structure preserved from the historical days. The building was an old theatre recently renovated. Inside the dining area that also served as an entertainment room, tables covered in golden cloths were set up along the middle of the main floor. On the way to our table, Saul stopped to greet at least fifty people. Most of his love-struck fans were females he brushed off as we passed by. Stares and more than a few glares came from all directions, but Saul didn't falter a bit and neither did I.

As the night wore on, I got the chance to meet the Governor, a few of Saul's local business partners, and more of what I figured were his female playmates. The women didn't make their annoyance with me too obvious, however, they found creative ways to let me know they had played a role in Saul's past.

After spending a couple of hours watching various plays take place on the stage situated at the head of the dining room, I started to get restless.

During the intermission, Saul leaned forward and said, "You eat like a little bird. You haven't even touched your calamari or your red velvet cake. I admire your ability to resist such temptations."

"Actually, birds eat twice as much of their weight. My grandmother used to always tell me I eat like a hamster. I pile things on my plate and then come back to munch on them later. That way I'm the one controlling the temptation." I held Saul's gaze this time, refusing to lower my eyes, even though my face was on fire.

After a long moment, he broke the connection and grinned. Even in the candlelight, Saul's brilliant smile lit up the table. "Are you not having a good time? We can leave if you're ready."

"Oh no. I don't want to interfere," I answered. However, I desperately wanted to break out of this crowd, a group filled with people who reminded me of my ex-husband's colleagues. And coming back to Castle Hayne made me think of Grandma Zee's little cottage sitting along the outskirts in the swampland areas. The memories of my grandmother perishing in a fire made me think of Baby B.

You don't deserve to be happy.

You let your little girl die the same as your grandmother.

Tell my story. Tell my story. Tell my story.

The voices assaulted me for the first time in over a week. Wincing, I studied my surroundings as the room pulsed in and out. The images of the partygoers around me changed from people dressed in suits and gowns to attendees dressed in petticoats and menswear from a time long gone.

Saul had disappeared and I no longer sat at a table. Instead, I stood inside a ballroom, one from several hundred years ago. My breathing increased and beads of sweat prickled my forehead. I spun around several times, trying to study and memorize the details.

"Flowers for the lady," a masked man said and held out a blue curiosa. I reached out, grasped the flower, gripping the thorn while doing so, and cried out. The scene flashed and faded just before Saul's concerned face came back into view.

"What the hell is happening?" I whispered as I glanced around. Was that a vision? Or something else? I'd never had the sight randomly attack me that way. The incident felt so real.

"All right, I've decided. We're leaving." Saul stood and moved behind my chair. He was always ready to be the gentleman.

"I'm okay. Really, we don't have to leave." A total lie.

He leaned in close, his spicy cologne drifting around him. "We're going. No arguments." If I didn't know better, I might think Saul was a knight in disguise or a prince coming to rescue the damsel. I stood and Saul took my hand draping it across his forearm.

On the way out, we were approached by several people who questioned our early departure. Just as he did the women from earlier, Saul brushed them off too.

Back inside the car, the air between us changed. Heated energy floated around us even before Saul made the first statement. "I'm sorry you didn't have a good time," he said suddenly.

"That's not true. I had a great time," I lied.

"Want to tell me why you're teary-eyed?"

"Not really."

He sighed deeply. "Tandie it's perfectly all right to open up once or twice a lifetime."

"My grandmother's old house isn't far from here," I admitted. "I haven't been there since I returned to the area."

"Why not? I'm sure your relatives would love to see you," Saul said.

"None of my father's relatives live here in this area. Grandma Zee's other son lives in Hawaii. My mother's people still live in Egypt, but she never talked about them. And I have no idea whether my father is dead or alive." I scoffed at the thought. Deep down inside, I knew he was still living. He'd slowly descended into a world inside his head as he looked for a way to find what I now understood to be Mama's pathway, claiming that's where she waited for him, on the other side of this world and inside the veil. He drove off one day and never returned. Only his car and notebooks were found along with a few bloody pieces of clothing.

Grandma Zee's funeral was mysteriously paid for and the house she left was partially restored. Why my father chose to hide from his daughter and mother was something I would never understand. The rejection left an ache, a pang that plagued my relationships, an aching need to find bits of father in the men I chose as mates. My grandmother spoke fondly of both her sons; but I could tell from the way her face lit up that my father was her favorite.

"My grandmother had a little garden I used to tend to for her."

"Where is this place?" Saul asked, making me curious about his questions.

"It's near the swamplands. Why do you ask?"

"Because we're headed that way," Saul said as if this were a trip we took together every day.

"I'm not ready to go back there," I said, tingles creeping up my neck. Saul continued driving toward the coastline. "You don't even know where the house is."

"No. But you're going to tell me how to get there, unless you'd like to ride around all night." He gazed over at me with an expression that said he meant every word of what he just promised to do.

Anger and fear and a strange sense of relief stirred in my chest. Since I'd already learned he was the kind of man who would do exactly what he said, I gave in and told him the address. The thought of driving around all night with Saul worried me, and I was ready to go home.

Twenty minutes later, the Mercedes eased to a stop in front of grandma's cottage. Part of the roof was still covered by the tarp father's estate lawyers had the workers put on it years ago. The small walkway leading up to the front door bore cracks in the cement. Before getting burned on one side, the Cape Cod style house had been painted a crisp white. Now the faded exterior gave the place a sad appearance. The siding was a dingy color, a symbol of the way my life had changed since I lost Baby B. Considering all the damage, traces of the lush garden my grandmother labored over still lingered along either side of the property's borders.

The day I received the call from Grandma Zee's caretaker six years ago was both the best and worst day of my life. I was sad because of the tragedy but happy because I had just learned I was pregnant with Breena. But the news brought bittersweet joy. The woman who took care of me for most of my life would never get the chance to see the baby.

"I'm not ready for this," I whispered, raking my gaze over the exterior. The strangely colored moonlight gave the house an eerie glow.

"Yes, you are," Saul said. He lifted his long limbs out of the car, walked around the front and opened my door.

"Why are you doing this? You barely even know me." I stepped out of the Mercedes and faced Saul, waiting for his answer. He wore the saddest look I'd ever seen on him, the oil tycoon who was always smiling.

"I understand what it's like to be a victim of your past. It's a clever way for fate to cripple you in the future." He gazed deep in my eyes for the longest moment, and I found myself wanting to know more about the millionaire with the sad face. "Now, let's go inside."

"What? We'll fall through the floor," I said, my voice rising the tiniest bit.

A subdued smile flashed across his face. "No, we won't. Looks like someone has already completed quite a bit of construction on this old house. Let's take a look."

I didn't want to go inside or notice anything about the house. Instead, I wanted to head home and get away from this man who wanted me to face things I wasn't ready to see.

A vision surged through my mind, a picture of Grandma Zee sleeping soundly on the sofa, her wrinkled brown skin looking peaceful. The coroner's report said grandma died long before the fireplace shot out the spark that set the house ablaze; so she didn't suffer. I never really knew grandma's age; but she seemed wise beyond her years. She told me that her mutt-blood made her look younger than other women the same age.

The vision faded, bringing back memories of Breena's death along with my grandmother's. The image was a small, but powerful one. Sobs started in my upper body, making me feel as though I might hyperventilate. "I can't go in there. I just can't." Leaning against Saul's chest, I found his embrace comforting as though I could allow myself to grieve for just one stolen moment.

Saul took my face in his hands, caressing my cheeks with a gentleness that made me feel safe. Why were his hands so soft? They were very different from Eric's weather beaten ones or even my ex's dry skin. Everything about Saul Chelby was different from any man I'd ever known.

"Don't let the sadness win. I'm here for you now and always," he mumbled so low I barely heard him.

Still willing the tears away, I didn't get a chance to utter a word before he lowered his head and kissed me ever so gently. He pulled back after a few seconds and gazed into my eyes. His baby blues were bright and glossy, a penetrating look that worked its way deep inside my mind. As though my silence offered a silent confirmation of some type, he lowered his head again, crushing his lips against mine, and deepened the kiss once he realized I wasn't about to protest or pull away. His tongue parted my lips, darting in and out and around my mouth as if seeking to consume me with his passion.

The lightness in my chest and the way his kiss stole my breath opposed one another. Part of me wanted to be touched this way, to feel normal as if I wasn't a freak hiding inside of a house and behind a novel that might never spring to life. The other half of my body screamed that all of this happened too fast.

It wasn't a secret that Saul Chelby played games with females. I'd be kidding myself if I thought for one second that I would be treated any differently. But the spell he held over me was as if I had lost all will power. His mouth eased away from my lips and traced a warm path down my neck, lingering on my collarbone and gently brushing across the sensitive skin. Waves of heat shot through my stomach and left me swimming in a dizzying swoon.

Somewhere deep inside, I found myself, the insecure little girl still hiding from a shadow monster, and fought whatever he was trying to do. "Saul, don't," I said through our gasps. "Please stop!" He didn't stop. Instead, his grip tightened around my arms, and his heated kisses became more aggressive.

Shoving his shoulders back a bit, I stepped away from Saul.

"What's wrong?" he asked, almost pleading and reaching toward me.

I moved away from his attempt to touch me again. "Please, just take me home."

"What did I do wrong?" Saul asked. A pained expression ran across his face.

"I don't want to be one of your harem girls, Saul," I said, still trying to recover.

"Ah, I see. The rumors about my lifestyle precede me." He hesitated and stared at his feet as if he were in some kind of trance. After a long moment, he sighed and stuffed his hands into his pockets.

"I have to say this. You take me out on a beautiful date, and convince me to do something I have no desire to do, and made me enjoy every minute of it," I said, caught up in the smile creeping across Saul's pouty lower lip. "Suddenly, I found myself hating that I believed all those things I heard about you. And then, you get all crazy, groping and kissing me like we've known each other for years."

He shrugged. "People do it all the time on a first date. Kissing that is," he said with emphasis on the last part.

Sure that's exactly what you meant, I thought.

"Well, call me a country girl, but I don't like being felt up like I'm in high school."

"You forget. I'm a country boy too."

"Then act like one, and be a gentleman. You're so used to getting your way that you don't even realize when you're manipulating someone. It's all right to take your time with a woman instead of marathon racing her to the sack." I pulled my shawl tighter around my shoulders.

"Tandie, I certainly don't want to make you into a harem whore," he said with sad sarcasm, his boyishly handsome face drooping.

A touch of guilt tugged at my chest. He stepped toward me. "I only wanted to help you feel better. I'll take you home, now." We turned and walked away from the steps, a strong gust pushing us sideways as if the wind were trying to keep us from leaving.

Returning to Grandma Zee's cottage had turned out to be a terrible idea. I didn't completely blame Saul for bringing me here, though. From what I could tell, he appeared to be somewhat interested in my past.

Back in the car, I studied his sad but determined profile. For being such a rich man, he came across as super lonely. His soul was a desolate one like mine. However, he was a man used to having his way with women.

Was I doomed to spend the rest of my life judging and pushing people away? If so, then that was a curse I needed to break. Just as Frieda said, I had been playing the victim for far too long. Without self-pity, I was losing the main reason for my dependence on anti-depressants and tears. And I was more than ready to accept something new in my life.

That was, until I looked down and studied my right middle finger, the one that had bothered me ever since I experienced the vision back at Thalian Hall. A small dot of dried blood had spread across my fingertip.

Chapter 18

E*ric*
Eric didn't realize he'd been grasping the steering wheel the entire time Saul and Tandie had stood outside the house until his hand went numb. What he also didn't understand was his urge to warn her about Saul's reputation. Relaxing his grip on the wheel, he felt the blood rush back into his palms.

"All right, first, you turn into an asshole," he said, thinking of the way he had dismissed her feelings since the night Virgil was killed, "and then you want to go beat the shit out of her date who happens to be your paycheck man. Real smooth, Fontalvo."

Parked just beyond the edge of the trees lining the property's borders, Eric watched the couple. All he needed to hear was the tiniest whimper and Saul Chelby was going to be sorry he ever touched her. But he didn't hear anything until Saul pulled away from her and Tandie raised her voice. Were they arguing?

He strained to hear what she was saying. No luck. They quieted down after a while. The area was too silent, now. The whistling breeze rustling through the trees didn't help matters either.

He had promised Abby and Shania that he would try to figure out the story behind the mystery woman people saw walking on the beach. What he didn't realize was that doing so meant resorting to following people around like a stalker.

His heart sped up. If Tandie wasn't screaming then that probably meant she was enjoying herself. He cleared away thoughts of a Chelby's hands all over her sweet body from his mind.

Long ago, the feud between the Fontalvos and the Chelbys turned brutal. Decades passed and as new children were born into the families, either they forgot the cause of the rivalry over time or didn't care. Still, the unspoken hurts and anger passed down throughout the years lingered over the last remaining heirs of either side.

Was Saul's bid for Eric a peace offering? Or did something sinister lurk behind his new assignment? Eric knew the Chelby's were linked to his family's curse. At one time, he would've thought thinking such a thing was paranoia. Now that his friend had been murdered and the woman residing in Saul Chelby's house happened to be linked to his final living moment, a new fire had reignited within in the long-forgotten feud between Bolivia's two oldest families. And time to save Javier's life was winding down. The Dark Souls Day celebration happened in a month.

Instinct told him to go and confront both Tandie and Saul. Pride kept him sitting inside the car. He drummed his fingers across the steering wheel, checked his watch and tapped his thighs. For some reason, they had pulled away from each other, Tandie looking less than pleased from the kiss they just shared. A little tingle flickered through Eric's chest.

"I bet that's a new one for your ego, Chelby. Rejection with a blue dress on," he said just before Saul opened her door. With a strained expression on her face, she appeared to be more than ready to leave the half renovated house. Relief washed over Eric and he found himself sinking down in the seat just in case one of them noticed his Jeep. They didn't. Instead, Saul revved the Mercedes' engine to life and sped away into the night.

Looking back at the cottage, Eric did a double take. At first, the light in the window to the far right side of the house made him think he was seeing things. He squeezed his eyes shut and opened them. The light shined even brighter, a vivid white, reminding him of an incident that happened one night a couple of weeks after his father died.

In his grief, he had awakened that night to a stomping noise on the steps. He was in the room with his youngest brothers, Nico and Juno, when a sulfuric odor drifted into the air. Outside the bedroom window, a bright light lit up the area and filled the room. Juno whimpered, ran over to Eric watching over Nico in his bed, and jumped under the covers. He hid his face under his brother's pillows. The two younger boys and their older brother sat huddled together long after the light faded away.

"Was that papa's ghost?" Nico had asked him.

"Don't be silly. Papa wouldn't scare his kids that way," Eric said and pulled the boys into his embrace. He stared at the window until his eyes dried out.

He couldn't look away that night just as he wasn't able to do so now. An invisible force held his gaze in place and his body had gone numb. The sensation felt as though someone or rather something was holding him in place so he couldn't turn away. *El mono en su espalda* ... the monkey on his back as his mother called the sleep demon that held children down in their sleep.

His blood ran ice cold and he released a shaky breath, opening his mouth a few times while doing so. A throbbing pain pulsed through his skull. Eric cried out, squeezing his eyes shut until the sensation eased up. The light coming from inside the little house moved until the beam was floating across the lawn.

"Damn," he gasped, sweeping a hand across his sweaty forehead as he broke away from whatever force had held his limbs in place. "No fucking way."

The light or whatever it was drifted over to the edge of the yard and lingered a moment. Eric inhaled sharply, deciding whether to sit and stare at the apparition or crank his Jeep and high-tail it in the opposite direction. The light decided for him. The blob of whiteness drifted down the road in the same direction Saul Chelby had taken Tandie until the glow disappeared around the bend.

"What the hell is going on in this place?" And for the first time in almost a decade, he was afraid of what he couldn't understand.

Chapter 19

T*andie*

The soprano's flawless voice sailed through the speakers like musical honey. Leontyne Price, one of the first African American sopranos, had skills that rivaled Carla Bruni's superb vocals. The deep, dreary bass inside the male tenor's vocals highlighted her insanely high notes in a haunting duet as I hummed to Aida while writing. I enjoyed listening to opera during moments of writer's block. However, I still found it hard to focus.

My mind drifted between three things: Eric the annoying, but talented contractor, Ella the screaming teenager with issues, and the return of my visions. Every now and then I thought of Saul. He hadn't even called to check on the renovations since the night I jilted him. Finding room in a clouded mind for such a strangely elusive person seemed a waste of time and energy, but I hoped what happened between us didn't taint his decision to sell the house. With Eric's help, I had turned the place into a showcase house the way Thomas Chelby did long ago.

To clear my mind, I attempted to mimic Leontyne's unearthly high vocals, but I ended up coughing in my hand, a tingle picking at my vocal cords. I set my work aside and leaned back in the chair, thinking of the way Breena had developed a love of opera at the tender age of five. Even with complexities of the foreign language the singers used, we learned to enjoy the complex vocals and lush musical arrangements.

"I need water, Baby B." I stood and looked down at Breena's picture. "Were you responsible for that vision I had at the Thalian?" Her wide, toothy smile beamed back at me. Silent in answer, but revealing much with her bright eyes.

Grandma Zee used to say that pictures carry little pieces of a person's spirit. That was why witches and voodoo priestesses held so much power over the victims after they were able to steal a lock of hair or a personal item.

I stared at the picture so long that I conjured the sound of imaginary giggles. Or so I thought. Another giggle echoed out of the photograph. Frowning, I tilted my head and reached toward the frame. Shaking off the delirium, I continued on the mission to remove the dust bunnies from my throat.

Prancing into the kitchen, I opened the refrigerator, pulled out the water jug and gulped the cool liquid straight from the pitcher. Doing so made me think about the last scene I had written in my novel. Maud Cropels, my unintentional heroine, had just found three dead bodies and her handsome hero was the number one suspect on the list.

The water washed away the tingle in my throat, but not the anxiety rolling through my chest, a sensation that had returned over the last few days. I missed Breena, and the horrible ache known as grief still trickled into my thoughts every day, sometimes clouding my head. One cure. One solution. Wine. And lots of it. Stepping over to the kitchen cabinet beside the sink, I removed one of my favorite blue-tinted glasses.

Thunk! Thunk! Loud knocks echoed from upstairs. My heart cartwheeled and I almost dropped the glass. The pipes in my bathroom. What else could make a noise like that? "Damn it! I thought Eric fixed those."

I stormed out of the kitchen, rounded the corner beside the stairway and started up the steps.

My breath caught at the sight before me, and the creepy chills surged across my arms like a million feathers tickling the skin.

Three ragged, dirty children—two older boys and a young girl around six or seven years old—stood at the top of the stairs and stared down at me. All three kids had black-rimmed eyes and pale skin. The girl, who appeared to be the youngest, wore a tattered colonial-style dress that might have been white at some point. The boys' pants were torn at the bottom, giving a clear view of their bare feet. Their shirts appeared to have plaid markings on the filthy fabric, but I couldn't tell.

The oldest boy took one step down toward me. I stumbled backward and dropped my glass, shattering the blue tumbler, keeping my gazed locked on the children. Each child wore amused expressions and covered their mouths, suppressing their giggles. Laughter had been coming from Breena's photograph too, or so I thought. I was about to ask the children how they got inside the house when the boy in the middle turned and faded as if someone had switched off his image. The tallest boy flickered and faded next, but the girl stayed and stared at me as I stood plastered against the wall beside the stairway.

"No freaking way!" I said, gasping. This wasn't just any old vision. Something else was happening here and I intended to find the source.

More giggles echoed and more feet thumped upstairs. The sound of children filled Chelby Rose's hallways as my heart pounded through my black tee shirt. I covered my mouth, afraid to move. At once, the hallway fell silent, my breathing the only noise in the area, my eyes fixated on the image of the little girl. The child's dingy dress, the matted hair, and ashen pale skin freaked me out. She stared at me with eyes that reminded me of the little boy I met at the Brunswick Town store. Eyes that made my palms sweat and my underarms prickle.

And then the two boys began to chant.

"Grandma wants a brier switch! Grandma's gonna whip somebody!" The two voices repeated the words like a mantra.

I gasped and was hypnotized by the chanting, an eerie tune of high-pitched voices that would haunt my dreams for sure. From inside the living room's sound system, Leontyne Price's voice hit the highest part of Aida, an insane note to compliment an equally crazy moment.

"What do you want?" I asked.

The little girl placed a finger to her lips. She answered in a whisper. "Shh. Grandma will spank us if we talk."

My lips quivered as I released a shaky breath. Without removing my gaze from the child, I stepped over the broken glass, made my way to the bottom step and started up the stairway. The wood strained under my step in the form of the loudest creak ever.

The child frowned. "You're making too much noise. She'll hear us."

The feet running overhead echoed through the house. It was almost as if there were ten children instead of two boys. Blood curdling screams sent shivers careening down my spine. I slammed my hands over my ears and stumbled backwards, barely missing the broken glass. I recovered and found the courage to face my tiny tormentors, ripping my gaze upward. Only the dark stairwell remained.

I raced back to the study, trying to think of what I'd say to the authorities. The male opera singer's voice sang an aggressive range of vocal dips paired with a medley of strings drumming through my ears.

"Okay. Breathe once. Twice. Three times and you're there. Okay. You can do this. Creepy little ghost kids are running around the house. The situation was enough to drive even the most savvy medium insane. Think!" One name flashed through my mind... Eric Fontalvo. I had programmed his number into my phone, so I jabbed at the nine button, my hands shaking.

Footsteps still pattered up and down the hallway. The children screamed as if they were being tortured. I jerked my head towards the noise, fear consuming me in a whirlwind of high operatic notes, screams, and panting breath.

"Get a grip, Harrison. You're used to this," I said through gasps. Who was I kidding? I had never seen ghosts physically manifest until the day I arrived in Bolivia. This new aspect of my pathseeker abilities both frightened and intrigued me.

Eric's deep voice sailed through the phone. "Hello—"

"Eric! I need you to come as fast as you can! There are screaming ghosts running around my house."

"—you've reached Fontalvo Contractor Services where every place is a restorable one, and we've got the tools to make your reno right." I dropped the phone, my throat raw from gasping. "Damn it!"

A frantic knock caught my attention. Now what?

"Tandie! Are you in there? Are you alright?" Eric's muffled voice was on the other side of the front door. Silence paralyzed me while I attempted to process this turn in events. Eric started thrashing his body against it.

I rushed toward the entrance, ripping the door open and flinging myself into Eric's arms, not caring one bit about what I'd just done.

"Talk about just in time." I buried my face against his warm chest. He smelled of the outdoors and faint cologne, a welcome aroma after experiencing the moldy odor that came when the children appeared on the stairway. In the background, the opera singers hit their final, long note, signaling the end of Aida.

"What's going on?" Eric's concerned voice asked. He held me a bit and massaged my arms and my back. Through chest-jerking sobs, I managed to huff out a few words. "The children. They're running upstairs."

"What children? Do you have kids over? I don't hear anything." Eric checked out the hallway and frowned.

If humans were able to start fires from within, then I was certain my heated embarrassment would've burned us both.

I eased out of his arms, turned around, trudged past the study and stopped at the stairwell. All was quiet now that Aida's singers had just finished singing their last note.

"They were right up there. I know I'm not losing it."

"I can't help unless you tell me what this God-forsaken place has done now." He stalked toward the stairway and followed my gaze, a disgusted expression on his handsome face.

I studied Eric with curiosity. "What do you mean by 'what has *it* done now'?"

"No one stays here, Tandie. This place goes through tenants like an oil rigger changes work boots. Let me go check around upstairs. Then we can hash things out." He started toward the stairway.

"You knew that all along? You could've warned me, you know." And Saul Chelby had to have known his old house was haunted. Yet, he never said a word. I made another mental note to call him first thing in the morning.

"I'm sorry. Things tend to slip my mind when I want to avoid scaring my new clients to death," Eric said.

"Fine, then. I'm coming with you." I followed close on his heels.

He looked back at me. "Maybe that's not a good idea. You seem pretty spooked. And I'm sure a couple of your little eight-legged friends are hanging around up there." Was that a smile creeping across his lips?

"You're so funny," I said, narrowing my eyes. "That doesn't mean I don't want to know what's going on in my own house."

"If you insist. One thing I've learned over the past month: don't argue with Mets fans."

I scoffed. "I'm not a Mets fan. Why do people think that anyone who lives in New York is a Mets fan? Besides, I only lived there for six years, okay?"

"You barely have a southern accent," Eric said. I could almost hear the laughter in his voice.

"And you hardly have a Hispanic accent. But that doesn't mean you're not Spanish. So annoying."

He stopped and turned back towards me again. "Did you say something else?"

"Nope. Not a word," I lied.

"Hm. Could've sworn I heard you call me annoying."

I shrugged. At that moment, it didn't matter what he called me. What did matter was that another living breathing soul was here with me.

The stairs creaked under the pressure of our double weight. A single set of dirty footprints about the size of a child's foot began at the top and tracked down the hallway. The imprints ended at the door to the fourth room on the right side of the hallway, the one I still hadn't opened.

I held on to Eric's arm. He stood right at six-feet-tall and his arm was pure muscle. If there were intruders upstairs, I had no doubt he'd make it hard for the unfortunate souls to get away. He glanced down at my hand, a smile flickering across his lips. "Okay, now you're going to tell me all this is explainable, right?"

He turned and stared into my eyes, his face with the perfect lips and intriguing hazel eyes was filled with concern. "No. This is the part where I take you back downstairs and fix something to calm both our nerves."

"Aren't you going to check the room?" I pointed at the door.

He hesitated and stared down the hallway. Was he afraid? After speaking with the store owner and hearing what Eric already knew about the place, I didn't blame him.

He stalked toward the door and turned the immovable doorknob. The handle gave way under his grip as if I had never struggled with the lock before. The foot prints in the hallway offered little comfort because I had seen ghosts. But the physical evidence suggested something else. I wrapped my arms around my shoulders and waited outside. Eventually, Eric emerged from the room, eased the door closed behind him and walked over to me.

"All clear. A window was open. Would you like to have a look?"

My heart flipped. The thought of going in that room threatened to bring on a panic attack. I shook my head.

"That's probably how your 'ghost' kid got out." He gave me his rugged-model smile, making me feel like a silly girl instead of an experienced woman. And then I thought about what he said.

"Kid? There were three children, Eric," I said and pointed at the footprints.

"Then where are the other two sets of tracks?" he asked.

"I'm not sure. Anyway, they were ghosts. Maybe the other two flew away." I could tell from the strained look on his face that he struggled with his own thoughts.

Feeling flustered and confused, I looked down at the footprints again. They weren't large tracks, or tiny ones like the youngest girl child would've made. They must've been the middle boy's tracks, the one who stood in the shadows so I couldn't see his face. My mind swooned from confusion, fear, and embarrassment. An image of the boy from the store flashed through my mind.

"Could the tallest child have been the same boy?"

This was all too much, and the children had brought back memories of Baby B. Cradling my forehead, I fought back tears. The last thing I wanted was for Eric to see me looking all puffy from crying.

"Okay. All right, now." Eric placed his arms around my shoulders and led me back toward the stairway. His voice was like honey for the ears and a calming presence surrounded him.

What was Eric's past story, his present life? He'd given me hints and glimpses. However, I wanted to know more.

Sitting back in Chelby Rose's living room, my mind raced. I'd always been able to see psychic images of the past. I mastered the ability to touch an article of clothing and see flashbacks of the victims in the pictures Sgt. Gomez brought to me. Up until the accident, I had never seen a ghost or been visited by spirits inside my dreams. And I didn't really consider the shadow monster from my past a ghost. My grandmother concluded that the darkness I'd nicknamed had been created to protect me, a way to block the identity of a serial killer.

I shivered at the thought and pulled the blanket Eric gave me close around my shoulders. September was right around the corner and the nights had already cooled off. The temperature wasn't really the problem, though. I needed something to ease the chill I got from thinking about the events of the night.

My pathseeker's eye, the ability to experience visions firsthand and find pathways leading to previous lives had awakened and was growing in strength. That would explain these new visions and definitely shed light on my ghostly visitors. Out of all the house photos Frieda had sent, I'd chosen Chelby Rose as my place to begin anew. Or maybe I didn't pick this house. Maybe Chelby Rose chose me.

The question remained, though: what did the house need me to do? Will doing so help me determine the culprit behind my accident, the event that took my daughter and jump-started my spiral into a vision less life. The answer had something to do with the children I saw tonight. I was sure of that part.

"If there are dirty footprints, then the children, or ghosts are real. I'm sure I saw three kids." I wanted to make him agree. If someone else, a calm and collected person such as Eric, would confirm what I saw, then I'd feel relief via validation.

"Then where did they go?" he asked, speaking in the softest of tones. The kind that feels sorry for the basket case sitting on the sofa.

"I'm not sure." My mind shuffled through memories of what I had experienced earlier this evening. One thing was certain... I needed to give Norma Atwater a call. She held vast knowledge about the pathseeker.

He stared at me a long time before he said, "You're not insane or even headed in that direction. Troubled, overworked, and a good possibility that maybe you've taken on a savings-buster of a house. You're not a basket case, though."

I tilted my head. Once again I felt as if he had heard my thoughts. But that was impossible, right? He looked so much like my main character: the wild dark hair, the strange hazel eyes, the way his jaw tensed. *Who are you? And when did you step out of my dream?* Oh shit. My mouth was hanging open. I needed a distraction. "You have your own troubles too. Did they figure out what happened to your friend?"

Sighing, he shook his head and wouldn't look at me for the longest time. I took advantage of the moment and studied his striking features: his caramel brown skin, black hair, the way he sat with his muscles tensed as if he were ready to tackle the next project at any moment. "What's your story? Why are you here all alone?" My inner thoughts escaped my lips before I could silence the words. Inhaling deeply, I met his gaze and held it.

Amusement filled his eyes and crept across his heart-shaped mouth. Such small gestures, but just enough to set my heart aflutter. "I should be asking you the same thing, Ms. Harrison. And no, they still haven't made any progress with finding Virgil's killer." He lowered his eyes and sighed. I didn't need to hear his thoughts to understand what he was feeling.

"You know what's funny? I promised myself that after I lost my father I'd never cry again. Not even when my mother dies or my brother. In my family, death is a given. I won't give the reaper the power to break me down. I have to be strong for my other loved ones. Damn it." He made a light laugh, shook his head and blinked a few times. Massaging the back of his neck, he turned away, but not before I saw the tears lining his eyes.

"Sometimes you have to let them fall. The tears, I mean. Or they'll pile up, blind you and keep you from seeing the beauty in things. Tears can be evil if you allow them to be. I don't care what anyone says." I thought of Breena and the car accident.

He leaned over and brought two fingers to my lips, tickling the skin with only the slightest touch. "Is that advice for me? Or for you?"

Time stood still for a moment, freezing all of my deepest thoughts, fears, and pains. His hazel eyes darkened in the light of the lamps and smoldered me. Two exotic jewels stared at me in a way that pulled me inside his soul as if I were a genie and those sparkling eyes were my master's bottle.

"You're like this house. A delicate piece of art, damaged by everything that has happened inside it," he whispered, reaching out to move my dark auburn hair away from my shoulders, exposing the skin of my neck.

Heart fluttering in my chest, I couldn't remember the last time a man made me feel this way. But what if I had attracted a bad spirit without knowing it? If that were the case, then I certainly wasn't going to put Eric in danger too. I moved my head back a bit, breaking the spell and freeing my mind from the lock contained in Eric's eyes.

"I'll make us both a good cup of raspberry coffee." He sighed, stood and strolled out of the room.

One thing was certain, Chelby Rose had work for me to do. But did the house want Tandie the psychic or Tandie the pathseeker? One aspect I could handle while the latter was still a mystery. And just how did Eric the contractor know that raspberry was my favorite coffee flavor without me telling him so?

Chapter 20

T*andie*
        "The wind here always sounds alive. Like a mangled animal caught in somebody's trap," I said to Eric. I'd always wanted to say that sentence aloud just to see how the words would affect someone.

Eric and I sat together on the sofa, listening to the storm outside while drinking raspberry coffee. The lights flickered and eventually lost power. My heart flipped a couple beats along with them. I was most definitely still recovering from the night's adventures. The idea of being left to spend the night alone made me anxious.

Eric made a small laugh. "You sound like Anne Rice."

"Oh, stop. You're making me blush. I'd like to believe I'm a great author. That is, if the pages of my book stop disappearing and reappearing." I regretted revealing the story of the missing pages as soon as the words left my lips.

Eric studied my face and frowned. "Pages of your book have disappeared before? How does that happen on a computer?"

All right, you might as well go on with the story. He probably already thinks you're crazy at this point, anyway. Even if he did just tell you how wonderfully sane you are in the most beautiful way you've ever heard from a man.

"I don't have a laptop, or anything," I said, watching a frown deepen on his forehead. "What? I want my writing to feel like I'm truly creating something."

He held up his hands, and said, "I didn't say a word. Continue."

"Anyway, the pages sometimes disappear after I type them, and then they'll show up in some odd area later on. Want to know the interesting part?"

"Why not?" He studied his hands a moment before turning his gaze back to me.

"I thought you took them. At least, I did at first."

"Why would I take pages out of your book?" Eric asked, giving me an incredulous look.

"I don't know. Why do you have almost the exact same name as the main character in my novel? I ask myself that every day too." A faint voice said: "you're pushing too hard."

"Some people might call it coincidence, but I don't believe in that word," he said, frowning. He was in deep thought about something. Thinking about his ancestors perhaps? Or the thing that he was holding back from me? My book Eric held secrets from Maud, dangerous ones that could cause tons of pain. I was willing to bet a leg that flesh and blood Eric bottled up a few dark tidbits in that gorgeous head of his too.

"Yeah, I thought so too. That was until the three ghost kids showed up. You see, the lost pages describe a scene I wrote where three people go missing."

"Let me guess. The victims disappear at the hands of my namesake—your villain guy named Eric?"

"Something like that."

He stood and peered out the window a long moment before he said, "Intriguing."

I expected to hear him say a lot of things, but intriguing wasn't one of them. Maybe he truly meant what he said; that he didn't think I was a loon. I appreciated the sentiment, and that he considered my gift an alluring aspect of my personality. My ex husband always danced around my ability, making me feel like an outcast in our marriage. I'd spent a lifetime trying to belong, to fit in. Here stood someone like me... lost and hurting.

"You know more about what's happening here than you're letting on." My question came out as a statement. He kept his gaze locked on something outside the window. The tension in his lean body gave him the appearance of a man in a lot of pain and I wanted to know why. "That storekeeper in town said the last man who lived here, Pontus Tomlinson, thought he saw the Chelby children running around before he died."

He turned back to me. A faraway look masked his handsome face until his eyes flickered back to the present. He'd returned from whatever hidden part of his mind he had escaped to. "Virgil told me all about old Pontus and his hallucinations. Again, aren't you psychic? Wouldn't you know if you bought a haunted house? I always figured psychics could feel stuff like that."

The rain drummed down on the roof. I was holding Mr. Smug, handsome, and super controlled in my palms and wanted to milk him for information.

"My abilities don't work that way. In fact, they haven't been working at all. At least, not consistently." I sighed deeply and propped my hands on my knees. "I believe those children used to live here. I've seen the grandmother they were running from. Or, at least I think they were running from the same woman. I also believe the kids need my help."

Eric strolled over to the hurricane lamp and adjusted the light. The small flame inside the glass responded with a brilliant blaze. "What else did you see?"

"I saw her in a vision, but the scene faded. Then there was only Ella outside," I admitted.

Eric stopped fooling with the lamp and passed me a sideways look, a sharp expression hardening his dark eyes. "Ella?"

"She's a little strange and pig-headed, but she's a good girl, I think," I said. "Why do you ask?"

"No particular reason," he said, blinking too much to be considered normal.

"I think you're lying." We held gazes and the grandfather clock's ticking was the only sound in the room. Eric had skirted around this secret that I'd be better off not knowing about for long enough. Time to come clean, Mr. Contractor.

"Well, you're the psychic. You tell me if I am." His voice rose a bit and he stood there with his arms folded. Sighing, he turned around, stalked back to the sofa and sat on the end farthest away from me.

"Okay, truce." I held my hands up. Weak muscles and a dull headache drained my energy and I wanted to cry for some reason. Plus I was tired and felt drained, typical post-vision symptoms.

Truth being told, I didn't understand my new visions. They'd been choppy and unclear ever since the one where I had seen the woman in the rocking chair, the person I assumed was the kids' grandmother because of her age. The returning visions signified a closing point; a truce with a life stolen from me, a sign that

I'd been blessed to be the mother of a wonderful little girl like Breena. I stared at the picture of my smiling daughter in the picture sitting over on the writing desk and choked back the emotion balling up in my throat.

"I'm sorry. I don't mean to be harsh." Eric softened his tone.

"I dreamed about my Baby B when I first got here. I think what I've been seeing are dead people who used to live in this house before me. Furthermore, I believe we're connected in some way," I said. When I worked with the NYPD, I would receive visions about the dead person's last moments. However, tonight I communicated with the little ghost girl by speaking to her.

"Baby B? Is that what you called your daughter?" Eric asked.

Covering my face, I knew the tears would fall no matter how hard I tried to hold them back; and they did. Eric scooted closer to my side of the sofa, the place where I woke up almost every morning since arriving in Bolivia. He placed one muscled arm across my shoulders and moved my hands away from my face with the other hand. In that small gesture, I found a comfort I had missed for a long time.

"I'm sorry I asked about your daughter," Eric whispered, his expression concerned. I could tell he was sincere. Yet, that didn't stop the ache in my chest whenever I mentioned Breena or anyone else for that matter. "I know how it feels to lose someone. Trust me."

Swallowing through the knot in my throat, I asked, "Can I ask how you made it to my house so fast? I mean, I'd just hung up on your answering machine." The question had drifted in my mind ever since he showed up at the front door. I'd been too relieved to see another living person to bother with the logic of the situation.

"I had this feeling I needed to stop by and check on you." He focused on the floor, avoiding my gaze.

I placed a hand on his cheek and turned his face toward mine. "You know what? I think you're the psychic one, and that's why you're so hard on me." I gazed deep into his eyes, losing myself inside them. Being in his arms this way felt so right. It was as if we had known each other longer than a month and a half.

"Trust me. It was a very unique feeling," he said.

"I want to trust you. It could be a mistake, but I feel like I can," I whispered. The pattering rain fought against the howling wind, and the smoldering light filled the room with shadows while the heat flying between our bodies set the scene flawlessly for what was sure to happen next.

Eric leaned over and brushed his lips across mine. Timid, hesitant, soft. "Do you accept me?" he whispered with his eyes closed.

I scoffed playfully. "Do I accept you? What kind of question is that?"

"Do you accept me?" He said with more eagerness in his voice.

"I haven't decided yet," I answered, feeling confused. It had been over two years since I'd last been with a man. My body ached to be touched. My soul longed to be caressed. Eric felt the same way. I could tell.

"Let me help you decide." He crushed his lips down on mine without any restraint this time. I opened my mouth and accepted his probing hot tongue and allowed my body to succumb to the fiery sensations coursing through my entire being. His lips traveled down my neck, and he gently nibbled the skin as he did so. Tingles erupted over my body, and my heart flipped and made cartwheels.

After a moment, he pulled back. His expression was distant as though he was lost in an inner thought.

"What's wrong?" I whispered.

"I can't do this to you." He looked away.

"I don't think a gun is pointed at my head." I felt confused and a bit rejected.

"There are things you don't understand." Eric moved away from my arms and stood.

Why do all men use that line when they're doing the "it's not you, it's me" thing?

"I'm the paranormal expert, remember? I'm pretty sure I can understand anything you want to throw at me," I said.

Eric hinted at a smile forming on his lips, but still refused to meet my gaze.

"Please stay a little while longer. Just until I fall asleep." I felt anxious about being left alone with the ghost kids, their eerie grandmother, and whatever else might be waiting for its turn to pick on me. There was something beyond hunches and visions stirring in Chelby Rose. I could feel the invisible forces waiting behind the old doors upstairs.

"I thought you said I was annoying," he reminded with a slight smile, his face still flushed. Moving back over to me, he sat down and eased his arms around my waist.

"Extremely annoying, but you're good with scaring away ghosts."

"I'll stay. I won't let anything happen to you. I promise."

I placed my head on Eric's shoulder. He stroked my hair and massaged my right ear, a different sensation in and of itself, but the small gesture still felt wonderfully sinful all the same. It wasn't long before I fell asleep.

IN MY DREAM, I WALKED along unfamiliar shores, a place called Sunset Beach according to the sign I passed. The cool breeze of nighttime swept across my face, ripping my attention towards the ocean. Breena! My Baby B. was dressed in white like her mom as her spirit drifted in front of a ship with about four layers of massive box sails and intricate details carved into the wooden hull. This was the same Spanish war ship that I'd seen before.

As in previous dreams, my daughter wasn't smiling. Her chubby cheeks hung downward, and I longed to reach out and touch her sweet face. I held out a hand toward my baby, but her image faded, teasing me. In return, Breena pointed at the words painted on the ship's hull. I tried to focus on the blurry white letters.

"I can't see them Baby, B. What do they say?" But there was no Breena. The scene faded away to another place I hadn't visited since I was a young girl. The sand became plush, green grass and the sight of the ocean disappeared behind a medley of trees. Only this wasn't a dream. This was me being ripped back in time to a fatal day in my past.

When the visions first started, I was only six-years-old. I had been playing outside with my babysitter and foe alike, Chelsea Woodard. She had led me into the thick woods behind a house my parents owned in Castle Hayne, the town located next to Bolivia.

I clearly recalled the memory of Chelsea's thick black ponytails secured by silky white ribbons. With her attitude of a prima donna, the girl could talk her followers into doing anything.

One day Chelsea and her younger sister, a girl everybody called Silver Teeth Carina because of her braces, along with me and four of their friends decided to play hide and seek. That game was the precursor to discovering all things lethal in an old forest. Especially one riddled with tales of headless damsels and jilted lovers roaming the woods. Never mind that Chelsea and her friends were all seven to ten years older than me. Throw in a river that seemed like a small ocean to the children, a rotting bridge, and you've got a game with a dangerous edge. The chase should have been exciting, but the adventure turned into a nightmare.

First, Chelsea's groupies blindfolded me that day. In my young mind, I couldn't understand how such a pretty girl could be so mean. But I had always believed that Chelsea had some other spirit in her body, dimming her beauty with a devilish haze. And that's why things happened the way they did.

"Now you got to wait exactly one minute after you finish counting. You can't come looking for us until then. Got it?" Chelsea's dark, fourteen-year-old voice still haunted me.

"I don't like it. Where are you taking me?" I asked, my voice cracking. The two boys in the group snickered. Chelsea and the others continued leading me through the forest, snickering at my ignorance of their plans.

"This will be the hide and seek of a lifetime for us," Chelsea boasted.

"Yep. Other kids will want to play all the time," another boy's voice echoed.

Tears stung my eyes, and I was glad the handkerchief kept the other kids from being able to see me crying. The older children would tease me into the next lifetime if they saw me crying. After trudging through the forest for about five minutes or so, I felt my body being lifted up to a set of stairs. I stumbled on the first step and my heart raced.

"Please tell me where we are." My request earned a rough tug and then someone shoved me into what felt like an empty space. A door slammed behind me and giggles echoed on the other side. I stood alone, fighting the fear tightening in my chest.

Behind the blindfold, shadows moved along the darkness. I snatched the handkerchief away and found myself alone in a cottage. Rotten beams lay scattered everywhere, the ceiling was filled with holes, and a large opening gaped in the middle of the floor. The old place was one of the numerous slave cabins still sitting in a few cities situated near the Carolina coastline. Grandma Zee had showed me many pictures of them.

Something shuffled in the corners across from where I stood. I gasped, and my heart beat too fast. The dim slant of light from outside made it hard for me to focus on anything. The darkness of the room swirled before my eyes, easing toward me with sinewy, crooked fingers, getting closer each second. I pulled on the wooden entry door to no avail. Locked. Someone trapped me inside the cabin.

I risked taking a look behind me. Something was rising in the shadows, a shapeless form, a blob with a pair of round yellow orbs for eyes. At once I turned back around, yanked on the old knob, and screamed. The door still didn't budge an inch.

The shadow blob rose and hissed one word: "Tandie." And then, "What happens to bad little girls who wander into dark forests all by themselves?"

Fear seized me and my mind shut down. I slumped to the floor in front of the door and stared as the thing glided closer. My mind raced and my heart was about to explode. There was no way out. The monster was going to end my short life. That's what I thought would happen up until the moment when I heard Grandma Zee's voice speak inside my mind.

"Tell that old shadow to get behind you, girl. Tell it now!" Grandma Zee's presence, even though she was only there in spirit, gave me strength I needed to face my fears.

"Go away, you ugly monster. Get behind me." The shadow slithered back into the dark corners. Before the demon or whatever I saw that day disappeared, I heard the words that would stay with me forever. They were the very reason I decided to join the NYPD's crime unit.

"Maybe I can't have you, slippery little rabbit, but I will have your little friends hiding out there in the forest." The shadow's hiss echoed on those last few words and faded, and the doorknob snapped, creaking open as if someone on the other side had pushed it. I bolted outside, grateful to feel the cool fall air on my skin, and happy to find a bit of light illuminating the forest.

In the distance, someone was burning leaves, the strong scent of the remains burning my nostrils. All I needed to do was make my way to the place where the smoke came from. I checked out the woods surrounding the cabin. The way back home seemed clear. Breathing heavily, I didn't have a clue about where the older kids had taken me. I was lost.

Tears flowed down my cheeks, blurring my eyesight. I had only taken a few steps toward heading deeper into the forest when a tightening sensation filled my head. White light blinded me and screams filled the air. In the vision, it wasn't light outside. Instead, the last bit of daylight trickled away by the second. A few feet away from where I stood, a child's red sneaker lay on the ground. The shoe belonged to Chelsea. Something bad had happened to her. And then the vision ended, but the headache I was left with blurred my sight.

Something large shuffled through the brush, and it headed straight toward me. Still unable to see, I felt my way to a large bush and dived inside the foliage, promising myself that if I got out of this situation then I'd never disobey my mother again when she told me to stay out of the woods. I hid in those bushes the longest time.

Eventually, my vision returned. I kept silent as I peeked through the small opening. Whatever was going to happen to me hadn't come to pass just yet. I wasn't sure how much time had passed when Chelsea and another girl ran past my hiding spot. With terrified faces, the girls screamed and kept looking back. My blood went cold when the shadow blob passed by my spot.

I gasped and covered my mouth. The shadow caught the first girl and tossed her to the ground as if she were a rag doll. The girl's flailing body whirled toward the rotten bridge across the way.

"And now, for my special pretty girl." The shadow's raspy voice filled my ears with dread. Chelsea turned and ran, losing a sneaker, the same one I had just seen in my vision. The girl didn't get far before she tripped, her body slamming face first to the ground. And then she stopped trying to escape. She moved her body into a fetal position as the shadow swooped over her, blocking my view of what followed.

The silence came next, and I sat alone in the quiet forest: no animals, footsteps, or Chelsea.

Fear forced me into action. Leaping out of the bushes, I ran toward a large oak with a hollow opening, crawled inside, and pulled my legs up to my chin, cradling them the same way Chelsea did. This was all my fault and guilt wrenched at my throat. Soon, I cried myself to sleep. Only moments passed, it seemed, before shouting voices woke me up. The deputy and my father's dark eyes peered in at me as I lay inside the tree's trunk.

Back safe in my bed that night, I learned that another boy had been beaten and tortured along with Chelsea's sister, Carina, and the other girl. Only two other kids besides me got out unharmed. No one ever found Chelsea's body. News reporters bombarded our house on a regular basis, and I experienced nightmares for weeks to follow, especially when I woke up and found my bedroom door closed.

A part of my subconscious mind still felt like the shadow monster waited in the corners. And if he were there then I wanted to make sure I had an easy way to escape.

Years later, I found out my shadow monster was actually a serial killer, a man who had eluded authorities for years, and the main reason I committed to use my gift to get justice for victims like Chelsea.

Chapter 21

E*ric*   Driving through the dark back roads, Eric focused on his jumbled thoughts. There was no way he would ever believe Tandie Harrison had a thing to do with Virgil's death. His thoughts were focused on that kiss: her soft sweet lips, the apple-scented fragrance she wore. In her presence, Eric felt wild and unrestrained; but she also stirred a dead portion of his heart. Something no other woman had ever been able to achieve.

Why did Tandie drive him insane this way? The pull, that unexplainable sway of the heart, the moment when you just know that you'd live or die a thousand lifetimes to save he one you love sweeps you up and twists your mind like a pretzel.

The connection with her was beyond looks, influence, and even money. She said ghosts were in her house. He probably should've told her about the thing he saw outside the cottage the night she visited it with Saul. Yeah right. Then she would've thought he was a stalker. That slant of light was the same thing he witnessed outside his house on the beach just before Tandie said she had called him. Right away, he had bolted out the door and raced to Chelby Rose in record time.

Something wanted to get his attention, but why?

He found it hard to think of the pain in her face after he rejected her. Why didn't he just tell her about the curse? As with previous girlfriends, he found himself doing what he always did best— pushing someone away for their own sake. Tandie wasn't like his ex-fiancée. No, she was strong even though she didn't know it. If anything, she will be the one to help him figure out how Chelby Rose was connected to the curse on his family. The time for saving Javier winded down each day. Dark Souls Day loomed around the corner. Eric needed to do whatever was needed to save his brother's life and fast.

Deep in his thoughts, Eric almost didn't see the girl standing in the street until his Jeep came within inches of striking her.

"What the hell?" It was as though she appeared out of nowhere. Eric swerved sharply to the left and then slammed on his brakes, his tires skidding to a stop inches away from the trunk of a large oak. His head banged against the steering wheel and waves of pain rushed through his skull.

"All right, seat belt next time, my man," he groaned.

Eric managed to sit up even with the stars swimming around his eyelids. He squeezed his eyes closed tight and waited for them to fade. A bright light seeped across his eyelids. Slowly, he opened his eyes and turned his head to the left, feeling the presence again even before he saw the source.

The blob of light stood within a foot of his window; only the beam wasn't just a blob anymore. The little girl he almost ran over stood inside it, her tiny frame and white clothing highlighted as though she were an angel. "What the fuck?" he muttered, his voice caught in his tight chest, his limbs quivering. Blood from his head wound trickled down to his mouth, easing through his parted lips. The metallic taste seeped across his tongue. Reaching toward him with her glowing index finger, she touched the wound on his forehead.

At once, a whirlwind of images surged through his mind: wings fluttering around a ship, a baby crying, a little girl drawing three circles in the dirt, and then that same child screaming for help, a woman's naked body writhing underneath him as they made love on a straw mat. The emotions he felt for the woman brought a sense of longing, an ache that crossed all boundaries, including time.

And then everything vanished, leaving Eric gasping and panting. There was only a dark street and a huge oak tree before him, now. The little girl was gone. What the hell just happened? His mind both accepted and denied what he'd just seen. The same phenomena had taken place outside the house Tandie visited with Saul. Truth be told, this same thing happened the night Eric soothed his cousin's fears.

The explanation was obvious... Eric witnessed one of Bolivia's ghosts. He thought back on what Tandie had said about the children she'd seen in Chelby Rose. Eric hadn't wanted to believe her. Doing so took the going ons of the past few weeks to the next level.

His mother had warned him to never return. Pastor Jeffries thought he was also making a terrible mistake by accepting Saul's offer. But Eric had never been the type of man to let unseen forces rule his life. Yet, the time to accept the inexplicable had arrived. To save his brother and find his best friend's murderer meant he must consider everything.

"All right, Bolivia. You've got my attention," he muttered. "What now?"

He eased the Jeep backward. His head was still swimming but the pain wasn't as sharp as it was before the strange girl touched him. *Unbelievable.* Eric was certain of one thing. The spirits of the little children in Tandie's house, Saul Chelby's old home, had something to do with what just happened. Most importantly, he hoped this occurrence offered clues to help him find out whom or what killed his best friend.

Chapter 22

andie

T Gentle taps echoed through the room. Someone was knocking at the front door. I bolted up on the sofa and looked around. No Eric. The room was empty. Traces of the raspberry coffee he brewed for me still lingered in the air.

The man was such a mystery. Sexy. Addictive. A fabulous kisser. Still somewhat annoying. I scratched that last thought. Although he had left me hot and bothered, he still gave me something fantastic to remember. One question haunted me, though: what freaked him out last night?

The knocks increased. I stalked to the door and opened it. An elderly black couple stood outside, smiling as if they were posing for a picture in a magazine.

"Morning there, Miss Lady," the man said.

I wasn't the least bit surprised to find the odd pair wearing old-fashioned clothes. The woman wore her hair back in a tight bun with loose strands of hair along either side of her head. She wore a prairie style dress and kept her hands dutifully folded in front at all times. The man appeared to have ripped his coveralls right out of a Mark Twain novel. What did Bolivia hope to show me in this duo?

"Did you make it through last night's storm all right?" The man gave me a huge grin.

"Yes, I guess I did." I shielded my eyes from the intrusively bright sun.

"I'm Lou and this is my wife, Ruth Ann. We're the Adams."

"Your house is so beautiful. Chelby Rose is alive again because of you." The woman's accent sounded proper as if she strained to make sure she pronounced each syllable with care.

"Thank you. But I can't take all the credit though," I said, touching my lips as I thought about Eric Fontalvo's kiss.

"We've been waiting a long time for somebody like you to come along these parts." Lou kept the wide smile plastered across his lips, making him appear to be somewhat manic. I looked back and forth between the two.

"Well I, um, Fontalvo's Contractor Services helped me out." I wanted to make sure Eric got the credit. After all, this was his old hometown and he'd get more business through word of mouth if I started spreading news around.

The couple passed a worried look between each other before refocusing on me.

"Something wrong?" I asked.

"Nothing at all." Lou's grin widened. I thought his cheeks might break if he kept holding that position. He turned to Ruth Ann and said, "Bet old Thomas Chelby would love to know Enrique Fontalvo had a hand in restoring his house."

"No. His name is Eric, not Enrique," I said, curious about the accusatory tone in Lou's voice.

"But they're both one and the same, honey." Ruth Ann's golden brown face glowed. I didn't need my psychic intuition to understand that she was insinuating something.

"Where are my manners? Would you like some tea? I have some tasty cold cereal in the kitchen, if you're hungry," I said to the strange couple.

"Why that's mighty kind. But we need to do something else first," Ruth Ann said. Suddenly the woman stepped forward and grasped my hands, holding them tightly. All right, so maybe the idea of cold cereal didn't appeal to them.

"What are you doing?" I tried to snatch my hands away, but it was almost as if they were glued to her skin. "Let go of me!" I moved my gaze to Ruth Ann's wide-eyed expression.

"He needs you. You two must accept one another. Stop denying what you see, what you feel." The woman spoke as if she were in a trance, tightening her grip on my hands. Lou's face was still frozen in that crazy grin. However, his eyes flickered just the tiniest bit. Was he afraid of his wife?

"You're hurting me," I said, my hand throbbing.

"He is your soul mate, girl. You know this. Why, oh why do you keep denying it?" Ruth Ann asked, her voice rising.

"What? I haven't denied anything," I snapped.

"Now, listen up. Find your way back to one another. You must do so, before it's too late." Releasing my hands, the woman slumped against her husband's arm and cradled her head as if she might faint. Lou's clownish smile faded, his body reanimating, and he caught his wife before she tumbled off the porch.

Behind the Adams, footsteps crunched across the gravel in the driveway. The couple looked back and then turned to me, their eyes wide. Ella pranced toward the house as if I hadn't said a word about calling before she came over. Wonderful. Just what I needed... two shots of insane within the same hour.

"G' day miss," the couple said in unison. Lou and Ruth Ann turned abruptly away and scurried along the path outside the gates, heading in the opposite direction as Ella.

My uninvited visitor turned and yelled after the pair, screaming at the top of her voice. "That's right! Scurry on, you old battle axes." She wore the same dress as usual.

"Ella! Don't speak to my neighbors that way." I stepped down and headed towards her and got the stare of death. For a moment, the girl's eyes gave off a red tint. I blinked and stepped backward. What the literal hell? Goosebumps I'd nicknamed the Creeping Willies eased up my spine and my mouth went a bit dry. I knew something about Ella was off but this revelation in the flesh shook my core.

"Just because you gave me my Chelby position back, doesn't mean I'll keep sparing you." Ella's narrowed eyes faded back to their normal sky blue.

Rattled by the gardener, who was probably the most unstable teenager I'd ever met, I crossed my arms and held my ground. "What could you possibly mean by that?"

"You know what I'm talking about," Ella said.

"This is my house. I don't have an obligation to you as my gardener." I stared the girl down.

"Are you trying to be an Injun giver?" Ella's pretty face twisted into a scowl. With her lips curled up and her strange blue eyes, she truly appeared dangerous.

"What? Are you trying to say *Indian* giver? No, it doesn't matter. I dismissed you," I said. The day had taken an oddball turn and I already wanted it to end.

"I'm staying." Ella folded her arms and held her head high.

"Not today, you're not." My ears heated and my chest burned.

"This is my garden, my job. I stay."

"And this is my house, my property, and you need to leave." I held the girl's blazing gaze. We stood that way for the longest time. Ella's strange eyes and her scowling baby face made me think of Chucky, the little killer doll from those old movies.

A group of ducks squawked and flew up out of the trees in the forest beside Chelby Rose, the part near the cemetery. Ella jerked toward the sound, her body tensed. Turning her terrified wide-eyes back to me, she opened her mouth wide and screamed an unnaturally high-pitched shriek, a noise that could rival a fire alarm.

An eerie chill settled over my skin and my mouth went dry. I closed my eyes and slammed my hands over my ears, drowning out the girl's wail, waiting for the rant to end.

At once, silence fell. I parted my eyelids and found an empty front yard. No Ella. There were only the rose bushes, a vacant driveway, and the trees whispering in the wind.

Chapter 23

T*andie*
    "I've always wanted to come inside this house," Shania said, taking a look around the outside of the entrance as if she were in Disneyland. She was my third visitor of the day, and perhaps the most shocking one considering we hadn't spoken since that night at the Aeneid. Oh yeah, and she indirectly accused me of being a murderer. Let's not forget that tidbit.

"Chelby Rose is a great place. Perfect for witches to hang out in," I said, feeling spicy and anxious to hear the explanation for her sudden appearance and hoping that at least this woman wouldn't start screaming or handing out fortunes.

"It's all quite fascinating, the things Eric has done. He must be very good with his hands," Shania said, her gray eyes boring into mine.

"If only you knew." I smiled, unable to resist the comeback. A slight breeze stirred between us. I half expected the voices of my psychic tormentor to gear up and start whispering sweet supernatural nothings of danger. No luck.

"We started off on the wrong foot," Shania said.

I scoffed and crossed my arms. "That's an understatement." Detective Leroy had sent me a summons a few days ago. I'd not been officially charged of any crime. However, Frieda told me the gossip mill had all but confirmed me as a main suspect. I intended to clear my name by any means necessary. My abilities hadn't fully reformed but if I pushed hard enough I was fairly certain I'd get something to surface.

"That's part of the reason I'm here. May I come in?" she asked.

"Sure." I stepped aside.

Shania walked over the threshold and closed her eyes, inhaling deeply. The loose brown tank dress she wore hung limply on her body. Frieda's friend looked as if she had lost ten pounds or more since I last saw her. "Fresh apples recently picked off a tree in an orchard."

"What?" I asked.

She opened her eyes and gave me a tight smile. "That's how it smells in here. I'm sorry. The poet always gets the best of me."

"Okay. Step into my study that's really a living room, the place where the writing tries to get the best of me, anyway." I entered the room, walked over to my desk and sat down. Shania took a seat on the newly upholstered sofa, still looking around as if she were a child about to hop on a new ride.

"I know I'm kind of late with this, but I'm sorry about your loss," I said, trying to remain civil even though I'd every right not to be.

"I'm taking things one day at a time," she answered, cupping her hands in her lap.

"Shania, I didn't have anything to do with your husband's death. I swear."

"That's not why I stopped by," Shania said, lowering her eyes. "Well, um, that's not completely true. I should know better than to try and fool a psychic. Ms. Harrison—"

"Please call me Tandie."

"You looked right at me that evening, Tandie." Shania's expression softened.

"But it wasn't me. I was right here, in this room, the whole day," I pleaded. The woman stared at me the longest moment. *Oh no, please don't start screaming.*

"I'm not saying you killed him. You couldn't harm a flea. I can see that." Tears clouded her eyes and she looked away. "I just want to understand why the man I love is gone. Why? That word is like a curse, isn't it? It teases you with the answers, dangles the solution in your face, and then snatches it all away. Just like that, you have to start over again. Do you understand what I'm saying?" Shania's eyes filled with tears. She lowered her head into her hands and started sobbing, her body jerking in hard spasms. I stood, moved over to the sofa and placed my arms around the grieving woman.

"I understand. I really do. Like you wouldn't believe," I took a quick look at Breena's picture. Why?—How many times had I asked that question over the last two years? Too many. And like Shania said, I was never given an answer.

Pulling back from our embrace, Shania wiped her eyes and said, "I'm so sorry."

"Don't apologize." I wiped away my tears.

"Do you have someone? If I'm not being too personal," Shania said.

Yes, I have a special person, but I'm scared to let him know how I feel. "No. Well, kind of. But not really," I said and tucked my bottom lip, thinking of the way Eric's kiss touched both my skin and my soul.

Shania made a light laugh. "I recognize that look. You don't have to lie."

"I'm not lying," I said, lowering my eyes.

"Yes, you are. I felt the way that you look right now on the day I first realized how much I cared for Virgil. I was scared shirtless at the thought of telling him. But he accepted me, even with all my faults. Your mystery man will feel the same way too." We shared a knowing look and made nervous laughs. It felt good to know Virgil McKinnon's widow didn't think I was some kind of crazy woman who possibly murdered her husband.

"I think it's time for a subject-change." Shania reached into the burlap tote she brought in, pulled out a flyer and handed it to me. "Outside of preparing mixed drinks and finger food, I do actually have another life. One of the other reasons I came here tonight. The Macon House Museum is holding a charity for the VA. Proceeds support a cause close to my heart. Orphaned children. We need a nicely worded inscription for a dedication plaque. It'll be the centerpiece for a sculpture we've created. For that part, we need a damn good writer. I was hoping maybe you'd be interested."

"Wow. The event is the day after tomorrow," I said as I read the date on the flyer.

"Blame it on Frieda. She told me you loved challenges." She touched my hand and said, "I've read your books. This will be a breeze for you. Oh, I almost forgot. There'll be a banquet after the showing. Frieda will be there to help. What do you say?"

"Okay. Deal," I said, feeling proud that my name will become a permanent part of the community. Plus this little gig will give me more time to spend with Frieda and less time to think about Eric Fontalvo.

"This is fantastic news. The committee will probably drink themselves silly once they find out you're on board with this.

Now all I need to do is get Chelby Enterprises to approve the sponsorship."

"Saul Chelby's company?" I muttered. And suddenly the good mood fairy flew right out the window.

"Is there a problem?" Shania asked.

I smirked. "I just didn't peg Saul Chelby as a charity guy. That's all."

"You might be surprised. Thank you, Tandie. For everything," Shania said softly, her eyes shining brighter now.

"Ditto," I said, and for the first time in months, I looked forward to being a part of something that benefitted others.

THE MACON HOUSE ART Museum's auditorium was filled with people from all over the state. The display of bronzed soldier's uniforms, guns, and boots that Shania had put together fascinated me. The sculpture was at least seven feet tall and just as much in width. A bust made of the heads of three soldiers was molded into the middle of the top portion. The dedication I wrote for Shania was now framed and the plaque hung below the three heads. The bust of the middle face and the way the man's strong facial features stood out made me think of Eric.

"Girlfriend, what are you doing standing over here? We've been looking everywhere for you," Frieda said walking over to where I stood and looking fabulous in her emerald green mini dress. She turned her attention to my plaque. Writing the dedication over the past couple of days had eased my slightly obsessive thoughts of Eric. However, the feelings he rejuvenated still haunted me.

"So it's like that, huh? The writer is making gooey eyes at her creation," Frieda said, a wide grin on her face.

"That sounds totally conceited," I said, wondering if there were some crazy-small chance that Eric got the text I sent him and might actually show up tonight. I squeezed my eyes shut for a bit, opened them and focused on my friend.

Frieda and I had been together for way too long to let my slight lapse of control slip by her sharp gaze. Of course, she read more into it right away. "Okay, baby, which one?" Frieda crossed her arms and tapped her foot.

I tried to laugh. "Whatever do you mean, Frieda?"

"I mean, this is a kick ass day for you. It's not every day you get your name tacked on a big ugly statue for people all over the world to see. You should be all jumpy and giggly."

"I am. It's just that, I'm..." I covered my mouth and tried to focus on anything besides Frieda's face.

Frieda narrowed her eyes, grabbed my arm and pulled me into the hallway behind the main room. "Saul Chelby or that contractor dude? Which good-looking ass do I need to beat the crap out of first?"

I scoffed a laugh. "Violence is not the key, Frieda."

"All right. Watch this." Frieda spread her lips into a wide grin. "I'm laughing at your joke. I think we can see that you can be funny when you're upset. Now, out with it."

"I feel stupid. I made something out to be a whole lot more than I thought it was with somebody. I don't know, Frieda. I kind of just want to forget about it," I said, the silly tears creeping up to my eyes. "Dammit, I feel like I'm turning into a well, these days."

"What did you do, baby? Did he forget to use a condom? I understand now. You lost control, ripped his clothes off and went at it all night long? Sex happens to everybody at some point, Tan. We all have red blood, and the Good Master didn't bless us with vaginas and penises just to make our mirrors feel good."

"Oh my God, Frieda, we're in a public place," I said, my face on fire. "Anyway, it's not like any of that. We just kissed."

"A kiss? I cannot believe you're about to cry over a kiss. Was is that bad, baby?" Frieda asked.

"It was beautiful, actually," I answered, thinking of the way Eric seemed to be so torn after we finished kissing. "It was for me, at least."

Frieda found comfort in talking about sex. However, I felt about as red as the dress Saul's date was wearing, a thin and racy number that made my black baby doll dress look pale in comparison.

He strolled through the doors behind us as if he were a king. Dressed in a charcoal colored suit with a white shirt underneath the jacket, he could easily pass as one.

Wearing four-inch red heels, the woman beside him stood at a level equal to Saul's height. Her streaked blonde hair was pulled back in a tight bun. The whole package screamed leggy fashion model all over the place.

Right away his gaze found me and Frieda standing off to the side. He motioned for his date to follow as he headed in our direction.

"How nice. The king and queen have arrived," Frieda said, raking a sarcastic gaze over the couple.

"You've got to be kidding me. The nerve of some people," I said, letting out a long sigh.

"Don't think you're slinking your way out of the talk just because Saul Chelby walked in," Frieda muttered and then turned a beaming smile on to Saul, the disappearing landlord who had the nerve to drag his leggy date over to where I stood.

"Welcome. So glad you could make it, Mr. Chelby and his date." I beamed through a tight grin.

"Evening, ladies," Saul said, smiling in a way that lit up the room. "The date's name is Sasha. This is Frieda Tyson. Without her and Shania McKinnon's talents tonight this gala would never have happened.

"We're thankful for you both then," Sasha purred.

"And this is the lovely and gifted Ms. Harrison," Saul said, holding my gaze only a touch longer than what would be considered inappropriate. Sasha, who was all smiles and giggles a moment ago, suddenly looked as if someone stole her hair pieces. Her green-eyed gaze bore mental holes in my head, and her posture stiffened. Her eyes came close to bulging out and her mouth hung slightly open. "This is *the* Tandie Harrison I've heard so much about? Interesting indeed."

No way. Saul discusses me with his dates?

How insane is that?

It was Frieda to the rescue. "Shania reserved a seat for you both at a good table. We don't want you to lose your spots. So, I'll say thanks for everything, Mr. Chelby. Tandie and I will scoot along on our way, now." She attempted to pull me away, but Saul interrupted.

"I'd like a moment with Ms. Harrison if the two of you don't mind," Saul said without moving his eyes away from my face.

"I mind," I said right away. A look passed between Frieda and Sasha.

"We'll only be a moment," Saul said to his date who was handling his inconsiderate behavior better than I could ever have done.

"Come along, Miss Sasha. I'll show you the way to your table," Frieda said and stretched her eyes at me just before she walked away. I turned to Saul. The grin on his face brought the devil out of me.

"The times when a man should remember his comrades become most significant in all matters of race relations whether it be an issue of war, peace, or prosperity. Let this statue sit forever in our midst as a reminder of the ones who fell for our country." They were the words to the dedication I wrote, and Saul had memorized every single one. "Stunning tribute, Ms. Harrison."

I was speechless. Clearing my throat, I said, "I've told you before. I'm not a grandma just yet. So no more Ms. Harrison, please."

"It's mighty good to see you again, Tandie," Saul said, studying my eyes, his narrowing the slightest bit. "You've been crying."

"I have not." I scratched the back of my neck, a tension relief tactic.

"The contractor I hired has done astoundingly beautiful things for Chelby Rose. Why did you flinch when I mentioned the contractor?"

Damn him. He doesn't miss a thing. "I didn't flinch, okay?

"I knew this would happen. No Fontalvo has ever been able to keep his hands to himself." He shook his head and made a scoffing laugh.

I challenged his gaze. "Really? So you set us up then?" I demanded, the blood surging through my body.

His face turned serious. "I hired a man to fix the plumbing in my house. I didn't however give him permission to grope my tenants."

"You know, Saul Chelby, you must have the biggest balls ever," I blurted before I could stop myself. Saul was probably about to receive some of my frustrations about Eric too. "You disappear for weeks. The damn house could've floated away with me in it by now. I put my sweat, tears, and money into fixing the place up without a word of thanks. You show up at a charity function with Barbie-Bad-Ass on your arm, something my good friends organized let me add. Then you have the nerve to question me about my sex life?"

"I only mentioned the contractor. You're the one who brought up your sex life," he said, a smile easing across his lips. "But if you'd like to make a test run of that first thing you accused me of then I'm ready when you are."

"There's something seriously wrong with you. Can you not see that?" I asked.

At once, a man came rushing toward the auditorium and bumped into me, shoving my body up against Saul's chest. My forehead bumped against something hard inside his jacket. I moved my hands up to the object, tracing the outline while Saul glared at the man.

"Watch where you're going, would you?" Saul hissed at him.

"I'm really sorry, Mr. Chelby," the man answered back.

"Right. So that corny banana-in-your-pocket joke doesn't apply here because your fruit's up too high. Want to tell me why you're carrying a gun around," I said.

"That's not a gun. It's a cigarette lighter," he said in a monotone voice.

"You don't smoke, and I used to work for the NYPD, remember?"

"Let it go, Tandie."

"No. What's going on?"

"You handled everything so well tonight, Tandie. And your wording is stunning," Shania said as she headed our way, breaking through the tension bouncing between Saul and me.

She frowned and then continued. "The function was a complete success, Mr. Chelby. We raised almost $550,000 dollars in donations. We can take care of our vets and orphans with money left over. We can use it to build a ceramic base for our sculpture."

"That's great to hear, Mrs. McKinnon. Time to celebrate with good food and wine," Saul said. "I'll see both of you inside." He nodded toward me and walked away toward the auditorium.

"Are you all right, Tandie?" Shania asked. Her mood was different now.

"Yeah, sure."

"He's not the one we talked about, right?"

"Oh, goodness gracious no," I said.

"Too bad for him. He has a serious thing for you. Any fool can see that," Shania said.

"I guess it is too bad for him then. Hey listen, I don't feel well, Shania. I think I'm going to head home. Please tell Frieda for me if you don't mind."

"Go home. Get some rest. And remember what we talked about, okay?" Shania embraced me.

Anxious to get to the car, I walked out of the museum and inhaled deeply. The crisp evening air filled my lungs and cleared my head. There would be no more sorrow on this night.

Chapter 24

T *andie*

"AH, THE INFAMOUS CHELBY Rose. Up close and personal," Norma said as she walked through the doorway. She looked around the hallway, her face bright and her eyes wide as she studied the photos of Saul's ancestors, the ones I'd yet to remove. We headed into the study, sat down, and drank the tea I prepared.

"Took some coaxing and promising to get this. But old Norma got it." Norma reached into her bag, pulled out a book and handed it to me. "This is the record book I told you about in our call last week. A history of Pathseeker magic among the Owanechee. The Angeni Diary. Instructions and photos drawn by the first pathseeker herself."

I took the book in my hands and ran my fingers over the cover. "It's beautiful."

The medium paperback-sized book was covered in brown leather and held the faint musty scent of a time long gone. A brown and gold Owanechee dreamcatcher was etched into the cover. I ran my fingers across the design, closing my eyes and waiting for a vision or something to happen. Nothing. I opened the book and flipped through the pages with care as though generations of Pathseeker secrets would be lost if I weren't careful. Norma and I spent the next hour or so going through the contents. There were passaged written in both English and some other language illustrated in symbols.

The amount of information in the diary overwhelmed me. Not only did it contain passages of Owanechee history, but it also held images of rituals and conduits used by Angeni to reach other planes.

It talked about how she used meditation and chanting to speak with spiritual beings and how she used certain plants and herbs in her rituals. It even had directions on how to perform a vision quest. Neither father nor Grandma Zee had never told me much about our ancestors or their traditions, so this was an incredible discovery for me.

I felt a sense of pride that I had been chosen to protect these ancient teachings and knew I had a responsibility to use them wisely. I resolved right then and there to learn everything I could from the diary.

Sighing heavily, I said: "It has a lot of information in it that I need to know if I want to finish this novel I'm writing," I said without thinking about what I'd just revealed— that my novel was key to solving a supernatural mystery and freeing Breena's spirit from what I suspect was the same spiritual plane where Mama disappeared.

"And it seems like every time I write something my visions become more intense. They hurt like hell when they happen and are still pretty sporadic, but..." My voice trailed off as Norma reached out and grabbed my hand sympathetically.

"I understand, Tandie," she said quietly. "You're looking for answers about what happened to your daughter years ago. Now you think this diary might be able to give them to you?"

I nodded slowly. "Yes, that's exactly what I'm hoping for," I said with a quiver in my voice.

Norma squeezed my hand and smiled. "Then let's figure out what's in this book together," she said. "I'm sure we'll be able to make some sense of it."

"What if I already messed something up?" I asked, thinking about the times I'd walked inside visions without knowing I'd done so.

"It's not what you screwed up. Cause you didn't. I believe you used the other aspect of the pathseeker, beyond the simple glimpses of her past life...the ability to travel back in time."

I opened and closed my mouth several times. Couldn't decide whether I wanted to laugh, cry, or shout hallelujah! Somebody's finally going to help me. "What do you mean by the ability to travel back in time?"

"First, you need to understand the origin of the Pathseeker itself. I've had time to do quite a bit of research. Contacted shamans from Owanechee circles across the state."

"We pretty much know they're time travelers, right?" I asked. Norma's research triggered the slightest bit of unease.

Norma raised her eyebrows and peeked over the rims of her glasses. "Knowledge, my girl. One can never pull enough of it. Especially when dealing with the supernatural. The origin of the first pathseeker came from a very powerful witch. One who spooked the Owanechee in this area so badly, they banded together to stop her from stealing their relatives for sacrificial offerings."

"Of course. A witch." Isn't that what the people of Bolivia had called me from day one. As though sensing my distressful thoughts, Norma continued.

"Now don't go downin' yourself just yet. Hear me out. Witchcraft involves spells and magic and such as you know. Pathseeking while a form of magic doesn't require a spell. The Owanechee severed the link from that witch by using their shaman's power. Took the witch's ability to create pathways in time. Here's where things get interesting. That shaman, a woman named Angeni, then mastered the art of seeking pathways. Henceforth the name pathseeker was given to those related to her afterwards."

"Wait. So that would mean I'm related to this pathseeker?"

"It would seem so. The real mystery is how the first pathseeker, this shaman severed the line to the dark witch. She had help."

The story of my ability bothered me. I couldn't place my finger on why it did. "So who helped the first shaman?"

That's where my mystical sisters' knowledge ends. Goes back hundreds of years, that battle of village witches and Owanechee shamans does. Over time, some very powerful Pathseekers have developed the ability to physically travel back in time. My grandmother told me she knew of one. That was a long time ago though. I hadn't met any descendants of that original shaman... until now."

She'd abandoned her tea and now regarded me with a curious expression as though seeing me for the first time. "What makes time traveling as a Pathseeker so truly unique is that you're able to go back and find your past lives. However, that's also the most dangerous aspect. Change something and everyone in the future could suffer the consequence. You could cease to exist. That is, is if you don't return within a specific timeframe."

"So I did briefly leave the Thalian that night at the Governor's ball," I said more to myself than Norma.

"Come again?" Norma asked.

"I think I've already traveled. A few times, I believe."

Norma raised her eyebrows. "You didn't mention this when we spoke on the phone. Could've told you the reason that was happening." Norma pushed her glasses up and focused on me. "Sounds to me like your pathseeker's eye has opened. According to my research, the pathseeker's eye fully develops around 25 years of age. A time of which Tandie you've already passed. The accident must've set it back. However, now it's demanding to be opened."

Her explanation made sense but was off in timing since I turned 28 in a few months. No, the entity that started this supernatural war played a role in delaying that ability. I was willing to bet my Dean Koontz novel collection on it.

"What does it mean for me?" I asked.

Norma sighed and leaned forward. "Could mean a few things. My ancestor had the eye. She could touch a person and something they owned and see their past. That's where it stopped for her, though. She wasn't related to Angeni. Your ability goes beyond the eyesight though. You've the ability to channel the path of your spiritual selves from past lives. I saw you using it the first time we met."

"What do you mean?"

"You faded in and out for a brief moment. Startled me too."

"You're just now telling me? Thanks for taking your time." I stood and started pacing. "I can travel across time." I spoke more to myself than Norma at that moment.

I knew something had happened at the library. The visions I'd experienced felt real. I could smell the smoke and odors on the wind as I summoned Chelby Rose's history. The same as I did the night Saul and I attended the Governor's ball. Had I traveled that night? Is that why Saul eyeballed me the way he did just before we left? If yes, then why didn't he say anything?

"If I was able to see Rose Chelby and her sons then that means..." I couldn't finish the sentence. The meaning behind it stole my words. I was a reincarnated version of someone from the Chelby line.

"I'll say it for you. One of your past lives pathways crossed with the Chelbys. Perhaps you were a Chelby family member."

I released a shaky breath, and my breathing increased. This revelation took my investigation to a whole otherworldly level. Jumbled thoughts rushed through my mind, and I now understood that Chelby Rose found me instead of the other way around. The frame of the puzzle clicked into place. Now it was time to work on the body.

"I want you to show me how to use it. To go back in time."

Norma gave me a sideways look. "Tandie... I um... Not sure if that's such a good idea."

"I'm a time traveling shaman, right? Then show me how to use my power. It's all here in the book." According to the diary we'd just read, the pathseeker has three main abilities: to see the past or the future, to channel spirits, and to travel through time to either one by using a conduit, places that held pockets of energy from times long gone. Breena's topaz ring was my key and

I was fairly certain Chelby Rose the conduit. All I needed to do was channel the energy. I could go back and stop the accident. Witness the devilry behind Virgil's death. What I'd give to be half of myself again.

"You cannot simply go back and change the past," Norma said as though she'd read my mind. "That is forbidden. You saw what the book said."

"You can help me. Or I'll do it myself." I crossed my arms, stilled my beating heart, and shoved the hell out of the butterflies storming through my belly. The thought of walking along a former life's pathway freaked me out. "But it would be easier if you helped me."

Norma studied me a long moment, shaking her head while doing so. "You stubborn young folks." She turned, lifted a small object from her bag and held it out on her palm. It was a red and black scarab, a jewel similar to an item I'd seen in my mother's trinket box long ago. "An Enochian scarab. Pretty little thing, isn't it?" she asked.

"What does it do?" I asked, my eyes widening as the ruby portion of the body glistened as though it were alive.

"This little baby does quite a bit. Without it, the MARAS wouldn't stand a chance of identifying and beating the nasties that show up on Dark Souls Day. Tonight it'll be our double conduit. This energy paired with the power in your necklace will help you travel along the pathway you find."

Of course. The unity of three... an occurrence common in pathseeker mythology according to Angeni's diary. Norma came prepared. As leader of the MARAS she was just as intrigued by my abilities as me.

Releasing a long sigh, she pushed her glasses up and stood, holding her hand out with the scarab in her palm.

"Give me your hand," she said. I did. Norma placed the jewel on my right palm. The ruby portion of the scarab lit to a bright red. A warm vibration coursed through my skin. "All right then. I want you to focus on something small and easy. The first image you see. No going back to find any demons or change anything. We'll get to all that. Together. Promise me?"

I nodded and resisted crossing my fingers. "Say the words," Norma said, widening her eyes as though she were casting a promise spell.

"You got it. No changing anything."

"Not sure I believe you. But okay. Place your other hand over the scarab." Norma stood in front of me. I did as she instructed as the scarab's body heated a bit more. "Now close your eyes and focus. Pathseeking power works in threes. In this case, it's your necklace, the third eye, and the scarab."

The room pulsed in and out. My body lit with a fire from within, a sensation that was hard to describe as my third eye opened and I saw the past, present, and future unravel before me. It was like looking into an infinite abyss of possibilities. Norma's voice came again from somewhere outside of myself. "Focus," she said softly.

I nodded slowly and tried to center my thoughts on the task at hand. I tried to focus on something small and easy. A white table lamp came into view, smothered by the darkness of the room. My vision slowly pulled away from it as if I was standing in its place, looking down at myself from the ceiling.

My heart raced as I felt a pulse within my chest that seemed to be coming from the scarab. It was so strong that it almost hurt. The sensation became stronger and stronger until it felt like something had taken over my body, manipulating me like a puppet on strings.

An image of the boy from the Catsburg store came to mind. "I see someone," I said inside the void, my voice echoing in the same manner as my ghostly tormentors had done for the past two years.

Norma gently urged me to focus on this thought and hold it in my mind's eye until it became clear as day. With each breath, my vision began to solidify until finally I could almost feel the boy's presence beside me in the room.

The energy coursing through me moved me forward until I found myself in a familiar landscape. Trees, rocks, and plants were spread out around me with streams of energy connecting them all together like spider webbing between them. I'd arrived in Chelby Rose's yard and was seeing the way it looked back in Rose Chelby's time. I stepped forward tentatively and noticed that each step caused the environment around me to change slightly; some trees wilted while others grew tall and green.

As I stood there mesmerized by the beauty of my surroundings, I heard someone call out my name softly from behind me. Turning around quickly, I noticed Rose Chelby standing with her hands clasping a bouquet of lavender roses.

"You made it!" she said excitedly before motioning for me to follow her deeper into this strange version of Chelby Rose I had stumbled upon after my pathseeking journey began. I grinned and ran towards the woman.

"Tandie! Wait!" Norma called out from within the void. However, I'd waited long enough, and didn't want the entity responsible for Breena's death to hold control over my life any longer. I needed to discover my identity. Ached for it with every ounce of life in my body.

I pulled on the sensation from within my head. A warmth spread across my body and the fields faded in and out. I now stood inside Chelby Rose. Only this wasn't the modern day version I lived in. The furniture and sewing machine and other items strewn throughout the room told a different story. I recognized the room. I'd been inside it many times before. A mirror. That's what I needed. Surely there'd be one situated along the hallway. I made my way out of the living room and into the hallway. No luck.

"Tandie! Come back." I heard Norma's voice calling from inside a void, a sound that seemed as though it vibrated from within the walls. Not yet. I needed to see my face. To understand whose body I'd found.

At once, my feet turned as though some invisible force moved me along. I drifted towards the stairway and made my way to the top, glide walking until I came to the door at the end of the hallway. The same door I'd yet to open. Whispers assaulted me, boring into my mind as though using tiny fingernails. The door pulsed in and out and cold chills spread across me, I felt my spirit rising from within the temporary body I inhabited. I was losing hold on the pathway, returning to my time.

"Not yet!" I yelled in an unfamiliar female's voice. I grabbed the doorknob and turned it. Success! And then something yanked me out of the woman's body and back through a dark void until I returned to Norma, Chelby Rose and my living room.

Chapter 25

andie

T Eric showed up two days later. His hair was messier than usual and the fine stubble of a beard and mustache grew on his face. His spicy cologne smelled the same even if the man I'd spent the last six weeks with seemed aloof and uncomfortable. But still, my silly heart flipped a bit when he walked through the door.

"I've been all alone the last few days. No phone calls, no nothing from you. Only Ella, the creepy gardener girl," I said. "You could at least have answered my text messages."

"I know, and I'm sorry I missed your showing." He placed his hands on his hips, gave me a serious look, and said: "I really think you should dismiss Ella."

My ears heated. "She's not the only one I've considered dismissing these past few days."

"Okay, I probably deserve that. I just needed some time to think." Eric stood by the door as if he expected me to toss something at him and would need an escape route.

"All men do. And for the record, I've already fired Ella. You don't have to be psychic to know she's bad news." I shuffled on my feet and crossed my arms. "Forgive me for assuming, but I kind of thought we were working towards developing something outside the discussion of paint colors and roof shingles."

"And we are. Please trust me." His intense hazel eyes filled with sadness. Whatever they hid must truly be grim.

"Does you being M.I.A. have anything to do with Enrique Fontalvo? Or maybe even the kiss we shared?" I went for the hardest blows. Eric stood there and stared at me, his expression guarded and his eyes filled with a sadness that floored me.

"Ah. I believe I'm one step closer to solving the great Fontalvo mystery," I said.

"To answer the first two questions, yes. But I'm not running if that's what you're thinking," he said with a strained expression on his face. He was struggling with something, perhaps an inner thought. His look turned serious just before he said, "It's not safe for a woman to get involved with the men in my family."

I held his gaze, studying those sexy hazel eyes that showed off more green highlights today. "What do you mean? Do the women suddenly blow up or disappear?" I asked with just a touch of sarcasm.

He gave me the strangest look, a combination between surprise and something else sad that made me want to take back my words. "Would you believe me if I told you there's a curse? At least, that's what I've been told. Hell, this vex even has a name." I could tell he was struggling with the decision to tell me about this curse.

"After what happened here with Norma the other day, I'd believe just about anything," I said truthfully. I stepped closer to where he stood and touched his arm. His muscles were like stone with all the tension inside them. "Got strange and odd? Good. I'm your go-to-girl. Talk to me, Eric."

Our eyes met. For the longest moment, the room silenced and was charged with a warm current, the power of the chemistry between us, a heated energy we always managed to create. My heart sped up and my body ached to be touched again. Did Eric feel the same way?

As if he'd read my thoughts again, he took my hand in his, lacing his fingers through mine and led me toward the study. "I'm sorry I left without saying goodbye. And for not calling. I was wrong to treat you that way."

"It was somewhat humiliating, and I was ready to beat the crap out of you; but I'll survive," I said. He was on the verge of telling me a crucial secret, and I didn't want to break the trust we'd worked to develop between each other.

Eric sat down on the sofa, guiding me to a sitting position beside him, squeezed my hand tighter and continued. "A long time ago there was a feud between the Fontalvos and the Chelbys. I don't know. Something about one of my ancestors. The one I told you about before, the one named Enrique. Apparently, he had an affair with Thomas Chelby's daughter, Alice."

I nodded. "Sounds feud-worthy so far."

"There's more to the story. See, Enrique arrived on a Spanish warship that attacked Brunswick Town. This happened in September of 1748. The survivors from the ship were either put in prison or did their best to blend in." He stopped and glanced at our entwined hands, his mind lost in that same deep thought as before.

"This isn't hard to figure out. I assume, Thomas Chelby wasn't too happy with his daughter sleeping with one of the soldiers who attacked his town," I said, gazing at Eric's profile and the way his thick dark hair framed his face perfectly. He was gorgeous, sensitive, strong...perfect.

"Chelby wasn't happy and neither were the Cropsey witches," Eric said.

"Cropsey witches?" I asked.

Eric nodded. "That's right. I only know bits and pieces of the story. I mean, after two-hundred plus years facts tend to get distorted."

"I always heard that the old witch stories about this area were true. But my mind works in strange ways. So..."

"You're naturally odd, which is why you want to hear all the gory details of my family's history," Eric said in a flirtatious voice. I pulled my hand away and playfully narrowed my eyes at him.

"Good one, Mr. Jokester, when he shouldn't be joking."

"I'm sorry, but with everything that's happened over the last week, I either have to make jokes or go insane." He sighed and smiled.

"I know the feeling," I said, losing myself in his gaze. "Okay, so one of the Cropsey witches fell in love with Enrique, who didn't love her back. That ticked her off and she wound up creating a curse to get back at him and Alice Chelby. A permanent one, so something bad happens on a certain day or time. Or even worse, something terrible happens to him or his wife."

Eric leaned in toward me, his mouth slack, and his posture stiff. "Did you just fool around in my head?"

"I—my ability doesn't work that way. Or, at least, not with someone close to me." Heat surged through my cheeks.

"You repeated the exact detail of what I was told is called the Broken Heart Curse. Seriously, how did you do that?" Eric asked, his eyes studying my face as if he'd just met me for the first time.

"I don't know. I just—My powers..." I swallowed hard and stood. Eric did the same. Norma had explained some of the Fontalvo family history. I somehow knew the rest. "Something is happening, Eric. I did see three children in this house, and they weren't alive. Pages from my novel disappear and mysteriously show up later. Just now, something whispered the answer I gave you. The same voices I've heard off and on since Breena died." I didn't tell him about the strange dreams where Breena walked on a beach and led me to a warship. Listening to him describe the circumstances surrounding his ancestor's arrival, I'd already linked the ship I dreamed about to the Spanish soldiers that attacked Bolivia hundreds of years ago.

"The 267th anniversary of the Fortuna's arrival happens in six days. Bolivia's infamous Dark Souls Day." Eric cradled my face in his palms. "I've already caused enough grief for my friends by coming back here. I don't want to be around you when that day comes."

"Can't you see that's exactly what we need to do? We have to work together. I can help you figure this thing out. Besides, it's too late to run, Eric. I'm already involved now." I stood on my tiptoes and placed my lips on his. He kissed me back.

After our kiss ended, Eric leaned back, his handsome face distorted by something painful going on in his mind. He nodded slowly and said: "You're right. We should figure out what's going on. Together." A faint smile touched his lips, and he wrapped his arms around me as he looked deep into my eyes. Even though things seemed overwhelming right now, I was certain that there wasn't a force strong enough to keep us from saving our loved ones.

Tell him about Breena. About that horrible story you've been summoned to write. He needs to understand how connected you are to this situation.

"The consequence of you being involved in this is what scares me the most. I—I have to go." Eric glanced at Breena's photo and headed toward the front door.

I followed him to the entrance. Touching his arm, I said: "Don't abandon Chelby Rose now, Eric. I'm scared."

His determined look softened. He turned and took me in his arms. I savored the familiar scent of pine mixed with a woodsy smell on his skin and ached to feel his lips on mine again. "I'm not abandoning Chelby Rose or its new owner," he whispered in my hair.

I pulled back and stared deep in his eyes. I thought about how great it would be to have my visions back. Then I'd be able to figure out the mystery known as Eric Fontalvo, the man who was very much like the dream character I had created in my novel.

However, the sweet victory of experiencing ecstasy inside of a second kiss wouldn't happen tonight. Eric's face twisted, and he turned around as if he were forcing his feet to move through the doorway. The wind howled the familiar song I had gotten used to hearing, a sound I had always found comforting in an odd way.

ERIC'S MIND TOLD HIM to leave Bolivia again, but his heart knew he couldn't run. Not this time. The curse on his family affected the Fontalvo men and the women who loved them as well. Tandie was right. The Chelby children she saw were ghosts, no doubt. His recent nosedives into the heart of Bolivia told him that there was truth in her revelation.

After his encounter with the ghostly girl on the street, he knew something bizarre was happening. The spot that the child touched had completely healed by the next morning, leaving a scar in its place. The encounter seemed like a dream, but it wasn't.

The photo of Tandie's daughter stuck in his mind. The similarity between the ghost child on the road and the girl Tandie called Breena rattled him. He didn't dare say a word to Tandie, though. She'd already experienced enough pain without him adding to her grief. Dark Souls Day loomed around the corner and he still hadn't managed to find a way to help Javier.

He eased his Jeep to a stop outside his beach house and sat listening to the ocean for a while. His family had always relied on him to be the voice of reason, the realist. What would they think about him now? Hell, Eric wasn't sure what he believed anymore.

He got out of his Jeep, walked into his cottage, and headed straight for the bar. He filled a shot glass and downed the Vodka in one gulp, savoring the burn as the liquid trickled down his throat. The phone blared through the silence, startling him back to the present moment. With hesitation, he answered it. His sister, Daniella's hysterical voice sailed through the headset.

"Eric! Oh God, it's awful," she said through sobs.

Cold dread washed over him. His baby sister held a special place in his heart. Her tearful voice tore at him in a way that no woman had yet to touch. "Daniella, please, calm down and tell me what's wrong."

"It's Javier! The doctors just confirmed he only has two weeks to live."

Chapter 26

T*andie*

I read and re-read the scenes inside the thirteen returned pages, the ones featuring my protagonist, Eric Fontaine. I'd assembled the framework of the mystery behind Chelby Rose: the living Eric Fontalvo, my novel's main female characters, and the spirits haunting the upstairs bedrooms. One piece felt out of place. The newspaper clearly described a fifth bedroom. Not even Eric had mentioned where it could be. Maybe the area was closed off or merged into one of the other four rooms upstairs.

Both Eric Fontalvo and myself were somehow linked to all these occurrences. Since I now understood my psychic visions were connected to my novel, I looked forward to seeing what direction I'd be pointed toward next.

I placed my fingers on the typewriter's keys and began pecking away at the next section.

Although Maud Cropsey felt relieved that her best friend survived Eric Fontaine's attack she knew he'd eventually kill again. He must be brought to justice so there'll be peace among the people.

"What were you trying to tell me by hiding these pages, little ghostly ones? How are my fictional Eric and screaming Ella related?" I massaged my temples and peeked at Breena's picture.

"Help mommy understand, Baby B?" I whispered, my attention a bit distracted by the groan coming from inside Chelby Rose's framework. The massive house not only made the loudest settling noises I'd ever heard, but it also accented my loneliness and all the anxiety associated with that emotion.

At once, a bright light illuminated the area around my desk. I inhaled deeply and turned toward the source. The girl ghost I assumed was Eliza Chelby stood in the doorway. She bore a serene but emotionless expression. My hands trembled and I dared not blink. I dropped my pencil and held a hand to my chest. Unable to move, I stared at the apparition.

"I can see you." I stood up slowly. "Eliza?"

The ghost girl nodded.

"Do you have the other seven pages from my book?" It was a farfetched question for an equally strange moment.

Eliza shook her head in a slow side-to-side motion.

"Did Samuel or maybe Joseph take them?" I asked. The child's spirit was shrouded in a sadness that winded me. Eliza had somehow suffered a terrible death. Maternal instinct gave me this feeling more than a psychic one. For some reason I longed to take the child in my arms and assure her that everything would be okay.

"It's quite all right. No one here will hurt you. Did your brother take my work?"

Eliza frowned and shook her head again.

"Oh boy. Can you talk to me?"

Eliza nodded and said, "I have something for you." The ghost turned and drifted into the hallway.

I trailed Eliza to the kitchen where she pointed at the wide china cabinet sitting at the far left wall. The massive structure was empty so I had never thought to move it before. I wanted to think of a nice way to tell Saul why I didn't want to keep the space-eating hulk. I took baby steps toward the cabinet and peeked behind the right side. A cool draft tickled my face.

"Wait a second. There's something...here..."

I moved to the left side. A small opening between the cabinet and the wall created a space just large enough for both my hands to fit in. Slipping my fingers into the crevice, I jerked and pulled on the edge until I created an opening large enough to fit my body inside.

"Mental note. Must join the gym next week," I said, situating my back against the wall. Gathering strength, I placed my hands on the cabinet and pushed.

The hulk of wood slid forward inch by inch. A hard push moved the massive structure out far enough for me to be able to turn around. One last shove and I found what I was looking for—the outline of a door that blended in with the kitchen's golden wallpaper. This new discovery called to me with its promise of hidden mysteries.

"How much do you wanna bet this door explains the missing bedroom?" I peeked around the cabinet until my gaze landed on Eliza's ghost. She stood still and silent, her light bright as a beacon in the dimly lit kitchen. The girl's only movement was the way she sucked her thumb, another gesture that tugged at my maternal instincts. I wanted to reach out to her, this memory of a child who reminded me of my round-faced daughter.

I turned my attention back to the hidden doorway, pierced the wallpaper with my fingernail and ripped the musty paper down until the hidden door was fully exposed. "Great. There's no doorknob."

The next challenge was to find a way to open the door. I trudged over to the pantry, pulled out Eric's toolbox and a screwdriver and removed the knob from the door. Praying that the knob from the pantry door wasn't as ancient as it looked, I headed back over to my new discovery, slid the screws inside the holes and attached it. The cams fit.

"Yes!" I exclaimed while Eliza still stood across the room, sucking her thumb and staring as if she were hypnotized by my discovery.

I placed my hand on the knob, hoping I didn't experience a repeat of the scene behind the door episode that had played out in the fourth room upstairs. To my relief, the weathered wood gave way. A burst of stale, wet air engulfed me. I fanned my nose and thought about picking up a can of Lysol before moving forward. The room beyond held the stench of an area that had been sealed for an undisclosed amount of years, reminding me of a neglected, moldy fish tank.

I examined the wooden steps vanishing in the darkness and assumed the pathway led to a cellar and no doubt what could've been considered a fifth room for servants back in the day.

"I can go no further. I have to leave you now," Eliza said with a frightened expression on her face. "Look for the magic brick. I must go."

"Wait! Magic brick? What does that mean?" I asked the fading spirit.

I now stood alone and faced exploring a gaping black hole with no light. The only sounds were whatever was dripping in the cellar combined with my ragged breathing. Chills flooded my body with a vengeance. Yet, I was determined to discover what secrets Chelby Rose held. I hadn't felt such passion since before the time I lost my sight. I wished Eric had left a flashlight lying around somewhere, though. What kind of contractor owns a tool box without a flashlight?

Swallowing hard, I reached into my pocket, lifted my cell and hit the flashlight icon on the screen. Using the phone's light, I felt along the wall and stepped down on one creaking step at a time. One wrong move and I would become a permanent spirit roaming the halls of Chelby Rose as well. My fingers passed across something wet and slimy along the way. Focusing on the area at the bottom of the stairs, I thought of Eliza Chelby's ghost and her hesitation about coming down to the cellar just before my hands raked across a switch on the wall.

"A light! I knew this room couldn't be that ancient. Please work." I flipped the knob up and the area sprang to dimly lit life.

I examined my surroundings. The room was about four hundred square feet or less. A small cot with sheets gray from dirt and years of grime sat against a far wall. A dingy white dresser with nicks and gashes in the wood and a cracked mirror sitting on top sat against the adjacent wall. I stood in what would've been considered the fifth bedroom back in Chelby Rose's glory days.

The room vibrated with energy of past memories, and something stirred deep in my stomach. The feeling was the familiar pang I'd experienced ever since that tragic day I entered the woods with Chelsea and the other kids. I could use my pathseeker's eye to see what happened here.

Closing my eyes, I placed a hand on the cot and gave in to my inner signal, the one that led to the birth of a vision, and concentrated on the youngest Chelby daughter's image, the first part of a larger scene. A brief flash of a clean, but frightened Eliza

Chelby running up the cellar's stairway played through my mind and disappeared just as fast. "Damn it! I lost the vision."

"Look for the magic brick," the child had said.

Caught up in the sight, I closed my eyes again and moved my ethereal self to the top of the stairway and followed Eliza's gaze as she peered down to whatever had frightened her. A laugh echoed in the darkness. The eeriness of the noise raised goosebumps on my skin. However, the scene warped and changed and we now stood in the cellar room. As if somehow guiding me, Eliza pointed toward an area between the cot and the dresser.

The vision cleared, leaving me with a light head. At once, I walked to the corner and examined the grime covered wall. At first glance, the bricks looked normal. On the second scan, I found one that jutted out about a half-inch more than the others. I wiped away the dirt from the brick and pulled on it. Groaning from years of disuse, the slab came out of the slot after some effort. Behind the brick, a book lay in a hollow area.

I inhaled deeply, reached in, pulled the book out, dusted the cover off, and read the name carved in gold letters on the front: Alice Chelby. The binding was a black leather diary with words written in calligraphy on the paper inside it. I flipped through the old pages and was amazed to find the sheets had been conserved well inside the airtight space over the past two hundred-plus years. Closing the book, I held my new discovery against my chest and smiled. Somehow, I knew this would be a turning point for everything.

I walked back upstairs, closed the door and headed toward the study, my curiosity eating away at me by the second. Settling in at my writing desk, I opened the diary and started reading.

December 3, 1748

My dearest diary,

It has been almost two months since the man of my life and I met and declared our love. He grows weary of my hesitation to marry him. I haven't the nerve to reveal the true reason for my deliberation, the fear of Ella Maud and her voodoo priestess mother. Oh how I fear Ella's jealousy and hate of our love.

Alice

I pulled a delicate yellow note from inside a gap between the pages and unfolded the thin sheet. The paper contained a poem written in a different handwriting from Alice's.

Mi Amor, I give thee all of mi.
To thy beauty, I pledge love eternally.
I wash thou hacienda in colors
like a sunset over sea.
Where the moon cradles our love,
I see she is flying free.
Mi Amor, how I love thee,
Under the hacienda moon,
shall be where you always find mi.

At once, a dizzying pressure thrummed in my temples just before the sight took my mind. Maybe the sensation was so strong because these were my first controlled visions in almost two years. Or maybe I was excited. Whatever the reason, the vision came on with a force that I had never experienced in any of the others.

In this new vision, I became Alice Chelby of 1748 as she ran through the woods to meet her lover, Enrique Fontalvo. With skin as pale as snow and hair as dark as the most sinfully sweet chocolate, I marveled at how different it felt being in another female's body and mind. Especially someone who was a different race from myself. None of that mattered in this place, and I embraced the spirit I had become.

I was a woman who would do anything to save the man I loved.

CHARGING INTO THE SECRET cabin, Alice bounded over to Enrique as he met her at the door. "I cannot stay long. I think she is following me," Alice said out of breath.

"We have to show her we are not afraid." Enrique pulled Alice into his taut arms. In his embrace, she felt as if they could take on the world that was so against their love.

"She does not care, Enrique. Ella wants you for herself. I think she has even convinced that voodoo priestess mother of hers to hurt us in some way," Alice said, her chest filled with worry, her eyes blurred with the tears she didn't want him to see.

Enrique released Alice, walked to the door and examined the woods. "Colonel Dryden's men know I have been hiding here."

Alice gasped and held a white gloved hand over her mouth. Dryden's men would show no mercy if they found Enrique. He was one of the soldiers from the Fortuna, the warship that attacked the city three months ago. "What? How could they find out? Do you think Ella told them?"

"I am not certain. Some of the other surviving soldiers are hiding in a place near Bald Head Island. They have a room for me." Enrique's soulful dark eyes pleaded with Alice's light brown ones for understanding. He had been through so much pain and heartache since that night the Fortuna was destroyed. He had worked hard to mask his Spanish accent and to blend in with the local citizens.

"Oh, Enrique, you cannot go. I found a way to trick the evil. Nanee gave me a talisman to ward off bad spirits and their spells." Alice buried her face against her lover's chest. A familiar scent of the deep woods filled her nostrils, making her feel secure and stirring the earth-rocking desire she had for him. The lovers were never able to get enough of each other, and she wanted him to make love to her right then.

"Alice, I must go. They will kill me if they discover our secret."

"And what about us?" Alice demanded.

"What do you mean?"

"Search your heart for that answer." Alice moved Enrique's hands to her stomach and met his gaze.

"A babe?" Tears came to Enrique's eyes. "Alice, mi Amor. You make me so happy with this news." Enrique pulled his lover into his arms and squeezed, but with a gentle care. After a long moment, Enrique moved back. His smile faded and a frown rode across his handsome, exotic features.

"What is it, my love? What brings this scowl to your face?" Alice's heart sped up. The woods seemed alive with Dryden's spies. The air was filled with an evil menace lurking in the shadows as if the darkness were ready to pounce on their love and crush all emotion.

"I must go for a while. There's so much more at stake now." He placed dark hands on her stomach. "I must provide for my family. Make you both safe. Will your father support this child?"

Sighing, Alice gazed deep into his eyes and said, "Only mother knows. But she promised no harm would come to either of us. Father will be insane with anger, but he will be fair." She didn't have the heart to tell him that she would receive the typical fornicator's punishment. Her parents would have the local pastor absolve her sins. And then she and her child would be locked up in the attic until her family was able to pair her with a proper suitor.

"Oh, Enrique. Don't go. I'll wither away if you do." Alice threw herself against his chest again. She hated being selfish and losing control. A well-bred lady of a manor should support her husband's decisions instead of thwarting them.

Enrique cradled her in his arms and rocked her like his baby, the symbol of love she would one day hold. "I shall return. I must see someone before your father finds out about our child. He would separate us for good if he knew."

"Where will you go?"

"I'll find the other soldiers. They shall assist us with making a good life for our babe."

"I love you, Enrique," Alice whispered, tears flowing down her face.

"I love you more, mi Amor," Enrique answered back and then kissed Alice, a passionate hungry kiss. She moved his hand to her breast and the other one to her thigh. He bent down, lifted her dress, slid his hand up underneath the chemise, exposing her bare thigh. And when he touched her sex the sensation rolled through her abdomen as if he had set her soul on fire.

He lowered her body down to a mattress made of soft hay, ever so gently, and slid her dress up to her waist. And then he positioned himself over her body and entered her. The way he made love to her: each kiss, every touch, each shove inside her sex was exquisitely gentle because now he understood that her condition was delicate, and Enrique accepted both Alice and their child. Ecstasy filled Alice's heart and her body as the couple thrust their way to orgasm.

The vision cleared and my body shook almost as if I were reacting to Alice's orgasm. I cradled my forehead and took a moment to steady my heaving chest. Enrique bore a disturbing resemblance to Eric. How could that be?

Yet, the kiss Alice received from Enrique was similar to the one I had experienced with Eric. The most shocking part was that both Alice and Enrique mentioned Ella's name. A riddle. Only this puzzle wasn't the kind created by geniuses. No. Something dark and angry spun this web of a nightmare.

A clang of metal came from in the direction of the kitchen. I thought about the cellar bedroom and wondered if I remembered to shut the door. I had been so excited about receiving the visions again and finding the diary that I had blocked out and neglected the rest of my environment.

Trudging back to the kitchen, I spotted the culprit. A stainless steel pot lay in the middle of the floor. I bent down, removed the pan from the floor and placed it in the sink. I examined the empty kitchen and assumed that the ghosts of the Chelby children were responsible for this latest mischief.

"All right, Eliza. I have the diary. I'm reading—and experiencing it." Even though I was alone, my face heated as I thought about how real the things Alice felt seemed to me.

I turned and headed back towards the study, anxious to return to the fire's warm embrace. September brought unusually cool weather along with it this year. I trudged through the hallway beside the stairwell, my mind caught up in thoughts of Enrique slash Eric's lips on my body, and stopped just before I entered the study.

Shocked beyond words, I stood in the middle of the floor and stared at the entrance. Several sheets of paper that formed an X were stuck on both the door and the rectangular-shaped picture window beside it. I inched toward this latest mystery of Chelby Rose, lifted a shaking hand and removed one of the pages from the top of the X, exposing a windowpane as I did so. I peeked outside, focusing on an area in the forest where the old Cape Fear swamp used to be before it dried out. And then, I shuddered.

Part 3

The dark ancestral cave, the womb from which mankind emerged into the light, forever pulls one back - but...you can't go home again...you can't go...back home to the escapes of Time and Memory. ...You Can't Go Home Again"

~Thomas Wolfe

Chapter 27

T*andie*

The bright afternoon sun beamed through the study's window, bathing my face in nature's warmth. The horror of the ill-fated love affair between the girl who lived in Chelby Rose and a man related to Eric filled me with a keen sense of dread. I'd placed the seven returned pages of my manuscript on my desk, keeping the sheets in view as if they might disappear again.

One thing I knew for certain, I chose this house and town for a reason. Correction. Chelby Rose and I chose each other. If what the librarian told me about the famed curse on the Bolivian residents held any truth then I had already figured out what that purpose might be... using my pathseeker ability to stop the chaos created by the Cropsey witches. The question remained though... How do I go about doing so? Grandma Zee's voice echoed through my head. "The trinity of love can stop those witches."

"What does that mean, grandma?" Time was running out. Dark Souls Day was less than 1 week away, and the date on my subpoena took place shortly afterward. The crossed timing of the two timeframes wasn't a coincidence. Somebody wanted me to fall. And something wicked was most definitely coming our way. According to Eric, Dark Souls Day jump started his curse. Translation: I had six days left to complete the body of my puzzle.

Along with my upgraded abilities, came a heightened emotional state. Alice's memories reeked with sadness and it was almost as if she and I had combined as one. Plus, I missed Eric in such a way that felt as if I'd known him my entire lifetime even though a short timeframe had passed since we'd last seen each other.

And since we shared another beautiful kiss. His hands are callous but gentle. His touch makes me feel treasured, and he caresses me as if I am made of glass and I am precious to him.

The landline phone's buzz-like ringer sounded out in the hallway. By the time I mustered the energy to head toward it the answering machine had picked up. Frieda's voice sailed through the speakers. I stayed on the sofa and listened.

"Hi, Tandie, it's Frieda. I'm worried about you. I haven't heard anything from you since Macon House. How's your revised manuscript coming along? Did you find those missing pages? Give me a call, girl. Geez."

The voice mails cycled through two messages left earlier in the day. "Shania here. Just wanted you to know the charity event was a huge success. We've enough funding to make this the most memorable Dark Souls celebration. Virgil would've loved being here to witness this. But... oh well. Thought I'd let you know. Talk soon."

In the next message, a male's voice filled the speakers. "I came on too strong, didn't I?" Saul's voice said, getting straight to the point as always. "Sorry about that. Let me know how things are going." Silence. Typical Saul... abrupt and focused.

I settled back on the sofa and pulled my blanket up to my chin, unable to face the day's word count. I'd fallen behind. Walking visions had consumed most of my waking moments ever since I discovered the diary in the hidden cellar-bedroom. I closed my eyes, fell asleep right away and stumbled into a deep hole. Falling through a dark abyss, I screamed and cried until I emerged in a forest on the other side of a vision.

A man ran through Chelby Rose Forest at breakneck speed. The men trailing him shortened the distance like a group of lions focused on a gazelle. I had somehow found a way to channel Enrique Fontalvo's nightmare as he ran from Thomas Chelby and the other townspeople, I'd channeled the pathseeker's ability to go back in time.

A GANG OF TOWNSFOLK had formed a lynch mob to capture the renegade who, according to local rumors, had raped and impregnated young Alice Chelby.

Enrique had managed to keep his identity secret for almost a year. And with the help of the Chelby's servant, a young girl named Nanee Atwater, he was able to sneak in and spend time with his beloved and their two-month-old son. That was until Ella Maud Cropsey and her horrid mother Mary Jean found out.

There was almost enough money saved from his turpentine business profits to leave this place and take care of his family. No longer would Alice be locked away in an attic as if she were a deformed step-child.

Fleeing through the forest, he cradled a small box under his arms and tried to avoid the tree limbs scattered throughout the area. Stumbling over branches made him lose precious time. He dropped the box, panic rising in his chest.

A bridge of time flashed and passed and now highlighted a very distinct patch of bluish-lavender roses surrounding the base of a tree—the same type of rose Saul wore on his suit the night he attended the Governor's Ball.

The blue curiosa.

Another flash. Enrique dropped to his knees and plowed into the dirt with his bare hands, making a hole large enough to hold the box. Placing the small container in the ground, he covered the box and slouched over, stilling the pain raging inside him, the anguish of leaving his family behind.

A final flash. The haze cleared. And he was gone.

Chapter 28

Tandie

I walked out the front door, my mind muddled and caught up in a trance, each step heavier than the previous one. The continual visions drained my energy. I'd never known the sight to be so frequent before. Headed toward the forest, I knew exactly what I hoped to find. Crickets, birds, and small animals continued to sing their praises to nature as the world unfolded for me one grim discovery at a time.

Following Enrique's path, the one from the vision or rather the journey back in time, I trudged deeper into the woods until I came to a circle of pine trees surrounding a cleared patch of forest ground. A single maple tree bordered by a halo of greenery stood in the middle of the area. I inched closer and inspected the foliage growing along the tree's base. Miniature blue flowers grew in the weeds. The blue rose, the curiosa Saul had called this plant. Alice's favorite. Seeing them brought tears to my eyes.

I examined the place where Enrique had buried the box he carried. Layers of dirt now covered its resting spot, almost three-hundred years' worth of deposits. Lifting the shovel I didn't remember picking up, I stabbed the ground and jumped on the tool, driving the head through the soft mud.

What would Eric think if he saw me now?

And will I ever see Eric Fontalvo again?

He seemed pretty spooked about the curse on his family and with good reason. In the calm little town of Bolivia, the living and the dead were all connected. The curse on his family was the binding factor for us all, a mystery I vowed to solve for Eric, Saul, Enrique, Eliza, and Breena.

After obsessively digging for an hour or so, I felt the shovel thud against something at the bottom of the chasm I had dug. I dropped the tool and hopped down in the three-foot deep hole, my chest heaving with the excitement. The mystery was becoming an obsession.

Dropping to my knees, I dug through the moist dirt with my fingers until they scraped across a box. I lifted the wooden container from the ground, brushed off as much dirt as I could and examined the Spanish words engraved on the top. Barely able to control myself, I lifted the lid. A necklace attached to a fingertip-sized heart made of gold lay inside the box. Dirty and disheveled, I worked my way out of the hole and examined the necklace during the trek back to Chelby Rose.

As I emerged from the woods, I felt someone or something watching me. I focused my gaze on the house. Two groups of about six or seven people stood in the trees along either side of Chelby Rose. The women wore clothing similar to the outfit Ruth Ann Adams wore the day I met her; but the men's outfits varied from coveralls to pajamas to suits that were fashionable decades ago. The crowd consisted of both black and white people alike along with a few children. The phantom boy from the Catsburg store stood among the group near the right side of the porch.

I froze as I looked on at my phantom visitors, a chill running down my spine. A middle-aged black woman with an extraordinary contrast of silver and black hair stepped forward, her body aglow with an ethereal light that painted her ghostly. Her eyes were alive with a passion that was undoubtedly real, and her raspy voice seared with urgency.

"Do not waver, child. Speak of Chelby Rose to the world. They must all be made aware. End this tale as it must be done, for only then can you show them the path to salvation!" she commanded.

"I don't know what else to write." I stood among the ghosts gathered around me. A different woman stepped forward this time, a blonde in her mid to late thirties.

"But you must know. You have all you need now."

"Why have you chosen me? I'm not a savior. Not even close," I said, feeling my insecurities rising up, "and I'm too scared of being wrong... again. Besides, I'm too dirty. Look at these hands." I held up my right hand and splayed my fingers.

The black woman's spirit stepped forward so she stood merely inches away from me. "Alice knows what to do. Be strong, pathseeker. Young Fontalvo will return if you act now, but the choice is yours." Her words pressed against my skin with the weight of an eternity of hope and despair. My heart was filled with conflicting emotions. I wanted to help these people, to be their savior, but at the same time I was scared of what I might find if I kept going down this path. Would I destroy their only chance at freedom the same way I caused Breena's death?

The woman's kind, round face and soulful eyes reminded me of Grandma Zee. My heart ached from all the losses I'd suffered over the past decade, but I felt strong in the presence of these people, these lost souls who looked up to me. For the first time in what seemed like forever, my life had a purpose.

"No tears. No more, baby girl. Save your strength." The woman beamed a kind smile, turned around and floated away.

I watched the other spirits drift away in a shadowed unison. Somewhere deep in my mind, I heard Norma Atwater's voice repeating what she'd told me about the Bolivian townspeople.

"Sometimes the spirits don't know they've moved on, the dead among the living."

I watched the lost souls until they all faded away in the light of the setting sun.

THE SHOWER WATER RAINED down on my skin and massaged away the events of the evening. The liquid flowed through my hair, over my eyes. I leaned against the shower wall and released my fears, tears, and burdens. Images of the face of the black lady's spirit combined with memories of Grandma Zee fluctuated through my mind. And then my grandmother's image fully materialized before my closed eyes.

I caught my breath.

"Hey, my baby girl, open your eyes. You gotta pay attention, now." After doing as she instructed, I found myself standing naked in a dark room, a single beam of light highlighting my body and the area around me. I crossed my arms and attempted to hide my nudity.

Grandma Zee came into view and stood before me. She was dressed in her favorite white gown. I wanted to embrace her, but I couldn't move. "The trinity of love can stop those witches: the rose, the heart, and the lucky one. Find all three things. Unite them as one." Grandma's gaze focused on something in the area to the left of me as her imaged dimmed.

"Don't go, Grandma. Please." My voice wavered as a small stream of water flowed over my lips. Grandma Zee reached out to me just before her image faded. From in the darkness, her voice echoed and said six final words: "Look up, girl! They're above you."

"What? Who's up there, grandma?" The room changed and started closing in until a wall had formed around me. Complete darkness came next. I felt along the surface until my fingers raked across the three-prong shower head and the faucets located beneath it. Somehow, I managed to turn the water off. Silence fell. Flashes of shower tile and darkness merged together, a medley of images taunting my troubled mind. The light went out, and I still stood in a deep hole, a mixture of past and present events enveloping me.

I swiped at my eyes and tried to focus on anything besides the darkness. At once ants and spiders started moving down my skin, crawling in my hair, and tickling my naked breasts and buttocks. Gasping, I cleared the water away from my eyes; but it wasn't liquid on my face. Something that had a grainy texture trickled over my skin. Forcing my eyes open, I focused on what should've been the shower walls. The faux marble tiles were gone. I spun around and found myself surrounded by a circle of dark brown walls. Dirt. I was standing in the bottom of a ten-foot deep hole.

"Look up! They're above you," Grandma Zee had warned.

With hesitation, I moved my gaze upward. A gaping hole had replaced the ceiling over the shower and I was no longer naked. As I focused on this new vision, a pile of dirt plummeted down on top of my head. I swiped the soil away from my pale-blue dress, Alice's favorite one given to her by Enrique. *How did I know that?* What I thought was spiders turned out to be dirt particles easing between the dress and my skin. The shower had turned into an open grave. More dirt shoveled down on my head and trickled into my eyes. The particles stung worse than being poked with a mascara brush.

"Stop! Somebody's down here. For God's sake, hear me, please!" I screamed in a voice that now belonged to a stranger ... Alice Chelby.

Ella's face—or someone who looked a lot like my temperamental little gardener—appeared over the hole. She glanced down at Alice, laughing hysterically.

"Whining is for babies, Alice. Should we be merciful, Mama?" Ella's high-pitched voice called to someone I couldn't see. Mary Jean Cropsey's face appeared over the grave. But her features were shrouded by the shadows.

"Thomas Chelby will pay for spurning my love. And your Enrique will pay for hurting my Ella," Mary Jean threatened. So that's what started all of this—two women burned by men who were in love with someone else.

"Please, don't do this. Oh God in Heaven! Enrique will find me. He'll kill you both for this monstrous act," I hissed.

"They won't find you, Alice. No worries, though. My Ella will comfort your ailing Latin lover," Mary Jean said.

Ella dumped more soil on my head. I raised my arms and attempted to block the dirt, feeling the true horror of a mother unable to defend her children: my two-month-old son left with Nanee Atwater and the second child inside my womb. I was thankful that I'd had enough sense to send my baby boy away with Nanee. My faithful servant and her father, Jacob, would protect Enrique's baby as if their lives depended on it.

"Please. I'm with child. Have you no soul?" I pleaded in Alice's voice, my words cracking from all of the screaming, my mind tortured by the image of a man who would never see the face of the child he loved ever again. Oh, the pain that Enrique will experience once word of this terrible moment reaches him. Thinking of his reaction ripped at my heart worse than the horrid act about to be committed by the two women above. Hysterical laughter and falling dirt were the only responses I got.

The soil turned into water flowing over my head, and the hole changed back to a ceiling and a shower head.

"They buried her alive." I gasped and slid down to a sitting position, sobbing for the loss of a girl's life and her unborn child, and I ached for someone to understand how I felt about losing my own daughter. Clenching my fists, I screamed.

Chapter 29

T *andie*

Later that evening, I sat in the study and examined the seven recovered pages of my manuscript while the burial scene played over and over in my head. My heart ran a marathon inside my chest. I made plans to head out and find Eric Fontalvo myself if he didn't show up soon.

I peeked outside the study's window and inhaled sharply. About fifty men and women stood along the edges of the forest on either side of Chelby Rose's driveway. A strange glow surrounded their bodies, and the ethereal beam wasn't a reflection of moonlight, either. The people belonged to many different races and genders, tortured souls brought together against their will by an entity with a power that could cross human barriers. I had never seen so many spirits at one time. All the psychic training in the world hadn't prepared me for this task.

"Poor souls," I whispered.

A whack-ker plunk came from the left side of the house, the part where the rose bushes grew, an area I couldn't see from the window.

I walked out of the study, shoved aside the curtains on the window beside the front door and scanned the yard. A manic Ella hacked at the rose bushes as if I had given her permission to do so. The girl held the ax high above her head and chopped the rose petals off with enough skill to rival Jason Voorhees. She swung at the bushes about three more times and then froze with the ax poised above her head. The tool thudded to the ground behind her, but Ella stood there with her arms extended as if she were still holding the handle.

A few more seconds passed and Ella released her imaginary ax, her body going slack as if she might fall over. She turned around in slow motion and faced Chelby Rose. I moved to the side a bit, out of sight to the crazed gardener, but in a spot where I could still see the girl.

The implications behind what I had witnessed in the last couple of visions rang inside my head, filling me with both courage and anger over what happened to Alice Chelby and her children, Eric's ancestors.

Watching Ella mutilate the roses, a vital part of Chelby Rose's history, fueled the flame inside me. I had been afraid of the world for almost an entire year, and I no longer cared to be the little girl running from a shadow demon in the woods. Pressing my lips together, I picked up Alice Chelby's necklace, cupping the delicate jewelry in my palm, and stepped outside.

"I told you to stay off my property." My voice rose as I headed toward Ella and my palm hurt from clutching the necklace so hard.

Peels of high-pitched girlish laughter echoed through the woods. The souls had floated back to whatever void they existed in. Ella took a step forward and picked up her discarded ax. She gave me one last insane grin, turned around and resumed her horror-movie chopping, paying no mind to a fuming, but shaky me standing beside her.

"I know what you did, Ella." The girl stopped moving as if contemplating whether to listen or not, and then started back chopping the rosebush, the delicate red petals flying in the air around her.

One of Eric's paint buckets sat behind Ella. The displaced gardener dropped the ax and turned toward a pile of branches she had cut away from the bush. Lifting an armful of roses and twigs as if she couldn't feel a thing, Ella turned around and dumped them in the bucket. She then picked up the ax and started to chop up the remains, sloshing the mixture around in what appeared to be water. The crazed way the girl moved along with my new knowledge of what Ella might be almost stole my courage to confront the girl. This was going to be my house, not Ella's or even the Chelby's, and this girl was no longer welcome on my property.

I spoke in a raspy voice. "I know who you are. What you are. You're not welcome here anymore."

Ella stopped moving as if I had cast a spell with my words.

She whirled around and said, "You think you can stop me? Ha! You couldn't even keep death's fetcher from taking your daughter." Peals of laughter filled the air.

"Don't you dare talk about my daughter! You're not welcome here anymore, Ella." I recalled the day I had heard Grandma Zee's voice in the slave cabin, and the way her soothingly strong vocals said, "Tell that demon to get behind you." I inhaled deeply. "I'm taking away your position. In other words, you're fired, for good, Ella. Now get off my property. Chelby Rose belongs to me now."

"Just what are you going to do if I don't leave? You don't deserve all my hard work, these flowers I bled to raise. I'm taking them back." She spun around, lifted the bucket of crushed rose remnants and poured the contents over her dress. The mixture of petals and prickly branches stuck to her dress in various places so she looked like a bloody doll created by a madman.

Going inside and calling for help was probably the most logical thing to do. However, I tasted revenge's bittersweet juices, and good sense wasn't in the recipe. Stepping away from the rose bed, I gathered strength from both Alice's necklace and Breena's ring, the one burning with life at my throat and the other in my hand.

"Demon, if you don't get off my property, I will send you back to the hell you charmed your way out of."

"You can't be calling me no demon. You're the witch girl who came back first!" Ella growled and charged at me, wrapping cold fingers around my neck. We toppled over and I found myself pinned underneath the girl.

"Not so brave, now, huh?" Ella hissed through gritted teeth, her hands firmly wrapped around my neck.

At once her gaze moved down to Breena's ring hanging around my neck and then to something beside my head. My gaze followed hers... Alice's necklace. I had dropped it just before Ella grabbed me. Her body tensed and her face twisted. Releasing the death grip on my neck, Ella scooted backward, her eyes fearful. The girl stood up and shook her head. "I'm so sorry. I didn't mean it. So sorry."

Without blinking or saying another word, Ella slowly turned around and walked away, leaving me gasping and shaking as I lay on the ground. What in Hades lair just happened here?

Chapter 30

*T*andie

After lifting myself up from the ground, I dusted my clothes off and headed back towards the house. Images of a tall glass of Duplin filled my head. From behind me, shuffling noises caught my attention. I spun around, ready to take on whatever insanity Ella harbored this time. Instead, I slammed into a wall of muscle... a six plus foot tall wall with blond hair and a crooked smile. "Saul? What the hell?"

"Lovely to see you as well, Tandie." He waggled his eyebrows and grinned.

I scoffed, headed up the steps and stopped at the front door, turning around after doing so. Saul followed me up to Chelby Rose's porch. He was silent and scruffy and strange: things that weren't normally associated with him. The Manolo Blahnik's on his feet were covered in mud and the edges of his trousers were wet. It was almost 10 o'clock at night and Saul looked like he just finished a hiking trip in the woods.

We sat down on the new white patio furniture Eric had brought home for me one evening, one of his many surprise gifts for Chelby Rose. Until Saul explained his odd behavior tonight, I wasn't about to invite him inside.

"Are you all right?" he said, leaning close and massaging my arms. Maybe one day he'd learn how to ask permission before touching someone. But with Eric away, a small part of me was glad Saul chose to come around.

"I'm—I...Saul, were you walking in the woods?" I asked, wondering if he witnessed my showdown with Ella.

Easing his hands away from my shoulders, he sighed and turned toward the forest. A grim expression masked his handsome features. "I still enjoy spending time alone in these woods. I'll be leaving to go back to Houston, soon, and I was feeling a little reminiscent." He gave me a sad but very enticing smile, one that would hold more power over me if he hadn't just done the creepy-man thing by walking out of the forest like a ghost.

"Why did you hire Eric to work on this house? And don't give me some sort of bogus southern charm answer about how I won't understand." We locked gazes and stared each other down. "You're hiding things. I can feel it. Please tell me the truth."

"The truth could hurt you," he said so softly I almost didn't hear him.

"And not knowing could kill me," I pleaded. It was time to tell him more. The key was to figure out just how much more. "Let's make a deal. I'll help you out by telling you a little something about me first. What do you say? Okay, here it goes. I'm connected to your family. I've had visions of Alice and Enrique Fontalvo. Hell, I think I even traveled back in time once or twice. I see her sister, Eliza, and her brothers' ghosts when I visit other parts of the town. They've disrupted things in the house. Should I go on?" He stayed silent, so I kept going.

"Now you expect me to believe you just decided to take a stroll through the woods? Right after I'm almost strangled to death by a madwoman, might I add?" I paused and pleaded with my eyes. "I think I'm going crazy, Saul."

He moved hair away from my neck and examined it. Closing his eyes, he said, "You should probably have called the authorities about that girl."

"Okay. That's a great idea. I tell the group led by a man who already considers me a murder suspect that someone who I believe is a reincarnation of a deity from the 1700's is stalking my house," I said. Saul flinched as if my words hurt him and focused his gaze back on my face.

"Tandie, I never meant for things to go this far. Let's go inside. I'll tell you what I can." He stood. I stayed. "Are you coming?" he asked.

"Saul, you're acting creepy. I feel like I need an escape route."

"Oh come on, Tandie. You can't be serious," he spat, sounding annoyed now. "If I were going to kill you, I would've already snapped your pretty little neck. Now get up and come inside." He held out a hand. I took it this time. Saul's intense blue eyes pulled so much out of a person. His business partners must jump at his every whim.

"Careful with that flirting syndrome. Your girlfriend, Sasha, might not like that so much," I said, hating the tinge of envy in my voice.

Grinning, he shook his head and said, "You're talking about Barbie-Bad-Ass again, I see. Careful, Tandie. You're starting to sound a touch jealous."

"In your wettest dreams," I said, challenging him with my gaze.

"Don't even go there with me," he said in an almost deadly low voice. I decided to take his advice. "Make a note of this. The woman you so lovingly nicknamed is my oldest sister."

"Sister? Right." Thinking back on that night, I could easily see the resemblance now. "Can I ask you something without you thinking I'm strange?" I asked.

"I probably won't answer it, but you can try."

"You're successful, good-looking, things like that, right? Why aren't you married? I mean, taking your sister out to functions is okay, but...Wow, none of this is coming out right," I finally said.

"Tandie, stop talking. Stop thinking." Even though he was smiling, the emotion didn't reach his eyes. "Right now, I wish I could take your mind away from this obsession with your visions, and be free of my own troubles as well." He seemed so sad and desperate.

"It's not that easy, I'm afraid," I replied. "I'm snatched back and forth between times. I feel like I'm caught up in an eternal vision, ripping me back through the past." And each hope, loss, and pain Alice Chelby felt was now mine. "Riding this wheel is torturous. "I can't just let it go, Saul."

"Come with me." Saul tugged at my hand, leading me through the doorway. Inside the hallway, he flicked on the light switch and led me up the stairs. How long did the confrontation between Ella and me last? Time had sped up during our spat... or so it seemed.

We continued walking until we came to the locked door that led up to the attic, the room that floored me with anxiety whenever I thought about entering it. The same room I tried to open during my first pathseeking venture into the past. He removed a key from his pocket and eased the relic into the lock.

"You had a way in the entire time?" I asked.

"You'll understand everything soon enough," he said in a whispery voice.

I took a step back and fought a strong desire to flee the place. "Are you hiding something up there? I don't know if I'm ready to go in that room."

Saul stepped in front of me, his movie-star face close to mine, and said, "You've come a long way, Tandie Harrison. You can do this thing. Trust me," he said in a voice that seemed sincere yet strangely untrustworthy. How could a man be so captivating but also be the source of so many troubling rumors?

As I stepped inside the musty air surrounded me and my psychic sensitivity was almost too much to bear. I stumbled a bit and Saul quickly grasped my arm, steadying me with his firm grip. "Again, I'm not sure I'm ready for this."

"Trust and confidence are the keys to the world's treasures," he said and led me toward the bottom stair.

I wanted to believe him, but something inside me couldn't shake the fear rising up in my heart. "Great. Remind me to use that line in my next chapter," I said, swallowing hard despite the tightness in my throat.

We climbed up eight steps and entered a room about the size of the kitchen. A strong mothball odor assaulted my nose. Emotions lingered in the room: sadness, laughter, fear, and the stolen joys of a woman making love to a man she could lose at any moment. And each sensation showered me with a force that made me gasp. This was the place where Alice Chelby spent almost an entire year of her life in hiding—scorned by a father who couldn't accept that his little girl had fallen in love with a fugitive.

"Thomas Chelby hired artists from all over the world to paint portraits of his family. At some point, they wound up wrapped and stashed away in this room," Saul said and ran his fingers over the top of a portrait of Eliza Chelby, my little ghostly friend in the flesh.

I gasped and examined each painting situated throughout the room. The people I'd seen during the escapades back through the past all sat staring at me: Thomas, Rose, Eliza, the two boys. One of the young males resembled the child I'd met at the Catsburg store. He wore the exact same outfit. However, his face was filled with life and his smile reminded me so much of Saul's.

Tingling with excitement and awe, I worked to control the multiple emotions shooting my way. One person was missing. The only Chelby I hadn't seen because I had connected to her body each time I went back to the past... Alice Chelby.

"Where is she?" I whispered, afraid to turn around. Saul eased over to me and gently turned my body toward the window facing the driveway. One of the larger easels sat beside the opening. The mystery portrait was covered in a brown tarp. We stepped toward the picture. My heart beat so hard I could feel the movement on my tongue.

Saul sighed deeply and yanked the tarp away, revealing the portrait of Rose and Thomas Chelby's eldest daughter.

The girl staring at us moved me with those brown eyes. Right away, I understood Sasha's reaction when Saul introduced the two of us the other night. Yes, the eyes of the girl in the picture were a different color from mine, but everything else about Alice was identical: the oval-shaped face, the small, but full lips, the pointed nose, the forehead that wasn't in proportion to the rest of her face, the black hair highlighted by auburn strands. It was as if I stared into a mirror. The only difference being the dark eyes and pale skin.

I took a couple of steps back, a flush of adrenaline tingling through my body. "What is that? Are you playing a sick joke?" I spat.

"Unfortunately, I'm not." He moved over to the closet and removed a cotton gusseted hanging bag, the kind used to store expensive clothing. Inside was a dress like the one Alice had worn in my vision, the scene I experienced in the shower. "This is what you wore the evening Virgil McKinnon was murdered."

"Stop it, Saul. This is too much strangeness for one night," I shook my head and turned away, my chest heavy with emotion.

"I don't want to hurt you, believe me, but you need to hear what I'm about to explain. You called me that night. Your voice sounded strange enough. Of course I was excited to hear it, as I always am. You told me to get over here and unlock the attic door. I did. You walked right over to this closet, removed the dress from inside a trunk, and put it on. You never said a word the entire time. At that point, I figured you were in a trance, a spell of some kind, so I played along." He stopped and cleared his throat before continuing. "You kept saying something about the beach over and over. I drove you out to Market Street. You told me to pull over just before we reached the Aeneid."

My heart beat so fast I was certain I'd have a heart attack. Although I wanted to believe Saul was making things up, instinct told me he was telling the truth. "And because my mind was consumed by Alice's memories, I walked out to the beaches, hoping to catch a glimpse of the ship in the water. I remember, now," I whispered.

Nausea and confusion fought inside me as I stared at Alice's face in the portrait, my twin from another lifetime. Connecting with a spirit was one thing, but finding out you were the reincarnated version of someone who lived almost three centuries ago was tough.

"Why didn't you tell me this before now? People saw me talking to Virgil. They think I had something to do with his murder."

He smirked and made a light laugh. "You would just have conjured it up to me trying to find another way to get you into bed."

"Don't show your true self, Saul. You've been doing well. What happened after Virgil approached me? That's the part that's still fuzzy." I anxiously waited for his answer.

"I spoke to him. Told him you were with me. He seemed well enough when he left us standing there. Besides cursing about some wine he needed to pick up from the store, he never once seemed agitated or scared."

The events of the past few days fell into place. Now Saul had confirmed Eric's suspicions: I was the woman Shania and Abby saw on the beach the night Virgil died.

I wanted to be alone and craved time to sort my thoughts without being influenced by Saul. The way he looked at me, that love-sick hopelessness in his eyes, made me feel uncomfortable now.

"My turn to fulfill my part of our deal. This attic was like a second home for me. My mother and father were never the types that would win parents of the year. And I wasn't the son who wanted to behave so that they could. I spent days at a time locked up here as punishment. What's an eight-year-old boy supposed to do with all that time on his hands?" His face was lost in a reverie, and his eyes held enough sadness to last a lifetime.

"The people in these portraits, especially Alice Chelby, became my best friends. My father despised me. My mother was busy keeping my sisters out of trouble. She forgot all about her worrisome son. My father remarried and lives in Houston now. You would think neither of my parents were living. I sometimes wonder. We have little to no conversation these days. These portraits became my world. I even started picking women who reminded me of Alice, the ultimate conversationalist."

"Just say it. The kind of woman who doesn't utter a word in protest," I said.

"Maybe. And then I saw you that first day a couple of months ago. The world was suddenly very different for me."

"I'm sorry they treated you that way." I felt a connection with this man, someone whose relationship with his father was even more broken than mine. At least I never really got the chance to know my dad before he vanished. Robert Jacobson took the dedication to his professorship to new levels. Saul was different, though. He'd always be forced to hold memories of being abused in his heart.

"That's the Chelby's cruel part of the Broken Heart Curse. Always pining for someone we can't have," Saul said. He stuffed his hands in his pocket and gave me the boyish sideways look. I had learned that when he hid his hands he wanted to say more. Staring at Alice's portrait, he said, "If I could help her find peace. If I could find her resting spot..." His voice trailed off, but I knew what he wanted to say.

"You mean, if you could find the place where the Cropseys buried her alive?" I finished for him. The look he gave me hitched at something in my chest.

"You know about that too? Of course, you would. Do you know why?" he whispered, moving closer so his spicy scent drifted all around me.

"Because I'm a reincarnation of Alice Chelby," I whispered.

"Can you be so sure?" He glanced at my lips, parting his own.

One thing I'd learned from divorce was I would never put another human being through the heartache I experienced. Eric was the only man on my mind. Even though I felt bad for Saul, and winded by the truth behind my dive into Alice's pathway, I refused to treat either of them the way my ex-husband did the two women in his life.

Tell my story, Tandie

Help me please.

The voices sailed into the room like a dark ballad playing on a gloomy day, a familiar medley that rattled my soul. This time, however, the voice was clear and sounded as thought it came from underneath the house. Or perhaps it came from inside the basement. Eliza called to me. I'd become familiar with her tones over the past few weeks.

"Did you hear that?" I asked Saul. He frowned.

"Hear what?" He glanced around the room.

"Nothing. It—it's nothing. I need time alone," I said. And to investigate the basement. "I'm sorry."

At once, Saul pulled back, studying my face as if I were a ghost or something fragile he shouldn't have touched. For the first time since we'd met, my heart actually ached for him. "I'll do as you say... for now." He turned and walked out the door, his shoulders slumped. Yet another good man haunted by a curse created by a mad woman and her daughter.

Chapter 31

E*ric* Eric got the call around midnight. Tandie said Chelby Rose's plumbing system had failed, and the faucets had gone nuts. She was headed downstairs to fix it but would need his help. She didn't sound like herself. Her high pitched voice sounded as though she were someone else.

Adding to the mysterious water problem of which he knew had been fixed weeks ago was Tandie's distress. She'd somehow gotten locked in the basement while attempting the repair. It took some fancy metal work to break through the lock. Eric strained with all his might, jimmying the ancient contraption until the clasp gave way.

"What the fuck?" Eric studied the situation. Water dripped from the basement ceiling as though someone had turned on a sprinkler system. There was only one problem, though. The plumbing running along the ceiling didn't have faucets. Right away, Eric knew a greater force was at play.

Tandie stood in an area at the far right side of the basement. She was wearing a thin light-colored nightgown that had somehow gotten soaked up to the waistline. Eric made his way over to her, trudging through ankle deep water. For a brief moment, her image faded in and out. Eric shook his head and thought he was seeing things for sure. Tandie's head turned his way, and she gasped once she noticed Eric. A faraway expression clouded her eyes as though she were looking at him and through him simultaneously.

"She's down there. In the water. We have to get her out!" she yelled as Eric came closer.

"Tandie—what? Who's down there?" Eric's studied the water. There was nothing but cement flooring.

"Eliza! She's in the water." Tandie shook her head and frowned. "I saw her. I'm not crazy."

"Course not." Eric put his arms around her, and she shoved him away. Eric stumbled back a bit, feeling startled by her strength.

"Look at me, Tandie. Look at me!" he demanded, grasping her head between his palms. She obeyed and focused on his face. That same heated sensation he'd felt the day he visited Abby at the Aeneid, that time when some invisible force had reacted to his anger surged through his body.

Her breathing evened out as she stared into his eyes. "There is nothing down there. It's all in your mind. Do you understand me?"

Slowly she nodded. And then he kissed her. The passion he released had been held back for too long. He no longer cared about any Broken Heart Curse, and tasting Tandie's luscious lips gave him all the resolve he needed. Her hands wound through his hair, pulling gently. The kiss lingered and Eric lost himself inside her touch, the taste, and the smell of her. And she gave off an intoxicating scent. With great hesitation, he pulled back and stared in her eyes, losing himself as each second ticked away. "Wow. I could never get tired of doing that, mi mujer bonita."

Tandie smiled. "How did you do that?"

"Do what?"

"You pulled me back from a nightmare. I felt you. Heard your voice."

"I've no idea," Eric said. Not a complete lie but not the total truth either. He'd always held this power of persuasion over people. This ability to convince others to do as he wished. It was only recently since his return to Bolivia that the ability had resurfaced.

"We need to get you out of here. Before you catch cold." With his arm wrapped around Tandie's soaked body, the pair headed back upstairs.

LATER THAT EVENING, Eric and Tandie sat on the sofa while recovering from the experience with Chelby Rose's plumbing.

"It was the Cropseys. You know that, right?" she said without taking her eyes away from the fire he'd started. The September weather had already turned abnormally cool. "I'm not sure how they're doing it. Reaching out from the grave. Screwing with my life. But I will stop them. Make them pay for what they did."

"The Cropseys? How so?" Eric asked. He'd heard his mother mention the name a long time ago. However, she had refused to go into details. Didn't want her family to be influenced by or give power to the entities by speaking their names.

"Those witches were powerful. More than we realize. I believe they're somehow linked to whatever killed my daughter... and they're right here in Bolivia. I believe the Cropseys hurt your friend. I've been assaulted by these waking visions. They're relentless as you can see. They never end. Been this way ever since I arrived in Bolivia."

"Do you think the frequency has something to do with Dark Souls coming around the corner?"

Several moments of tense silence drifted between the couple.

"I do. And time is winding down. I've no control over these new visions. They come in sporadic bursts. Norma warned me about using the ability without assistance." She turned towards Eric. "Your voice brought me back. Pulled me out off my pathway. How did you do that? Tell me the truth, Eric."

He hesitated and massaged the area between his eyebrows. How much should he tell Tandie? Would the truth spook her or cause her to harm herself the way it did the last girlfriend to whom he'd confessed?

"I'm a warlock. At least, according to my mother. Oh yeah, and half the townfolk around here. Surprise." He scoffed a laugh, and quickly turned serious once he looked at Tandie's expression. She hung on his words. "Kidding, Tandie."

"I didn't say a word. What's you story, warlock?"

Sighing deeply, Eric debated on how much he should confess. He settled on an abbreviated version of the misfortune he met twice, the month his father passed away, the reason he'd been branded a black sheep.

"A long time ago, shortly after my 24th birthday, my father passed away. I was angry and out of control. Didn't care whose feelings I hurt. You see, he was trying to find me that night. We'd argued over me not taking over the business. Even though I wasn't the oldest. Papa held high regard for my business sense. The curse took him that night. While he was out looking for me.

My girlfriend, Jenna, called me. Gave me the news. My mom was too heartbroken to talk."

"Eric, I'm so sorry." Tandie took my hand in hers.

"You won't be after you hear the rest."

"Try me," she said and settled down in her spot.

Eric shook his head and continued. Too late to turn back now. "The anger didn't go away. It intensified. I blamed myself. Hated myself. Took my frustration out on Jenna. She had her own issues. Battled depression on the regular. Making a sad, horrid story short, I said things to her a few nights after his funeral. Terrible things I can't ever take back. She took my words to heart. Sped off in her car. She'd told me I'd get my wish. To have her disappear. I didn't want to see her hurt. I was dumb as fuck. Saying something like that. Nevertheless, her car somehow slid off Lake Pontchartrain Causeway's bridge. No one knows how such a thing could happen. The bridge is secured by guard rails. She didn't deserve that fate. Word spread back here to Castle Hayne, of course. The black sheep son, the rebel finally did it. Killed his dad. Took out his girlfriend."

"And because both your father and Jenna passed away the same week, the lovely inhabitants of Castle Hayne and Bolivia blamed you. Or rather your powers as a male witch," Tandie said as though she'd taken the last thoughts out of my head.

"I might not be a warlock. But something shoved Jenna's car from the bridge." Eric wanted her to understand. Did he reveal too much?

"It's all tied together," Tandie said. "I'll figure it out. I promise."

Chapter 32

C helby Rose Swamplands
      September 1, 1749

"Mi Amor. I am so relieved to see you again. The past two months have been torturous since Colonel Dryden's men chased me away." Enrique held his fiancé close to his chest, basking in the scent of apples drifting around her auburn hair.

"I cannot stay long. Nanee told Mother and Father that I was asleep. Father will beat her if he finds out she told a lie for me. Or even worse, Grandmother will take a switch to her legs. My parents are too focused on my sick brothers to notice me. But I am almost certain I was followed by Ella. She frightens me so," Alice said.

"I will die before I allow them to separate us again, mi Amor. We will pour our love into this talisman." Enrique dangled the golden heart before Alice's eyes. "A gift my father gave to my mother long before he began sailing the vast seas."

She ran her fingers across the charm, her eyes marveling at the brightness of the gold. Turning around, Alice lowered her head and exposed the downy hairs hanging against her nape. "Put it on. I want this reminder of your soul to be close to my heart."

"Of course," Enrique said, reaching around Alice and fastening the necklace so the charm rested in the space between her bosom.

Alice turned around and beamed a smile at her lover. "I have the best news. Mother is on our side."

Enrique placed his calloused hands over her smooth ones, his handsome face beaming. "This is such good news. I pledge my eternal love to you, Alice, and our children."

"Let no one take this joy from us. With this golden heart as a shield, our love will be bound for eternity." Alice smiled at her secret fiancé. And then Enrique kissed her with a passionate fervor, a gesture of affection that sent electric sparks up and down her spine.

At once, dog barks broke the fiery spell. Their owners were still far off in the distance, but getting closer.

"Oh no, they followed me. Dryden will arrest and hang you. Flee, my love," Alice said, her chest tightening with worry. How could the Fates be so cruel? Could they not allow them just one moment of stolen bliss?

"This is the voodoo woman and her daughter's doing. We must leave," Enrique pleaded.

"No. I'll only slow you down. You must go on without me," Alice said, even though her heart was breaking.

"Never." Enrique tightened his hold on Alice.

"They won't hurt me. I'll find you later. Please, don't make me beg." Easing out of his grip, Alice reached behind her head, removed the locket from around her neck and placed the trinket in Enrique's hands. "For protection."

"And what will protect you?"

"I have love and faith on my side. What else do I need?" Alice said bravely.

"I will lead them in the opposite direction. Rush back to Chelby Rose as fast as you can. I am a soldier. I will throw the dogs off our trails. And then, I will return for both you and our son. I swear to it." Tears streamed down Alice's cheeks, but she still found enough courage to smile.

Struggling to control the grief raging inside, Enrique pulled her up against his chest. "We will be free to love, Amor. No matter what may come. We shall be together. I swear it," Enrique said, his eyes fierce with strong conviction.

"Yes, free to love our entire lives along with our children. I told Jacob to meet us tomorrow night. He will show us the way to reach the underground leaders. They will take us to our new lives up in the northern territories," Alice said.

She grasped her fiancé's hands and positioned his palms over her stomach. Their second child was developing well inside the womb. Alice could already feel the flutters of life. Enrique embraced his fiancée, clinging to her as if his very soul depended on how well he'd remember this moment.

"Now flee, my love. Imagine my face as inspiration along your journey," Alice said. Enrique pulled away from her body, turned around and ran out the door. Alice moved to the doorway and stared until his form disappeared in the trees.

Walking out of the cottage, she inhaled deeply and headed in the opposite direction, dodging tree limbs and fighting the fears she held for the safety of her unborn child. Out of breath, she stopped and leaned on a large oak tree. Sharp pain ripped through her abdomen. Crumpling her face, she bent over and clutched her stomach. Fear seized her mind. Something was wrong with the baby, but she needed to hurry back to Chelby Rose. By thinking of her fiancée, she found the strength to keep moving.

AT THAT MOMENT, MY pathseeker's spirit left Alice Chelby's traumatized body and drifted upward, the vision focusing on an oak tree growing in a spot across from where Alice had stood. A girl with a familiar head of blonde ringlets stepped into view from behind the trunk... Ella Maud Cropsey.

"Yes, go. Flee, my love." She mocked Alice's voice. "For you shall never see yours again."

ENRIQUE FOUND OUT ABOUT his second child the night before Alice was murdered. Could the story of the two star-crossed lovers get any more tragic?

While Eric was away the following morning— he'd gone to buy a wet-dry vacuum for drying out the basement—I kept reading Alice's diary, falling into a vision each time I ventured into a different entry. This new way I could use the sight both terrified and intrigued me. To figure out the next part of this puzzle, I needed the help of someone outside the main group. At the library, I'd managed to channel Rose Chelby's spirit and I needed to do that again.

There was no way to deny I could see Alice's memories without reading the whole entry. The news that I had sleepwalked my way on to a murder scene and while I was dressed up in a dead girl's outfit messed with my head. And the vision I experienced after I found Alice's diary was so real that it gave me the first orgasm I'd had in years.

I had created characters based on the people of this town before I even heard of Chelby Rose, shaped the perfect male protagonist and then fell for the man I modeled him after, someone I'd never met until we ran into each other at the Aeneid.

The one element that didn't fit in the story was my daughter's spirit. Breena watched over me while I slept, speaking to me through dreams. Why? What did I need to do to help my daughter's spirit move on? A selfish part of me wanted Breena to stay, but the maternal instinct was still there. That part of me wanted to see my daughter resting in peace.

The next entry started where my last vision left off. This was the final segment in the diary. The events took place sometime after Alice made her way back to Chelby Rose, and just before Mary Jean and her daughter, Ella, buried her alive. There was only one paragraph where Alice wrote about Enrique's arrest. She had intended to go see the warden himself and beg for his release. The jagged letters, the short sentences, and the raw emotion in this entry gave me enough details to sense Alice's desperation. I inhaled and prepared for an emotional ride.

Closing my eyes, I concentrated on the way I felt the first time I linked to Rose Chelby's spirit. The sense of being a weightless soul drifting through history came faster this time along with a what felt like a shock of electricity, a bothersome side effect that worsened each time I used my pathseeking ability. I slipped through a serene white void, a place where the living and the dead crossed paths. Sailing out of the darkness, I connected with Rose Chelby's spirit.

CHELBY ROSE: SEPTEMBER 4, 1749

Mary Jean Cropsey's daughter, Ella Maud, died two nights ago. The virus took her out just the same as the sickness did many other children in the colony. Rose suspected that her death came as a surprise to Mary Jean, the witch that created the disease. Now she wasn't only a woman with a dark heart, she was also a mother hell bent on revenge.

Rose Chelby and her youngest daughter, Eliza, stood on the porch. An unusually strong wind howled around them and blew Rose's fiery red hair around her face. She'd sent Alice out to find Thomas. Her husband and daughter should've been back with the doctor long before now.

Sammy and Joseph's virus had gotten worse over the past three days. The epidemic had spread through the community like a plague, attacking mostly young children first. But this wasn't a disease caused by animals. This was the work of a witch's hand, a curse created by a dark soul.

Rose turned to her daughter. "Eliza, you must find Alice. Keep to the trees and stay quiet. You don't want to attract the wrong attention." She didn't want to frighten the girl by telling her to watch out for the Cropseys.

"Are Sammy and Joseph going to die?" Eliza asked.

"No, baby. Your father will return soon. He'll bring the doctor. Do not fret. Concentrate on finding your sister." Rose coughed in her handkerchief, hiding the blood she knew was on the cloth away from her daughter's eyes.

"I'm scared, Mama. What if I get lost?" Eliza asked.

"You are a child of nature. Use God's gifts to help guide you. The same way we always do when we take our walks through the woods."

Eliza nodded, her eyes wide. Rose scanned the area beyond the forest. The daylight would fade in another hour or so. "Just pretend Mother is with you. If you do not find your sister on the path, then keep going. Do not stop until you reach Jacob Atwater's cabin. I pray that you dare not look back. No matter what. Do you hear me, child?"

Eliza's face crumpled and her tears fell. Upstairs, Samuel and Joseph's wails sailed through the house like a crescendo of death, the music of a mother's worst nightmare.

"It was them, wasn't it? Those two bad women made you, Sammy, and Joseph sick," Eliza said. She was gifted with a great deal of wisdom for such a young child.

There was no reason to hide the truth from her any longer. "Yes, my daughter. The bad women did this. You must hurry. We cannot let them know you are not sick. Go now. Keep to the big oaks as I instructed. Look for your sister on the other side of the swamp," Rose said.

"I don't want to leave you, Mama." Eliza's voice cracked.

"I'll walk with you to the edge of the forest," Rose said.

Rose and Eliza scurried to the swamp's edge, the place where she believed Alice went after she heard her Spanish lover had been arrested. Alice loved with all her heart just as her mother did, even when loving someone often brought pain and heartache.

Rose loved her grandson, Enrique and Alice's lovechild. It did not matter one bit that he was illegitimate. But Thomas was harder to convince. Two months passed before he found enough forgiveness in his heart to even venture up the stairs to visit with his daughter let alone her child. From inside the house, the boys wailed louder.

"I love you, Mama." Eliza threw her arms around her mother, her tiny frame trembling.

"I love you too, baby. Now go before I throw myself into the swamps out of despair," Rose said, her chest burning with both sickness and heartache. Eliza choked back her sobs, turned and bolted into the woods.

Rose stared after her daughter a moment and then forced her feet to move back toward the house. Just knowing that one of her children would be safe from the virus renewed her strength. However, the comfort of victory was a fickle creature. As Rose moved closer to the porch she fought the despair that resulted from seeing what awaited her return. Mary Jean blocked her path to the doorway.

"Stand aside, devil's wife," Rose demanded, a cold chill easing its way through her veins.

The woman clucked her tongue. "You think your little girl escaped? The fever took my daughter. And it'll take yours too. Both of them. Too bad you don't know how to bring them back." A wicked smile played across the woman's face, but it was a shaky one.

"Your black soul will not bring anything back but the devil himself. Now stand aside." Rose shoved past Mary Jean, walked up the steps and opened the front door, feeling thankful the Atwaters had given her a talisman to keep the Cropseys out of the house.

"I cannot take the curse back now. It will be yours and your sons' lives for Ella's. Thomas loved me best. He loved me and he loved our daughter. Do you hear?" Mary Jean screamed as she stood outside the doorway.

Rose stopped at the stairway, turned around and gave Mary Jean a look that made the woman take a step back. "You were nothing to Thomas, but a mere fling with a desperate whore. Your daughter died because of you." Rose narrowed her eyes.

"Throw your high and mighty words at me all you want, Rose Chelby. But you all will pay for how my Ella was treated at the end."

Samuel's scream jerked Rose back to reality. She turned and rushed up the stairs, taking them two at a time.

ROSE'S PIERCING SCREAM echoed throughout the void and sent a chill down my spine. All the while, Mary Jean's last words continued to linger in the air, ringing in my ears as the connection to the past faded away. The next moment, I felt a sharp stab of pain coursing through me, and I was jolted back into reality.

Mary's voice had called out, echoing through the ripple in time. "That's right. Run and scream, Rose Chelby. Tonight, you lose everything. Know that your daughters' spirits will forever roam the swamplands. Humility walks among the mighty Chelbys on this night. Feel the pains of a mother scorned by the death of her broken-hearted daughter."

Chapter 33

andie

T I sat at the bottom of Chelby Rose's stairway, rocking back and forth, my chest pounding with grief, my legs too weak to stand. Feeling like a prisoner of the past, I held both Alice's heart necklace and Breena's topaz ring in my right hand, the combined charms of two ill-fated souls. Eliza never stood a chance against the Cropseys. And like his daughter, Thomas had fathered a child outside of wedlock which meant that Ella and Alice were both enemies and sisters in love with the same man, Enrique Fontalvo.

Lowering my head, I closed my eyes and tried to ground the spinning sensation. Fear and sorrow had won. Being ripped between the past and present was too much. I should never have come here. Taking on the wrath of two witches was something beyond my ability.

Knocks echoed around me. Were they real or part of a vision? I couldn't tell the difference anymore, and I didn't have enough strength left to answer the door even if they were genuine. The intensity of the pounding increased. Slamming my fists over my ears, I willed the taps to stop and they did. For the longest time, silence filled the space between the front door and the stairway.

And then I lifted my head, slowly opened my eyes and focused my teary vision on Eric Fontalvo kneeling in front of me, sadness in his handsome face. A flush of adrenaline tingled through me. "You came back to me," I said and threw my arms around his neck, being careful not to drop the charms. Embracing me with reassuring strength, Eric pulled my body up against his.

"Oh my God, where have you been?" I whispered in his ear, enjoying his woodsy scent and wanting to savor the taste of him. "I thought you were never coming back."

"Are you kidding? And miss the chance to see you suit up in the paint shorts again? Don't think so." He pulled back, stared in my eyes and wiped away my tears with his thumb. "We still have to clean up all that water, and the—"

"Shut up and kiss me before I scream." I barely finished the sentence before he scooped me up in his arms.

On the way up the stairs, Eric parted my lips with his, exploring my mouth with his tongue. A groan or something like a moan or maybe even a growl came from the back of his throat. It was a hungry kiss, one that had crossed over centuries of time, waiting to be experienced again.

I inhaled and held the breath as Eric carried me towards the bedroom I hardly ever slept in. And for the first time since arriving at Chelby Rose, I looked forward to being in the master room. This house belonged to me now, and it felt right for us to consummate our relationship this way.

Moving closer to the bed, he deepened our kiss. With my free hand, I ran my fingers through his thick hair, something I'd wanted to do since we first met. The strands were soft and silky just like I knew they'd be. A fire ignited in my belly, spreading through both my body and my heart filled with joy, an emotion I hadn't experienced in forever.

Suddenly, my feet touched cold floorboards. Coordinated as always, Eric managed to set me down without breaking our kiss. The moment was as if we had created two lifelines, one providing the air to keep the other going. Two people scarred by a past colored by relationships with the wrong people were getting to know one another on an intimate level. Tonight was well worth the wait.

With hesitation, I broke our kiss and lifted my right hand between us. Eric's gaze moved to my palm, his face darkened by lust. "I need to set these down." He nodded, lowered his head and nibbled my neckline as I turned toward the table beside the bed, being careful to set Alice's heart necklace and Breena's ring down so the two trinkets lay close together.

Focusing back on Eric, I tugged at the white tee shirt he was wearing, my fingers grazing over his six pack abs as I grasped the bottom. He shuddered and moved his face away from mine, allowing me to pull the shirt over his head and toss it to the side. Moving his lips back to mine, he continued our kiss with even more passion. His hands slid over the contours of my hips and down to my thighs where he grasped the hem of my shirt dress. Outside the window, the annoying tree tapped against the side of the house and the infamous Bolivian wind howled on, but nothing could stop the sinfully sweet sensations flowing through my body.

Eric's hands grazed the bare skin of my thighs and then my abdomen as he slid the dress up over my breasts, stopping at the point underneath my arms. He moved back for yet another second, his gaze lingering on the contour of my breasts. "Raise your arms," he whispered. I obeyed right away. He finished sliding the dress over my head, tossed it aside and pulled me up against his body, his bare skin setting all my nerve endings on fire at once.

I moved my hands down to the button on his jeans, unsnapping them. Eric wiggled free of both his pants and briefs in a flash, and I was grateful for his assistance. I would never have gotten them off without busting up the moment. We shared a small laugh as if he'd heard my thoughts and fell backward, our bodies thudding on the bed.

Our legs and arms tangled together, and I found myself caught up in a kiss like none I had ever experienced before. Eric's sleek hands popped the hook on my bra and his mouth left mine, leaving my swollen lips yearning for its return. He worked his way down to my nipples and covered the delicate skin in heat from his mouth as he kissed, tugged and sucked. I arched my back up to him, losing myself in the moment.

Gasps of pleasure escaped my lips as I called out his name in between them. In response, he moved to my waist, slid his fingers between the elastic on top my panties and slid the delicate fabric down my legs and over my feet. And then he crushed his body down on top of mine, lifted my left leg over the back of his thigh and moved his hand between my legs, gently massaging my sex that was wet with pleasure.

"Damn, you're blowing my mind," he whispered. "Put your hands on me." I did as he asked. Ran my hands up and down his cock, feeling him jerk each time my thumb grazed the sensitive tip.

Lifting up a bit, he positioned his erection between my legs. However, the expression on his face was a pained one and his eyes were closed. A struggle. That's what he was doing. Deciding how far to go. Or maybe even if this was the right thing to be doing. "If we do this, I don't know what might happen," he whispered.

"And if we don't, then do we wait another three hundred years?" I asked, watching him frown, waiting for him to understand the meaning behind my words.

"I dreamed about you before I ever met you. You're everywhere. My mind, my visions, my book. We're soulmates, Eric. Reincarnations of people who lived long ago... Enrique and Alice." There, I'd said it. He smiled and a flash of recognition moved across his face. "You've seen something too, haven't you?" His silence answered for him. What did he see?

He moved closer, his lips brushing my ear, and said in a low voice, "We are the same, you and I, Tandie." I looked up into his gaze and knew, right then and there, that he believed it. He believed what I did. That this was more than just physical attraction. It was a connection beyond anything we could comprehend. We had been connected since another time and another place.

"Take away my pain, this loneliness. Show me that you believe I need you," I whispered. His mouth came down on mine just as intense as before and not weakening at all.

"Protection," he said, bringing a hitch of reality back with him. He hopped off the bed, fumbled in his pants and returned with a foil packet.

"Do you always carry condoms around?" I asked.

He gave me a wicked look as he straddled my legs and ripped open the packet. "Tandie, I wasn't exactly a priest before I came here."

"Oh. Okay," I said, watching him work the rubber up his enticingly gorgeous shaft and feeling a touch jealous of the other women. His entire body was perfect: dark hair tousled over smoldering eyes, ripped abs, muscular arms, and satiny dark skin...a Spanish Adonis.

Bending back down, he clamped on to my right breast, and I turned into a waterfall again, my love a liquid feeding a higher power. Eric worked his way back to my lips, kissing and exploring my mouth until I writhed underneath him. "No more waiting," he said, plunging inside me with one well-timed thrust. I cried out and grasped his buttocks, shifting his fullness in and out of my sex in a rhythm that rocked every organ in my body. No other man existed. I had found my soul mate, the one who completed me. Against all odds, we had returned to each other.

Eric and I came together many more times as we swept away two and a half centuries' worth of waiting.

ERIC HAD ALWAYS BELIEVED he would never again feel the mind-blowing ecstasy he felt when he and Tandie shared their bodies. Like himself, she was lonely, hurt and rejected. A dark part of her soul called to him. Why? Because he felt the same way. Tortured by a curse that kept him at a distance from the women in his life, Eric's relationships had suffered. That was until the day he spotted Tandie. Life as he knew it changed. There was an instant connection, a charge that rattled something in both his mind and heart.

Tandie not only ignited him sexually, she also set his heart to beating again. Her body so perfect and superbly responsive called to him. The things she said last night drifted through his mind. She had wanted to know if he'd experienced anything supernatural. He never mentioned seeing the ghostly light outside her grandmother's cottage or the little girl who healed his wound with a single touch. And he most definitely didn't utter a word about the dream he had of a man making love to a woman as they lay on a mattress made of straw, or the sexual feelings that rocked his body after he woke up.

Tandie wanted him to believe the two of them were the reincarnated spirits of Enrique and Alice. Even though he didn't say a word when she asked for his thoughts last night, a deep part of him did believe the concept of soul mates could be true. What other explanation might there be for his dream about making love to a woman who bore an incredible resemblance to the one lying beside him?

He would try hard to believe for the woman sleeping so peacefully next to him. For Tandie he would fight through a lifetime of curses just to see a smile on that beautiful face. And he was going to find a way to keep her safe no matter what he had to do.

After watching her sleep for the past hour or so, Tandie finally began to stir. Her face was calm, and she barely tossed or turned as she slept last night, a breathtaking beauty. The painful way she looked when he found her slumped on the stairway had vanished. Eric made a mental promise to make sure she never suffered again.

"Wow. The sun is super bright this morning." Tandie draped an arm over her face.

"I'm pretty sure we fired up the curse last night," Eric said jokingly, trying to hide the worry in his voice.

He propped up on his elbow and stared down at her. She moved her arm away and gave him a sexy smirk. How could he think clearly with her looking at him that way? And those eyes, one light brown and one hazel-green, could hold him under her spell forever. As if she heard his thoughts, she smiled and closed her gorgeous irises.

"I know what happened to Alice, Rose, and the Chelby boys," Tandie declared, her eyes still closed. Sighing and focusing her gaze back on Eric, she described the things that took place in her vision with Rose Chelby. She told him about Alice getting buried alive while she was pregnant with Enrique's second child, and she mentioned how her grandmother's spirit had explained the way to break the Cropsey curses. There was a trinity: Breena's pinky ring, Alice's heart, and something else called the lucky one. The items represented the three babies who met early deaths.

Each cruelty, everything she told him, dug deeper into his soul. Clenching his jaw, he thought of his brother, Javier. He should be with his family right now. Yet he wasn't. Instead he was chasing ghosts and false leads all while dealing with Virgil's death... or rather his unsolved murder. Eric had no choice but to succeed. Failing to find the answers now would mean he'd failed his family twice.

"You saw all of that in a vision?" Eric said, his mind swimming with curiosity.

"Not everything. I still don't know what happened to Eliza Chelby. For some reason, I feel like I have to know."

"And Enrique?" Eric asked.

"Cursed by Mary Jean's words."

"The words of a witch," Eric said, his face hardening. "They're what killed my father. We're always leaving widows to raise children by themselves." He studied her expression, making sure he got the point across. No one should be put through that. That damn curse was why he resisted Tandie for so long. "My parents always believed the Cropsey curse was responsible."

"I believe they've somehow returned," Tandie said.

"Doubtful," Eric said. But something quivered in his chest. A small part of him wanted to believe she spoke the truth. The logical man in him wasn't trying to hear it.

"Why do you think it's doubtful? You didn't sound that way last night. Besides, I've seen Mary Jean Cropsey before," Tandie said, lifting up on her elbow. "Just like I saw the Chelby boys. And don't forget Eliza, the ghost girl who led me to the cellar downstairs, the one you never found, Mr. Contractor."

"That's because I wanted to trick your ghosts. Make them think they did something special for you," Eric said, trying to lighten the moment for his sake as well as hers.

"Don't be mean," Tandie said and paused. She was in deep thought about something, or maybe someone. He couldn't help but to wonder if that person was Saul Chelby. "I think powerful spirits can be reborn as someone else. Especially malevolent deities like dark witches."

"I believe they can too," he said in a low voice, recalling the way he'd felt last night when they were caught up in passion. The admission was a start, a small victory for Tandie. The smile she gave him touched his heart, and he could feel the heat in his growing erection. "I'm sorry I left the other day. I had to sort some things out."

"What things?"

"About us. My past. My brother."

"How is he?" she asked. Pulling Tandie over to him, he turned her body so their chests were against one another. Eric savored the feel of her velvety soft skin up against his, and he was certain she felt his hardness against her leg.

"He's about as good as he can be given the circumstances." He buried his face in her hair, moved his free hand between their chests and cupped her breast. She responded by grinding her hips against his leg.

"You should've told me about the curse long before now. We could've worked things out sooner. Together," Tandie said in a small voice.

"I think we've worked things out together very well," Eric said, a mischievous smile spreading across his lips. He turned his face away from the bright sunlight coming in through the window, the one with the tree tapping against the panes.

"We'll find a way to end that curse," Tandie said. "Your brother will be fine. So will my Baby B." She muttered the last sentence so low that he barely understood the words.

Eric sighed. Trouble clouded his mind. If there were one thing he inherited from his father, then that would be how to fully appreciate the mind, body, and powerful allure of a good woman. This time, he was in deep and for the long haul. He lifted her chin so she stared in his eyes and then he kissed her. Lost in Tandie's embrace, Eric purged his mind. Soon, trouble became nothing more than a word blowing away in the wind.

Chapter 34

T*andie*

Later that evening, Eric and I reluctantly emerged from our haven. We headed outside and stood on the front porch. Rose Chelby's voice flooded my mind as I examined the front lawn for evidence of the shadow people. The somber thoughts disappeared at once as Eric pulled me into his arms. I intended to put all the power I had in me toward finding a way to free his family of the Broken Heart Curse and to help Saul find Alice and Eliza's bones. One family's release meant freedom for the other one. In the end, doing so will save both mine and Breena's spirts as we end the terror reign created by the witches that started all this.

"It's time to put Bolivia out of its misery. The Chelby spirits deserve to rest as well as our own," I said, leaning my forehead against Eric's chest.

Moving his hand down my left side, Eric found mine and laced our fingers together. Lifting my chin, he kissed me. "I love that I can kiss you freely now," he said with our lips still touching.

"So do I," I said, kissing him again and parting my lips. His tongue laced with mine, filling my body with warmth and tingles. Damn this guy is addictive.

Eric's breathing increased and his skilled hands moved over my body, caressing all the right places in the most seductive ways. The sudden surge in hormones sent me whirling on both a mental and physical level.

Something vibrated in his pocket. He pulled away, his face flushed and his breathing ragged as he removed his cell phone from his pocket. Frowning, he slid his finger across the screen and passed a hungry, dark look my way, a sexy gesture that made me want to smash the phone for interrupting us. After listening to the caller a moment, Eric's face changed.

"What's wrong?" I asked, the damned anxiety sneaking back in.

"It's the hospital calling. Hold on." He held up his index finger. "Detective Newman, my favorite person. How is your day going so far? I hear you enjoy harassing—" He stopped mid-sentence and turned my way. A different kind of darkness clouded his handsome face. "I'll be right there."

Sighing, he closed his eyes, placed both hands on the back of his neck and lifted his head toward the sky.

Damn. He even makes stress look sexy.

"What happened?" I asked, dread creeping along my spine.

It took a few moments for him to answer. "Abby's in the hospital. Leroy thinks she was attacked by the same person who killed Virgil."

"You mean the Cropseys?" I asked. "Or whatever this thing is they're controlling."

Eric closed his eyes and sighed. "Perhaps. But I was referring to the psycho who murdered Virgil."

"Perhaps? How can you stand there and act like none of the things we said last night matter today?" I demanded, my insides clenching.

As if he heard my thoughts, his face softened even though his body was still tense. He pulled me into his arms and buried his face in my hair. "I still remember everything. We kind of complement each other. My stoic hard assness to your ghostly visions." He pulled back and glanced deep into my eyes. "It's kind of like good and evil. For one to exist, the other has to hang out somewhere in the equation too."

"Why, Mr. Fontalvo, I do believe my poetic nature is rubbing off on you," I said. Staring in his eyes, I felt a pull in my stomach and the beginnings of an ache between my thighs, the kind of sensation that brought us together as a couple. "I can go to the hospital with you."

"I don't think that's a good idea. If there are people... or— or spirits connected to the Cropseys, they seem to be most interested in me. You said that Rose Chelby placed a protection spell over this house, right?"

I nodded. Eric was trying to show me how much he wanted to believe in my theories. Was he starting to believe I was his reincarnated soulmate? I never discussed the extent of his relationship with Abby before. Obviously something happened between them.

"Do I just sit here and twiddle my thumbs? You know that's not my style, Eric."

Sighing, he moved his lips into a thin line and said, "You're not sitting or pining. I'm keeping you safe. Promise me you won't go looking for Eliza Chelby's grave until I get back?"

No way do you get both the cake and the girl, Eric Fontalvo. I nodded and crossed my fingers behind my back.

"All right. I'm holding you to it." He looked deep in my eyes.

"What about you? I think we should avoid splitting up tonight." My heart sank. I hated feeling the way I did about Abby, but deep wounds take longer to heal than the smaller ones.

"I can take care of me. Now stop worrying." Eric leaned over and brushed his lips across mine. "Go back inside. I'll call you from the hospital." Eric turned, hopped in his Jeep and disappeared around the bend in the driveway.

Standing on the porch under the darkening evening sky, I struggled to control my anxious mind. A shuffling sound came from the woods to the left side of the house, and a light flashed in the area near the old swamplands, the same place Saul emerged from a few nights ago. This time Eliza Chelby's ghost appeared outside the trees.

She waved her arm for me to follow.

Chapter 35

D*ark Souls Day*
     Eric

"She's lucky to be alive. The doctors said the wounds on her neck were close to her main artery," Detective Leroy Newman said.

Standing outside the window to Abby's hospital room, Eric massaged his temple as he watched his best friend's sister fight for her life. Tubes extended from all over her body. Her face was bruised and a large gauzy bandage covered her neck. The dressing reminded him of the kind used to treat whiplash victims. Her right leg lay above the covers, and the cast on it extended in the air. Vibrant Abby had been reduced to something he didn't even recognize. What tore at Eric the most was that he suspected the attack was somehow related to him and that godforsaken curse.

"It's interesting. The people you know keep winding up dead or injured, Fontalvo," Leroy's voice said beside him.

"Yeah, well I'm cursed. If you're not careful, I just might toss a dose of bad luck at you next," he said meeting the detective's critical gaze.

"Is that a threat?" Smiling, the detective reached into his pocket and pulled out a blowpop, taking time to carefully remove the wrapper before he popped the candy in to his mouth.

After a beat, he removed it and said: "I'm about tired of getting threats from all of you people. That freak master, Saul Chelby, threatened me when I questioned his little psychic a while back. Now you're doing the same thing. Makes me want to believe your girl really is a witch."

Eric stiffened. The slippery detective caught his change in mood right away. "Whoops. Did I say something shocking?" He gave Eric a hard stare. "The way I figure things, is that you didn't do this. Nah, your balls never grew that big. But either Chelby or our little psychic celebrity knows who did. That is, if one of them didn't try to take out the victim's sister themselves. No, I got it. They're working together. What do you think?"

Eric narrowed his eyes and clenched his fists. "That's enough."

Yeah, Detective Newman's news took him by surprise. Tandie had never mentioned how she was able to get inside the locked attic. Or why she believed Saul wanted her to find the bones of his ancestors. Hearing the news from the sarcastic know-it-all detective made his stomach boil. "What's your point? Why are you even here, Leroy?"

He moved closer to Eric, closing the distance to less than a foot. "That little lady lying in there all busted up. She's the reason I'm here. Our killer slipped up. They left her for dead in the woods by the old swamplands. She found her way back to the road. When I got here, she managed to tell me one last thing before she passed out. She said: 'Tell Miss Harrison I know she didn't mean to do it.'"

Every drop of blood drained from Eric's face.

"Tomorrow I'm hauling her ass in. And there isn't a damn thing you or Saul Chelby's lawyers can do to stop me." Leroy turned and stalked away, shoving through the doors at the end of the ward. Eric moved his gaze back to Abby, his mind whirling, and his heart screaming that he'd been a fool to trust emotion again.

Deep in thoughts of how he'd been such an ass the last time he and Abby spoke, he almost didn't feel the fingers on his left shoulder. He spun around and found Shania McKinnon's face staring back at him. Puffy, red eyes studied his face and she looked as if she'd lost a few pounds since he last saw her.

"I heard what the detective said. I'm sure he's wrong about Tandie," she whispered, embracing him. This time, he welcomed the attention. Things had turned on him, and now he wasn't sure where to begin... or who to believe. Pulling apart and taking a step back, he examined the face of Virgil's widow.

"I've been here ever since they brought Abby in," Shania said. "The doctors aren't sure if she'll make it through. I could lose the last connection I ever had with Virgil if..." She broke down and started sobbing. Eric embraced his friend's widow and let her cry on his shoulder.

She glanced up at him after composing herself. "I'm sorry, I didn't mean to attack you again. A little Abby humor."

"She's tough, Shania. Stronger than any of us," Eric said truthfully.

"But I'm not. I could really use a break from all the hospital odors," Shania said, attempting a weak smile. "Wanna go grab a beer or something?"

"Sure, why not. I need a few minutes with Abby first, though."

"I'll meet you in the lobby by the parking garage." She smiled again and walked away. The way she moved made her seem like a ghost walking in a formerly vibrant woman's body.

Eric turned, walked through the door of Abby's room and stopped at her bed. Her makeup-free face wore a peaceful expression. He couldn't remember the last time he'd seen her so calm. Maybe back when they were in elementary school. Sometime before adulthood entered the picture. Sometime before her brother was mauled by a maniac.

He reached out, moved a long strand of auburn hair away from her face, kissed her forehead and positioned his lips beside her right ear. "I will find whoever did this to you. I swear on my life, I will." Standing tall, he turned, left Abby's room and headed toward the parking garage.

The lobby beside the elevator was empty. No Shania. No anyone. Figuring she must've needed fresh air, Eric trudged out to the parking lot, stopping just before he reached his Jeep. Shania's small gold purse lay on the ground, the contents scattered. A handwritten note was attached to the side of it. Eric picked up the bag, pulled the yellow paper off and read the words, his heart racing:

If you ever want to see your dead friend's wife alive and in one piece again, then you'll be at the Old Catsburg Store across from Sunset Beach by midnight. Bring the psychic, the librarian, and Saul Chelby.

No police.

Chapter 36

T*andie*
I followed the little girl through the yard and deep into the woods surrounding Chelby Rose. The child's bright light filled the forest around us. This trek took me even further than my previous venture, the day I found the heart necklace. I inhaled deeply and examined my surroundings. Eliza Chelby had disappeared.

Soon, I'd be alone in complete darkness, and I was standing inside a forest where a serial killer could be hiding out.

Each bush, every cricket, even the unseasonal mosquitoes swiping at my skin added to the strange atmosphere. Somewhere in the distance, an owl hooted. The situation reminded me too much of the time I got lost in the forest surrounding the slave cabin. A small part of me wanted to believe Eliza's spirit led me into the woods and abandoned me on purpose. Deep inside, I knew better. Eliza Chelby had been nothing but helpful so far. I was certain that me being led into the woods wasn't done with ill intentions. The child wanted to show me something.

"Okay, Eliza. You have to help me. What do you want me to see?" I said, my voice quivering. A snap to the right made me jump and my heart thudded. The darkest areas within the trees played tricks on my eyes. If I had to hide I was pretty sure this ragged breathing would give me away.

"Eliza!" I called out louder this time.

Another snap! The woods around me were almost dark now. Stupid idiot for not bringing a flashlight.

I turned in the direction of where I believed Chelby Rose was situated just before the area around me lit up. Eliza's ghostly light wasn't doing it this time, though. I had been transported into a vision.

I now stood inside a scene that happened during the daytime in another time period. The trees in the forest were smaller but denser and there was an embankment with a six-foot dip in front of me. A scream coming from the opposite end of the dirt slide caught my attention. Eliza Chelby had slid down toward a hole. She was using a branch to hold herself up, but the limb was about to snap.

Oh, God, no. Not that hole.

"Eliza!" I yelled, forcing my feet to move. They didn't budge an inch. This was the same thing that happened in the dream on the beach, the one where Breena had led me to the warship sitting in the water.

The child stopped screaming. One hand slipped off the branch, and she turned her face toward me.

"No, don't let go!" I warned the child.

Eliza said, "The bad lady will hear you if you keep screaming."

"Who are you talking about?" I asked. As if Eliza's spirit suddenly ripped itself back to the correct time period, the little girl resumed screaming just before she slid into the hole, the same one the Cropseys had just buried Alice inside.

"No!" I yelled, my heart ripping at my chest as if I were truly the little girl's sister. The vision cleared, leaving me alone in the dark forest.

Dropping to my knees, I allowed the sobs to come. For so long, I'd been numb to the pain, all of it. The emotions raging through me now weren't only about Breena's death, but this breakthrough was also about aching for a father I never knew, a mother I lost way too soon, a beautiful grandmother, and the affections of a man I may never be able to fully enjoy because of a curse. Life didn't get any darker than this. I'd bet my book advance on that fact.

At once, my body went airborne, snatching my voice away before I could scream. I sailed down in to a hole at least ten feet deep and thudded to the bottom. A crack sounded as I hit the ground, and a stabbing sensation surged through my left ankle. I cried out and lay paralyzed with pain, biting my lower lip as each wave shuddered through me.

"Fascinating history lesson, wasn't it? Ella glanced down in the hole and shined a light in my face. "Too bad we didn't ever become best buddies. You could've showed me how you do that crazy witch thing. You know what I'm talking about, right? Those visions you make."

"How do you know? About my visions."

Ella smirked and cocked her head to the side. "Oh, a little bitty ghostly birdy told me."

I didn't have time to decipher what she meant. I needed to toss something out there as a connection for us. "We can still be friends. Just help me up," I pleaded.

Ella shook her head. "No, we can't. I don't believe you. Mama said you and your boyfriend wanna send us away. My mama owns this town. The townsfolk here have accepted that fact for the last two hundred-something years. So, I'm sorry, but we can't be pals."

"No one else in this town will become your victim. It'll all end tonight, Ella." I wanted to feel as confident as my words sounded.

"Don't be so sure about that. You want to know what they went through, right? Those Chelby girls."

I shuffled to my feet, winced at the razor sharp sensation passing through my foot and slumped back down to the ground. Grabbing my sprained ankle, I gagged and fought nausea. Laughter peeled through the air.

"You should feel honored, Tandie like Candy." Ella's face appeared at the top of the hole again. "You got what you wanted."

"You know, Ella with no fella, you really should go put yourself out of our miseries again. Go and drink some fresh poison, or something," I hissed and examined my surroundings while I still had a fraction of light. If I were to meet death tonight then I wasn't about to go without at least a word fight. However, I didn't intend to leave this world yet. I'd survived a car crash the doctors claimed was impossible to do. Yet, I was alive and was given a second chance to make things right. The tiniest light found its way into the recesses of my dark mind. "I'm going to find a way out of here, Ella."

More giggles came from the girl. "No you won't. Unless you got wings to go with that vision thing you do. I know what you and the carpenter wanna do. You plan to send poor little Ella back to the other place."

I had no idea what Ella was referring to and couldn't see this girl ripping someone's throat out the way Eric said the victims had been mutilated. No. She had help.

"I'm not afraid of you, Ella."

"Probably not me. But who's not afraid of getting buried alive?" She laughed again, grating my nerves.

I didn't answer her question. Instead, I pushed my back up against the dirt wall and used it to work myself to a half-standing position. Just as I came to my full height, placing pressure on the ankle which felt more sprained than broken, I felt dirt trickle down over my head.

"What are you doing?" I yelled.

"Only giving you a taste of what's to come," Ella said in an amused voice. But first, I'll be tending to business elsewhere. Or should I say with someone else. Two guesses who that might be with."

Rage surged through me. I scooped up a handful of the fresh dirt Ella dumped on my head and threw the soil up toward the top of the hole.

"Leave the Fontalvo's alone, Ella. Leave all these people, or—"

"Or you'll do what with your handicap body? In case you haven't noticed, you're pretty far down in a rut, I'd say."

"Well, you're wrong. I can walk just fine," I lied.

"Not to worry though. My sissy, Alice, will keep you company down there."

Up above, the girl shuffled around. She truly intended to leave me in the hole. I shuddered at the thought and examined my surroundings that were now highlighted by moonlight. A large pile of dirt dropped on my head.

The panic set in and I screamed Ella's name, my stomach rolling at the thought of being buried alive.

"Give some love to my little sisters buried down there, won't you, Candy Tandie? Now, I have a date to attend with one handsome Latin lover," Ella said and disappeared from over the top of the hole, her footsteps fading in the forest.

"Come back here, Ella. You can't leave me down here." However, I knew that only the trees heard my scream.

Chapter 37

E*ric*
    Eric raced to Chelby Rose, his heart pounding. Norma Atwater was the leader of the MARAS, and the only one he could turn to for help. He knew without a doubt that whatever or whoever had taken Shania McKinnon, was what they were all up against.

He quickly placed a call to Norma, and as soon as she answered he blurted out, "They took Shania McKinnon."

"Gracious! What do you mean?" Norma asked, her voice rising.

"Somebody kidnapped her. They left a clear message—no police. Told me to gather a group of people and bring them to the old Catsburg Store. Norma, you're one of them."

Norma was quiet for a few moments before she said, "But why? Does this have something to do with the Cropseys?"

He nodded even though he knew she couldn't see it. "More than likely," Eric said.

Norma hesitantly responded with words of courage and strength, "So be it. What time do we meet?"

Eric paused, shocked by her willingness to help despite being an Atwater and the only family never cursed by the Cropsey witches. Payback time had arrived. And Norma was the only

Atwater left in the area. He knew this would be the chance for revenge against the her family. "

You don't have to do this, Norma. It's too dangerous."

"Yes, I do. I read up on some things. I can help you. Freedom has come for Bolivia. The psychic—"

"You mean, Tandie?" Eric interrupted.

"I have some ideas about the trinity she mentioned. But all that can come later," Norma said. "Let's focus on getting your friend back."

"I called Saul Chelby five times. No luck. So I left an encrypted message, hoping he understood we needed his help without giving too much away. I'm almost at Tandie's house now. I have this bad feeling about her I can't shake. We still don't know who these people are or if Shania's all right and..." His voice trailed off. A heavy weight settled on his chest. Were something to happen to Virgil's widow then Eric was certain his friend would come back from the grave and exact revenge.

"Don't worry, Eric. We'll find Shania, and I'm sure Ms. Harrison is just fine, too."

"I can drive you to Catsburg, Norma," Eric heard Gus's voice say in the background. "I didn't mean to eavesdrop."

"How kind of you, son," he heard her say to Gus. "Don't worry about me, Eric. I won't be there alone. What time?"

"Was that Gus Taborn's voice I just heard?" Eric asked. He shuffled his phone from one hand to the other, and tried his best to ignore the sinking feeling settling his stomach like boulders. Something about Mr. Handyman Taborn just rubbed him all wrong. The urge to warn his friend flickered through his mind. "Norma, listen to me. I think you should—"

"What did I just say? Go get Tandie. We'll see you at the store in an hour," Norma said and ended the call.

Eric was already pulling into Chelby Rose's driveway by the time she hung up. He didn't even bother turning off his lights before he got out and dashed past Tandie's Camaro. He stormed through Chelby Rose's entrance. A keen sense of dread crept its way along his body, eating away at his resolve to be strong no matter what he faced tonight. He felt her fear before he even realized she wasn't in the house.

"Tandie!" he called as he trudged through each room. The house where they had connected with each other seemed so different now. It was as if the heart of the manor had been ripped out. Tandie's presence filled the place with a new life, and with her gone, emptiness haunted Chelby Rose once again.

Clasping his hands behind his neck, he glanced around. Surely, she wouldn't have gone out into the woods by herself. If she did, then where would he look first?

"Don't panic. Just stay calm. She's here somewhere," he said aloud, his breaths increasing. He rolled his shoulders back and forth, focusing on rational thoughts and not the last memories of his dead best friend, images he'd never forget.

"Call her again. She'll answer this time. I know it." He removed his phone from his pocket and punched in Tandie's number, his posture stiff as he waited to hear her voice. No luck. Instead, the rings echoed around him. He followed the sound. Her cell phone was on the table in the hallway. "Fuck!"

On Tandie's writing table, the little girl in the photograph smiled back at him. Her daughter might be gone from this world, but she left a vivid image to watch over her mother. His scalp prickled as he reached up to the breast pocket on his shirt and fingered the golden clover through the fabric.

Something was standing behind him.

Inhaling, he slowly turned around. The light coming from the little girl— the same child that was in the picture on Tandie's desk—throbbed in his eyes. The glow surrounding her body was brighter than the last times their paths crossed, the night she healed him after the accident.

Eric stared at her, unable to speak. She held out a hand toward him. Instinct told him to run, but logic made him realize he'd never see Tandie again if he did. He glanced back at the photograph and then moved his gaze back to Breena's ghost. The child's smile reminded him so much of her mother.

She lifted a finger and pointed at his pocket, the one that held the golden clover, his family's heirloom. What was the child trying to tell him? Pastor Jeffries had said he'd know what to do when the time came. Eric didn't doubt he'd stumbled onto that exact moment.

Reaching into his pocket, he removed the clover and held it in his palm. A heated feeling spread through his hand as though someone lit the metal. Yet, he felt no pain. He turned back to Breena's ghost.

"I can save your mother with this. That's what you're telling me, right?" The child nodded and pointed towards the doorway.

Her body stayed planted firmly on the ground as if she were a living human. Taking one cautious step in front of the next, Eric slowly walked over to Breena and took her hand, a strange coolness filling the spot where her ghostly fingers rested inside his palm. Their journey had begun just before the growl of the beastly element hidden inside the curse sliced through the air.

Chapter 38

T*andie*

I stared at the top of the hole, my courage fading. The harsh reality of the nightmare I'd stumbled across clouded my mind. Ella said this was the place where Alice and Eliza were buried. No special sight was necessary for me to know she spoke the truth. It was as if I could envision the remains of the two sisters buried in the dirt. Even though I fully understood what happened, numbness eased its way through my body and calmed my mind but not the ache in my heart.

I only recently learned about this ability to connect with spirits of people who had lived in the past. But the link I shared with Alice wasn't just an impersonal reading of her former belongings. Eric and I were the reincarnated spirits of Alice and Enrique. I knew that statement to be true, and felt the weight of the meaning vibrate through my heart.

"Oh Eric, I've failed. Baby B, Mommy failed you too." My voice cracked and I slumped back down to the ground.

Closing my eyes, I waited for whatever might come. Ella intended to bury me alive. Why was she prolonging the agony?

Part of me wanted the Cropseys to follow through on the threat. Then I'd be with my daughter. I hummed the tune I'd heard the old woman singing during one of the first times I experienced a vision in Chelby Rose. The flat, sorrowful notes threatened to bring the tears again, but they never did. Something else came instead.

Bright light lit up the inside of my eyelids. I opened my eyes and inhaled sharply. Sensing a warm vibration over my head, I turned my attention to the miracle happening above me. The smiling spirit of my Baby B floated a foot or two above my head. I held my breath and didn't dare move a muscle for fear of frightening her away.

"You haven't failed me, Mommy." Breena lowered her hand and placed what felt very much like a small hand over my chest. A surge of warm emotions flooded my heart. This was the first time I'd ever seen my daughter outside of a dream or a vision. "I've been right here with you the whole time."

"You're really here? This isn't just a dream, too. I'm so happy to see you." My voice cracked.

"Please don't cry," Breena's smile faded as my tears fell. Even among the angels an emotional connection ruled the heart and linked souls across a void that crossed both time and spiritual boundaries.

"A very bad spirit wants to hurt you," Breena said, her full form kneeling before me.

"I know, baby," I whispered.

"Don't let them."

"I can't stop them. I don't know what to do. No one knows where I am," I said.

"You know what to do. That's why we're both still here."

Breena smiled and then drifted upward. Panic seized my chest. I felt as if the dirt walls were closing in around me.

"Where are you going? Please don't leave again," I pleaded.

"Don't worry, Mommy. I'm going to bring help. I love you."
Breena's voice faded in the wind. How could she assist me? What
did Baby B mean?

Another ten minutes or so passed. The moonlight moved
away from the opening, leaving me in darkness, silence, and pain.
I squeezed my eyes shut and prepared to accept the inevitable.
Breena's tiny spirit wouldn't be able to bring someone. Or would
she?

Suddenly a deep voice called my name.

I moved my gaze back to the opening and focused on the
silhouetted body of Eric Fontalvo.

"TANDIE?" ERIC SHINED a light in my face.

"Eric! I'm down here!" I yelled.

"Did you decide to go treasure hunting again without me?"
he said, his handsome face strained.

"I did, but I'm done. I got a little too excited and dug so deep
I couldn't get out," I said, laughing and crying at the same time.
Breena kept her word. After all the oddities, I was still learning
that anything was possible in this game of supernatural surprises.

"I have to find something to pull you out," Eric said.

"My ankle is sprained. I don't think I can stand."

A long pause from Eric sent flutters through my chest. The
night had worn my nerves down and panic made me think he
had decided to leave.

"Hang on," Eric said after an agonizing pause.

"Please hurry," I said.

Getting rescued by Eric reminded me of an old fairy tale I
loved to hear Grandma Zee tell. She told me about the phoenix

rising from the ashes of the earth. The phoenix's life was ugly and wretched before he fell into the volcanic ashes. But after his ascent into the world as a new creature, he became beautiful, feared, and legendary. That was how I felt as I waited for Eric to return. I was a phoenix rising from the ashes of a bland existence to conquer the dark demons of my past.

"All right, Tandie. Guide this tree limb toward you. I'll pull you up after you grab it." Eric eased the branch down in the hole. The jagged edge scraped my forehead and I cried out.

"Everything all right down there?" Eric's panicked voice asked.

"You just whacked me a good one." I grabbed hold of the large branch, wondering if Eric would be able to lift me.

"Sorry. Hold on." Eric tugged and pulled, lifting my body inch-by-inch. If I were to let go, or if he weakened, I would fall. The walls of the dirt prison receded, and I inhaled the scent of cool fresh air. At the top of the hole, Eric tugged my body towards his and abandoned the branch. "Can you stand?" I nodded. He gave me one final tug, using enough force to pull me out so I wound up collapsing on top of him.

"Well, Mr. Fontalvo. I should say you really know how to grab a girl's attention," I said through panting breaths.

"Likewise, Ms. Harrison." Eric eased his arms around my neck, pulling me to him in a kiss. I'd never been so happy to see and feel a pair of lips in my entire life.

I pulled back and stared into his eyes. "Baby B told me she'd bring help. She kept her promise," I said, savoring his scent and not ever wanting to let go.

"I told you to stay at the house. Are you hurt anywhere else?" he asked in a raspy voice.

"No. I didn't hurt you, did I?" I asked.

"Maybe in a few places, but you can take care of those later. Deal?"

"You got it," I said. He gently rolled me off the top of him, sat up and helped me do the same. "Eric, they're down there. I felt sadness and pain. Eliza's last moments and Alice's terror. Her agony over knowing she'd never see Enrique again." Despite the things I'd suffered, I felt re-energized instead of sad.

Eric leaned over the hole and peered down in it as if he were trying to envision what I just said. "So this is where they buried them? At least, Saul got what he wanted out of this," he said dryly.

I didn't understand his sudden change in attitude. "I saw everything. I even felt her pain."

"I should never have left you." Eric took my hand, spread my fingers and placed a golden four-leaf clover in my palm.

"It's beautiful." I studied the relic. The leaves were made with the same kind of gold as the heart I wore around my neck.

"It belonged to Enrique and the Fontalvos who came before him. It was passed down through the generations."

"This was your ancestor's piece?" Eric's implication hit me like a club. The link to the persecuted child of Alice and Enrique lay in my hands, the lucky one. "Okay, so the trinity is complete now. But I have no idea what happens next."

"We don't have much time to figure it out," Eric said, taking the clover and returning it to his pocket. "I promised Pastor Jeffries this little gadget would stay with me. Always."

"What's happening? Is it Abby?" I asked, trying to look brave for Eric who looked as if his best friend's sister had already died.

"Someone kidnapped Shania. They're holding her at the old Catsburg Store near the coast. The note gave me specific instructions to bring you, Norma, and Saul."

He paused and studied my face. "I believe you now. God only knows how I fought it all these years. I do believe an evil force of some kind is at work here. But there are good spirits there, too."

"We'll beat this thing, Eric. Our combined faith can do anything," I said. Did he also believe we were the reincarnated spirits of the two ill-fated lovers? I wanted to ask, but decided against doing so. Instead I said, "How did you find me?"

Eric placed an arm across my shoulder and gazed deep in my eyes. "You know how I found this place. Breena came to see you, right? She made me a believer again, too. Now, let's get going." My aching body craved his support, and the pain in my ankle dwindled a bit.

"I'm not sure what to do here. Ella isn't going to let us ask her out for an exorcism date," Eric said.

"I think I have an idea." He pulled me to my feet. A sharp ache surged through my foot. I walked two steps and stumbled. Eric caught me before I fell.

"My ankle is going to make this difficult."

"Hold on to this," he said, placing the lantern in my hand. At once, he bent down and scooped me up in his arms. "I've got you." He started walking back toward Chelby Rose.

"We do have a connection, Eric," I said, trying to ignore my anxiety.

"I know," he answered. That was all I needed to hear.

Chapter 39

T andie

In the distance, a bright light silhouetted the trees. At the end of the road sprawled in front of Eric's Jeep, Sunset Beach awaited. Even though I couldn't see or hear the ocean, I could almost taste the strong salt water scent. My chest tingled and my body buzzed with nervous energy. Grandma Zee's prophetic advice, the words she'd whispered to me several times was complete. The trinity of love consisted of Alice's locket, Eric's clover, and my pathseeker conduit... Breena's necklace. All chess pieces now sat on the same board. Only the night knew whether we'd successfully defeat the witches and free Bolivia's trapped souls now that the trinity's key players had gathered together in one place. Every move I'd made since the accident led to this night.

"What are those lights coming from?" I asked.

"I'm not sure," Eric answered and eased the Jeep to a stop across the street from the Catsburg Store. He looked just as worried as I felt.

Images of the last time I came to this place flashed through my mind. There were no wandering souls drifting around tonight. The store looked the same. The only difference was the four five-gallon cans sitting under the window to the right side of the door. Outside the store, Gus and Norma Atwater stood beside one of the two wooden pillars that supported the ten-foot awning over the door.

Norma approached the Jeep as Eric hopped out and helped me step down. We managed to shuffle around the Jeep and headed toward the store. The librarian's face looked both nervous and happy. "You found her! I'm so happy you're all right, hun. Well, as fine as you can be, I guess." She studied the way I was leaning on Eric and moved to my free side, supporting my weight as we headed over to where Gus stood. "Someone is inside the store. But we don't know who it is. Maybe we should try to call Detective Newman. That wouldn't be like calling the police."

"No police. Why do you think they wanted to meet us at this old store?" Eric asked Norma. A strange look passed between Eric and Gus. I couldn't help but to remember the last time we crossed paths, the night he hummed the same tune I had heard back at the store. Tonight, his slicked-back hair paired with the dark coveralls gave him an alarming appearance.

"This is where Thomas Chelby set fire to the little cottage that belonged to the Cropsey's two hundred and sixty years ago." Norma paused, reached into her blazer's right pocket, pulling out the Enochian scarab, and said, "With Mary Jean inside. All our ancestors are coming together for the first time in hundreds of years. I can feel them. The lost souls trapped by those Cropsey witches. Can't see them. But they're here all right."

"So it all started at this place," I said, my hand drifting up to my neck, clutching the trinkets. "And will end here as well."

"Yes, naive people. This is where the fairy tale began and where the nightmare ends, no doubt." Shania emerged from in the store, a gun pointed at me. She was as calm as silk with not a scratch on her. All heads turned to where she stood.

Her glare raked through me. "Do you think you've outsmarted me, Alice?" Shania said, stopping just before she reached the end of the bottom stair. She wore a skin tight white suit unlike anything she'd previously worn and no frilly dress. Her hair was pulled back into a tight french braid, and her face cemented the negative energy flowing from her body. Nausea rolled in my stomach. There was no trace of the kind-hearted woman I now considered to be a friend left in this person standing before us.

Eric stepped toward Shania, but Gus moved into his path. "What the hell are you doing, Shania?" Eric said in a pained voice. He stared at his friend's widow as if he'd never seen her before, as did Norma. I blamed myself. If the sight had worked properly, then I would've seen this coming. Did Frieda know her friend had issues? The only person not affected by this new Shania standing on Mary Jean Cropsey's burial grounds was Gus. He stood there smiling with a grin that made me even more nervous than Shania's gun.

"Where's Chelby, Eric? You still can't follow directions. You're as dim as your godforsaken ancestors," Shania said.

"Gus, what are you doing, son?" Norma's shaky voice asked. Gus pulled out a gun and aimed the barrel at her head. Norma stumbled backward, tripping over a large stone. Eric started toward him.

"Go ahead. Be a hero you frigid bastard. I'll be happy to place a bullet in her head before tonight's grand finale," Shania said, taking a step towards me, her once beautiful face twisted by a scowl.

"Why, Shania?" I said through the lump in my throat.

"Patience. We're getting to that part. Give our nosey town librarian the ropes, Gus," Shania ordered and turned to me. "And you, the lovely star, move over to the old water tub here beside this stairway." Shania motioned with her gun. I locked gazes with Eric. He made a slight nod. Somehow, I hobbled over to the tub a few feet away from Shania.

"Oh, you're so obedient and boring," Shania said to me. "I want you to tie Eric to the post, Atwater, and then Gus will tie you up to the other one. Don't look so worried, everyone. I promise this is going to be unforgettable fun."

Norma followed Eric over to the beam about fifteen feet directly in front of the water tub and tied his hands behind his back and around the post. She apologized the entire time as he grunted. He never once moved his eyes away from me. Gus stalked towards Norma next, grabbing her by the forearm and leading her away from Eric.

"Gus, this isn't you. I know it's—" Norma said, slipping the scarab conduit back into her blazer's front pocket before anyone noticed the gesture.

"You don't know anything about me, librarian," Gus interrupted, speaking in a low voice. Then, as instructed, Gus secured Norma in a sitting position against the post across from Eric's. He walked over to Eric and yanked his ropes tighter. Eric winced and made a small gasp as he wrapped another one around his throat, securing the rope around the post. Next, Gus approached me and did the same, his fingers brushing across the top of my hand as he did so.

At once, a small vision surged through my body, the familiar jolt of electricity rendering me blind for a moment. Images of ripped throats taunted me, and my pulse quickened. Closing my eyes, I saw a vision of Gus as he stalked a few steps behind Virgil McKinnon. I'd seen his photo in the news enough to recognize Eric's best friend in my vision. Both men walked along the shores behind the Aeneid, the section cloaked in darkness.

However, Gus held a weapon... a pitchfork. *Oh God no.* Lifting it, he brought the pronged end down on Virgil's head, rendering the man unconscious. Eric's friend fell to the ground and rolled over so he now faced his attacker. Gus raised the weapon and slammed it onto the man again and again, laughing while doing so. Nausea rose in my gut even though I was inside a vision.

"Tandie! Come back to me," Eric's voice said. I fell out of the reverie and focused on my surroundings. "You all right?"

"I'm fine," I whispered, still catching my breath. I passed a quick glance at Gus. In return, I received a crazed, yet somewhat normal grin, as though he knew what I'd just witnessed him doing.

Shania scoffed. "She's just fine for now. You are truly pussy-whipped, Eric. Amazing."

"What will you do now?" Norma asked, ripping through the leftover fog and bringing me back to the dilemma at hand.

"*What will you do now?*" Shania mimicked with as much venom in her voice as she could gather. "Ask the fortune teller standing here beside me. Wait, she doesn't have any powers. She's about as worthless as an old mule, isn't she?" Her off beat statement gave me hope. Obviously, she didn't know my abilities had returned, giving me a sudden advantage. An ember lit inside me along with something else hard to describe.

"We know you're grieving, Shania. If you let Norma and Tandie go, then I won't tell anybody about what happened here," Eric pleaded, wincing with each swallow. However, I didn't need to glimpse inside this woman's past to see inside her dark soul. How could I have been so blind?

"I'm not grieving, you idiot. The only thing I'm sad about is that you were too stupid to get Chelby out here," Shania spat back at Eric. Thinking about Saul made me angry. Eric said he left messages for him, detailing this situation. Surely Saul didn't want to see anyone get hurt. He couldn't be that selfish and cold.

"Besides, why would I let the reason I've managed to survive the last twenty years of hell prance out my door?" Shania asked. That statement echoed in my chest, and a dark cloud of realization set in.

Tied to the post on the other side of the stairway, a distraught Norma started praying. A raging look darkened Gus's face. Fear for Norma's safety raced through me. Clearly, the librarian had cared for this guy, but his soul was just as dark as Shania's. On my last visit to Catsburg, I spoke with a woman who said her name was Minerva. From the vision I had experienced as Rose Chelby, I knew that I had somehow channeled the pathway of Mary Jean Cropsey. If I'd once lived a life as Alice Chelby then that meant the ill-fated woman standing before us was Mary Jean Cropsey. A powerful witch who could easily cast a spell such as the one that caused my accident. Fire lit underneath me and I clenched my teeth.

"Let them go. We can leave here together the way you wanted to do a few days ago," Eric suggested. Gus perked up and frowned at Shania. Under different circumstances, I probably would've glared at Eric too. However, I suspected his statement caused just the right amount of tension he intended to do.

"Look at what I have standing here beside me," Shania said, moving to put her arm around Gus's waist. "Do I look lonely?"

"No, but I'm sure you could do better," Eric stated.

Before Shania could respond, Gus picked up what looked like a pitchfork, turned the tool around and rammed the handle up against the side of Eric's head. I started toward the two men. Gus shoved me back, and with my bad ankle it didn't take much to make me fall.

"Leave her the fuck alone," Eric hissed. And then, Gus aimed the the pitchfork at his head again.

"Gus, chill!" Shania yelled, her chest heaving.

"Did you kill your husband? And hurt Abby?" Eric asked, ignoring a fuming Gus standing over him. Blood trickled down the side of his face, and the pain in his voice radiated in his expression. It took all my resolve to stay away from him.

Shania gave Eric a calm, dark look and a smile, the markers of an insane mind. "They deserved to be forgotten. Especially Virgil. If Abby hadn't been such a nosey little wench the night her brother was handled, then Gus would never have had to bother with her. How does it feel to know your best friend was nothing more than a pawn in a higher game?"

"About the same way it feels to know his widow is a psychopath," Eric said bravely. Gus raised the pitchfork again, but Shania grabbed the handle and said, "No. I'll make the last move in this game. He will regret those words. Once he realizes there's nothing he can do to save his beloved from burning alive in that store." Gus lowered the tool, but kept his gaze locked on Eric. And for the first time since I met Eric, he looked terrified.

"Bullseye!" Shania said, throwing her head back in laughter. "You should see the look on your face, Eric."

"What do you want from us?" I demanded.

"No, it's more like what I need," Shania said, turning back to me. "You really don't remember me do you, Tandie? Probably not. Let's start the memory game. Twenty years ago, I was playing in the woods just outside of Castle Hayne. There were six of us teenagers."

"Oh no," I closed my eyes, feeling thankful for my seat on the ground, my body numb as if the muscles had been drained of all blood. The past was reaching out with those greedy claws, yet again.

"Yes, you're starting to remember, aren't you?" Shania hissed. "There were four girls, two boys, a little snot-nosed six-year-old who should've stayed home, and a psychopath on the loose."

She bent down to the ground beside me, the barrel of her gun pointed at my heart. "My sister felt bad about leaving the little girl in that old cabin. I tried to warn her, to tell her that I saw someone hiding in the bushes. But Chelsea never listened to anyone. The moment my sister grew a conscience was the day I'd always regret. We heard her cry out. One of the boys went back with me to find her. The other one ran away. Fast. Damn coward." She stopped, took a deep breath, stood and looked off in the distance.

"Virgil took Abby and her friend with him. They left Gus and me to fend for ourselves. I was right about the psychopath. He beat my sister, and—and raped her. I watched every excruciating moment. Chelsea spotted me hiding in the bushes and signaled for me to run while the monster had his way with her. But I didn't run. No. Gus picked me up and carried me off. We weren't fast enough, though. The psycho caught us. He moved fast and quiet like a ghost. That sick bastard tortured us and almost beat us to death." She stopped and took in a few gasping breaths.

Her face softened and she looked more like the person I shared a private moment with the day we sat together in Chelby Rose's living room. I also now understood Abby's question regarding my memory of her. That was the night we first spoke to each other at the Aeneid. Her witch accusations now made sense.

Gus moved over to where Shania stood and massaged her shoulders. She frowned and her stony face resurfaced. "Don't do that," she snapped at him. He dropped his hands as if she were a piece of hot coal and lowered his head.

"My mother, God rest her soul, told me that we're cursed. She said one of our female ancestors, a woman named Mary Jean, made a deal with the devil. The Cropseys didn't get off blood-free no more than the Fontalvos or Chelbys did. To create the Broken Heart Curse meant making a deal with an entity even more powerful than all of us here. More vicious than the devil himself. It meant sacrificing something in return. In Mary Jean's case, that meant giving up her daughter's soul. Now it's the same for every generation after hers. At least one little girl must die. Mary Jean gave her daughter up to the darkness. I will not let the same thing happen to mine."

I caught my breath. Norma had stopped praying and was listening too. Bullyish Chelsea was Shania's sister. Mary Jean Cropsey's relatives had been linked to me throughout my life.

"But how could that be? I clearly remember Chelsea calling her sister, Carina," I said, thinking back on that day.

"My first name is Carina. My full name is Carina Shania Woodard. Silver Teeth Carina, the ugly sister with the braces and the glasses. Do you remember me now?"

"My family moved us away after my sister died. But the pain of what I experienced and what I saw my sister go through still haunts me. I lived and breathed the plan for my revenge against Virgil and his skinny sister—the ones who ran. And you... the one who made my sister go back in the first place. That's why I used my powers to call you back here to Bolivia."

"You've been the voice in my head all along," I said with venom. "You sent that light too. Blinded me and killed my daughter." I kicked out missing her body by a few inches.

"Voices? What voices? I sent a locate and bait spell. One of the Cropsey's specialties. I'd no control over where it landed. You should've stayed in New York. Could've simply ignored my call. But no, you just had to come back here, didn't you? I knew you couldn't resist the temptation. No one does." Shania's eyes filled with rage. However, I no longer cared. Her validation of what she'd done gave me strength in the mouth of madness.

"Real smooth to blame a little kid for something a bunch of teenagers started," Eric said. "Tandie, none of this is your fault. Don't you dare start blaming yourself."

"What would've been smooth is if she had stayed put that day in the forest. We were going to come back and get you, idiot girl." Turning to Eric, Shania said: "Keep running that flap trap mouth of yours and I won't stop Gus the next time he lifts his pitchfork."

"You've seen my pitchfork art, haven't you, Fontalvo?" Gus grinned. Eric growled and tugged against his restraints.

"Tell you what," Eric said, his chest heaving. "Remove these bonds, and I'll show you mine."

"I'm sorry," I said, feeling guilty for Eric and Norma's suffering. As much as the next words pained me, I had to do something for my friends. "I understand your pain. Really, I do. You have every right to be angry with me. But, please let everyone else go."

She scoffed and snorted. "Is this Dark Souls night? Or did somebody change it to Be A Martyr day? No one is leaving. You see, there's another task on tonight's list. The curse on my family can be broken. All I have to do is get rid of you three... the last relatives of the original families. Doing so will satisfy the master and then the Cropsey's obligations are filled. No more sacrificing Cropsey girls in future lines." Shania aimed both the gun and her wild-eyed gaze toward me. "I want to save my daughter. Surely, you can understand that, Tandie?"

"Your daughter?" Eric asked.

The door to the store creaked open. All eyes turned towards the doorway. My screaming gardener girl, Ella, stepped out of the door and stopped when she saw me sitting on the ground. Examining the heart around my neck, her face crumpled and she wrung her hands. "You were supposed to stay in the hole," Ella hissed at me.

"This is my sixteen-year-old daughter, Ella Leanne Woodard. We were recently reunited because she'd been in foster care. Virgil knew about her. Helped me get her back and pay for her homeschooling. He kept my secret, even from you, Eric," Shania said, her voice determined. "Say hello, Ella."

Now I understood why Ella acted the way she did. Her mother was just as psychotic as her daughter.

"Hey y'all," Ella said and lowered her head. She was dressed in a tee shirt and jeans, a normal teenage girl's wardrobe.

Shania walked over to her daughter and placed an arm over her shoulder. "Now tell me, my dearest girl. What do you mean by asking the sacrifice why she isn't in the hole?" With each measured word, Shania's voice became deadlier.

"I don't mean nothing by it. I was just talking," Ella said, shrugging.

Something about the girl was different tonight. Maybe it was the way she kept staring at the necklace around my neck. Or maybe it was the fear in her voice when she told me that I should've stayed in the hole. Either way, something was up with Shania's daughter.

"I'm sick and tired of all this babble. Ella, it's time. Help the psychic get inside the store." Now I understood the gasoline cans. Shania intended to burn the store down with me inside. Eventually, the fire would reach Norma and Eric still tied to the posts too, but not before they watched the store burn.

Ella bent down and touched the heart hanging on my necklace, shaking her head and staring as if she were consumed by a deep thought. "No, mama," she replied in a low voice.

"What did you say?" Shania asked, her eyes narrowing.

And then the face I had seen Ella use so many times before, the face of a girl possessed, turned toward her mother. "I said I'm not gonna do bad things. I won't be hurting my sissy no more."

"What the hell are you talking about? She's not your sister," Shania answered back, the gun lowering.

"She is my sissy. Don't you see the heart?" Ella grasped Alice's golden charm and turned to me and whispered: "I was the voice in your head. It was a warning. I tried my best to get you stay away."

"The girl I saw in the light that night on the mountainside. That was you." It all made sense now. The daughter, Ella, had sent an interference spell to stop her mother.

"What's she talking about, Ella," Shania said. "Explain."

At once, something in the woods behind the store began to stir. Faint lights glowed in the dark areas among the trees, and I knew what was gathering around the resting place of the Cropsey witches... spirits of the lost souls, people cursed by the Cropseys back in the day. They'd gathered on previous Dark Souls Night for the last few centuries. However, this night proved to be a special one.

Eric stopped picking at his rope, studied the area and frowned. Could he see the spirits too? Norma had her eyes closed. And even though she wasn't speaking out loud, her lips moved, quietly forming the words of a strange chant, the creed of the MARAS no doubt.

Gus ripped the belt out of his pants and stalked toward Ella, his arm raised, his face crumpled with rage. "You respect your mama, or I'll skin you right here," he griped at the girl.

I shuffled around in front of Ella. "You will not touch this girl, you fucked up psycho." That strange tingle I felt each time Alice's memories took over trickled through my arms and legs.

Gus frowned and lowered his arm. "All right then. We'll just get this over real quick. I always felt like Shania was too dramatic, anyway." He dropped the belt, pulled out his gun and aimed the barrel at my face.

"No, you fool. This is my night, my revenge. It's going to be done my way!" Shania yelled.

"Your way? Or his way?" Gus nodded his head toward Eric. The statement Eric made earlier about Shania coming on to him hit the mark. Gus's creepy, long face turned a fiery red and his body trembled.

Shania scoffed and sneered. "It has always been about him. He's the master's favorite."

While the crazed duo argued, I passed a quick glance to Norma. Her alert gaze locked on mine as if she were trying to speak with her eyes. On the far side of the stairway, Eric moved his arms up and down. What was he doing? I forced my attention back to our captors, Bolivia's version of Psycho.

At once, Eric freed his hands, ripped the cord away from his neck and surged toward Gus, knocking him off balance. Gun shots thundered through the air. One bullet hit the old water pump about two feet away from my head and the second one zipped past Ella. The two men struggled for control of the gun—Gus's height versus Eric's muscular build.

Feeling wretched, I covered my mouth. Ella draped an arm across my shoulder and caressed my hair. "It's gonna be all right, now, Alice," Ella said, her calm eyes pulling at something deep inside me.

A choking noise ripped my attention back to the fighting men. Gus fell backward on the pitchfork, the prongs jutting up through his neck, a mockery of the way he had mutilated his victims. Blood spurted over the area around him, a demon's waterfall. His body thrashed on the ground for about thirty seconds and stopped.

"Gus!" Shania cried. The agony in the wail raised the level of her scream to a deafening pitch. She dropped to her knees beside Gus's body, pulled his head into her lap, closed her eyes and started swaying. The chill in the air deepened. Something was happening to the woman, and I was certain that it probably wasn't a good thing.

Eric made his way over to Norma and started cutting away her bindings. The first part of her rope fell just as a hissing noise came from Shania. She snapped out of her trance and passed me a death glare.

"Curse you, Alice Chelby!" She lifted her gun and aimed at me.

"Damn it, Shania. No more!" Eric ran and dived in front of me and Ella. The bullet shot out of the gun and thudded in to his chest, a sickening clank as if you could hear the metal striking a bone. Eric's body struck the ground, sliding a bit before it came to a stop.

I shuffled over to his motionless body. And this time, I allowed the screams to leave my lips. Pulling his body up in my arms, I cried out until my voice cracked. Ella made her way to my side, shielding me from her mother.

"Are you satisfied now?" I snarled at the mad woman.

"Not quite yet. Ella, move back," Shania said.

An image of a blurry face flickered around her head. It was the woman I had seen in my visions—Mary Jean Cropsey. I'd somehow locked onto the witch's pathway. Could see the image of the reincarnation that was Shania McKinnon just as I suspected. If I would've paid attention, I wouldn't be holding a lifeless Eric in my arms. Once again someone's death was due to my shortcomings. If Shania's bullets didn't kill me, then the pain closing in on my heart soon would.

Shania aimed the gun at me again. I didn't care what happened now. My soul, the very reason I'd found for leaving a meaningless existence was gone. Feeling as dead inside as the man lying in my arms, I looked down at Eric and waited for the bullet. Nothing. There was only clicks and a growling woman. Shania's gun malfunctioned. Of course, that would be the case.

"Tandie, watch out!" Norma shouted.

I tore my gaze away from Eric's face, so peaceful in his eternal dream. Shania charged toward me with Gus's pitchfork held high above her head. The reaper didn't favor the Cropsey's ancestors on this night, though.

Instead, something else did.

Chapter 40

Tandie

The lights in the woods shifted to one side and drifted towards the front of the store. Underneath the glow of the full moon, the forest became a supernatural stage. Several of the orbs surrounded Shania, ripping the pitchfork out of her hands—the souls of the shadow people. Only they weren't dark this night. The lights of the victims Mary Jean Cropsey and her descendants had sacrificed over the years burned bright, and Alice Chelby aka me was the one calling them back for vengeance.

Spinning around in all directions, the woman screamed. The sight entranced me as my breathing increased. I closed my eyes a moment and focused on Alice's pathway. Bright white light filled my mind and ignited my body as though someone hit me with a strong bolt of electrical current. My eyes flew open and I refocused on the area around me.

From beside me, Ella stared at her mother, her eyes wide and her face innocent like a small child. Just as Shania did moments ago, I began to sway in a circle, never once releasing my grip on Eric's body.

"Come over here and help me finish untying this rope, child," I heard Norma's voice say to Ella.

However, Mary Jean wasn't ready to lose. She wanted her revenge, to save her daughter, and she'd do anything to get both those things. Shuffling through the lights that stuck to her body like fireflies, Shania snarled and reached toward the pitchfork lying on the ground a few feet away. "Your dead family won't stop me, Alice Chelby," she said and lifted the tool.

The lights faded as if the orbs had entered her body. For a moment, Shania stood completely still, her eyes wide and her mouth open. She passed a quick look towards me, but her face softened when her gaze landed on Ella crouched beside Norma.

"Mama, don't do it," her daughter whispered. Even her daughter's pleas couldn't stop the vengeful reincarnation of Mary Jean. Shania's eyes rolled upward and widened as they focused back on me. With my pathseeker's eyes, I saw the original identity of the woman standing before us, Mary Jean Cropsey herself.

"It's over, Mary Jean," I said in a higher-pitched tone... Alice's voice. Both Ella and Norma stared at me. "You've still lost your daughter, and the spirits you wronged have taken control of this situation. Give it up for God's sake."

"I will. But guess what, little Alice Chelby? My master will avenge me. His end game is bigger than all of us little minions." She passed a quick glance towards Eric and refocused back on me. "For now, you're coming with me." Shania snarled and positioned the pitchfork to strike, even though her face crumpled as if she were in pain.

"Please don't, mama. It's over," Ella pleaded.

I leaned over Eric's body, shielding him from the blow that never came. Instead, a gunshot boomed through the air. Ella screamed.

I focused on Shania. Blood oozed from out of a wound just above her heart and seeped through the light colored pantsuit she wore. The ruby-stained fabric reminded me of the night Ella poured crushed rose petal water all over herself. Shania's body slinked to the ground in a movement as graceful as a swan. Her daughter hobbled over to her, threw herself over her mother's body and sobbed.

Sirens sounded in the distance just before Saul emerged from inside the trees to the left side of the store. He still had a smoking gun aimed at Shania as he approached us.

"Tandie, are you okay?" Saul asked, coming to a squat beside me.

"No." I tightened my hold on Eric's body. The world spun as the leftover embers of my powers faded and the reality of the situation took hold of my mind. My chest tightened. There was no way the world could be this cruel.

"He's going to be all right," Norma said, bending down beside me. "Look at his chest. It's moving." I did as she instructed. Right away, Eric's lips parted and he inhaled sharply. Every cell in my body shot to fiery life as his eyes fluttered open, those beautiful hazel eyes.

"But—but, I don't understand," I said.

"See. Both of you will be just fine," Norma reassured, reaching into Eric's shirt pocket. She pulled out the golden clover. The charm bore a slight scratch in the middle, but the heirloom still managed to keep Shania's bullet from piercing Eric's heart.

Grandma Zee's prophecy was complete. The ring kept Breena's spirit around long enough to help me. Alice and Enrique's golden heart reminded the reincarnated spirit of Ella Maud Cropsey that she had a sister. And Eric's lucky charm, a golden four-leaf clover passed down through his family saved his life. Together, the three items ended Mary Jean Cropsey's terror reign and the Broken Heart Curse.

"It took you long enough, Chelby," Eric said through gasps. Sweat beads prickled his forehead. He was still in a lot of pain, even though he was trying to sit up.

"I wouldn't move around too much, hero," Saul said. "An impact like that had to either crack or break something." He met my gaze, gave me a slight smile and then walked over to inspect Shania and Gus's bodies.

Eric's gaze drifted up to mine. He gave me the lazy smile, the one that made my silly heart flutter like crazy. "While I was unconscious, I dreamt of you," he said. "But it was another time, some other place. We were at a party and you wore a royal blue dress that I gave you. You had the blackest hair and your smile... so beautiful. You were the prettiest girl at Chelby Rose. I hate to admit this, but I do believe, Tandie. You are my soul mate." I took his hand and placed his palm against my cheek.

Tears streamed down my face. Happy ones. The time had come to say goodbye to the sadness. I leaned over and placed my lips on Eric's, giving him a deep kiss, anything to keep him from trying to sit up.

The sirens turned out to be an ambulance and a fuming Detective Newman. Saul must've called them in sometime before he handled Shania. The detective stormed right over to Saul, who was standing over Gus's body as if he were making sure the man wouldn't move again. A traumatized Ella was still lying across her mother's body.

"Where is it? The evidence. You better have one hell of a testimony to make up for those three dead bodies lying there," Newman said.

"Ah, those of little faith and imagination," Saul said, smirking.

"I'm not kidding around, Chelby."

"Check under the edge of the water tub." Saul crossed his arms, shook his head and smiled as if he were listening to a private joke. Newman felt along the edge of the tub, cursing when he came up empty-handed. The two uniformed officers that had arrived after the detective took a step toward Saul.

Saul smirked and said, "Hello gentlemen."

Detective Newman felt along the edge of the tub. Even Eric turned his head so he could look. Cursing under his breath, the detective turned back to Saul and held up a fancy recorder, the kind that uses Bluetooth to transmit signals. He had recorded every gruesome detail of the night's events along with Shania's confession that she and Gus orchestrated the death of Virgil McKinnon and the attempted murder of his sister, Abby.

"I assume you know how to use one of those?" Saul asked, his eyes gleaming along with his smugly boyish grin.

Detective Newman twisted his lips, sighed and pressed the silver button. The last hour's nightmare sprang back to life on the recorder as he replayed the taped events. The detective pointed at Saul. "This isn't over yet."

"Careful, Newman, I'm starting to think you're anxious to see me in handcuffs for some reason," Saul said. "People talk about things like that these days."

"Don't push your luck, Chelby. And don't leave town. Any of you," Detective Newman warned as he stalked off toward the other officers.

The paramedics rolled a stretcher over to Eric. The woman who examined him confirmed Saul's theory. Three ribs around the area where the bullet struck were cracked and possibly broken. They didn't want to take any chances with him trying to sit up because the bones could move and pierce his heart. After loading Eric on the cot and moving the stretcher over to the ambulance, the other paramedic secured my foot and ankle in a temporary brace. I felt instant relief and even managed to hobble back over to the ambulance before they lifted Eric's stretcher up.

"He won't let us put him in there until after he talks to you," the female paramedic said.

"We need three body bags," one of her partners said. Surely, they didn't still think Eric needed one. The energy in his kiss indicated he was nowhere close to dying. Across the road, I spotted Norma standing beside the coroner as he took pictures of Gus, Shania, and Ella who still lay across her mother, their hands laced together.

"Oh no," I said. Lying on the cot, Eric followed my gaze over to where the small group stood.

"I had hoped I was wrong," Eric said, squeezing my hand. "The second bullet that Gus shot hit Ella. At first, I thought it struck you until I saw Ella clutching at her side."

Now I understood why Ella's face was so pale and why she hobbled over to her dead mother. Like Eric, she was in pain, but unlike the man I loved, Ella's wounds turned fatal. The girl had scared the crap out of me, rearranged my rose bushes and threatened to bury me alive so she could save my life. In the end, Ella was one of the brightest lights among all the souls I'd encountered along this journey. She was just a young girl aching to have the love of someone who cared about her.

Bending down, I kissed Eric again. I craved a distraction from the heart-wrenching scene behind us. "Do not ever scare me that way again," I said. "If you do, then I will burn all your tools." We shared a small laugh and stared in each other's eyes.

"All right, sugar. We have to take him now." A female paramedic placed a hand on my shoulder.

"Norma's going to drive the Jeep for me," I said, moving sweat-soaked strands away from his face. "I'll be right behind you. Always."

"I know," he answered, smiling with his eyes.

"Okay, Romeo. Time to leave Juliet for a bit," the female paramedic said. She and her male partner lifted Eric's stretcher up into the ambulance, shut the doors and sped off down the road.

A gentle set of hands touched my shoulders and turned me around. "You all right?" Saul asked. "I don't know what I would've done if anything had happened to you."

"I'm fine. Thank you, for everything," I said.

"Don't thank me like I'm one of the suits. Make no mistake, none of this was about saving Fontalvo. Looking after you is all I care about. You knew I'd come, didn't you?" he said. I didn't want to lie, so I redirected our conversation.

"I found Alice and Eliza's bones. Your family can find peace, now," I said, feeling anxious to leave for the hospital.

Scoffing, he shook his head and said, "Do you really think things will go that easy? We all just walk off into the sunset. Life never works that way, Tandie. Nothing has broken inside me. I hate to tell you this, but waving the magic wand didn't work. Maybe the curse broke for Fontalvo, but I'm still a moth looking for a way to touch the flame."

"I'm sorry, Saul. I think you should know I've fallen in love with Eric," I said, chewing the inside of my lip.

"Think? That doesn't convince me. The word 'think' shouldn't even be in the equation." He took my hand and kissed it gently. "As I said before, my heroics was about you and me. Period. I don't do Mr. Nice Guy so well. And I am not giving up, Tandie Harrison. I can't," Saul whispered, his blue eyes blazing a strange hole through my soul.

There was one last question that had eluded me ever since Saul arrived. "How did... You knew exactly where to put the recorder. How did you know where Shania would be?"

Saul smiled. A wicked one almost and said: "My lovely curiosa. You and your warlock aren't the only ones walking an ethereal plane."

"What does that mean?" I asked. Instead of answering, Saul smiled with his eyes.

He had saved me from a crazy woman. And in a way, he was the reason I started to believe in myself enough to give Eric a chance. Before I could ask any more questions, Saul turned and drifted away, walking down the deserted road the same way he did the night Detective Newman was at my house.

"There goes a young man with a tortured soul. I don't need to be a psychic to see that," Norma's voice said behind me.

"I know. I was just like him not too long ago," I said, staring out into the darkness where Saul had disappeared. Sighing, I turned to Norma and said, "But that's all in the past now."

"There'll be others like the Cropsey's," Norma laced her arm through mine, supporting me. "As a pathseeker, you can free those poor souls terrorized by the darkness."

"Did you use some kind of enchantment earlier?" I asked as we hobbled toward Eric's Jeep.

Norma tilted her head back and laughed. "That wasn't magic. It was a little something I learned long ago."

"And what was that," I asked.

"The Lord's Prayer in Latin. Now let this old woman get you to the hospital." Norma smiled and shut my door.

Examining the woods where the shadow people had emerged, I lifted a hand to my throat and fingered Breena's ring and Alice's golden heart. Ella, Eliza, and the two Chelby boys' spirits stood amongst the trees. Holding hands, the two girls smiled and waved at me. Neither Alice nor Breena's spirits were anywhere to be seen as it was to be expected. Breena had said goodbye sometime after she brought Eric to rescue me. She was free to move on, and I no longer worried my daughter would spend an eternity roaming the veil between the worlds.

And Alice...well, she was headed to the hospital to meet the man she'd spent almost three hundred years trying to find again.

Chapter 41

C helby Rose, one month later...
Hacienda Moon was picked up during a bidding war by several publishers. My story was projected by top reviewers to be a literary sensation. Surrounded by friends and colleagues: Norma, Frieda, my literary agent, Marsha, and a few other townsfolk, I felt as if I might explode with happiness. The party wasn't just to celebrate a book launch, but the gathering also marked a change in Chelby Rose's ownership.

Standing in the kitchen that now sported a sleek new stainless-steel sink and faucet set, Frieda and I prepared deviled eggs and mini hot dogs. We poured Chianti and prepped a few bottles of Duplin's muscadine wine.

"Girlfriend, now I know you didn't pick this," Frieda said, waving a bottle of Duplin in the air. "Eric picked this out, right? Speaking of devilish, where is that stud of a man?"

"Frieda," I scolded, my cheeks heating.

"Why are you blushing? It's true," she said. Her face changed. A concerned expression spread across her strong features. "Tandie, I did not know Shania was crazy as a lard cake. You have to believe me. I didn't know Ella was her daughter. I just thought she was mentoring the girl." Her eyes pleaded for understanding.

Stepping closer to my friend, I embraced her. "I know it wasn't your fault."

Pulling back, Frieda still didn't look convinced. "She was a client off and on for the past five years. How could I not know? You could've been tortured or killed."

I placed two fingers on my friend's lips. "But I wasn't. Come on. People are waiting on their wine. And you don't want an alcohol deprived Marsha on your hands, trust me."

We shared a hearty laugh, gathered the entrées and shuffled back into the living room. I refused to let any part of the past cripple my future, and helping Frieda understand she wasn't at fault for introducing me to Shania was a huge step in the right direction.

Eric still hadn't arrived by the time most of the guests left. Since his contract with Saul was done, he had taken some time to go home and see his brother. Javier's cancer was in full remission. The day Eric had called with the news, he both laughed and cried on the phone.

The next morning brought a bright October sun along with some unusually warm fall temperatures. Stepping out on the porch, I glanced toward the cemetery where Alice and Eliza's bones now lay along with the rest of their family. The blue curiosa roses I'd ordered from the florist gleamed under the light. I walked off the porch and headed down the path to the left side of the house. Saul had ordered a complete cleanup of the cemetery in the woods beside the house. The vault that contained Rose and Thomas's bodies was no longer covered in vines. And the angels sitting atop the younger children's graves stood upright, guarding the tombs below them.

Bending down at Alice's grave, the only one with a polished marble headstone, I placed three roses atop her plot and one each on Eliza and her brothers' graves. I closed my eyes and pictured the faces of my own missing loved ones: my mother, Grandma Zee, my beautiful Breena. And for the first time in two years, there was no sorrow wrenching in my chest. Instead, there was a surge of life and longing for new days ahead.

Bushes shuffled. I turned around and found Eric standing behind me, smiling.

"Continue with whatever it is you're thinking. Daydreaming looks stunning on you," Eric said.

I threw my arms around his neck, kissing him passionately beneath the sunlight. We pulled back and stared at each other in silence for a short moment. I didn't need to hear what he was thinking because I felt the same way too. It had been over a week since we'd last seen each other and there was a matter of making up for lost time to discuss.

"Were you able to help Abby fix the Aeneid's roof?" I asked. Virgil's sister wanted to carry on with the McKinnon legacy and ordered a full renovation of her brother's nightclub. Of course Eric planned to assist.

"I sure did."

"And Abby? How's she doing?"

"She's a fighter. Throwing herself into this management role is just what she needed."

"That's good to hear."

"Why do you think Ella went against her mother?" Eric asked as we strolled back toward the house.

I leaned my head against Eric's shoulder, recalling the way Ella and Eliza's spirits held hands that night a month ago. "Even though Mary Jean sold her daughter's soul to the darkness, it didn't kill the light inside the girl's heart. Life is funny that way, sometimes," I said.

"True. Funny and cruel," Eric said, his muscles tensing a bit. He was thinking of Virgil again.

"Norma said there are others waiting to be rescued from curses by witches like the Cropseys," I said, turning to face Eric.

"So what you're saying is you want to hunt souls?" he asked.

"I think so," I answered.

"Well, if that's what you want."

"It is."

"Do I need to make a sign that says Tandie Harrison, extreme ghost hunter?" He asked, barely containing his grin.

"Maybe, but you can leave the extreme tidbit off. That's more of a Van Helsing kind of thing, I think."

"We'll find them all and set them free."

I sighed. "That could take years."

"Not a problem for me," Eric said. "As long as you wear those painting shorts while we're fighting the damned."

"All right, Fontalvo. You're on." I didn't wait for him to kiss me. Reaching behind his neck, I moved his head down to my lips, kissing him the way he did the night we first made love.

My life was no longer drifting along a dark and dangerous highway, and I was no longer afraid of the world hidden by the rainstorms in my life. Instead, the path I chose steered my life straight ahead, giving me no reason to ever look back.

Dear Diary,

I found him, the man from my dream.

My waiting is over.

Eric and I will sit outside on the porch tonight, enjoying the serene glow of the moonlight, feeling comforted by the way it cradles Chelby Rose... Alice and Enrique's Hacienda Moon.

THE END

Eric and Tandie's story continues in Book Two
The Emerald Isle: A Pathseekers Novel

About the Author

KaSonndra Leigh lives in the City of Alchemy and Medicine, North Carolina. She loves to play Life Is Strange and Tomb Raider and lives in an L-shaped house with two sassy cats that were both human in previous lives. She has created a secret library complete with fairies, Venetian plastered walls, a desk made out of clear blue glass, and a garden dedicated to her grandmother, Nezzetta Tomlinson Wall...Rest in peace lovely lady.

If you enjoyed this story then please leave a review at:
http://www.amazon.com/Hacienda-Moon-Path-Seekers-ebook/dp/B008QAY0BQ
or
Connect with KaSonndra on her author website at:
www.kasonndraleigh.com
or
http://twitter.com/kasonndraleigh
or
http://www.facebook.com/kasonndraleighbookspage
or
https://www.tiktok.com/@kasonndraleigh

Dedications

No ending is ever complete without acknowledging the people who stuck with you until THE END.

Although there were many who helped me during this journey, I must mention a few names. They were the people who brought this book to life and encouraged me to dream the impossible. LM Preston for sending me that first email, encouraging me to begin my journey in the warrior's way. My first proofreader, Greta Maloney, for dressing up like Spiderman so that she could help pull the spider scene between Tandie and Eric out of my head. A round of applause to Maggie Maguire for being the best beta/writing coach ever! I loves ya woman!

I'd like to send a special thank you to the expanded edition's editor, Caroline Acebo, who helped me take this story to the next level so that I can tell Tandie's story the way it was meant to be done the first time around.

Shoutout to Professor Potter at National University for helping me understand that classic gothic romance is not the same thing as horror. Professor Janet Jeffries for reading/editing Hacienda Moon when it was a screenplay. To Sylvia, Adriana, Marni, Brooke, Erin, Mari, and everyone in the Never Too Old for Young Adult Goodreads group for being such awesome supporters of my work. To my readers, bloggers, and fans all over the world. I'm working hard so that I can bring my books to all of you someday soon.

Special shout-outs to my X-men and sons (Xavier and Xevandre) for being so patient with mom's trips to make-believe land.

And to my hearts and the lights of my life forever...my grandmother, Nezzetta Tomlinson Wall who told me the voices of the flowers are the way and my mother, Doretha Lee, who encouraged me to follow every single dream that brought me here. May the angels guide you forever in the house of the Lord.

Rest in power, my loveliest ladies.

Other Works by KaSonndra Leigh
The Prelude
An Aria in Venice
Coming in July, 2023
The Emerald Isle

Printed in Great Britain
by Amazon

22229260R00205